A SONG UNSUNG

FIONA CANE

Cover design by Adrian Newton
Cover image: LongQuattro

For Dad, in loving memory.

You can tell the history of jazz in four words.
Louis Armstrong. Charlie Parker

Miles Davis

1

Soho London 1958

It would have saved time if she'd changed in the café, but she hadn't dared risk it. Giovanni noticed everything, even when he wasn't looking. Sometimes when he wasn't in the room, which was quite some talent. He'd have asked questions. Annoying questions at that. It's what he did. Another talent. And she wasn't ready to answer them. Not by a long shot. So, she'd gone back to her lodgings. Fair dos, she'd allowed enough time. The mistake she'd made was putting on the shoes. She should have worn her saddle shoes and carried the stilettos. Irresistibly shiny and oh-so elegant, she'd waltzed out of the house in them without a second thought.

But now she's paying the price. The tight new leather is pinching her skin. Her heels are blistered, and her toes, squashed into the pointy end, have been rubbed raw. Blindingly obvious, in hindsight. Brand-new, high-heeled shoes equals pain. Why is it always the little details that escape her?

She hobbles into Berwick Street. The market is chaotic as ever; the air pungent with the sickly-sweet aroma of bruised apples and overripe oranges rotting in the gutters. Deftly avoiding a scattering of carrots, she inches past a large wooden wheelbarrow, weaves an awkward path through a gaggle of loud-mouthed traders and their customers, and skids on a decomposing cabbage leaf into a boy carrying a can of film.

'Watch where you're going, luv,' he says and, deaf to her apology, hurries on his way.

Damn these shoes.

Last night, as she'd strutted in front of the mirror, she'd been bowled over by how pretty they looked with the sky-blue polka-dot frock. It was 'The Look' she'd dreamed of but couldn't afford. She was behind with the rent a-*gain*. Two months this time. But really, that unfortunate detail was beside the point. She needed to impress, and to do that she had to have the perfect outfit. It was hardly a gamble. She'd landed the job on the spot.

Hadn't she?

'Darling girl, have you ever thought about modelling?' said the woman, beautiful, blonde, and with a bouffant hairdo.

'Who, me?' She glanced over her shoulder at the various customers seated in the café, but no one seemed to be paying them the blindest bit of notice.

The woman smiled and patted her hand. 'Why not? You're adorable. Cute as a kitten. Just what we're after, as a matter of fact. Stan's camera will absolutely love you.'

Adorable. Stan's camera. A model. Me? It didn't seem likely. She was a waitress and—

'It's well paid. Two pounds an hour.'

'Two pounds?' Somehow, she managed to place the woman's cappuccino on the table without spilling a drop. Quite some feat given her trembling hands.

'You sound surprised?'

'I—'

'Drop by our studio on Thursday. Give it a go. God knows, you only live once.' And with those words of encouragement, the woman thrust her hand inside an expensive-looking handbag and whipped out a business card.

A knot of nervous apprehension brings her crashing back to the present. What if the woman is wrong? What if Stan's camera doesn't like her? She'll have wasted a lot of money and be in even more debt than she was before.

She shakes her head. Negative thinking never got anyone anywhere. She hasn't wasted her money. She's invested in her future. A brighter future. A better job. Not that she minds working at the café. Despite needing to know everything about everybody, all the time, Giovanni Fiori is a decent boss; the pay is good, the hours reasonable, and the work easy enough. It's just that she wants more out of life. She wants to make something of herself. That's why she'd run away to London. Not that she'd ever imagined being a model. Who'd have thought? Strange the way life works.

Only now she's late because of these ridiculous shoes.

She glares at the unsightly red V carved into her skin by the too-tight leather, grits her teeth, and veers into Wardour Street. Tears of pain prick the corners of her eyes. The shoes are agony, her feet are blistered, but so what? Her life is on the up. She's going to be rich. And once she's paid off her debt, she'll buy one of those electric fires so that next winter she won't have to sleep in her coat. After that she'll buy a chest of drawers. There are loads going cheap on the Portobello Road. A rug maybe, and then she'll save. One thing she's sure of. She isn't going back.

She'd left home without a word, eighteen months ago, a change of clothes, and her twelve precious jazz 78s packed into a tatty cardboard suitcase. She couldn't stay. Not after what had happened. And she couldn't tell her parents why she was leaving either. They wouldn't have understood. They'd have been angry, screamed at her that she'd let them down.

'You brought it on yerself, my girl,' her mother would have said. 'Nowt good ever came from telling lies.'

She rolls back her shoulders and staggers on. She's better off out of there anyway. Life had become intolerable. She loves her kid brothers, and she misses them terribly, but the tiny terraced house was too cramped with the six of them living on top of each other, especially since they were growing so fast. It was damp and dirty, too. Mildewed walls, rotting woodwork, and a misshaped front door that rattled in the wind, combined to make a mockery of her mother's endless cleaning. She'd had enough of nannying, washing, shopping, and cooking, too, chores she'd fitted in around school and her Saturday job at the grocer's, a position she'd got by chance when she'd noticed old Mr Hargreaves was limping.

'Looks like you could use some help,' she'd said.

'Happen I might, dearie. When can you start?'

In hindsight, that was another reason she couldn't go back. She'd left poor old Mr Hargreaves in the lurch as well.

Still, the job had been a lifesaver. Well, not the job exactly, but the shillings she'd earnt. Enough money to buy a few of the 78s she'd been eyeing up in the Swing Store, an Aladdin's cave of a shop in the city, a short bus ride away. More precious than jewels, she'd treated them reverently, taking care not to touch the vinyl as she slipped them in and out of their cardboard sleeves. Lucky for her, she'd saved a few extra pennies, too. Intent on putting the past behind her, determined to forge a better future for herself – a future she'd be proud of one day and, who knows, that Ma and Pa would be proud of as well – she'd bought a ticket, jumped on a train, and wound up in Soho.

On the corner of Old Compton Street, a punter wins the three-card trick a swindler has set out on an old wooden crate and crows with delight. The swindler grimaces and pays him his due, and the stooge, his work done, melts away. Oblivious to the con, a well-dressed man steps out of the crowd that has gathered, hands over a crown and, smirking, chooses a card. But, of course, it isn't the queen. Undeterred, he relinquishes another crown and promptly loses again.

Incredible anyone would fall for it. She smiles wryly and, spotting a gap in the traffic on Shaftesbury, totters across the road. She throws a longing look at the Flamingo Club and heads into Gerrard Street, bustling with Chinese traders as usual, the smell of exotic spices lingering in the warm spring air. A black man in a sharp suit, shades, and pork pie hat, sucks leisurely on a panatela as he leans against a lamppost outside a shop selling brocade pyjamas. A musician most likely, she thinks, enviously. The cool cat get-up and the battered leather case, a dead giveaway.

'Nice day for it,' he says, swiping the cigar from his mouth.

'Well, yes, I suppose it is.' If her mother taught her anything, it was manners.

'Whatever *it* might be.'

She dithers, wrong-footed by his response.

'Ah, I see. Well, good luck to you den.' The man sighs and shakes his head.

She follows his gaze to the end of the street, and the platinum-haired woman frantically windmills her arms. Her pulse quickens. Stay calm, she tells herself and, biting the inside of her cheek, scurries towards her as fast as her painful feet will allow.

'Daaarling, I'm so glad you came,' the woman purrs.

She takes in the low-cut black dress, a snug fit for the woman's hourglass figure. Her insides shrivel. She's got 'The Look' all wrong. 'Oh. I … Thank you.'

'Stan's ready and waiting, so follow me. We're up the end here.'

She trails the woman – Lucy, is it? Or Lydia? Loretta? She's hopeless at remembering names – to the end of the street and through a door into a damp-smelling hall, its red walls plastered with framed black-and-white photographs.

'Up here,' the woman – Loretta. Yes, she's certain now – says, heading towards the stairwell in the corner.

Her eyes adjusting to the dim light, she pauses to scan the pictures – row upon row of bikini-clad girls. No, it can't be. Can it? Oh God. Her eyes flit to the door. With Loretta halfway up the stairs and out of sight, it would be so easy to make a dash for it.

'Darling?' calls Loretta. 'What's keeping you?'

Her cheeks are burning, her heartbeat erratic and tuneless. Run, her body seems to be saying. Get out of here, quick. 'I was … I was … admiring the photographs,' she hears herself say.

'They're beautiful, aren't they? Although not entirely typical of Stan's work.'

'Really?'

'God, no. Stan Waterfield is famous for his glamour portraits.'

She breathes a silent sigh of relief. 'Well, yes. That's what

I thought.' Her equanimity restored, she continues up the stairs, content once more with her choice of frock, her shoes. 'That's why I came.'

'Well then, isn't that splendid,' Loretta purrs.

Taking a deep breath, she follows Loretta into the studio and is immediately struck by how shabby the room is. Bare, uneven floorboards. A large speckled patch of mould on the ceiling. Dirty-white walls, moist with mildew. And an incongruous hay bale plonked in front of a wooden fence, a couple of spotlights standing sentry-like beside them. Another prickle of unease runs through her. She'd expected something more … well … glamorous.

'You're such a pretty young thing I was worried you might need coaxing. Most of our new girls generally do. Honey,' Loretta says, glancing over her shoulder at a man hunched over a light box.

'Hmm?'

'The new model's here, and she's raring to go.'

The man, in a baggy brown corduroy jacket and thick-rimmed glasses, jerks upright and sashays over. 'Marvellous. Absolutely first-class.' His bushy moustache twitches as his eyes devour her body, greedily committing every line and curve to memory. 'Stan Waterfield. Pleased to meet you.' He holds out a hand, unpleasantly damp to the touch. 'Darling Loretta is such a fine spotter of talent, and you, my dear, have it in spades. Now, if you'd like to step behind that screen over there and slip off your clothes, we can begin.'

Her heart skips a beat. She's not sure she's heard him correctly. She can't have. That would mean … And she can't do that, God knows, she can't. She shivers, her heart a withered walnut.

Stan raises a finger. Eyes widening, he reaches for his

camera. 'And might I suggest that you keep your shoes on. Such fabulous shoes. And so very … *red*. My, my what a beautiful girl you are. Our readers are going to love you.'

2

I first met Martha Palmer in the winter of 1975, although I didn't know it then. In those days, she went by the name Martha Fairchild, not that it would have made any difference. I'd never heard of Martha Palmer. Perhaps, at fourteen, I was too young, although at times I felt far older. It had been a difficult time for our family. Everyone said so: friends, teachers, relations, my father's patients. Especially my father's patients.

'How are you, Natasha dear? It can't be easy. Such a difficult year for you all,' they said.

To make matters worse, my mother, previously the busiest most energetic adult I'd known, had confined herself to her bedroom, closing the door on the real world. Every night she'd lie awake and, exhausted, she'd sleep all day. She wasn't well, apparently. But she wasn't ill, either, at least not in the medical sense.

'She's lost hope,' my father said. 'She needs time to heal.'

I knew that, of course I did, but as far as I was concerned, my once vibrant mother had given up. I tried to see it from her point of view, I really did, but it wasn't easy. Life wasn't exactly rosy for me either. With my mother tucked up in bed and my father hard at work, the longed-for summer holidays had dragged. I'd been lonely and bored. No visit to the fairground for me, no cinema outings, and worse, no trips to the seaside. Still, it wasn't all bad. No one nagged me about my homework or bothered me about singing and piano practice anymore. No one forced me into itchy homemade dresses, or insisted I tidy up my room, or dragged me around boring museums and art galleries. Contrary to my mother's belief, the world hadn't ended. It went on just as it always had and always would whether she was around to appreciate it or not. It wasn't the same, that's all. Life, like my mother, had changed forever, and I think it was because of this, and it being the dawn of my teenage years, that I was ripe for changing, too.

The Fairchilds had moved to our village from London, which was exciting in and of itself. London was a remote and exotic city; a place we travelled to on bone-rattling trains, with scratchy moquette seats and doors that only opened from the outside. With its museums, bridges, art galleries, theatres, and shops, London was a place to wander around, admire, absorb, and then to leave. It seemed improbable that anyone would actually live there but at the same time extraordinarily glamorous that this family had.

Everyone was talking about the Fairchilds. The sale of Greystones, their new home, had gone through two months ago but, as yet, no one had met them, or clapped eyes on them either, for that matter, although this was not for the want of trying. A procession of villagers had dropped by with homemade cakes and jams to welcome the new family, only to find a house covered in scaffolding and overrun with workmen. There were builders and roofers, painters and decorators and, according to the local busybody, Mrs

Bracken, whom I overheard talking to Mrs Jones, the po-faced post mistress, in my father's waiting room, a very large hole in the garden.

'I heard they're building a nuclear shelter,' said Mrs Jones.

'Well, you can't be too careful these days, can you?'

Despite the absence of fact, conversations about this mysterious new family were rife. Dialogue consisted of observations, questions, and wild assumptions.

How many Fairchilds were there? *Oh, at least five or six.*

How would they adjust to village life? *It would be very difficult for them, coming from London.*

What did Mr Fairchild do? *He's a solicitor. An accountant. A stockbroker.*

Were they rich? *Undoubtedly. Greystones wasn't cheap.*

Would they fit in?

And that was the six-million-dollar question. The village was a harmonious place. It was run efficiently without obvious hierarchy. Everyone had a part to play and everyone committed to it. The villagers were on tenterhooks.

And then on the 21st of December, a crisp white card, edged in gold, landed on our doormats. The Fairchilds were throwing a Christmas Eve party, and the entire village was cordially invited. Although idle conjecture continued apace, the sense of relief amongst my father's patients was palpable. The waiting was over. They were excited, too, unlike me. It didn't feel appropriate to party, not when it still felt so raw. And it was Christmas, which somehow made it worse.

'Kind of them,' my father said, handing me the invitation.

I screwed up my nose. 'But we're not going, are we?'

'Well, here's the thing, Natasha. It would be rude not to.'

It was typical of my father, a man of integrity and honour, although the way I saw it that day, a slave to duty also.

Rolling my eyes, I sprang up from the breakfast table, grabbed my coat from the peg, and opened the back door.

'Where are you going?' he asked.

'Out,' I said, and slammed it closed behind me.

Half an hour later I was ambling down the twitten with Rafferty, Mrs Pocock's beloved Old English Sheepdog. A diminutive, white-haired widow in her seventies with a jolly outlook, Mrs Pocock was, quite probably, as lonely as me. Her house backed onto the twitten, an uneven, paved path that led from my house all the way to Greystones, via The Laurels where my best friend, Hayley Taylor, lived. Hayley and I had taken to visiting Mrs P a couple of years ago. This wasn't out of kindness, I'm ashamed to admit, although I'm sure she looked forward to these visits as any pensioner living alone would, but because we thought Rafferty was the best dog in the whole wide world. The fact that Mrs P rewarded us with an endless supply of sweets was a happy coincidence. It was unusual for me to visit her alone, but Hayley and her family were away for Christmas, staying with her maternal grandmother in Wales, and I had nothing better to do.

'Oh, you'd love a walk, wouldn't you, Rafferty?' Mrs Pocock fondled his ears, and Rafferty duly responded with a wag of his tail.

It was cold. Last night's frost still clung to the grass, but the sun shone weakly in a washed-out sky. By the time I'd reached the hole in Hayley's hedge we used as a shortcut between our two homes, my mood had improved dramatically and I was singing. It wasn't unusual. Singing was as much a part of me as my crooked front teeth and the freckles on my nose. Something that just happened, as though the music bubbling inside me was simply waiting for an opportunity to break free. I was about to hit the high note when a hard object stung my cheek and, instead of a high F, I let out a sharp squeak. Rafferty's tail stopped wagging, and he barked. I clutched my smarting face and glanced around angrily. The path was deserted.

'Well, that's odd,' I said, and bent down to stroke Rafferty.

Another sharp pain. On my bottom this time. 'Ow!'

I straightened up and rubbed my left flank. Another pellet caught me on the back of my head. I spun around, got tangled up in the dog lead, fell over, and let go. Rafferty bolted away, yelping, and disappeared through the hole in the Taylor's hedge.

'Rafferty! Rafferty! Here, boy! Ouch!' Another pellet hit me as I scrambled to my feet, this time on the arm. 'Oi! Stop that!' My eyes darted around, but whoever was attacking me was well and truly hidden.

I dashed towards the hedge, but the sound of muffled laughter high above me made me pull up sharp. I tilted my head. Two pairs of legs were dangling from the overhanging branch of the Taylor's sycamore.

'Stop it!' I said to the legs. 'It's not funny. It hurts, and you've upset Rafferty.'

A boy's face appeared, upside down, his white-blond hair standing on end, a peashooter in his mouth.

'Don't you dare,' I said.

Too late. One puff, and another pellet struck me on my forehead. 'Ow! Stop it.' I stamped my foot. 'Stop it now!'

The branch shook, and another dark-haired boy swung on it for a moment before dropping down beside me with a thud. He grinned. 'Don't worry. It's only paper.'

'And spit,' added the blond, still hanging upside down. 'We chewed it first.'

I screwed up my nose and wiped my flaming cheek. A self-satisfied smile settled on the blond boy's lips. Job well done, it seemed to say, but it was hard to tell, him being upside down.

'You're trespassing! And you've upset Rafferty.'

'Okay. Okay. Keep your hair on.' Blondie grabbed the branch in both hands, turned a somersault, let go, and landed, expertly, on the ground. He folded his arms and stared at me through narrowed, pale-blue eyes.

'Hey, Rafferty.' The dark-haired boy wandered over and fondled the dog's ears, who had reappeared and was sitting by my side. 'I'm sorry. We didn't mean to frighten you. It was only a joke. I'm Louis, by the way,' he added, and Rafferty wagged his tail, far too enthusiastically for my liking. 'Louis Fairchild. And that idiot is Charlie, my twin.'

I glanced from one to the other. It had to be a joke. 'But you're nothing alike.'

'You don't say,' said Charlie.

'We're fraternal twins,' Louis said.

I frowned.

'It means, non-identical,' he added, smiling.

'Well, you're still trespassing. That's not your house.'

The boys shrugged.

'It's illegal,' I added.

They exchanged knowing looks and exploded with laughter.

'Come on, Rafferty.' I gritted my teeth and reached for his lead. But when I looked up seconds later, the twins had gone.

Searching for my father on Christmas Eve, I found him hunched over his desk. His hair, which he wore swept back, was frosted with silver streaks, I noticed, as was his moustache. He was thinner, too, more stooped. I stood in the doorway of his study, waiting for him to register my presence, but he continued to stare at whatever it was on his desk. I was about to remind him I was singing in the carol service in a couple of hours, when his shoulders heaved. Was he crying? No, he couldn't be. My father didn't cry. Only that once. And we'd all cried then. My mind raced. Had something happened to Mum? Or had he had enough and was going to leave? I couldn't bear it if he did. I really couldn't. I scanned the room for clues. The family photograph on the fireplace was missing. Was it the cause of his grief? A memory of how life used to be before things had gone so catastrophically wrong.

The week, which had started dismally, was getting steadily worse. My father's stiff-upper-lip strength and unshakeable optimism was the glue that held my life together. I backed out of his study as quietly as I'd entered and crept upstairs to my room. It was bad enough that, aside from my solo, Christmas was going to be a non-event this year. Was this how it was going to be from now on? Was my father going to give up, too? And if he did, what would happen to me? Fighting back tears, I made a beeline for my small Whimsie collection laid out on my kidney-shaped dressing table. It had been a surprise present for my twelfth birthday. I'd never forget the moment Mum had unveiled it, whipping off the sheet like a conjuror doing a magic trick. I couldn't believe my eyes. The floral skirt matched my curtains – and it was mine. A sewing supremo, my father called her every time she revealed her latest creation. She could make anything she put her mind to. But that hobby had died along with her enthusiasm for life.

I picked up my favourite, the puppy, flung myself on my green candlewick bedspread, and stared at the ceiling, aware of the all too familiar pain behind my eyeballs. It wouldn't help to cry. It never did. So, I turned, instead, to the three Davids – Bowie, Cassidy, and Essex – a patchwork of posters of my three heroes, Blu-Tacked to the wall. But not even David Cassidy's brilliant white smile could lift my mood.

'What would you do?' I asked The Thin White Duke, who was staring at me intently, a cigarette dangling from the corner of his mouth. 'Perhaps I should take a leaf out of your book and reinvent myself. I could dye my hair red and take up smoking. It's not as if my parents would notice.'

I let go of the puppy, rolled onto my back, delved into the pocket of my jeans, and pulled out the remains of the packet of Spangles Mrs P had given me on my last visit. I unwrapped a sweet without checking the flavour and popped it into my mouth. Hmm. Pineapple. My favourite. Whoopee do. Ugh! It wasn't fair. The concert was a big deal. It would have been my first ever solo. My big moment. All those hours of practice made worth it. A tear trickled down my cheek, but I brushed it away angrily, grabbed hold of my knees, and curled myself into a tight little ball. A lump caught in my throat, and I almost swallowed the sweet.

'No. No. No,' I muttered. 'I will not cry. I will not cry. I will *NOT*.'

'You will not what?'

I uncoiled rapidly and sprang upright.

'Sing?' My father's eyelashes were wet, but there was no other evidence of the desolation I'd witnessed earlier. 'Well, now, that would be a shame.'

'You remembered,' I whispered.

He sat on the bed and put his arm around me. 'You don't honestly think I'd have forgotten? I've been looking forward to it all day.'

I closed my eyes, breathed in the soapy smell of him, and managed a watery smile.

'It'll be all right, you know,' he said.

I wanted to believe him, I really did. But when it came to Mum, I didn't know what to believe. I'd asked her, yesterday, if she'd wanted to come to the concert, but she'd said she was too tired. Tired from what? I'd wondered. Sleeping? And when I'd suggested she might feel better tomorrow, she'd insisted she wouldn't. It was as if some sad, pathetic stranger had taken over her happy, sprightly body. I didn't recognise her anymore.

'Will it?' I asked.

'Yes, poppet, it will. These things take time, that's all.' He kissed the top of my head and leapt to his feet. 'Now get a move on, Natasha, or we'll be late.'

It was a mild night. The cold of a few days earlier had given way to a warm front that threatened rain. I was still high on the success of my solo and enjoying the walk home, when my father announced we were going to drop into the Fairchilds' party. My heart plummeted to my shoes. The last thing I wanted was to come face to face with the twins again. Not after they'd humiliated me so spectacularly.

'It's on the way. Well, sort of,' he said.

I screwed up my nose. 'Must we?'

'We must. It's the neighbourly thing to do.'

'But we never go out.'

'We never get asked.'

It was true. We didn't. Not since my mother had taken to her bed. Prior to her collapse, she'd been the driving force behind our social life and, being in possession of an enviable joie de vivre, could light up the dullest party. I motioned to the jeans I'd changed into after the concert. 'But we can't go like this?'

'I don't suppose the Fairchilds will care one jot what we're wearing. They'll just be grateful we showed up.'

'You can't possibly know that, and anyway, Mum will be cross.' It was true. Back when she was a fully functioning adult, she'd been the best-dressed woman in the village, a fashion icon. Friends had sought her advice. Strangers sometimes, too. She'd have expected me to wear the maxi-length pinafore I'd begged her to make last year. I'd have fought her if she had. I loathed that stupid dress now.

'Mum isn't here.'

I sighed, as if I needed reminding.

'There'll be others, Natasha,' he said, squeezing my hand as we turned into the twitten. 'She won't miss those.'

'You really think so?' It had been months since my mother had left her bedroom. The idea she might leave the house one day soon seemed unlikely.

'Oh yes, sweetheart. I'm sure you'll be performing lots of solos in the future. You were wonderful tonight. Everybody said so. I was incredibly proud of you.'

He'd misunderstood me, but all the same my heart swelled. My father wasn't one for handing out compliments.

'Here's a thought. Why don't you perform it for Mum tomorrow? Or we could record it on the 8-track and play it to her after lunch.'

'Hmm … Well …' I was loath to commit. A nagging question had presented itself. What if she refused to listen?

'No need to decide now.' He winked at me and smiled. I smiled back, grateful he was going to let it lie.

'Oh look! Aren't they marvellous?' My father pointed to the flaming torches illuminating Greystones' long drive, just as the bleat of a trumpet broke through the still night air. Eyes shining, he drew to a halt. 'Well, I never. That's my boyhood,

Natasha. Right there in those sweet, sweet notes. The great Satchmo himself. Seems the Fairchilds have taste.'

The trumpet solo gave way to the vocals, and the great Satchmo sang about being alone with 'his fancies'. I listened, intrigued. It wasn't music I was familiar with, which was odd given Dad loved it so much. Although, thinking about it, apart from the records I played in my room and my singing, there was never any music in the house these days. Even on the odd occasion my father switched on the wireless, it was permanently tuned to Radio Four.

'You like it?' my father asked.

'Yeah. It's really cool.' Cool really didn't do it justice, though. This Satchmo was something else. His voice was growly, gravelly, and yet velvet. He seemed to be smiling, too. I grinned. I couldn't help it. His voice and the mood it conveyed were infectious.

'What say I dig out my old jazz records later? I've got quite a few of Louis Armstrong's, from what I remember.'

'I thought I recognised the voice. Why did you call him Satchmo?'

'It's his nickname, short for Satchel Mouth because his is so big. When it comes to jazz he's the king, but there are plenty of others. Charles Mingus, Ornette Coleman, Ella Fitzgerald, Charlie Parker. We could have a listen together. It might be fun.'

I beamed, buoyed by his words. If it meant spending precious time alone with him, I could think of nothing better. 'I'd like that a lot.'

He thrust out his chest and straightened his tie. 'Come on then. Let's go meet the new neighbours.'

The front door was open, which was why we'd been able to hear the music, but once we'd stepped inside, the song was swallowed up by the sound of a hundred conversations. My father was wrong about the turnout. The place was packed with partygoers. The modern, L-shaped hall led to a sunken sitting room which had a wall of cream-curtained windows and a raised circular fireplace, just off-centre, with a black teardrop hood. Life-size canvas paintings of musicians covered the walls, and huge cream lampshades which looked like upturned bowls, hung from the ceilings. My eyes were on stalks. I'd never seen anything like it.

'They'll regret the choice of colour tomorrow,' he said, sounding a lot like my mother.

We weaved our way through the guests, down the stairs onto a spongy cream carpet. A tall, jolly-looking man in a floral shirt, cravat, and jeans hurried over carrying two fancy glasses with green stems.

'Teddy Fairchild. Welcome. Welcome,' he said. 'I've brought you both a drink. White wine for you, sir, and lemonade for the young lady here. Not much of a choice, I know, but the carpets dictated the beverages this year.' He rolled his eyes. 'I'm a beer drinker myself.'

'Thank you,' we chorused.

My father offered his hand. 'Gordon James, and this is my daughter, Natasha.'

I braced myself for the inevitable question about the whereabouts of my mother.

'Ah, the local doctor, if I remember rightly.' Teddy shook my father's hand, warmly. 'Delighted to meet you. And your daughter, Natasha. Smashing.'

I smiled with gratitude. It was unlike an adult not to probe.

'You seem about the same age as my boys. They're in the games room at the back if you fancy joining them. I hope you approve of what we've done with the place,' he added before I'd had time to respond. 'It's not to everyone's taste.'

My father raised his eyebrows. 'It's very … modern. Very … stylish. A complete transformation. Clever, actually.'

'Ha. How tactful. It was Martha's doing. My wife. I must introduce you. She's here somewhere.' He glanced around. 'Ah. There she is. Martha, darling,' he said loudly, and beckoned her over with an enthusiastic wave of his hand. 'Come and meet Gordon James, the local doctor.'

A slim, dark-haired woman in a chic black halter-neck jumpsuit, cinched at the waist with a silver patent-leather belt, inched her way through the crowded room. Her face, though striking, wasn't perfect; russet eyes framed by bushy brows, a sensual mouth, the lower lip fuller than the upper, high cheekbones, a slender nose sprinkled with freckles, and long, dark, glossy hair, parted down the middle. Imperfections so infinitesimal they were superseded by the whole. I was hypnotised. She was the first truly beautiful person I had ever seen.

'My wife,' said Teddy, beaming with reflected pride.

A flicker of recognition registered in her eyes, and her lips parted into a beatific smile. 'Donny?'

I winced, embarrassed this gorgeous creature had confused my father for someone else. I turned to my father and pulled a face, but he didn't notice. He was staring at this vision of loveliness, slack-jawed, as though he'd seen a ghost.

'Darling, darling Donny,' she continued breathily, as she clasped his hand. 'My dear old friend. What an extraordinary surprise.'

'Goodness me. Martha Palmer. Is it really you? Here, in my village, after all these years. Well now, fancy that.'

The wide-eyed wonderment, which had settled on my father's face, had stripped the years from him, and I saw him then as he might have been in the days when he and Martha Palmer had been friends.

3

M artha hurries down the stairs. She's trembling all over and can't get out of Stan Waterfield's shabby studio fast enough. How foolish to believe she had what it took to be a model. She should have left when she had the chance. It would have been easy; a simple apology and a quick goodbye. Nobody was forcing her to pose naked, not Loretta, not Stan.

Glamorous. So that's what it meant. What an utterly ridiculous description for such a sleazy, degrading job. But she needed the money. Her landlady had her good points. Mrs Wilson was fair, she was discreet but, as she was always pointing out, she was not a charity. If you were late with the rent, you were out. Those were the rules. End of.

She pauses on the stairs and takes a deep breath. Best to look on the bright side. She has the princely sum of four pounds in her pocket, which means she's not only out of debt but fifteen shillings in credit. Crisis over. Lesson learnt. So why, oh why had she agreed to sit for Stan again tomorrow? Was it because, in the end, she hadn't had to pose naked? She couldn't. She wasn't that kind of girl. Not that she'd actually said as much, just something along the lines of *I don't feel ready*. She couldn't remember. She was having an out-of-body experience, as though the horrific scenario was happening to somebody else.

'Actually, we'd prefer it if you posed in your dress. Coy country girl is precisely the look we're after,' Loretta said.

Gritting her teeth, she followed Stan's directions and bent over the bale – which on closer inspection was merely a wooden box covered in a thin layer of hay – legs straight but parted, frock hitched up to reveal her knickers and the stockings and suspenders Loretta had provided. On Stan's command, she glanced coquettishly over her shoulder and pressed a finger to her pouting lips.

Click, click, click, click, click.

'My dear, you're a natural!' he exclaimed.

'Adorable,' agreed Loretta. 'And so provocative.'

'I can see it now,' continued Stan, licking his lips. 'We'll lead the readers on for a bit before the big reveal. Your future as a glamour model is golden er … I'm sorry, I don't think I caught your name.'

'Martha … Martha … er … Parker.'

'Martha Parker. Marvellous. Marvellous.'

She'd been flattered, momentarily, her humiliation forgotten. She wasn't used to compliments. Perhaps Stan and Loretta were right. Perhaps a career in glamour photography was all she was good for. God knows what the pose would have looked like without her clothes, though. Ugh! It didn't bear thinking about. She would never, ever pose naked, not even if Stan offered her a hundred pounds. She'd left home to make a name for herself, to make her parents proud. Well, she would certainly make a name for herself if she carried on like this. But as to making Ma and Pa proud. No chance. The incident in Yorkshire notwithstanding, they'd be appalled if they found out she'd posed even once as a *glamour* model, never mind she'd never intended to.

Not that they ever would find out.

Would they?

She shivers. What if someone her parents knew were into this kind of thing? Thank God she'd had the presence of mind to give a false name. Ah, but what if someone recognised her? Oh, dear Lord. Did her parents have friends who bought dirty magazines? Did Pa? She ups her pace, but her heel catches in a hole in the floorboards of the hallway. Damn it. She wrenches her foot free so sharply, the heel parts company with the shoe and knocks her off balance. Righting herself, she bends down, yanks the heel free, and limps outside.

'Hey, little lady. Looks like it didn't go so well.'

Oh, brilliant. The cat with the cigar. She wipes her cheeks with the back of her hand and very deliberately removes both the broken and the unbroken shoe. Ignoring the pitiable state of her feet and the cool stone of the pavement, she tilts her chin and strides barefoot into Wardour Street.

'Whoa, little lady! You're gonna rip your skin to shreds.'

She throws up her hands. 'So what?'

'So, you won't be able to walk any more. Dat's what.'

What is it with this fella? she wonders. Can't he see I want to be left alone? She wishes she could break into a run, but cars, taxis, and Vespas keep chugging down Shaftesbury Avenue no matter how hard she wills them to stop. With no choice but to wait, she pivots around to face him. 'Who the hell cares?'

'Hey now. I'm concerned, dat's all. Feeling bad, too, coz I should've warned you dem studios is no place for a pretty little lady like you. You is a class act. Anyone can see dat.'

A class act. Is he insane? She shakes her head and concentrates on the traffic. Just this bubble car and she'll be able to cross. C'mon. C'mon. After what seems an eternity it drives past, and Martha makes a dash for it.

The man follows, quick as a flash. 'But I'm tinking you already figured dat out.'

Ignore him, she tells herself as she strides up Rupert Street. And keep going. But even though she increases her speed, the man keeps pace.

'What say I take you for a sandwich? Di Nosh Bar in Windmill Street do di best salt beef sandwiches you will ever taste. And den I'll fix your heel. Little lady, you're sure gonna feel a whole lot better after dat.'

She steals a peek out the corner of her eye.

'Okay?' He smiles at her, a toothy, white smile.

The fight goes out of her. 'Okay.'

'Hop pan den,' he says, crouching.

'Eh?'

'Piggy back.'

She narrows her eyes. 'I'm not a child.'

'I see dat,' he says, but he doesn't budge.

'And you couldn't possibly manage me and … and … your instrument.'

He laughs, a big booming bass. 'Couldn't I now?'

She blushes. 'Thank you, I'm sure, but I'm fine walking.'

'Suit yourself, but be careful now.'

They head into Archer Street, past the crowd, congregated, as usual, on the pavement outside the Musician's Union.

'Got a gig, Cee Cee?' a blond man in a trilby asks.

'Uh-huh,' Cee Cee replies. 'Work still scarce den?'

'Damned electric guitars. They'll put us all out of a job.'

'Hell, I hope not.'

'Yeah, well, good luck to you anyway.'

Cee Cee doffs his hat, and they turn left into Great Windmill Street. 'Here we go, little lady.'

She glances at the sign, HOT MEALS SERVED ALL DAY, spelled out in blue lettering above the door, and the Star of David painted on the window. Strange choice, she thinks as he opens the door. The delicious aroma of cured beef wafts towards her, and she salivates. She eyes the meat laid out, invitingly, behind the counter, and her stomach rumbles. She hasn't eaten anything since the cheese sandwich she toasted last night.

'Salt beef pan rye wid mustard twice, please, Phil.'

'Would you excuse me for a minute,' she says, spotting the sign for the ladies.

'Ya, mon. Gimme your shoes, and when you're done there'll be a sandwich pan dat table over by di window.'

Half an hour later, Cee Cee breezes back into the café. He sets his case on the floor, sits down opposite, and whips out her shoe from his inside jacket pocket, to the amusement of a trio of pretty girls sat at a table beneath a poster of an East End boxer. Windmill girls, most likely, judging by their pristine makeup and enviable figures. They nudge one another, smiling coquettishly, as they try to attract his attention.

'Your shoe, little lady. Good as new.'

Martha fidgets with her napkin, a flush creeping across her cheeks. 'Ta very much. You really didn't need to.'

'I know dat, little lady. I know.'

She reaches down and, grimacing, eases her painful, battered feet into her shoes but jumps when Cee Cee slaps the table and bumps her head. The girls giggle again, louder this time, covering their red-lipsticked mouths with beautifully manicured hands.

'Little lady, how 'bout I take you home,' Cee Cee says, his attention firmly fixed on her.

'What? No!'

His eyebrows shoot up above his sunglasses. 'Hey now. What kind of man do you tink I am?'

She waves her hand. 'I didn't mean…' she begins. Is he teasing her? The dark lenses make it impossible to tell. 'What I meant to say is *already*. Before … before you've eaten your sandwich. They're delicious, by the way.'

'I was going to take it wid me. But if you don't mind, den I will.' He takes off his hat and places it on the table, and removes his sunglasses, folding them and slipping them in his inside pocket. His hair is closely cropped, and he has a small scar above his right eye. She wonders what brought him to England, a country where a black face can stir up resentment and racial hatred, no matter how skilled a musician or how polite an individual you happen to be.

'I'm guessing you're not from around here,' he says. 'You don't talk the same.'

'I'm guessing you're not from around here either.'

He chuckles and flicks his wrist. 'Ain't no flies pan you.'

The waiter, an old man with brilliantined hair, saunters over. 'You want cheesecake? It's good.'

She shakes her head.

'You're missing out, I tell you.'

She shrugs, and the waiter scowls and moves away.

'Is Cee Cee your real name?' she asks.

He clears his throat. 'My dear departed mother, Horatia Campbell, may di Lord bless her soul, christened me Clive.'

'Pleased to meet you, Clive. I'm Martha. Martha Palmer.'

Eyes twinkling mischievously, he reaches for her hand and kisses it. 'Enchanted, Miss Marta.'

The girls giggle again.

'You're making fun of me.'

Raising his eyebrows, he lets go of her hand. 'Who me? Never.'

'Hmm.' She nods at the case. 'You're a jazz musician. I mean, you look like a jazz musician.'

'Oh, I do. Do I?' He grins, revealing a set of white, evenly spaced teeth.

'It's the suit. A dead giveaway. And the hat.'

'You a jazz fan?'

'I'm a massive fan. I love them all. Ella, Sarah Vaughan, June Christy, Billie Holiday. But Delilah Moore, she's my favourite. Not that I could ever sound like her. She's out of this world, isn't she? A brilliant, shiny bright star.'

'You a singer den?'

'Yes. I mean no. Ugh. I mean, I love to sing. And I want to be a singer. It's why I left home. Well, sort of. Only I haven't got very far. A few auditions, that's all. I work in a coffee shop. The Grind in Greek Street. You may know it. But I've bought too many records recently, and clothes. Up to my eyeballs in debt, as it happens. It's why I ended up … well, you know.' She stops, aware she's rambling, something she does when she's nervous. Biting her lip, she fiddles with her napkin again.

A smile plays on the corner of his mouth. 'But you won't be going back there now, will you?'

She rolls her lip between her teeth. 'No, of course not.'

He clicks his fingers. 'So, what say you come listen to us instead?'

'Us?'

'Di Bo Rivers' Five.'

'Oh!'

'You heard of us den?'

She racks her brains. Has she heard of them? Think, Martha, think.

'Not good enough, eh?' He shakes his head and, laughing, slaps the back of his hand into the palm of his other.

'No of course not. It's … Well, I—'

'You'd be my *guest,*' he says slowly.

'Flippin' 'eck.'

'Is dat a yes?'

'Yes, please. I'd love to. That is, if you really mean it?'

'You have to stop doubting me, little lady. It's not nice. I mean what I say, and what I say, I mean. You heard of di Flamingo?'

She blushes. 'Yes, of course.'

'Drop by ten-thirty tomorrow night. Ask for Cee Cee.'

Martha leaps out of bed as the first hint of morning sneaks through the gap in the curtains. She scoots across the room, peers out of the attic window, and watches the sun's rays crawling tentacle-like around the chimney stacks and over the rooftops towards her. She tips back her head, stretches out her arms, and spins round in the orange spotlight. She's barely slept a wink all night and yet she's bursting with energy because tonight, she is going to a jazz club. And not any old club, but the Flamingo of all places, as a guest of a bona fide musician. She's read countless articles about the incredible music played there, but with an entry price of almost half a week's wages, could never afford to go.

She skips to the dressing table, picks up this week's *Melody Maker*, and flicks through it until she reaches the article she's searching for.

Delilah Moore will be performing at the Flamingo Club on Saturday with little-known jazz quintet, The Bo Rivers' Five. The delightful Miss Moore has nothing but praise for these talented young men, led by trumpet player, Bo Rivers, 25, having first seen them perform in a Croydon jazz club almost two years ago. Her return to the London stage has been widely anticipated, with dates at the Palladium, the Royal Festival Hall, and the Albert Hall, as well as appearances at The Marquee and The London Jazz Club. A late addition to a busy schedule – Miss Moore's first UK gig after eighteen months on the road in Europe – the Mingo is expecting a huge demand for tickets. Fans are advised to book early to avoid disappointment ...

Beside the large black-and-white photo of Delilah Moore, resplendent in a scarlet evening dress and pearls, is a smaller, grainier photo of the band: trumpeter, bass player, pianist, drummer, and saxophonist, the pork pie hat the only clue to Cee Cee's identity. Funny he didn't mention he'd be backing Delilah Moore. But then again, he didn't seem the bragging type. Who cares? Tonight, she'd be seeing her idol perform in the flesh, and for free.

She squeals, drops the magazine, flits over to the wooden tea chest, and rifles through her ever-growing pile of records until she finds her favourite Delilah Moore LP. She slides it out of its cardboard sleeve and, holding the disc between her palms, places it on the Dansette and sets the needle, gently, onto the vinyl. As the tenor saxophone strikes up the first few bars of 'Mean to Me', Martha dances over to the dressing table, picks up her hairbrush, and starts to sing.

Bang. Bang. Bang.

Becky's broom handle beating an altogether different rhythm from the room below, Martha lifts the standard lamp, slams it down three times, and a sliver of plaster flakes off the wall. Point made, she returns to the record player and cranks up the volume. She still hasn't forgiven Becky for her remarks yesterday. And why had she been watching them in the first place? Didn't she have better things to do than stare out of windows? There was a name for that sort of behaviour. Snooping. What business was it of hers anyway? It had been a chaste kiss. Nothing more than a peck on the cheek, a courteous gesture from an impeccably mannered man who'd come to the aid of a damsel in distress, buying her lunch, mending her shoes, and walking her home. Not that Becky knew about any of that. All she'd seen was the kiss.

She'd been lying in wait on the third-floor landing, hands on hips. 'What are you doing kissing that coloured man on the street?'

'Why say "that coloured man"? Why not "that tall man"?'

'Because he isn't particularly tall but he *is* coloured.'

'No, he isn't, he's black.'

'In broad daylight, Martha. Anyone could have seen.'

'So?'

'So, you know they're only after one thing.'

'They?'

'Col … black men.' Becky said, following her up the stairs and into her room. 'You want to watch yourself or you'll be getting a reputation.'

'You want to watch yourself, too, Becky. You sound like a racist.'

'I do not. I'm concerned, that's all.'

'Well, you're wrong. Clive is the perfect gentleman. He was only kissing me goodbye.'

'Oh, it's Clive, is it? I see.'

'No, you don't. You're jumping to conclusions. As usual.'

Becky had crossed her arms. 'Feel free to enlighten me

then. Why were you kissing a black man on a street dressed up like Dorothy Gale? What have you been up to, Martha Palmer?'

'Flippin' 'eck. You sound like my bloody mother.' It wasn't true. She didn't sound anything like her mother. But Martha had had enough. It had been a long day. 'Now if you don't mind ...' she'd said and ushered her friend out of the room.

It wasn't like Martha to keep secrets from Becky. Since they met eighteen months ago, in a café on Oxford Street, she's been Martha's confidante, her sounding board and, at times, her conscience, too. It was the day she'd arrived in London; a bitter winter's day, the gunmetal sky heavy with the threat of snow. A terrified teenager alone in an unfamiliar city, freezing cold, with nowhere to live and only £5 in her purse, Martha wandered into the crowded café only to find the tables all taken. Taking pity on the trembling waif with the big brown eyes, Becky gestured for her to come over and ordered her a coffee – a cappuccino, as it turned out, the first Martha had ever tasted. They got talking – well, not so much Martha as Becky. Smartly dressed, with scarlet nails and lipstick to match, she explained she was on a break from her job in the department store next door.

'I don't normally go out dressed like this,' she said.

Martha was glad of her coat. Although heavy and shape-less, it covered up her drab woollen frock. There was a two-year age gap between them but, Becky, oozing confidence, seemed considerably older. She was also in possession of a highly developed sixth sense.

'So, are you going to tell me what happened to make you run?'

Martha blushed a livid red. It was still too raw. She

couldn't talk about it, and certainly not with someone she'd just met.

'That bad, huh?'

Her lip wobbling, Martha nodded.

Becky placed a hand on her arm. 'There's a room going at my place if you'd like it. It's women only, absolutely no men allowed, and I mean *ever.* Crazy really, because two of the girls are clearly on the game.'

'The game?'

'My, my, we are innocent, aren't we? Ladies of the night. Prostitutes.'

'Oh.'

'No Irish, no blacks, and no dogs either. And if living like nuns isn't bad enough, you have to be in by eleven. There's no way round it. Mrs Wilson will lock you out if you're not. She calls herself missus but she's not actually married. Thinks it's more respectable. Still, she's not a bad old soul. And she likes me, so I could put in a good word, if you're in need of somewhere to stay.'

Martha was grateful. The room was larger than the one she'd shared with her brothers, even if it was lacking a view. It had an iron bedstead with a lumpy mattress and a green paisley eiderdown. There was a gas ring, a wardrobe and full-length mirror, a bedside table, standard lamp, and a three-bar heater that appeared to have seen better days and, when she turned it on later, clearly had because it didn't work.

They'd been friends ever since, shared all they owned – which wasn't much – and told each other everything. Fate had thrown them together, and it was down fate's path they now walked, arm in arm. So why, last night, had she shut Becky out? Why not tell her about the modelling shoot, Stan, her broken shoe? How Cee Cee had come to her rescue – a black knight in a well-cut suit? She'd been shocked by Becky's reaction. She hadn't seen that side of her before.

Deep down, though, Martha knew the reason she'd kept quiet was due to shame. Crazy really. Becky was hardly going to judge her. She might even be impressed because she was short of cash, too, and had been toying with the idea of auditioning as a Bunny Girl at the brand-new Raymond Revuebar. A second job that paid well, what with the tips and everything, would more than supplement her extravagant life-style. Their wages from the café and the department store covered their rent and food, enough for three meals a day, but they were young. They were living in London. The world was changing. Not for them the dreary life of their parents. They wanted to live life to the full. There were records to collect, shows to see, clothes and shoes to buy, sweets, magazines, and endless coffees. They wanted to have fun. There was jazz to listen to and, in Becky's case, rock 'n' roll. But despite being the most uninhibited person Martha had ever met, Becky hadn't summoned up the nerve to apply for the Revuebar job.

Not that it mattered. The shoot with Stan was a one-off.

Becky bangs again, violent enough this time to rattle the glass in the panes.

'Stop it this instant, Rebecca Turner,' shouts Mrs Wilson as she thumps on Becky's door. 'Have you no care for other people's property? I won't stand for it, I really won't. And you, Lady Day. You can keep it down, too.'

Martha sighs, turns down the volume, and wanders over to the mirror. She takes in her too-big eyes, her mismatched lips – the top one thinner than the lower – and her overlap-ping front teeth, her shoulder-length tangle of chestnut hair, and dimpled cheeks. Turning side-on, she pulls her nightdress flat and studies the ample outline of her breasts. *A natural,*

Stan had said. *Your future is golden.* Would it be so bad if she posed a second time? If she was going to a jazz club she really ought to dress the part. Becky was right. The polka-dot frock was old-fashioned and twee. She needed something to show off her figure. A chic black dress like Loretta's, only shorter. Yes, definitely shorter, like the one she'd seen in the window of Bazaar the other day. A neat little blazer to go with it, and another pair of stilettos, black this time to set the outfit off. She'd need a haircut as well. Something modern and classy. Something big and bouffant. Or a pixie cut, perhaps, like Delilah Moore. Trouble was, she only had fifteen shillings left. One more session with Stan wouldn't hurt. And then she'd stop. No one need ever know. It would be her secret.

She bites her lip. No. She can't. She mustn't. She'd promised Cee Cee she'd never go back.

4

It's a warm night, and the air is humming with conversation and laughter as the people of Soho prepare to party. Drinkers at the Blue Posts have spilled out onto the pavement and, outside the Flamingo Club opposite, a group of black GIs are smoking and drinking rum straight from the bottle.

Martha glances at the downward-pointing arrow beneath the illuminated Coca-Cola logo. This is it, she thinks. Unsteady on her heels, she totters past the Americans. Acutely aware of their eyes on her back, she stares straight ahead and, ignoring their whistles and invitations for a good time, makes her way slowly down the stairs.

A man in a booth asks to see her ticket.

'Cee Cee Campbell invited me,' she says.

He scans the clipboard on the desk. 'Martha Palmer?' He studies her cautiously as if she doesn't quite fit Cee Cee's description.

She bites her lips and nods.

'Okay, duck. Go on through.'

The room is crowded and hot – too hot – and reeks of

stale beer, sweat, and the smoke from countless cigarettes, which spiral into blue-tinged clouds and hover beneath the low ceiling. A few feet away on the small stage, a sallow-faced man in an ill-fitting suit and open-necked shirt is playing an upright piano. She recognises the tune, 'April in Paris', and hums along silently until he begins another, sprightlier piece she doesn't recognise. She takes in the dark-red walls, the coffee bar in the corner, and the jazz enthusiasts, clad head to toe in black, but there's no sign of Cee Cee. What if he doesn't turn up? She can hardly hang around here on her own. With no one to talk to she feels awkward enough as it is. But she can't go home either. Mrs Wilson will have bolted the door by now. She should've asked if Becky could come. She should've …

'Hey there, little lady.'

She spins around. 'Clive. I mean Cee Cee.'

He cocks his head. 'Oh, so it is you. For a moment I wasn't sure. You look … different.'

She fidgets, shifting her weight as he studies her neat bob, the black dress and jacket. Has she gone too far?

'I like it,' he says eventually.

She stares at him, tongue-tied. He is dressed as stylishly as before, the same well-cut black suit and sunglasses.

'I tink you need a drink.' He winks and, linking his arm in hers, steers her through a door she hadn't noticed to the left of the stage, into a small, dimly lit room, unfurnished apart from a scattering of chairs, one of which is buried under an untidy pile of coats. Kit bags and music cases are dotted around the floor, and a double bass is propped up against the wall.

'Rum okay?' Cee Cee asks, and closes the door behind them.

Is it? She has no idea. But she nods anyway.

'Good. Coz it's all I got.' He shakes his head and, chuckling to himself, rummages inside a well-worn canvas bag. 'Here.' He hands her a couple of enamel mugs, dips back in and pulls out a bottle. He twists out the cork, sniffs the contents and, humming appreciatively, pours.

'Cheers!' He holds up his mug.

Martha raises hers to his. Eyeing the amber liquid, she takes a tentative sip. The fiery scorch of it burns her throat, and her eyes water.

'Hmm, mm. Now dat is one mighty fine Jamaican rum.'

'Yeah … tis,' she whispers, hoarsely.

'Glad you approve, little lady.'

The door swings open, and a tall slender man storms into the room. He's dressed similarly, though not identically, to Cee Cee, in a neat black suit, white shirt and tie, and is carrying a trumpet case, which he slams down. He kicks out wildly, spitting expletives, and a chair topples over onto the floorboards with a crash.

'Hey, cool it, mon,' Cee Cee says. 'Dere's a lady present.'

The man stops swearing, turns, and glares at Martha.

She smiles awkwardly. 'Hello.'

'Marta Palmer,' Cee Cee says. 'A friend of mine.'

The man narrows his eyes and squashes his lips together in a thin line. Sensing he's about to explode, Martha takes a precautionary step back. But instead of erupting, the man exhales loudly, his jaw relaxes, and his lips return to their normal size.

Cee Cee chuckles. 'Bo Rivers. Mi bredrin and mi band leader.'

'Oh!'

'You sound surprised,' Bo Rivers says.

She is surprised. For some reason she'd assumed he was black.

'Apologies. I'm not normally this rude.' He raises his

hand in a brief salute and slumps into a chair. 'Had some bad news.'

Cee Cee's smile gives way to a frown. 'Go on.'

'It's Lila.'

'What about her?'

'She can't sing.'

'Oh no. Poor thing,' says Martha.

'She's not ill,' Bo snaps.

'Well, thank goodness for that,' Martha says. 'Oh, but she's not hurt, is she?'

He throws up his hands and groans.

'What is it?' Cee Cee asks. 'What's happened?'

'The stupid b…' Bo Rivers stops and takes a couple of long deep breaths. 'We're fucked. Apologies to your friend, Cee Cee, but that's how it is.' He springs out of the chair and paces the room, the metal heels of his boots clip-clopping on the floorboards.

Martha watches in a daze. This is not the stuff of which her dreams are made.

Cee Cee clicks his tongue. 'We may not be.'

'Oh, come on. We're up shit creek, not a paddle in sight.'

'Marta can sing.'

Bo stops pacing and squints at him. 'Who?'

'Marta Palmer.' Cee Cee gestures to her with an elaborate sweep of his hand.

Bo pulls a face. 'Her?'

'Me?' Her heart is in her mouth. Has he gone mad?

'Yeah. Why not?'

'Because I've never heard of her, that's why not.' Bo Rivers clears his throat and turns to her. 'No offence, mind.'

Martha shrugs. 'None taken.'

'I tink we should at least hear her. Lila is her idol. She knows all her songs. Don't you, little lady?'

'You do?'

'I—'

Bo scowls. 'No, Cee Cee. It's ridiculous.'

'C'mon, Bo. Let's at least have a listen. Here, take dis.' Cee Cee hands him his mug, snaps open his case, takes out his saxophone, and places a reed in his mouth.

Martha's jaw drops. She thinks she must be the butt of some elaborate joke. Cee Cee can't be serious, putting her on the spot like this. He only met her yesterday. He hasn't heard her sing. Not a single note.

The reed damp enough, Cee Cee attaches it to the mouth-piece with the ligature and blows. It's a little off, so he fiddles with it and blows again. A perfect A. He repeats the procedure, this time an F sharp, hooks the strap around his neck, and clips it to his sax. 'What harm can it do?'

Oh my God, he's serious. Hands clenched, she stands frozen to the spot, aware of Bo's eyes darting every which way across her body, as if the answer to Cee Cee's question lies hidden about her person. Her palms are sweating. She unclasps them and folds her arms instead. How did she get into this mess?

'Okay. Fine.' Bo flops into a chair three feet from where she's standing. 'We'll give her a go.'

What? Really? After everything he's said? Her knees tremble, and her breath is coming in short bursts.

His eyes still glued on her, Bo Rivers takes a packet of cigarettes from his front pocket, eases one out, and pops it between his lips without lighting it, all the time tapping his foot impatiently.

This really is happening. She thinks if she doesn't faint from shock, she'll fall over anyway.

'What'll you sing?' Cee Cee asks.

Her mind is blank. She looks at him despairingly, rolling her lower lip between her teeth.

He smiles. 'How about "Tenderly"? You know dat one?'

She nods and clears her throat.

'Go ahead, Martha,' Bo says, the cigarette still clamped between his teeth. 'The floor is yours.'

5

The Bo Rivers' Five is playing 'Round Midnight'. Martha knows every note. She's sung along to June Christy's haunting version often enough, trying to imitate her phrasing and husky tone. The band is playing it well. Bo Rivers' and Cee Cee's solos, alongside the piano, have captured the soulful, after-hours feel of the piece. But the fact no one is singing is driving her crazy. It would be so much better with the vocals; more melancholic, more mysterious.

Why am I still here? I shouldn't have hung around. I should've walked out when I had the chance. She'd been on the verge of doing so. Had wanted to leave but hadn't, out of respect for Cee Cee. How could she when he'd been so kind?

If only she knew what had gone wrong. Bo Rivers sitting opposite her, his expression unreadable, arms folded, left leg crossed over right, unlit cigarette between his lips – lips which seemed too plump for a white man – eyes fixed on her. Strange eyes, barely blue, almost colourless. Or grey, perhaps. They'd bored into her, unblinking, as if she was an enigma he was attempting to crack. It was unnerving yet, somehow, she'd managed to hold his gaze and complete the audition without a hitch.

She'd smiled – a small one, mind, barely perceptible. And why not? Despite her nerves, her voice hadn't betrayed her. In fact, it had sounded louder than usual, bolder, as if someone else, someone better than her had possessed her, temporarily.

But how she regrets that smile. Long after she'd finished, Bo Rivers had continued to stare at her, his unlit cigarette dangling from slightly parted lips. Certain she was blushing, she'd lowered her head and stared at her hands. Her senses seemed to be on high alert. She could taste the Marmite from this morning's breakfast; could smell the lingering odour of sour sweat, the wood polish and mothballs, Cee Cee's musky aftershave; could hear the paint peeling off the walls, the light bulb swinging from the ceiling in time to the music from next door, but which jarred with the uneven beat of her heart.

Cee Cee, ever the gentleman, had congratulated her immediately. Kind of him, but it was Bo Rivers' opinion that mattered. Why didn't he speak? Was he still scrutinising her? By the way her scalp prickled she was sure he was, his laser-like stare penetrating her skin in search of her soul.

She raised her head. Their eyes collided, and the cigarette fell from his mouth. 'Good God.'

Her stomach lurched. He hated it. She should never have agreed to sing. Stupid. Stupid. Stupid. Heat flooded her cheeks, and her heart struck up a fearful rhythm, urging her to make a dash for it while what remained of her dignity was still intact.

'See! I told you she was special.'

Cee Cee spoke as if he'd heard her sing a hundred times. What faith he had. She wanted to hug him. Perhaps she would when this whole horrible ordeal was over.

'You have the purest tone I've ever heard,' Bo said. 'Thank you for that.'

Wait. What? Had she heard right? 'I—'

Bo Rivers held up his hand. 'But you can't sing with us.'

'What do you mean, she can't?'

'She isn't Delilah Moore, Cee Cee, and it's her they're expecting.'

'When she starts to sing, dey won't care.'

'Maybe not. You'll stay, though, Martha? Listen to our set?' Without waiting for an answer, he backed away and began making strange buzzing sounds.

She should have left then, but the rest of the band had wandered in, and Bo, who'd picked up his trumpet and was warming up with a soft G as if nothing out of the ordinary had happened, had paused to introduce them: Mike the drummer, skinny and soft-spoken; tall, bearded Frankie on the double bass; and Roly, a rotund Jamaican pianist. They'd been friendly, welcoming but distracted, their minds focused on the job in hand. She'd understood entirely. The evening was a big deal, complicated by Delilah Moore's absence. Why would they be interested in Cee Cee's new friend?

As the band was called to the stage, Cee Cee suggested she sit behind them. He was being kind again, treating her as an insider. She tried to say no, that she was happy to watch from the floor, but he wouldn't hear of it. Her self-respect in tatters and feeling every inch a hanger-on, she took her place on a dilapidated sofa on the stage behind them.

The trickle of applause for 'Salt Peanuts' brings her back to the present. The audience is underwhelmed. It's a cruel reaction to a good performance, but she's not surprised. They're not here to listen to some unknown sideshow. They're here for Delilah Moore. They're her fans. They feel let down, understandably so. Delilah Moore is a star. Bo

Rivers, for all his good looks, subtle improvisations, and impeccable timing, means nothing to them. He's simply another musician hoping for a break.

Just like her.

Behind the piano, Roly shifts in his seat and adjusts his braces until they lie flat over his belly. Frankie throws a worried glance at Mike, nervously twirling his drumsticks. Mike gives an almost imperceptible shake of his head and looks away. In the centre of the stage, Bo dabs his mouth with a white handkerchief then opens the valve of his trumpet. A stream of saliva trickles onto the stage as he steps back to the mic where he pauses, perhaps scanning the room for a friendly face.

'Thank you,' he says eventually. 'And now here's one I know you're going to love. "A Night in Tunisia."'

A crowd-pleaser, for sure, she thinks. This should get them going.

A man whistles his appreciation, another claps, but that's all. She glances at Cee Cee, his face a study in concentration, his forehead glistening. He's not sweating from the fast tempo. It's fear. They've bombed, and he knows it. Roly's chins are on his chest and, judging by Mike's and Frankie's faraway expressions, their minds are elsewhere. She sympathises, she really does, but she's also mighty relieved. Truth is, she's had a lucky escape. If Bo Rivers hadn't been such an arrogant pig, she'd be up there with them, her career over before it had begun. Serves him right.

She glances over at him. Eyes closed, knees bent, he leans back and blows hard for a moment before tipping forward at the waist. Righting himself, he takes the head and plays a burning solo, hitting the high notes with confidence and inter-spersing the melody with the occasional growl. He's working his socks off, using every last ounce of energy in his effort to entertain the crowd. To no avail.

Thank God, she thinks. It might have been me.

Half an hour has passed, although it seems much longer. Bo Rivers is introducing the band to the audience again, but Martha is wondering what she'll do when the set is over. She can't go home. Mrs Wilson won't unbolt the door until six. Still, it's an hour earlier than she used to since she's now the proud owner of Elsie, a little white poodle.

'Oh, the irony,' Becky said, when they spotted them walking down Old Compton Street. 'She could be one of the French prostitutes she detests so much.'

All the same, Martha will have several hours to kill. The basement beneath the Freight Train Coffee Bar stays open all night. Or the Top Ten Club below Sam Widges, opposite, if she can get in. Becky keeps telling her she should try.

'It's full of musicians smoking marijuana as they wind down from gigs,' she'd told her. 'Perfectly safe and a lot of fun. You'll be in your element.'

A warm burst of applause interrupts Martha's thoughts. The audience are smiling. What on earth has Bo Rivers done to so dramatically alter the mood?

He winks at her and grins broadly. 'You ready?' he mouths.

For what, she starts to say, but Bo Rivers, now holding out his hand, has turned to face the crowd.

'Ladies and gentlemen, I'm delighted to introduce to you the delightful and extremely talented, Miss Martha Palmer.'

6

The Fairchilds, as I was to discover in the months to come, adored people. Or to be more precise, Martha Fairchild – although everyone always called her Martha Palmer – adored people, and the rest of the family were happy to be carried along on the wave of her enthusiasm. She was a persuasive character. Irresistible, too. Why else would I have let her take my hand that night and lead me to the diabolical twins, meek as a lamb?

She turned to me and smiled knowingly. 'They're the most darling boys. Mischievous and fun. But I have a feeling you already know that.'

I nodded, a dumb mute, too overawed to speak.

I didn't realise it at the time, but in hindsight it was obvious. It was love at first sight, if you could label a teenage infatuation with an older woman love. I'd fallen under Martha's spell, as so many others had before me, and so many more would in years to come. There was something magical about her, some ethereal charm which rendered her more exquisite, more essential than us mere mortals. She was the person I hoped to be, the air I wanted to breathe, and that was even before I'd heard her sing.

But I digress. Throughout that long hot summer, the Fairchild's house was always packed with guests – long-lost friends, casual acquaintances, television personalities, dancers, musicians, and exotic strangers – who, like the weather, came and went without invitation or warning. It was a house bursting with energy, a place where things happened, where life was lived to the full. There were parties which lasted well into the early hours of the morning. Wine flowed, the barbecue sizzled, and men and women of all shapes, ages, and colours, played trumpets, clarinets, saxophones, double basses, and the piano Teddy sometimes wheeled out onto the patio. Jazz emblems with their skilfully crafted improvisations and embroidered rhythms, at times dark and muddy, at others pure and bright, became the soundtrack to an unforgettable summer. A lonely teenager adrift in the big wide world, I envied the musicians both their freedom and their sense of place. More than anything I longed to escape the confines of my dull existence and become a part of it all.

But I am jumping ahead. Let me return to that Christmas Eve, and the moment Martha Palmer deposited me at the games room door.

'Dear child, you have no idea how pretty you are.'

It was an odd thing to say and took me by surprise. An out-and-out tomboy who preferred jeans to dresses, climbing trees to playing with dolls, I paid little interest in my looks but, all the same, it got me thinking. Pretty? Me? That's good, isn't it? But as I mulled her words over in years to come, it occurred to me she'd meant it as advice or, perhaps, a warning. She stared at me, solemnly, for a moment, stroking my cheek with the back of her hand, and then she was gone. I wanted to follow her but was concerned she might think less of me if I did. So, I took a deep breath and walked into the room.

It was dripping with Christmas decorations – a large tree in the corner, laden with baubles; twisted stripes of crepe paper stretched across the ceiling; shiny foil curtains hanging from the walls – and full of excitable children. The twins were playing a frantic game of table football with Barney Bracken and Peter Fitzwilliam, two fifteen-year-old boys from the village. They had their backs to me, but even so they were far too engrossed in their game to notice my arrival, whooping with delight and spinning the handles so vigorously the legs rose off the floor. Head down, I made for the corner where a group of girls I knew were playing French elastic. The craze had swept through our school last summer and had proved so popular we'd continued to play it indoors. I'd been practising like mad between two stools and, having managed to master the more difficult 'hipsies' level, welcomed any chance to show off my skills. I was hard at it when my father came to find me, a couple of hours later, to tell me it was time to go home.

Judging by the twinkle in his eye and his enormous grin, he'd been enjoying himself. And, as we strolled home, he rattled off a series of jokes, chuckling mischievously each time he delivered the punchline. He hadn't been this happy for far too long and, his mood contagious, I was soon laughing along with him.

'I'm going to dig my old jazz records out of the attic,' he said as he turned out my light, something he'd taken to doing since my mother's self-imposed confinement. 'We could listen to them tomorrow if you'd like.'

I told him I would like it very much and, for the first time in ages, fell sleep with a smile on my lips.

The following morning, I rubbed the sleep from my eyes

and was surprised to see the familiar striped stocking draped over the end of my bed. I'd assumed, things being the way they were, my father would have put an end to this family tradition. The Christmas Day lunch with fifteen members of my mother's family certainly wasn't happening this year, and neither was the Boxing Day drinks party she threw for half the village. But there was the stocking. Same as ever.

It's going to be okay, I thought as I pulled it towards me. This is the start. Life will get back to normal now.

Alongside the traditional chocolate coins, the tangerine, Jelly Tots, and bag of nuts, was a bottle of bubble bath decorated like a sailor, a tube of bath salts, three slightly babyish cotton handkerchiefs printed with lucky charms, and a bottle of mustard which, when opened, released a screaming snake, and I giggled and squealed at the same time.

After I'd eaten the edible gifts, I joined my father at the breakfast table. The first thing that struck me was how physically altered he was. For starters he'd shaved off his moustache, which had taken years off him, but there were other, more subtle differences, too. He was discernibly taller, his shoulders pinned back, adding a good inch in height. The dark shadows beneath his eyes had vanished, and he was brimming with energy. He danced around the kitchen, smiling and cracking jokes as he sliced the bread and broke eggs into a bowl, which he whisked with as much enthusiasm as he spoke. It was as though someone had waved a magic wand and transformed him overnight into a younger, more vibrant version of himself. My old father, minus the facial hair, the one I'd longed and prayed for these past ten months.

'I found those records in the attic, by the way,' he said when he served up the toast and eggs. 'They were buried in the old trunk. I hope I didn't keep you awake rummaging around for them.'

The discovery had clearly surprised and excited him, as if he'd expected my mother, during one of her many tidying splurges in the good old days, had thrown them away. I'd lost most of my treasured toys that way and dozens of my favourite books, all deemed to be taking up valuable room in the cavernous space.

'Louis Armstrong, Charles Mingus and Parker, Stan Getz, Ella Fitzgerald, Billie Holiday, Chet Baker, Thelonious Monk, and every one of Martha Palmer's LPs.'

I gasped. 'The woman we met last night? She's a singer?'

'She is indeed. Would you like to listen to one of her records while we peel the sprouts?'

I nodded and gobbled up my scrambled eggs. I could think of nothing better.

Fifteen minutes later, as I watched my father tease the vinyl disc out of the dog-eared sleeve with the same tenderness he treated his patients, a funny feeling came over me. Martha Palmer had made such a huge impression on me, what if I was disappointed? What if her voice didn't match up to her beauty, her charm? It seems crazy now because I can still recall, with alarming clarity, the warmth that coursed through my veins the moment I first heard her sing. Silky smooth and pure in tone, her voice was at times wistfully husky, at others, determinedly bombastic. Listening to Martha with my father, peeling vegetables at the kitchen table, made for a very different start to Christmas Day, and even when my mother, citing yet another migraine, refrained from making an appearance, an unexpected and enjoyable one. With no strict timetable to adhere to, we played three more Martha Palmer LPs before eventually tucking into a later-than-usual lunch.

'It really was a joy to see her again after all this time. An absolute joy.' My father, relaxing in his armchair by the fire later that evening, reached for his pipe. 'What an incredible voice she has. She really is magnificent.'

And that was it in a nutshell. Martha Palmer *was* magnificent. She was beautiful, talented, and magnetic, too, but more than anything she was infinitely memorable. Why, then, had my father never mentioned her before? I opened my mouth to ask but one glance at my father – a smile on his lips, his fingers strumming the arm to the rhythm of the music – I knew now was not the time. Martha Palmer had transformed our life, and for that I was grateful. There'd be plenty of time for questions later.

If I thought Martha Palmer was going to become a fixture of our lives from now on, I couldn't have been more wrong. Christmas and its momentary magic over, life continued gloomily. Father returned to work to be consumed by his patients, while my mother remained in her bedroom, doors locked, curtains drawn, like some crazed character in a Gothic novel. The tiny bud of optimism I'd sensed, instead of blooming, as I'd hoped, withered and died. No further invitations from the Fairchilds were forthcoming, and clearly my father had no intention of reciprocating. To make matters worse, Hayley telephoned on the second day of the New Year to tell me she and her family had moved to Wales to be near her ailing grandmother for the foreseeable future.

'It's two years till O levels, and my parents are sending me to a new school. My life is over.'

My life, on the other hand, was doomed. Isolated, miserable, and desperate for another slice of the glamorous lifestyle I'd tasted all too briefly, I took to sitting on the wall beneath the bank outside our house after school. I longed for a glimpse of Martha Palmer, walking a dog perhaps, or out and about in her car. Wishful thinking, of course. I had no idea if she had a dog, or what car she drove, let alone its colour. Too scared to drop in, I reasoned if Martha saw me it might provoke her into inviting me over. The plan was sound. Every time she left home, she'd pass by me. And if I wasn't there when she did, I hoped our paths might cross at the small shopping precinct down the road. I was always popping in to spend my pocket money or run errands for my dad.

One day, we came tantalising close. My father was exiting the car park when a woman in a long Afghan coat and a floppy hat dashed in front of the car. He slammed on the brakes, but the woman disappeared into the newsagent's without so much as a glance in our direction.

'Was that Martha Palmer?' I asked.

She'd been tall and stylish enough, but I'd seen her only fleetingly and wasn't sure. I craned my neck, but the woman was gone.

'Goodness, I hope not,' he said as he pulled away. 'I almost ran her over.'

Back home, I dug out my father's binoculars and returned to my cold, damp perch, hoping to catch her on her way home. Staring intently at the driver of each passing car, I was rewarded with a barrage of V-signs and other unspeakable gestures in return.

My father's patients grew increasingly concerned by my behaviour. This was entirely due to their misreading of the situation.

'You'll catch your death if you carry on,' Mrs Bracken said one day when I returned to the house after dark. 'Or, at the very least, piles.'

'Piles?'

'Ooh! Ghastly things, piles,' Mrs Fitzwilliam said and

shook her head knowingly. 'You don't want them, Natasha. Not at your age.'

'It's perfectly natural to be sad,' Mrs Bracken continued, 'but sitting out there in all weathers isn't going to bring him back. What you need is a hobby.'

You have no idea what I need, I thought and, clenching my jaw, hurried to the kitchen.

It was a Thursday evening in early May, and the weather had been unseasonably warm all day, a harbinger of the dizzyingly hot summer to come. The Taylors, still living in Wales, had employed me to water their plants until the threatened hosepipe ban was put in place. It wasn't a difficult job, but given the number of flowerbeds, the prized rose garden, and the vast vegetable plot the gardener still tended once a week, lugging the hose from one area to the next was time-consuming work. Not that I cared. I was pleased to be out of the house. With nothing to occupy me after school except homework, singing practice, and the endless patter of my father's patients, I'd been bored out of my brain. But it wasn't the only reason. The Taylor's house backed on to Greystones, so even though I wasn't actually *with* Martha Palmer, I felt closer to her there.

Rafferty was with me. He was lying in the shade, head on his paws, ears occasionally twitching, and watching me. I was singing with more gusto than usual because there was a point to my practice now. My teacher, Miss Hendrik, had asked if I'd like to do another solo, this time in the summer concert. I hadn't hesitated for a second. If I'd learned anything from Christmas, it was that I loved to perform. I knew exactly what song I would choose, too – 'At Last', the Etta James version my father also adored – but first I had to convince Miss Hendrik. There was no point simply telling her. She was bound to say it was inappropriate. But, if I practiced it to perfection, there was a chance she'd agree. Well, that was the plan anyway, and that was what I was doing when the shot was fired, shattering an empty milk bottle I hadn't noticed, inches to the right of me. I jumped out of my skin, and the jet of water from the hose squirted into my face. Rafferty leapt to his feet, barking, and dashed across the lawn. I spun around, heart thumping, half expecting to see a masked IRA soldier lurking in the bushes. It wasn't so crazy a notion. There'd been a spate of attacks on the mainland recently, and our local theatre had been evacuated last week following a bomb scare. But why would the IRA want to shoot me?

Hackles raised, Rafferty was snarling at a rhododendron bush. My mind screamed run, but my legs refused to budge. But then somebody snickered and the leaves shook. Rafferty stopped growling and wagged his tail.

Oh great. The twins. Who else could it be?

Intent on revenge, I dragged the hose across the lawn. The gun didn't bother me anymore. Clearly, they'd meant to frighten me, not kill me. I hadn't quite reached their hiding place when out they sprang. I upped my pace, but they were already scrambling onto Choppers, way too small for them, and pedalling furiously, their bottoms out of the saddle. I aimed the hose in their direction, but they sped through the hole in the hedge and down the twitten, Rafferty in hot pursuit. My cheeks smarting, I stamped my feet, furious they'd managed to humiliate me a second time.

After a few minutes I'd calmed down enough to sing again and was well into my stride when, like a vision in a dream, Martha Palmer appeared. Barefoot in a white sundress, she was holding a small posy of lily of the valley and smiling at me. The sun behind her, the shapely outline of her long, slender legs through the diaphanous material of her dress was visible. Her chestnut hair was curled into waves, her russet eyes framed with kohl.

'Forgive the intrusion,' she said, 'but I was enjoying listening to you. I do hope you'll continue.'

Rafferty nuzzled my leg, and I patted his head absently, gaping like an idiot, my hair tangled and wet.

'Oh no! You won't. Well then, I shall go.' She laughed, a light tinkling sound like the high notes of a piano.

'No! Don't. I mean, stay. Please stay.' My voice was hardly more than a squeak. Worse still, I was fighting back tears. This wasn't how it was meant to be.

Martha laughed her pretty little laugh. 'I'm sorry, I've startled you. You have such a lovely voice, I felt compelled to tell you.'

The bottom of my neck to the tips of my ears burned.

'There now. No need to be embarrassed.' She touched my arm, and a strange fluttering sensation in the pit of my stomach only heightened my discomfort.

'What a gorgeous dog.' She bent down and fondled Rafferty's ears. 'Oh! Your feet are soaked.'

I glanced at the now translucent white canvas of my sodden shoes and wondered if it was actually possible to die of shame. Feet squelching, I marched over to the tap and turned it off. Martha followed. Half of me was glad she did, half of me wished she hadn't.

'I'm Martha Fairchild, by the way.'

I wanted to tell her I knew exactly who she was, that she was not only unforgettable but also the most beautiful person I'd ever met. But the nearness of her continued to render me dumb, so I bent down and unlaced my shoes instead.

'And you are?'

My heart sank. She'd forgotten me. Of course she had. There was nothing special about me. I was completely and utterly forgettable. I slipped out of my shoes and mumbled my reply. 'Natasha James.'

'Pleased to meet you, Natasha.'

'Actually, we've already met,' I said, finding my voice at last. 'At Christmas. You had a party. You know my father. Dr James.'

Her eyes swivelled to the right.

'Gordon. Gordon James.' I willed her to remember. Our only connection, it was important she did.

She exhaled loudly and shook her head. 'Nope! Mind like a sieve.'

'You knew him. You … you called him Donny. No one ever calls him that.'

It was as if I'd flicked a switch. 'Donny? Darling Donny. Oh, my goodness, why didn't you say? How is he? Is he well? My, my! Donny's girl. Yes, yes, of course I remember. It was so unexpected seeing him again after all this time. I mean, what are the chances? Ah, but we were so different in those days. Young and pretty, just like you. I've been meaning to drop by. Do you think he'd like me to? When I didn't hear from him again, I didn't think he would. I'd hate to intrude. We were friends such a long time ago, you see. People change. It would be mortifying if I showed up unannounced and he didn't want to see me.'

Her words were sweeter than any song she'd ever sung, although I could hardly believe them. Never mind that she seemed genuinely fond of my father, this woman – more brilliant and more beautiful than anyone I'd ever met – had doubts and insecurities, just like the rest of us. She was a superstar but she was also real.

. . .

Thirty minutes later, after I'd returned Rafferty to Mrs Pocock and still a tad star struck, I sat on a stool in Martha Palmer's kitchen, watching her make bread, her long slender fingers balled into fists as she pulled and pummelled the dough. It was a light, airy room, twice the size of ours, with modern blue cupboards, wooden worktops, and blue-yellow-and-white geometric wallpaper. The surfaces were cluttered with magazines and records, dirty plates and glasses, and a vase of meandering pink and white tulips which were dropping their petals. A pearly-white shell mobile, hanging from the ceiling, chimed in the occasional breeze drifting in through the open window, and a Dinah Washington LP played on the stereo – although I knew this only because she'd told me. Outside, the pale-blue water of the swimming pool shimmered in the late afternoon sun, and beyond, a scattering of chickens pecked for corn in a dusty pen. There was no sign of the twins, and no mention of them either, which suited me fine. I couldn't have been happier.

'I can't send you back to Darling Donny without at least making you a cup of tea. Imagine how cross he'd be if he found out I hadn't even offered you a biscuit, not to mention what your mother would think.' She paused and bit her lip. 'I'm so sorry, I'm assuming you have a mother.'

I didn't have the heart to tell her my mother wouldn't give one jot whether she gave me tea or not and, for a split second, deliberated about denying her existence. How easy it would be. But what if Martha found out? She might think less of me, and I'd hate that. I nodded, and her mortified expression gave way to something resembling disappointment.

'And what does she do? Is she a doctor, too?'

The idea my mother had a job, let alone one as important as my father's, was so ludicrous I wanted to laugh. With a great deal of effort, however, I managed to restrain myself.

'My mother is ill,' I said, as if describing a profession. 'She's been ill for months.'

She stopped kneading again and regarded me earnestly. 'Oh dear. Oh dear, dear, dear. I'm sorry to hear that, Natasha. How awful.'

I slipped my hands in my pockets and focused on the set of animal mugs, hanging from hooks above a long wooden breakfast bar, which split the vast room in two. An elephant, a toucan, a lion, and an owl.

'Queen of the Blues they called her,' Martha said.

'Who?' Not my mother, surely?

'Dinah Washington.'

'I didn't know,' I said, relieved to be focusing on the music. How could I? The first I'd heard of Dinah Washington was ten minutes earlier, when Martha had put the record on.

'I adore her voice, don't you? It's so gritty.'

'Hmm. Very gritty.'

'She had perfect pitch, of course. This song, "Mad About the Boy", is my absolute favourite. I used to sing it, too, back in the days when I knew your dad. I was a singer, you see, not a patch on Dinah but a singer all the same. Donny was quite a fan. Loyal as well. He used to come and listen to me in the remotest of places.'

I wanted to tell her my father was her *greatest* fan, that he'd kept all her records, that he thought she was magnificent, but Martha was glancing at her watch, her mind elsewhere.

'Goodness, look at the time.' There was a light dusting of flour on her left cheek, I noticed, as she plonked the elastic dough in a bamboo basket, and traces in her hair. 'I'll leave this to prove while I go and find those boys of mine. I was so taken with your gorgeous voice earlier, I completely forgot I was looking for them. Where on earth have they got to, I wonder? They do have a habit of getting up to mischief. It's the twin thing, I suppose.'

My spirits sank. I'd forgotten all about them, too. Perhaps this was the time to tell her about the gun. I opened my mouth but thought better of it. No one likes a sneak. Fortunately, Martha, who was washing her hands under the tap, had her back to me and couldn't see.

Grabbing a tea towel, she whirled around. 'It was lovely to meet you, Natasha. Now, promise you'll mention me to your father.'

It was time to go, even though the tea and biscuits she'd offered hadn't materialised. I nodded, disappointed not, I hasten to add, by the lack of refreshment, but because this miraculous encounter had reached its conclusion. I followed her to the front door, where she picked up my hand and smiled at me coyly.

'You will do that for me, Natasha, won't you?'

7

The Gaggia machine is playing up as it does most Mondays. Giovanni Fiori, proud owner of The Grind, is trying his hardest to fix it before the first customers arrive. He is brandishing a spanner, in anger rather than with skill, banging a pipe while swearing loudly in Italian. '*Che cavolo!*'

Martha, who is buttering bread in the kitchen, giggles. The sound of a middle-aged Italian screaming *what cabbage* to a kitchen appliance never fails to amuse her. She wouldn't be chuckling if she was anywhere near him, however. She's seen what happens if you did, although, in all honesty, Luca had asked for it.

He'd arrived for work one morning, still drunk from the night before, and decided to fix himself a reviving coffee before opening up. Clearly not in the fittest state to be working the temperamental Gaggia, he failed to snap the basket firmly into place. When he pulled the shot, the muddy-brown liquid, instead of trickling into the cup, sprayed in every direction, over the pine counter, over the buns and sandwiches, and over Giovanni who was carefully slicing a large chocolate cake. One glance at his coffee-splattered boss, and Luca exploded with laughter. Grabbing a stale baguette, the nearest object to hand and cursing loudly, Giovanni struck Luca repeatedly on the back. The bread shattered into a thousand pieces, and Luca howled even more. His face now puce, Giovanni snatched a cream horn from the counter display and hurled it at Luca who ducked, just as Sofia Fiore arrived home from the school run. The pastry landed on her nose, splattering her face with cream. With impressive calm, Sofia removed the confectionary proboscis, ordered Giovanni, who was as biddable as a dog when it came to his wife, into the kitchen, and gave him a proper Italian dressing-down.

Despite his outbursts, which are as regular as his clientele, Martha has grown fond of her boss. Not a man to suffer fools, he is firm but fair. Staff must be punctual, polite, and tidy at all times. But he is generous with tips, and kind and patient when the occasion demands. On her first day, as she warily eyed the gleaming Gaggia, which spat and hissed and spewed out steam like a demented dragon, he took it upon himself to teach her how to make the perfect espresso.

'It is vital to use the right amount of coffee at the correct temperature, with beans ground to the proper consistency. Too coarse, and the water runs through too quickly and the coffee will be too weak. Too fine, and it packs too densely and the coffee will be bitter and without the crema. No crema, no good.'

'Crema?'

He pointed to the golden-brown froth. '*Questa*! The natural oil from the bean.' He showed her how to attach the basket securely and where to place the cup before turning on the machine. 'If you have done everything correctly, there will be a slight pause before the first drops trickle through and, when it is finished, *presto!* The crema will have settled on the surface. Delicious.'

The most popular drink by far was the cappuccino so named, Giovanni explained, because the milky foam resembled the white cowls of the Capuchin monks. 'My customers, though, they call it frothy coffee. *Che palle!* Why, I ask you? Why?'

The cappuccino consisted of one-third espresso, one-third steamed milk, and one-third frothed milk, with a light sprinkling of powdered chocolate on top. Steaming the milk wasn't as simple as it sounded. She had to stretch it to double the size, swirl and blend it, before finally heating it to the correct temperature so as not to overcook it. Martha found this the most challenging of all the beverages. She's had her share of spillages, mini milk explosions, and scalding burns, to which Giovanni almost always turns a blind eye – much to the irritation of Luca whose own mishaps never pass without criticism – but after twelve months she can honestly say she's tamed the beast.

The brass doorbell jingles, signalling the first customer of the day. One of the regulars, most likely – Iron Foot Jack in his black cloak and wide-brimmed hat, Dipper Da Costa the out-of-work actor, or Milton Hyde the raffish poet – all of them skilled in the art of slow coffee consumption, a single cup lasting up to three hours.

'Soho is a village,' Giovanni explained when she asked why, given the café is so small, he tolerated their behaviour. 'And in villages people look out for one another.'

This care for the community, however, did not extend to the sandwich-board men.

'All this talk about flying saucers and the end of the world is not good for business. Crazy mad, the whole lot of them.

And they … how you say, *puzza*?' He clicked his fingers and screwed up his nose. '*Puzza, puzza …*'

'Smell?'

'No, Martha. These people do not smell. They stink.'

Of course, it might not be a 'villager' at all but some teenagers searching for the 2i's Coffee Bar, around the corner in Old Compton Street. She pictures Giovanni, shrugging effusively while pleading ignorance, before furtively placing a Tommy Steele or Marty Wilde record on the Dansette he keeps hidden under the Formica counter, precisely for such occasions. The teenagers, their auditory senses satisfied, duly take their places at the proffered table and order cappuccinos and cake. This he calls, Giovanni Magic. Not for the first time she wonders why he hasn't bought a jukebox like all the other coffee bars. But following the crowd is not Giovanni's style.

'Martha! *Visitatore!*' Giovanni's voice is insistent and sharp.

Who on earth would call on her here? Becky? It must be. Nobody else knows where she works. Oh, wait a minute, Loretta, Stan Waterfield's assistant, does. She shivers. Would she call in on her at work? Better get out there quick before Giovanni begins his interrogation. Finding out who people are and what they do is another special talent of his.

A knot of apprehension in her belly, she puts down the buttering knife and rushes into the shop. A tall man in a fedora and raincoat, the collar turned up, is staring intently at a large canvas of a jazz saxophonist on the far wall. He has his back to her and is clearly riveted by the painting, which like all the other art on display is for sale, because he doesn't look around when she enters. The knot gives way to a frisson of excitement. Cee Cee. She told him where she worked the first time they met, a throwaway line she hadn't expected him to remember.

'I tell him you are busy, but he is most insistent,' says Giovanni, vigorously drying a coffee cup.

The man swivels around. His face, which is set in a stern expression, lights up on sight of her. 'Martha!'

She steps back in alarm. Bo Rivers! 'What are you doing here?'

Giovanni slams the Pyrex cup on the Formica counter. 'Looking for you. Like I said.'

Bo Rivers removes his trilby and clutches it to his chest. 'The thing is … I mean, what I'm trying to say is … well … thank you. You were amazing. Incredible, really. You totally and utterly saved the day. I can't thank you enough but—'

'Save the day?' Giovanni hooks the tea towel over his arm and runs his hand through his unruly hair. '*Che cazzo dici?* Can this not wait? I have a business to run.'

'I'm sorry, sir, this won't take long, but there's something I need to ask Martha. Would you mind giving us a minute—'

Giovanni bangs another coffee cup on the counter. 'A minute! Really, Mr Bo …' Giovanni gives a disparaging flick of his tea towel. 'Bo! What kind of a name is Bo?'

He shrugs. 'It means "friend" somewhere in Africa, I gather.'

'*Uffa*! Big place, Africa.'

Bo raises his eyebrows and turns back to Martha. 'It's a bit short notice, but are you free on Saturday?'

'*Basta! Basta*!'

He glances nervously at Giovanni. 'I'm sorry, I don't speak—'

'Enough, it means enough,' Martha says. *What's going on here? Is he asking me out on a date?*

'Oh right. I see,' Bo Rivers says, although it's plain he doesn't because he presses on. 'So, Martha. *Are* you free?'

'*Che cavolo*! Are you deaf as well as dumb?'

Bo winces as if physically struck. 'To sing, that is.'

'Sing?' Thanks to Giovanni's expletive-laden interruptions, Martha has got lost somewhere in the conversation.

'Sing?' echoes Giovanni. 'What do you mean sing? She is a waitress.'

'At The Marquee,' says Bo.

Martha can hardly believe her ears. 'The club?'

'The Marquee?' Giovanni stares at Martha, eyes wide.

Clearly bewildered, Bo glances from one to the other. 'That's right. At ten o'clock on Saturday night.'

Resisting the urge to whoop, Martha clasps her hands. 'I'd love to. Thank you.'

Bo Rivers takes her hands in his. They are soft and warm, she notices. Her heart flutters. Out of excitement? Or fear?

'No, no. Thank *you*. You won't regret this, Martha. I promise you, you won't.'

'*Mama mia*!' says Giovanni. 'Would someone please explain what is going on?'

8

Today, it seems to Martha as she takes Milton Hyde's unusually large order of a coffee, a cheese-and-pickle sandwich, *and* a Chelsea bun, is a day full of surprises.

'Are you sure?' she asks the poet.

'Perfectly. You see, Martha, I'm celebrating.'

'That's nice.'

He makes a show of studying his nails; smooth and clean, the pronounced half-moons a lustrous white. 'I rather hoped you'd be the tiniest bit curious.'

She bites her lip to stop herself giggling. 'I'm sorry, Milton. What are you celebrating? Is it your birthday? Your wife's birthday?'

'Wife? Good God, girl, what on earth do you take me for? No, no, no.' He brings a fisted hand to his mouth. 'Ahem. Since you're kind enough to ask, I will tell you. I have sold, for publication, you understand, not one, not two, but three of my poems.'

'Congratulations, Milton. No wonder you're celebrating.'

'Why thank you, dear girl.'

She hurries over to the counter with his order. Luca is

topping up the tank on the counter with squash, the plastic orange bobbing about as he pours the liquid in.

He puts down the jug and raises an eyebrow. 'And he can afford all this, can he?'

'He's sold three poems.'

Luca whistles. 'So, the old queen isn't a fraud after all.'

'Seems not.' She takes a tray and a damp cloth and skips across the wooden floorboards to a recently vacated table by the window. She piles the cups, saucers, and plates into a tidy stack, wipes the red gingham plastic tablecloth, taking care to pick up the glass sugar dispenser, the vase with the two white carnations, and the stainless-steel ashtray to clean underneath as Giovanni has programmed her to do.

'If you do not do this every time,' he warned, 'I will notice.'

Not that she cares about such trivial matters today. Bo Rivers turning up at the café, genie-like, to ask her to sing with them again has given her confidence a much-needed boost. He'd been nervous, which surprised her. Was that because of the way he'd treated her the other night? Turning her down flat then thrusting her into the spotlight without so much as a *would you mind*?

She drops the cloth on the tray and casts her mind back to the Flamingo. Unsure of what was being asked of her when Bo Rivers introduced her to the audience, she glanced at Cee Cee who nodded and smiled encouragingly. Her heart was thumping so fast she thought it might burst out of her ribcage. The nerve of the man, putting her on the spot like this. It wasn't fair. She wavered, but the audience were whistling and clapping. What choice did she have? Sing or be laughed out of the club. Knees knocking, palms sweating, she walked slowly to the mic.

'Ladies and gentleman, and now, in her own inimitable

style, Miss Martha Palmer will perform Walter Gross and Jack Lawrence's 1940's classic, "Tenderly".' Bo Rivers picked up his trumpet and nodded at Roly, who struck up the melody on the piano. The audience applauded. Adrenaline surged through her body. She counted the beats, took a deep breath, opened her mouth, and sang.

The end of the number was greeted with cheers. The audience stamped their feet and begged for more. Martha couldn't believe her ears. They liked her. She was a success. She felt as if she was floating on air. She was in heaven. This was what she wanted, what she'd dreamed of …

Of course, she would sing with them again. It was a no-brainer.

His question answered, Bo Rivers thrust a card in her hands, made her promise to call him later, and left, leaving her to explain to a bewildered Giovanni, who was pacing the room while wringing the tea towel into a stiff knot, what had just happened. Was she a singer or was she a waitress? Was she handing in her notice?

'What, Martha? *Che cosa*?'

She'd assured him she had no intention of leaving. She was simply helping a friend.

'That man is your friend?'

'Er … no. He's a … a friend of a friend.'

Giovanni groaned and held his head in his hands. 'But you sing, Martha? You do sing?'

'Yes, Giovanni. I sing.' There was no need to go into any more detail, not that she reasonably could. The incredible situation hardly made sense to her either. All that mattered was she'd been given the break she'd craved. Finally, her life was on the up.

'Martha Palmer!'

The woman's voice is shrill and loud. Martha's attention,

along with everyone else's in the café – the dozen or so customers, Milton Hyde, Luca, and Giovanni – is drawn towards a petite woman, standing a foot inside the doorway. Draped in a fur coat, she is brandishing a rolled-up magazine. The briefest of silences, shattered by a collective intake of breath, confirms the instantly recognisable beauty of Delilah Moore.

Could this day get any better? Martha wonders as she admires the face which has adorned the front pages of so many magazines. Brightly lighting up the café's drab interior, casting shadows over the occupants, it is both familiar, yet unfamiliar, the almond eyes and flawless caramel skin fleshed out and brought to three-dimensional life. Martha holds up her hand, noticing, a little too late, the steely glint in her idol's cinnamon irises, her full, glossy lips pressed to a thin angry line.

'You!' Delilah bares her teeth and points an exquisitely manicured finger.

Twenty pairs of questioning eyes swivel in their sockets to settle on the source of Miss Moore's disapprobation.

Martha gulps. *Me*?

'YOU EVIL LITTLE BITCH!'

9

I suppose it was inevitable, following my conversation with Martha Palmer on that sunny May afternoon, that we'd receive another invitation to Greystones. And so, when a card duly landed on our doormat a fortnight later, inviting us to lunch the following Sunday, I wasn't altogether surprised.

My father, however, was astonished. 'Well, now. Isn't that kind of her?' His face lit up as he handed me the card. 'I'm sure she won't mind in the least if we don't go.'

'What? Why?'

'I thought you didn't like her boys?'

I'd returned from my visit to Martha on a high and had told my father everything; the circumstances surrounding our meeting; the prank the twins had played on me – although I substituted the peashooter for the gun. I wasn't completely stupid. Not only would he ban me from Greystones if he knew, but also it would reflect badly on Martha; how eager she was to see him again.

The truth was, up until that second, I hadn't given the twins a second thought. I only cared about seeing Martha. My admiration for her – I did not consider it an infatuation yet – was unconditional. Of course, I could tolerate her offspring if it meant another afternoon in her company. No one else matched up. No one else came close. No one else would do.

I shrugged. 'They won't be nasty to me in front of their parents, though, will they? So, yeah, I'd like to go.'

He eyed me quizzically. 'Are you sure?'

'If it's okay with you.'

'That's brave, Natasha. I'm proud of you.'

Years later, I wondered if this was when it finally dawned on him that, with Hayley gone, I was lonely outside of school. He couldn't possibly have known it was Martha Palmer's attention I craved.

'That's settled then.' My father flashed the broadest smile I'd seen since Christmas. 'We'll go.'

It was another warm day in mid-May, the sky a picture-post-card blue, cloudless apart from a smattering of rabbit tail puffs.

'Martha was most insistent we swim,' my father said, handing me my familiar striped beach towel. 'I seem to recall she can be very persuasive, so I think we should, at least, show willing.'

Delighted by the prospect of splashing around with her in her swimming pool, I dug out my costume buried deep in a drawer, rushed down the stairs, and set off along the twitten with my father, chattering excitedly. Sounds of the party reached us well before we arrived; a distant hum of music, conversation, and laughter which grew louder the closer we got. My heart sank. There were other guests, which meant I'd be bundled off with Louis and Charlie and all the other kids.

Martha met us at the door. She was barefoot again and

looked a million dollars in a slinky, primrose maxi dress. Her hair had been curled, and a cerise peony was tucked behind her ear. Mortified by our overly casual appearance, I glanced at my beaming father who, unabashed, was handing her a bottle of wine.

She laughed her delightful tinkle, threw her free arm around his neck, and kissed him on the cheek. 'Oh, Donny, I'm so pleased you came.'

'Wouldn't have missed it for the world.'

'And dear, sweet Natasha.' She took my hand and drew me in, so close my head came to rest beneath her shoulder. She smelt of lily of the valley, sweet and fresh as a spring garden. 'It's such a pretty name, Natasha. It really is,' she said as she released me. 'But rather long. Would you mind if I shortened it?'

'My friends call me Nat.'

She screwed up her nose. 'Like the nasty insect? Oh no, sweetheart. I was thinking, Tasha. It's far prettier. Would you mind?'

I blushed. I didn't care what she called me, only that she spoke to me. 'No, not at all.'

At the warm, mellow sound of a saxophone striking up a ballad, Martha held up her hand. 'Recognise him, Donny?'

My father cocked his ear, and a smile crept over his lean face. 'Cee Cee Campbell? Surely not?'

She laughed her tinkly laugh and, cradling the bottle, spun round on her tippy toes. 'The one and only, *and* his Crusaders.'

Outside on the sunken patio, the party was in full swing. A pig was roasting on a spit beside a barbecue, heaped with sausages, steaks and skewers of vegetables, and attended to by a man in a fawn apron, dripping sweat. Trestle tables covered in starched white cloths and decorated in vast swathes of flowers, were laden with salads, coronation chicken, bread rolls, and bowls of exotic fruit. Behind a wooden bar, a caramel-skinned man with jet-black hair, dressed in a white open-necked shirt and a striped waistcoat, was pouring multi-coloured drinks from bottles of all shapes and sizes. Women in exotic dresses and wide-brimmed hats smoked cigarettes and sipped cocktails decorated with paper umbrellas, and chatted to men in linen suits, flared jeans, and patterned shirts, none of whom I recognised. On the grass in front of a small circular stage, people swayed to the sultry rhythm of the music from the four-piece jazz band. My gaze swooped to the saxophonist in the dark glasses and pork pie hat. Cee Cee Campbell, the first jazz musician and black man I had ever seen, here, in our village. I watched in wide-eyed wonderment, drinking it all in. It was all so incredibly exotic; the energy of the musicians and the smoky, plaintive sound they produced.

'Hi, Natasha. Want a Coke?'

My reverie broken, I turned to see Louis. He was smiling at me, a tumbler of iced cola in each hand. His dark hair was longer and curlier than before and, up close, I noticed a smattering of freckles on his nose, a full lower lip, and overlapping front teeth. Exactly like Martha.

'Peace offering,' he said.

'Thanks.' The glass was freezing cold, so I passed it from hand to hand, but it was also dripping with condensation, and I was worried it would slip out of my grasp. Perhaps this was Louis' aim. Another prank.

'I told Dad there was too much ice, but he insisted. He's worried we'll all get too hot.'

'Right.' Unconvinced, I took a quick sip and put it on a nearby table.

'Fancy a swim? Unlike the Coke, the water is warm. Dad put the heating on. So, you see, he's not a total idiot.'

The pool was a little way off, up four or five steps. Several teenagers were already swimming, and a couple of girls were floating around on inflatable chairs. Martha was there, too, standing on the water's edge with my father. She was holding him by the arm, leaning in and whispering in his ear.

'Okay,' I said. 'Why not?'

'Great. I'll show you where to change.'

My father's eyes sparkled at whatever it was Martha had said. Neither he nor Martha heeded us as we strode past, and although I was pleased how happy Martha made him, I felt a pang of jealousy it was he and not I who'd captured her attention.

The changing shed was lined with floral paper and had a wooden bench along one side and a row of hooks above. I hung up my clothes and slipped my costume over my feet, but I'd grown a lot in the last year and it took a lot of wriggling and writhing to get it on. It was uncomfortably tight. The straps cut into my shoulders, and the leg holes stretched above my hip bones.

Undeterred, I wrapped my towel around me and waddled awkwardly towards the pool. Martha and my father were no longer there, but Charlie was. Standing on a low diving board, he was smirking in his cocksure way. With his blond hair and his lean, tanned body, he cut a striking figure in his red shorts, more attractive even, than the girls bobbing about in the deep end, flicking water at him. His attention, however, was focused on me. Satisfied he'd caught my eye, he ran down the board, bounced into the air, and jackknifed into the pool with barely a splash. Seconds later, he exploded through the surface and shook the water out of his hair. The girls shrieked and clapped, but Charlie ignored them, his gaze firmly fixed on me.

'What are you waiting for, Natasha James?'

A pretty blonde, bobbing about on one of the inflatable chairs, turned to me and smiled. She was slim and had on the skimpiest bikini, constructed of three tiny triangles of white fabric.

Another girl pulled herself out and sat on the side. 'Don't be shy,' she said as she adjusted her equally skimpy top.

My cheeks flared. I couldn't go swimming. Not with them. Not in this too-small monstrosity with my too-flat chest. Two peas on an ironing board, Barney Bracken had called my budding breasts. Why hadn't I tried it on for size? What was wrong with me? Drawing my towel tighter, I backed away. This was too awful for words. And, thanks to Charlie, I didn't even have the luxury of anonymity.

A sudden jerk, and my towel was wrenched from my grip. Someone pushed me from behind. A whoop was followed by a loud splash. Water shot up my nose and down my throat. Through the bubbles, I saw a dozen legs treading water above me; heard the muffled laughter. My foot touched the bottom with a thud. I pushed off hard, shot up and popped out, gasping for breath. I swam to the side, but someone grabbed my leg and yanked me under. I twisted free and bobbed up, but I'd barely gulped a mouthful of air before a hand on my head was pressing me down again. I thrashed and kicked, but I couldn't escape. I panicked. My lungs were burning, fit to burst. I was going to drown. I stopped moving. At last, the hand released its hold. I scrabbled free, coughing and spluttering, my hair a tangled curtain over my face. I tried to scrape it back, but a sheet of water cascaded over me, blinding me. Disorientated, choking, I flapped my arms about. My head hit the concrete edge with a sharp jolt. People sniggered. Something whined. A dog?

No, it was me.

The laughing stopped. The music and chatter from the party continued, but in the pool all was quiet. Everyone was staring at me. I wanted to run and hide, but if I got out, everyone would see my stupid costume. So, I tucked a handful of dripping rat's tails behind my ear, clung to the side, and stared blindly at the wall, trying my hardest not to cry.

'For God's sake, Charlie!' Louis voice broke through the silence.

Charlie! Of course. Who else?

'It was a joke.'

'Why do you always have to take it too far?'

'Seriously? It's never bothered you before.'

I held my nose and tipped my head under the water to drown out the noise and to sort out my hair. By the time I resurfaced, the swimmers were chatting and splashing around again. I glanced over my shoulder to check where Charlie was, but someone put their arm around me. I froze.

'You okay?' Louis asked.

I frowned and pressed my lips together. Why couldn't the pair of them just leave me alone?

'Sorry about my brother. He's such an idiot.' He placed his hands on the paving and leapt athletically out of the water.

He made it seem easy, but there was no way I was going to try it, not in this costume and not after the ducking. I'd made a big enough fool of myself already for one day. Quietly and unobtrusively as possible, I swam over to the steps and clambered up them. Louis was waiting at the top, my towel open and ready. He wrapped it around me, but instead of letting go, he held on. My cheeks aflame, I stood still as stone. After what seemed an eternity, he let go.

Without uttering a word of thanks, I scuttled back to the changing room and locked the door. My head in my hands, I sat on the bench and cried. How stupid I must have seemed in my too-small suit. Ugly and childish and nothing like the other girls with their enviable figures and fashionable bikinis. No wonder Charlie had picked on me. I couldn't face any of them ever again. Not the girls. Not Charlie. Not Louis, whose sympathy had been almost as excruciating as the ducking. I wouldn't stay here a minute longer. I'd get dressed and make a dash for it, sprint past the pool in case Charlie tried to shove me in fully clothed, and go home.

I wriggled into my shorts, slipped on my t-shirt, and rolled my costume in the towel. There was still a lot of noise coming from the pool. To be pushed in twice would be mortifying. So, I sat on the bench and waited.

After a few minutes, someone knocked. 'Can I come in? I need to change.'

I unlocked the door and inched it open. It was the girl in the white bikini. I groaned inwardly. 'Sorry. Lost track of time.'

'Don't worry about it.' She pulled it open and looked me up and down. 'You going out or staying in?'

I shifted awkwardly. 'I'm … er—'

'Feeling better?' Louis was seated cross-legged on the grass behind her, a concerned expression on his suntanned face.

I cringed. Could the day get any worse? 'I'm fine,' I mumbled as the girl shot into the shed and shut the door.

He leapt to his feet and, smiling sheepishly, held up a daisy chain. 'Here, I made you this. Thought it might cheer you up.'

I stared at it in surprise. It was an odd thing for a boy to make. Perhaps Martha had taught him. 'Thank you.'

He grinned and hung the chain around my neck. 'Lunch is ready. Are you hungry?' Before I'd had time to reply, he took my hand and led me past the pool.

Charlie, his feet dangling in the water, was engrossed in conversation with two pretty girls, but I lowered my head anyway and allowed Louis to lead me down the steps onto the patio. Weaving a way through guests, he steered me towards the barbecue, where he grabbed a bun, slipped a sausage inside, and handed it to me.

'Better get out of here,' he said. 'Mum's about to sing.'

'Martha Palmer?'

He grinned. 'That's the one. Surprised you've heard of her, though. She's not exactly famous nowadays.'

'My father's a fan. He's got all her records.'

Louis made a face. 'Really?'

'They're old friends.'

'They are? Cool.' He spoke without feeling, as if their past was of no consequence.

'Don't worry about me,' I said, waving him away. 'Go and join the others.'

'What, and leave you to Charlie's mercy? I don't think so, Nat. Come on, we'll go watch from the grass over there, under the trees.'

How to describe that afternoon? There were ropes of fairy lights, Chinese lanterns, and strings of paper bees and butter-flies strung from the trees on the fringes of an apple orchard. Enveloped by the sweet scent of the pale-pink blossom, Louis and I lay on our stomachs in the dappled shade, sipping champagne from a bottle Louis had swiped from the bar, listening to Martha Palmer sing. The bubbles went straight to my head, but instead of dulling my senses, they seemed to heighten them. The early summer leaves seemed greener, the flowers more colourful, the pollen more potent, and Martha's voice more heavenly than the recorded version I'd heard so often. Soft as velvet, rich yet powerful, it caressed and seduced us, at times breaking our hearts. She was irresistible; an addict, I was hooked.

The last song, 'Someone to Watch Over Me' – the raw emotion of the lyrics, Martha's mellifluous tone – held me in a kind of trance. I closed my eyes and let myself drift away.

All too soon, it seemed to me, it was over. Martha bowed and turned to applaud her band. The saxophonist winked at her, and she smiled. I sprang to my feet, clapping loudly. The other guests joined in. A few whistled their appreciation. Teddy bounced onto the stage beaming, gathered her in his arms, and kissed her on the lips. Their friends cheered and whooped.

'Ew!' groaned Louis. 'Get down.'

He pulled at my shorts so hard I lost my balance and toppled to the ground. I lay on my back and flung my arms over my head. Above me, the sun was setting in a cloudless pink sky. Time, like the daylight, had evaporated.

Louis propped himself up on his elbow and peered down at me. 'You like jazz, Nat?'

Did I? I rolled onto my side and stared into his russet irises – so like Martha's – and sighed. 'I love jazz.'

He grinned. 'You're in the right place then.'

The party had taken a different turn. Steam was rising from the pool, now lit from beneath with a soft yellow light. The adults, in high spirits, howled with laughter as they sprinted from the changing rooms and leapt into the water. Was Martha swimming, too? Or was she taking a few moments to recover, inside perhaps, alone? I had this sudden urge to seek her out and tell her how much she'd moved me.

How I thought she was the most brilliant, talented, wonderful human being in the whole wide world. How *magnificent* she was, but Louis was yanking me to my feet.

'Come on,' he said.

Drunk on champagne as much as Martha, I let him lead me away from the party, into the orchard that backed onto the Taylor's garden. The still warm air was ripe with the fragrant scent of apple blossom, and the long grass we waded through glistened with dew. The stars were coming out, but they were little more than diamond flecks in the indigo sky and, with only a sliver of moon to see by, we kept tripping over hidden roots and giggling.

'Here we are.' Louis stopped so abruptly I bumped into him. 'Now, up we go.'

'Up where?'

'The tree.'

'You're kidding? It's too dark to be climbing trees.'

He grinned. 'Don't worry. There are candles up there.'

'Really? In the tree?'

'In the tree*house*. Follow me.' He took hold of an iron rung nailed into the bark inches above his head, placed his foot on another, lower rung, and climbed.

I followed, buzzing with excitement. By the time I emerged, panting, through the hole which accommodated the trunk, my vision had adjusted to the dark. Roughly hexagonal in shape, the house was Arcadian in design, with crooked windows, a lopsided roof, and the odd gap between the planks; minor defects which added to its charm. It was simply furnished with a rocking chair, a small table, a pair of stools, and a couple of rudimentary bunks.

'Do you like it?' Louis asked. 'Dad made it. That's why it's a bit rough around the edges.'

'I love it.' Of course I did. It was the stuff of dreams. I

peered through the window. The fairy lights, the lanterns, and the yellow glow of the pool shimmered in the distance.

Louis put his arm around me. 'I'm glad,' he whispered, inclining his head until our foreheads touched. His eyes were shut, his long dark lashes sleek against his cheek. His lips parted.

His breath on my cheeks was warm and sweet. I closed my eyes. I wasn't sure why. Butterflies flittered in my belly, and the hairs on the back of my neck stood on end. What was happening to me?

A twig snapped in the undergrowth beneath us, loud and sharp, and I jumped.

Louis let go and crept over to the window. 'Someone's down there?' he whispered and, pressing a finger to his lips, backed away from the window.

'Charlie?' I mouthed. Had he followed us? I trembled, overcome with a sense of dread.

Louis shrugged and glanced around the treehouse. But there was nowhere to hide. We were trapped, two flies in a web. I strained my ears, but all was quiet. I was about to say that it was probably just a fox, when the low hum of voices rumbled. Louis gestured at me to stay quiet.

'... the love of my life really, not Teddy.' The first part of the sentence was little more than a murmur, but I caught the second part. 'It was Delilah Moore's doing, of course.'

'I'm so terribly sorry, Martha. I shouldn't have left you that night. If it's any consolation, I've regretted it ever since.'

I recognised my father's voice and gasped. Quick as a flash, Louis slapped his hand across my mouth. Beneath us someone shushed. I listened, desperate to hear more, but neither Martha nor my father spoke again. The only sound was the soft thud of departing footsteps.

10

Martha is slumped, head bowed, knees bent, on the kitchen lino, trying to ignore Luca who is fanning her with a laminated menu. She wishes he wouldn't. She isn't hot. She isn't about to faint. Humiliation has reduced her to this pitiable state. Stranger things have happened, but not to her.

'Do you think Delilah Moore was wearing anything under her coat?' Luca asks. 'Bet she wasn't,' he adds when Martha doesn't reply.

Giovanni hurries in from his flat upstairs. 'Here, Martha. Sofia says this will help.'

She raises her head, reluctantly, and takes the cold, wet flannel. Mumbling her thanks, she places it gingerly against her cheek. Up until now, she hasn't registered the pain. She assumed the burning sensation was down to embarrassment. One minute she'd been floating around on a cloud of happiness, the next she'd been dragged back to earth with a monumental thump. Why had a woman she'd never met, set upon her so violently and so publicly? Delilah had known her name, but she clearly didn't know her from Adam. Had Cee Cee told her where to find her?

'For a tiny lady she packed a mean right hook,' Luca says. 'You must have really pissed her off. What did you do?'

Giovanni snatches the menu from Luca and hits him over the head with it.

'Ow! What was that for?'

'For being an idiot.'

'I was just saying.'

'Well don't. It's not helpful. That woman, *uffa*, she has crickets in her head.' Giovanni kneels beside Martha and hands her the magazine Delilah Moore had been brandishing, unrolled and open. He points to an article. 'Read this. It might explain the *piccola* diva's outburst. A review of your performance last Saturday,' he says, at once saving her the bother. 'Apparently you went down *una tempesta*. Look at the headline.' He slaps the page. '*Complete Unknown Steals the Show. It takes guts to sing songs immortalised by the jazz greats,*' he continues, reading over her shoulder, '*but Martha Palmer is bold enough and skilled enough to pull off what must surely go down in history as the debut of the decade. Her voice with its authentic, unsullied, and soulful tone, subtle, relaxed phrasing, and impeccable diction, is the finest I've heard in a long time. Talented and alluring, the young woman, who up until now has been working as a waitress in a Soho café, is someone to watch out for. A star in the making. Move over Delilah Moore, The Bo Rivers' Five has no more need of you.*'

Luca whistles. 'Hey, cool, Martha. I didn't know you could sing.'

'Nobody did,' says Giovanni. 'Apart from *Signor* Bo.'

Martha flicks back to the cover. *Melody Maker*. Could this day get any weirder? She has a review. A glowing review as it happens. In *Melody Maker* of all places. She is liked. A critic thinks she's going places. She has a future. Her spirits lifting, she focuses on the print and reads it again, savouring every word.

'So, let me get this straight,' says Luca. 'Despite being one of the most famous and celebrated singers in the country, Delilah Moore has lost her job to a waitress. No wonder she's angry. That takes some nerve, Martha.'

Martha rubs the back of her neck. 'I didn't steal her job. She never showed up. I sort of ... stepped in. At the last minute. It wasn't planned or anything.'

'As I always say, it is truth that makes a man angry.' Giovanni arches an eyebrow. 'Or in this case, a woman. *Bravissimo*, Martha. I congratulate you, but perhaps it would be wise, in this case, to heed the words of Mussolini.'

'You've got to be kidding.' Luca rolls his eyes and receives another swipe across the head with the menu for his trouble.

'"It is good to trust others but not to do so is much better."'

Martha frowns. 'I don't understand, Giovanni.'

'Who does?' mutters Luca, sidestepping out of the way.

'*Signor* Bo has hit the iron while it is hot. And why not? He is ambitious. Talented, perhaps. But, Martha, you must be careful in the choices you make from now on. A man's ambition is a perilous thing. Give him a finger, and he will take an arm.'

It's another warm evening, and almost dark, the violet sky and lavender clouds reduced to a mere stripe above the horizon. At the end of Old Compton Street, some fifty yards away, old Reggie the lamplighter is busy at work with his long pole, sparking the gas with the wick. Bo Rivers' card in her hand, Martha hefts her weary body off the bench, where she's been sitting since her shift ended an hour ago, and makes her way towards the recently vacated phone box. Her mind a jumble of indecision, she stalls. Should she call him or not?

On one hand, this is her childhood dream come true. She'd been seven years old when her father wound up the phonograph, lifted her onto his lap, and played her his latest 78. It was Sunday, so he was clean as a whistle, apart from his nails which, despite his best efforts, were stained with strands of soot.

'Tha'll nowt hear owt as wonderful as this as long as tha live,' he said.

She was intrigued. It was unlike her father to wax lyrical. 'Who is it?'

'The Divine One.'

'Tha mean God?'

'Might as well be. A' reight least a pitch-perfect angel. This lass's voice has wings. Listen to how she bends t' notes, a' top 'n' bottom of her range. I'm talking four-octaves, mind. Tis t' voice of a lifetime.'

She was young, but Martha instantly knew her father wasn't exaggerating. It truly was the voice of an angel, soaring and diving like a great bird in flight, its feathers occasionally skimming the water.

'Sarah Vaughan, that be,' he said when the record ended. 'Happen she's the best there is and the best there'll ever be.'

The song, Martha later discovered, was the first recording of 'Tenderly'. They must have listened to it a dozen times that afternoon, long enough for Martha to pick up the lyrics and the tune. She took to practicing it when she was on her own, testing out her instrument, its range and tone. And then, one day, following a pit fall at the mines and on his way home earlier than usual, her father overheard her.

'Proper champion, that, lass,' he said. 'Keep it up and who knows, tha might be a singer one day.'

Her heart swelled. 'Tha reckon?'

'Aye, Martha. Reckon I do. Imagine that? A somebody in our family, not a nobody like uz.'

'Tha aren't a nobody. Tha's a brilliant miner, Pa.'

'There's no miner what's brilliant, lass.'

She might not miss home anymore but she does miss those precious moments on a Sunday, alone with her father, listening to his latest record. She lets out a long sigh. No point crying over spilt milk. She's got a decision to make. Is she going to ring Bo Rivers or not?

Truth be told, there's only one thing holding her back. Delilah Moore. The review, though glowing, was short, and yet, by some miracle, she'd spotted it. But to seek out Martha because of it and land a fist in her face was taking things too far. What if she did it again? What if she kept on hounding and humiliating her? Was that likely, though? Delilah Moore was the star, not her, and that kind of behaviour wouldn't do her any favours. Martha thought less of her now. No longer an exalted jazz singer, she'd transformed into a vulgar, histrionic diva.

I'll do it, she thinks. What have I got to lose?

She opens the door, chucks her bag on the shelf, and digs out her purse but, as she roots around for some pennies, Giovanni's incoherent warning pops into her mind. What did he mean by *give him a finger, and he'll take an arm*? And what was all the stuff about Mussolini and ambition? Did he mean Bo Rivers was taking advantage of her? It didn't make sense. Bo was doing her a favour, giving her a break. Wasn't he? Honestly, Giovanni's crazy proverbs and misplaced fatherly advice were infuriating sometimes. Unless it was some highfalutin tactic of his to persuade her to stay on at the café.

She groans. Forget Giovanni. Dad would tell me to follow my heart. And my heart is saying phone the man. And quick before he changes his mind. Clasping the handset under her chin, she feeds the pennies into the slot and dials the number. A voice answers, so quickly, she almost drops the receiver.

'Hello, Bo Rivers speaking.'

She takes a deep breath and, with a trembling hand, presses button A. 'It's me. Martha.'

There's a loud exhalation. 'I'm so glad you called. I was worried you'd change your mind.'

'You were?'

'Well … We didn't exactly get off to a good start.'

'No, we didn't.'

'I'm sorry about that, Martha. Truly, I am.'

'It's okay. You'd been let down.'

'Yes, and I panicked. It's not much of an excuse but—'

'I understand.'

'You do? Good. That's good. So, we need to meet fairly quickly.'

'And rehearse?'

'What? Yeah. Are you free tomorrow night?'

'My shift finishes at six.'

'Cool. I'll pick you up—' There's a muffled sound, like he's placed his hand over the receiver. Was someone with him? Cee Cee, perhaps?

'Bo? You still there?'

'Terrific. Terrific. Thanks for calling. Bye, now.'

There's a bleep as the line goes dead.

She stares at the receiver, nonplussed. Talk about abrupt.

What was it with this man? Blowing hot one minute, freezing cold the next. Not that it mattered. It wasn't as if he was her friend. What they had was a working relationship.

With a shrug, Martha grabs her bag and backs out of the phone box. Dusk has well and truly fallen, the mellow light from the lamps eclipsed by the blazing neon signs of Soho's bars, restaurants, and clubs. Fashionably clad Bohemians – musicians, writers, painters, and gamblers – have downed tools and come out to play. She pauses outside the Algerian Coffee Shop to listen to a skiffle band playing on the pavement. A pimp gives her the once over and offers to show her a good time but scurries off when a couple of Teddy Boys, their hair greased into a Tony Curtis ducktail, stop and ask her for a light.

'Sorry, I don't smoke,' she says and sets off again.

A gurgling drunk meandering through the deserted market doffs his cap to her, and a couple of working girls say hello, but other than them, nobody takes much notice. They rarely do. Despite its criminal reputation, Soho is one of the safest places on earth.

She reaches her digs. A wave of tiredness washes over her. What she wants now is to lie on her bed and sleep. It's been one hell of a day. With a bit of luck, Mrs Wilson won't be on the prowl. An inveterate talker who pays more than a passing interest in her lodgers' lives, she's a nosy old so-and-so. But she's not a bad soul, and her busybody behaviour clearly stems from loneliness, hence the arrival of Elsie the poodle. Martha holds her breath, sticks the key in the lock, and opens the door as quietly as the ancient hinges allow. Ears on high alert, she pauses, but the house, unlike the rest of Soho, is unusually quiet. She slips off her shoes, tiptoes up the four flights of stairs to her room, and lies down fully clothed on the bed. Within seconds she's asleep.

. . .

She comes to with a start. She's not alone. Somebody is in the room. She's sure of it. She hoicks herself onto her elbow, her heart beating like the clappers.

A figure emerges from the shadows. 'Oh, Martha! I've been so worried about you.'

'Flippin' 'eck, Becky. You frightened the life out of me. How long have you been standing there?'

'You disappear without a word. Hang out with strangers. Cut your hair. Buy new clothes. Stay out all night. And now this.' Eyes widening, she gestures to Martha's face. 'What happened? Did someone attack you?'

'It's nothing.' Martha fingers the welt absently and winces.

'No, Martha. It's not. And I refuse to be kept in the dark one moment longer.'

'Well, turn the bloody light on then.'

'I'm being serious. I thought we were friends.'

'We are friends, silly.'

Becky plonks herself on the bed. 'Well, then. What's going on?'

Martha sighs and switches on the lamp. 'It's complicated.'

'Isn't it always? Please, Martha. I promise I won't judge. I'm concerned, that's all. The col ... Cee Cee called round for you, earlier. Bit of a nerve actually, given Mrs Wilson's sign. Fortunately, she was out walking Elsie.'

'Cee Cee?'

'Yeah, Cee Cee. He seemed disappointed you weren't in.'

She frowns. He'd said he'd call. She'd been looking forward to seeing him again. He'd been so kind to her the other night at the Flamingo. Had told her she was one in a million. And when he'd wrapped his arms around her in a big bear hug and whispered in her ear, *I knew you were special. From di moment I first saw you, I just knew it*, her heart had swelled fit to burst. He'd insisted on walking her home. Dawn had long broken, but it was still early, not quite six o'clock, when they'd arrived at her lodgings. He'd leant in to kiss her, a lingering, more passionate kiss than the first, which had agitated her body in a way she'd never experienced before. *I'll take you to dinner to celebrate*, he'd said, and kissed her again. And all because of a chance meeting. She'd had to pinch herself. It was unbelievable.

Becky's shoulders slump. 'I honestly thought we were friends.'

'We are.'

'Funny way of showing it.'

Martha cringes. She should have told Becky, but things had happened so fast: the photo shoot; meeting Cee Cee; the unplanned gig at the Flamingo and the invitation to perform again; Delilah Moore's shock appearance. Her life had taken on a dreamlike quality which hardly made sense to her. How could she hope to explain it to Becky?

Her gaze wanders to the crumpled magazine lying on the bedside table. The review. A tangible piece of evidence. She reaches across and picks it up 'Here,' she says, handing it to Becky. 'This might help.'

11

The red gingham tablecloths remind Martha of The Grind, but the crowded, white-tiled restaurant is grubbier and dingier and has a musty subterranean smell. She's not in the best of moods. She's been sat here, opposite Bo Rivers, for almost an hour, and there's still no sign of Cee Cee, or any of the other band members either, for that matter. They've eaten, too, the house speciality, a huge plate of moussaka, salad, and chips, washed down with tumblers of stringent red wine. It tastes foul, and her throat constricts with every mouthful, but at least it has helped her to relax.

The absence of band members is unsettling, but that's only the half of it. As if Delilah's appearance at the café yesterday hadn't been hard enough to stomach, Loretta turning up out of the blue had knocked her for six. Fortunately, she'd been making sandwiches in the kitchen when Giovanni, who was in one of his darker moods, loudly proclaimed that no one called Martha Parker had ever worked here. Loretta must have contradicted him because Giovanni repeated himself in a voice not far off a shout. Nervous as hell as to what might happen next, Martha sneaked a peek in time to see Giovanni shoo the photographer's assistant out of the café as if she were an errant hen.

Why was she looking for me? she wonders again and shivers.

'Are you cold?' Bo Rivers asks.

Martha shakes her head. Unable to hold his gaze, she glances at the barrel-shaped ceiling instead. Something about Bo Rivers unnerves her. Not the split lip he's sporting today – has he been in a fight? – but his intensity. The slow, deliberate manner of his speech. The way he listens, his unblinking eagle-eyed stare boring into her as if searching for something deep within her even she is unaware of. He's been firing question after bullet-like question at her all evening, too. So many of them, she's grown bored of the sound of her voice.

Swing, Trad, Bebop, or Modern? Swing, I suppose.

Dizzy, Miles, or Louis? Well, they're all very good.

John Coltrane or Bird? Both, I think.

What about singers? You must have a favourite? Goodness, I couldn't possibly narrow it down to one.

What age did you start singing? Seven.

Do I detect a slight accent? No, you don't.

He's interrogating me, she thinks, and takes another sip of wine. Less inhibited, thanks to the alcohol, she studies him critically. Tall and slim, with white-blond hair and colourless eyes, he's startlingly attractive in a supernatural-being kind of way. Slanting cheekbones, square jaw, triangular torso, his body seems to be a series of diverging angles. Apart from his mouth. The pillowy lips, the only softness amongst all the hardness.

'So how long have you worked at The Grind?' he asks brightly. 'And is your boss always that cranky?'

It's two questions too many.

'What happened to your lip? Somebody punch you?' she asks sharply, and the diners on the neighbouring table turn and stare.

A half-smile forms on Bo Rivers' mouth. 'Too many high notes. It's a common injury for us trumpet players. Seems my lip muscles weren't up to it.'

'Oh!' she says, blushing. 'I'm sorry, I—'

'Don't be.' He reaches across and touches her on the arm, but when she shifts awkwardly, he quickly retracts his hand. 'I've offended you.'

'No, you haven't. I'm … I … I wasn't expecting dinner. Just the two of us, I mean. I thought we'd be rehearsing … I thought Cee Cee would be here.'

Bo Rivers frowns. 'Ah! Cee Cee. Right.'

'What's that supposed to mean?'

'Are the two of you … you know … dating?'

'I don't see what it's got to do with you.'

He leans on the table and laces his fingers together, eyes fixed on hers. 'It's a question of dynamics.'

'Dynamics?'

He shrugs. 'It's my band, and I want everyone to get along.'

She tries not to squirm.

'We're virtual strangers, Martha.' He leans back and smiles. 'That's why I asked you out tonight. We're going to be spending a lot of time together, so I want to get to know you. Find out what makes you tick?'

He's got a point, she thinks. I don't know the first thing about him either. 'Okay, so now it's my turn. How did you meet her?'

'Who?'

'Delilah Moore.'

Bo Rivers sighs. 'At a jazz club in East Croydon. She was

there with a friend and we happened to be playing.' He says it off pat, as if tired of explaining.

'Some might call it luck.'

'Nah! Don't believe in luck.'

'Fate, then?'

He shrugs.

'You obviously impressed her, though. What did you do?'

His frown deepening, he rummages inside his jacket for his cigarettes, flicks the packet, pulls one out, and holds it between his fingers. 'My attempt at "West End Blues". You know it?'

She shakes her head.

'You'd recognise it, for sure. It's an old King Oliver song, hellishly difficult,' he says, waving the unlit cigarette around. 'Louis Armstrong and his Hot Five recorded it in Chicago, June 1928. Whenever I play it, I feel connected to them somehow. My uncle played it to me when I was nine. He was a massive fan of Satchmo. Absolutely adored the man. There's the dizzying opening solo, Louis' scat singing, the second solo, when he holds on to a top B flat so loud and for so long it seems to be saying: *listen to me, I bet you can't do that*. From the second I heard that note, I was gripped.' He pauses, transferring the cigarette to his other hand.

Martha waits, willing him to continue, eager to hear more.

'For months, I pestered my parents to buy me a trumpet. They must have got bored in the end because they bought me a cornet, a tarnished old thing with a couple of dents they found buried in a junk shop. They thought I'd play it for a week, get bored, and give up. But I was determined. I polished it till it gleamed and, thanks to my uncle, had lessons. It took a year to get the embouchure, buzzing the lips and playing with the mouthpiece. But the hardest thing was learning how to hit the high notes. I split my lips several times until I managed the C I was aiming for. My lips and jaw are stronger now, and I use lip salve, but I have to be careful, as you can see. Anyway, after ten years, although I was nowhere near Satchmo's brilliance, at last I could play it. So, come the Croydon gig, I thought: *now's the time*. Next thing I know, Delilah Moore is backstage and asking me for my details. Nothing happened, and I forgot all about it. But two years later, her agent calls and invites us to play with her.' He stops abruptly and slides the cigarette he's been fiddling with back in the packet.

'Wow! It's some story.'

'Yeah.'

'Too bad she let you down.'

'Is it? If she hadn't, we wouldn't be having this little chat.'

Martha frowns and clears her throat. 'What about Louis?' she asks hurriedly. 'Have you heard him play?'

'Two years ago, with his All Stars at the Empress Hall. He was sensational. The best I've ever seen.' He signals to a waiter who wanders over. 'Two coffees, please.' Drumming his fingers on the table, he turns away.

There's something he isn't telling me, she thinks, as the waiter returns with the coffees. She takes a sip. It's thick and sweet and not to her liking at all, or Giovanni's come to that. She glances at Bo Rivers, studying his cup as if it contains the answers to all the questions in the universe. 'Why did Delilah stand you up the other night?'

He presses his lips together and blows out his cheeks, releasing them with a sharp puff. 'I told you already. She was indisposed.' Frowning, he taps the cigarette out again and slips it between his lips.

'She dropped by the café yesterday.'

Bo straightens up.

'She had a copy of the review. She seemed angry about it. No, she *was* angry about it. She hit me.'

He swipes the cigarette from his mouth. 'Christ!'

'Why would she do that?'

Bo Rivers blows out his cheeks three, maybe four times. She watches, amused, wondering if he's stressed enough to smoke the wretched cigarette now.

'She has issues.'

She pulls a face. 'Like what?'

He bats the air dismissively. 'Just issues.'

'Thing is, I'm concerned what she'll do if I perform again.'

'If? There's no question of if. Listen to me, Martha.' He reaches over and grasps her hands. 'Forget Delilah Moore. You have a great future. Saturday's gig at the Mingo was only the start. Next stop, The Marquee. We're going to make a great team. Trust me, Martha. You and I are going places.'

12

I was convinced Louis would want to talk about the exchange we'd heard from the treehouse between my father and his mother. But he didn't. Not immediately, anyway. Instead, he muttered something about being tired, that champagne always had this effect on him.

What a load of rubbish. I'd have lain bets he'd never tasted it before.

He was going to go to bed. Did I mind?

It wasn't really a question. He had a foot on a rung of the ladder already, a hand on another. It was infuriating. I was itching to discuss why my father had left Martha that night. Was he the love of her life, or was it someone else? And if so, who? It didn't occur to me Louis might be in a state of shock. After all, we'd just heard his mother admit she'd loved someone more than she loved his father. It couldn't have made for easy listening. But perhaps my insensitivity stemmed from my own predicament. My mother had withdrawn, and Martha Palmer had replaced her in my affections. I was too excited about the possibility of a past romance between her and my father to give a thought to Louis' feelings.

My father was waiting for me when we got back to the house. He didn't ask where I'd been but said it was about time we went. Not those words exactly, but rather, *Mum will be we worrying about us,* which amounted to the same thing.

He was quiet on the way home, reflective, perhaps mulling over Martha's confession. I wondered if it had taken him unawares. It certainly seemed so. But there was no way I could ask outright. He'd be furious if he knew I'd been listening in on a private conversation. What was needed was tact. I had to think of a way to broach the subject without being too obvious. Coax the information out of him some-how. So, I steered the conversation onto Martha, declaring her to be the very best singer who'd ever lived. He agreed wholeheartedly, then clammed right up, uttering not another word until he turned off my light and wished me goodnight.

Try as I might, I couldn't sleep. My mind was a jumble of unanswerable questions. Where had he and Martha been that night? Were they in love? Who was Delilah Moore? And what had been 'her doing'? Why had my father left Martha? Where was he going? Or was it more complicated? Did he have another girlfriend, my mother perhaps, who he had to go and see? It seemed unlikely. My father, being a decent man, wasn't the two-timing type. So, I glossed over that little detail and tried to account for the inexplicable. If Martha was in love with someone else, why had she married Teddy? To a fourteen-year-old with no understanding of the peculiar machinations of the human heart, it simply didn't make sense.

∾

The following day was Sunday. My father went about his household chores, bright and breezy, as was customary on his day off. It was as if nothing out of the ordinary had happened. I wasn't surprised. It was his default reaction, head down and carry on, no matter what. Of course, it was also entirely possible he wasn't the least bit bothered by what Martha had said and I'd made something out of nothing. I doubted it. Either way, I wasn't going to give up. Determined to find out exactly what had happened all those years ago, I decided to wait until supper when I'd try a different tack.

'Did you and Martha ever go out together?'

My father lowered the newspaper he was reading, something my mother would never have allowed at the dinner table, and laughed. 'What on earth gave you that idea?'

All the whispering and handholding, that's what. I smiled sweetly. 'She seems very fond of you.'

'Well, yes, I suppose she does. But she's fond of a lot of people. She has a big heart.' He raised the paper and continued to read.

'You were friends, though?'

'We were,' he said absently. 'For a time, anyway.'

I rested my elbows on the table, my chin on my hands. 'Go on.'

He peered at me over the top of the newspaper. 'What do you mean, go on?'

'I want to hear all about it? What you got up to? What she was like?'

'Goodness, Natasha, we didn't get up to anything. And you know what she's like. You've met her.'

Exasperating. 'Did she have many lovers? Apart from Teddy, I mean. I bet she did.'

My father raised his eyebrows. 'Ha!' It was a short, sharp

bark of a laugh. 'Lovers? Goodness. Have you been reading Mills and Boon?'

As answers go it was frustrating, not least because I'd never read any Mills and Boon. They weren't my kind of books. 'Louis was surprised I'd heard of her,' I ploughed on. 'He said she isn't that famous anymore.'

My father put down the newspaper. At last, a reaction. 'Louis is right in a way. She's not as famous as she was.'

'How famous was she?'

'How long is a piece of string?'

I frowned and let out a frustrated sigh. 'Dad, please. I'm interested.'

My father smiled. 'Well, back in the late fifties, which was when I knew her, she was at the peak of her fame. She was performing in jazz clubs the length and breadth of the country, night after night. She made records. Hit after hit. Her face graced the cover of countless magazines. She had spots on the radio, appeared on various television shows. After she married and had the twins, she branched out into musicals. I saw her Maria in *West Side Story*. The critics adored her, and rightly so. She was magnificent, the talk of the town.'

That word again. 'So, what happened?'

My father paused. 'She was incredibly famous, Natasha. Her every move scrutinised. It must have been difficult.'

'So, she stopped performing because she was too famous?' I screwed up my nose. It seemed unlikely. But what about the love of her life? I wanted to ask. Where does he fit in? And who's Delilah Moore?

'Life is rarely straightforward, Natasha,' he said, disappearing behind his newspaper again and bringing the conversation to an end.

❧

When I was a child, life was either black or white, people either good or bad, behaviour, right or wrong. Grey and all its multiple shades simply didn't exist in my world. Not so my father. Life to him was at times straightforward, at others like a tangled ball of knots which, no matter how hard you tried, could not be untied and therefore should be left well alone. In his irritatingly taciturn way, he'd sidestepped my question. If he knew the reason why Martha had withdrawn from the limelight, which I suspected he did, he wasn't letting on. Did it have something to do with him? Was he an integral part of the mystery? And what exactly had happened after he left her that night? My curiosity piqued, I was determined to find out. Perhaps Louis knew. Perhaps all I had to do was ask him. We'd got on well at the party. Surely it would only be a matter of time until he contacted me. I had to be patient.

I heard nothing from Louis the next day, or the day after. Maddening, since the entire village seemed to be talking about Martha. Her true identity unmasked, she was, once again, the subject of gossip. My father's patients, who could never be accused of reticence, were more than happy to voice their opinions to anyone who would listen, me included. Top of the agenda this week were her parties. Why did she have so many? Why were the locals not invited? And who were the strange people who frequented them?

Mrs Bracken folded her arms across her ample breast. 'Drug-addled jazz musicians and the like, I gather.'

'You don't say?' said Mrs Percival, the butcher's wife.

'You must have heard the music, Marjorie?'

'Well, yes, I have, Penny. But drugs. Are you sure?'

'Quite sure. Alfie Jordan smelled marijuana, and his house is at least two hundred yards away.'

'Marijuana? Oh!' exclaimed Mrs Jones, whose po-face had paled.

'And that's not all,' continued Mrs Bracken, well into her stride. 'Apparently, when it gets dark, all the guests leap into the pool, naked and high as kites.'

Mrs Fitzwilliam who, along with Mrs Bracken, seemed to be a permanent fixture of my father's waiting room these days, shook her head and tutted loudly. 'It shouldn't be allowed. It really shouldn't.'

'I agree,' said Mrs Jones. 'It's too sordid for words.'

'Disreputable, that's what it is,' said Mrs Bracken. 'She'll give the village a bad name. It's time Reverend Josephs put his foot down. I've spoken to him, but he says there's nothing he can do.'

Mrs Jones stuck her nose in the air and sniffed loudly. 'Doesn't surprise me in the least. The man has no backbone.'

'None whatsoever,' agreed Mrs Fitzwilliam.

'It's to be expected, though, isn't it,' added Mrs Bracken. 'Remember the nasty business in the sixties?'

My ears pricked up. 'What nasty business?'

'Ooh, I'd forgotten all about that.' Mrs Jones covered her mouth with her hand.

Mrs Fitzwilliam sighed. 'I felt rather sorry for her, truth be told.'

'Why? What happened?' I persisted.

'It's her children I feel sorry for,' said Mrs Bracken. 'And her husband, the darling man. A leopard doesn't change its spots.'

My father popped his head round the door. 'Penny Bracken.'

'Oh, hello, Doctor.' She picked up her handbag and beamed.

'Hello again, Penny. Do come in.' He gestured to her and caught sight of me. 'Ah, there you are, Natasha. Your mother's asking for you. Could you take her up some tea?'

There was a general cooing among the women as they asked me how she was, and would I send the poor woman their love. And that was that. Dispatched to my mother's sickbed, I had no option but to leave the room, none the wiser.

The following day I devised a plan. It was ingenious, fool-proof, and had come to me the moment I woke up. Just like that. Never mind Louis, I would go around to the Fairchilds' and ask Martha to help me with the song I'd chosen to sing at the Summer Concert. It wasn't my original choice. I'd changed my mind after hearing her sing. She'd told me she liked my voice. With a bit of luck, she'd be flattered. Then, while she was coaching me, I'd ask her about her career, where she'd sung, and with whom. And when the moment was right, I'd ask her why she'd stopped. Simple yet brilliant. What could possibly go wrong?

I knocked on the door, but there was no answer. The windows were open, however, so I strolled around the back of the house and peered in through the kitchen door, in case they hadn't heard me. The room was deserted, so I carried on past the chickens and the pool, and down to the patio. There was no one out here either, but the sliding doors to the large, cream sitting room were ajar. I was about to stroll inside, when I caught sight of a couple, locked in an embrace. On closer inspection, I realised it was Martha and a black man in a familiar hat.

I froze. What if they saw me? How would I explain myself, creeping around the house like some peeping Tom? The sun was hot on my back. Sweat prickled my armpits, my palms, the creases behind my knees. I was thinking if I didn't move soon, I might faint from the heat when it suddenly dawned on me with the sunshine streaming in, it would be like staring out of a lit-up room into the dark. They wouldn't be able to see me. In a flash I'd run up the steps, past the pool, and was sprinting towards the orchard. Only when I was convinced I was hidden amongst the trees did I stop to catch my breath. I knew who the man in the hat was. The saxophonist who'd played at her party. But why were they hugging one another? What about Teddy? I thought back to that idyllic afternoon, the music, Martha's voice, the band. The saxophonist had winked at her, and a look had passed between them.

I clasped my cheeks. That was it. The look. It was complicit, like two lovers who knew each other well. Martha had been delighted he was there, happy my father had recognised his playing. Oh my God, was he the love of her life? Was the romance back on? Had he come to claim her? Was she going to leave her husband?

'Stop right where you are, Natasha James.'

I started at the voice, some twelve feet above me. Lost in my thoughts, I hadn't realised I was standing at the foot of the treehouse. But which twin was it? Their identical voices made it impossible to tell. I tipped back my head. Charlie leant out of the window, grinning. My heart sank.

'You're trespassing,' he said.

'I'm not, as it happens. I knocked on the door, but nobody answered, so I decided to take the shortcut home.'

'You're lying. Mum's inside with Cee Cee.'

I winced.

Charlie stabbed the air with his finger. 'Ah ha! I knew it!'

He did? I wasn't sure whether to be relieved or appalled.

'Sneaking around after lover boy. Your secret is out.'

'*My* secret?'

'*My* secret?' he mimicked, batting his eyelids. 'Yes, *your* secret. 'Fraid he isn't here.'

'Who isn't?'

'Oh, don't play the innocent. Louis, of course. Who else?'

'Oh! No. I wasn't. He isn't. Oh!' I stamped my foot. This was unbearable.

'Well, he's not here, so hard cheese. You'll have to make do with me. Come on up. Don't be shy.'

I clenched my fists and glared at him. 'Why do you always have to be so mean?' Without waiting for an answer, I turned on my heel and sprinted towards the Taylor's gate, the sound of Charlie's laughter ringing in my ears.

Miss Hendrik was ill the next day, and my singing lesson cancelled, so I caught an earlier bus home. The back door was unlocked as usual but, when I called out to my father, there was no answer. It was an hour before his evening surgery, and still sunny, so I wandered into the front garden in case he was pottering about out there, something he often did before work.

He wasn't in his shed, and the wooden trug he used, when he was weeding or deadheading, lay abandoned on the York stone path by the side of the house. Certain he'd been called out on an emergency, I was about to go inside when a few bars of music floated towards me from the terrace at the back.

I crept along the path until the bricks gave way to the glass of the sunroom. Careful, so as not to be seen, I peered through and almost cried out in surprise. Seated at the round teak table, my father was drinking tea with a woman in a crimson dress and a wide floppy hat. She had her back to me, but I knew full well who it was. Martha Palmer. No woman in the village dressed as stylishly or as flamboyantly. All the same, I didn't budge. Up to the moment I'd stumbled upon her in the arms of Cee Cee the saxophonist, she'd seemed to have been above reproach; beautiful, talented, and generous to a fault. My discovery had upset me. I'd been disappointed, too, because it meant my father wasn't the love her life. They were deep in conversation, but the song on the record player, parked on the rattan floor, drowned out the words. What were they talking about? I wondered, straining my ears. Was she confiding in him about Cee Cee?

Martha dabbed her nose with a handkerchief, and my father placed a reassuring hand on her shoulder. She inclined her head and put her hand on his. I held my breath. Nobody moved. Not my father. Not Martha. Not me. The only sound came from the record player, from Peggy Lee – I knew my father's record collection inside out by now – singing about the man she loved. Leaning in, my father lightly brushed away the tear trickling down Martha's cheek. An intimate gesture. My hand flew to my mouth. He'd denied being anything more than friends. Had he lied to me? Was my father in love with her after all? Was she in love with him? It certainly looked like it. But what about the saxophonist? Where did he fit in? Such a complex puzzle, my brain ached with trying to solve it.

A door slammed inside the house, and I jumped. Out of the corner of my eye, I saw movement inside the sunroom; a blur of floral fabric.

My father leapt to his feet, smiling, his arms outstretched. 'Darling.'

Mum? I turned and gaped, horrified by the lurid yellow-and-green kaftan she was wearing and the weird turquoise monstrosity on her head. A turban? What was she thinking? Her face, hauntingly pale from lack of sunlight with dark rings beneath her eyes, was fully made up. Over-the-top green eye shadow, smudged mascara, and a smear of pink lipstick which overran her lips. She looked like a faded version of herself. A woman with ideas of grandeur, detached from reality. What was she doing here? She hadn't stepped a foot outside her bedroom for months, let alone dressed and come downstairs. Had my father told her Martha was coming? Had he persuaded her to join them? Was she drunk? Or had my father upped her medication? Whatever the reason, it was awful to watch. I wanted to run away, but I mustn't. I had to see this through.

'Darling, you look wonderful,' my father boomed.

It was the forced encouragement he used in difficult circumstances, which I understood to mean *you'd better believe it or else*. Clearly, he'd been expecting her. Assuming the role of dutiful guest, Martha rose elegantly to her feet and brushed my mother's cheek with the briefest of kisses as if it was the most natural thing in the world. Was it sincere? Was she pleased to meet my mother? Somehow, I doubted it. She was smiling, and showed no sign of having been upset. My mother said something and giggled. Dad and Martha laughed, too. They were play-acting, all three of them. A farce. My father pulled out a chair for my mother, who sat down, demure as a nun, and the three of them started chatting.

Notwithstanding the oddity of the situation, I sighed with relief, grateful that, despite her deranged appearance, my mother hadn't caused a scene. Martha's visit seemed to be having an edifying effect. With a bit of luck, she would weave her magic and breathe some permanent life into my mother. We would be a proper family again, and life would return to normal. It was what I'd longed for this past year, what I'd prayed for. And yet I was far from happy. In fact, I'd go so far as to say I resented her intrusion. Martha had filled the gap my mother's absence had created. She'd got my father and I out of a hole. She was ours. Except, right now, she wasn't mine. She was nothing to do with me. She was a friend of my parents, another adult who had no interest in me.

My father glanced first at his watch then back at the house. He was expecting me home from singing practice. It was that time of day. I slunk further into the shadows, not wanting to be seen. It was obvious he was hoping I was about to join them. It would make his day when he saw how delighted I was my mother was up and about and chatting to Martha, a woman I held in such high regard. But I couldn't. I wouldn't. Not today. It was all too weird. I was angry and confused. I needed some time to make sense of my emotions. So, I did what I always did when I needed to think, I crept back along the path and headed off down the twitten to Mrs Pocock's house to take Rafferty for a walk.

I didn't know Mrs Pocock's exact age but, if asked, I'd have said the mid-seventies. A diminutive woman with a sprightly manner, I was surprised when she greeted me at the door in her dressing gown, back bowed and clutching a walking stick. Close on her heels, Rafferty clattered over the parquet floor, wagging his tail. Her tiny hands with their beautifully mani-cured nails were gnarled and arthritic, I noticed, and she was struggling to hold on to the handle. She was delighted to see me, however and, having apologised for her appearance – the dressing gown and her unbrushed hair, (although her blue-white curls seemed perfectly neat to me) – explained she'd fallen and hurt her hip.

'It isn't broken,' she said. 'Just badly bruised.'

'Is someone looking after you?' She lived alone and took great pride in keeping her house spotlessly clean.

She winked. 'Don't you worry about me, Natasha. Mr Jordan is keeping his beady eye on me. He's arranged for his daily to call in most days. I've never been so pampered in my life.'

It was common knowledge Alfie Jordan held a torch for Edie Pocock. Despite his best endeavours, Edie had refused to succumb to her neighbour's charms. She was, she said, too old and therefore too set in her ways. They enjoyed frequent cups of tea together, seaside strolls along the promenade, trips to the theatre, and the occasional pub lunch. Anything more, she insisted, would only spoil a firm friendship.

'I'm pleased to hear it, Mrs P.' Rafferty rested his feet on my belly and licked me on the chin. I smiled and fondled his ears and immediately felt better. 'Hello, boy. Hello.'

'He's very excited to see you, aren't you, Rafferty. Poor darling hasn't had a walk all week, although dear Mr Jordan did offer.'

'Would you like me to pick up some shopping, too?'

'How kind of you, Natasha, but Penny Bracken dropped by with a box of groceries, a fish pie, *and* a casserole the other day. Goodness only knows how I'm supposed to eat it all, but she means well, does Penny. Very thoughtful, that one, notwithstanding her wagging tongue.' She winked at me again and chuckled.

I smiled. 'Well, if you're sure.'

'Oh yes, dear. Quite sure. It's Rafferty who needs attention. You've timed your visit perfectly.' She delved inside her pocket and pulled out a handful of change. 'Buy yourself a packet of Ringos and a can of the Tab you and Hayley love so much. Can't stand the taste myself, but there we are. The world would be a boring place if everyone liked the same things.'

'Oh, Mrs P, there's no need to pay me. I love walking Rafferty.'

'I know but I insist. Now, don't go staying out too long, Natasha dear. It's a school day tomorrow, and your father won't thank me if you're tired.'

Rafferty tugged at the lead, his tongue lolling out the side of his mouth as we headed towards the shops. It took all my strength to hang on to him and a great deal of concentration, which took my mind off my worries. It wasn't until Mr Barton, the newsagent, had given him the usual handful of doggy drops, that Rafferty quietened down enough for me to choose how to spend the shiny fifty pence piece Mrs P had pressed into my palm. After much deliberation I bought Ringos, a Tab, a Sherbet Fountain, and this week's *Jackie*, because it had a free pull-out poster of David Soul inside, my new and fourth 'David' crush. Truth was, I had a crush on Paul Michael Glaser, too, and was desperate for a poster of him to add to my collection.

'Perfect,' Hayley said, during one of our weekly phone calls. 'Starsky's Christian name is David, too.'

Armed with my paper bag of purchases, we headed back the way we'd come, Rafferty trotting calmly by my side. 'Let's go have a picnic,' I said. We were passing the new housing development which had sprouted up in the fields beside the railway line these past few months. Rafferty, who enjoyed wandering around the building site as much as Hayley and I did, gave an enthusiastic wag of his tail.

The one hundred or so properties would, eventually,

urbanise our village, but were still a long way from finished and, with the builders often absent, the piles of mud and rubble and the empty rooms had become a giant adventure playground. It felt odd being there without Hayley, though, and with Rafferty in tow I couldn't climb the ladders, so I sat on the doorstep of the one nearest the railway, opened my Ringos and Tab, and began an article entitled *Are you Afraid of Boys*? I wasn't, but I was intrigued some girls might be.

Rafferty sat by my side watching the journey of each Ringo from bag to mouth, occasionally slurping the drool, dribbling from his mouth, with his tongue.

'You can have *one*.' I held it in my palm, and it disappeared with a smack of his chops, his eyes still glued to the packet. 'No more. They're too salty.'

I drained the last of the Tab and was about to tackle my Sherbet Fountain when Rafferty leapt to his feet and whined and pulled on his lead. I stood up and allowed him to drag me to the house next door. At the gap that would become the front door Rafferty stopped, looked at me, and wagged his tail. I was wondering what he was trying to tell me when I smelled cigarette smoke. I rolled up my magazine, crept around the side, and peered in through the window hole. Seated against the wall, legs drawn up, head bowed, a half-smoked cigarette in his right hand, was a boy. He had dark hair, and when he tipped back his head to take another puff, I caught a glimpse of his face.

Louis? I wondered as I ducked out of view. Had he seen me?

I was a bit shocked. Stupid really, since everyone smoked nowadays. No doubt he was under pressure from Charlie. I'd already worked out he was a bad influence on his brother.

Oh God. Was he here, too, lurking out of sight with his

wretched peashooter? I scanned the area. Our last encounter had left a bitter taste in my mouth. Last thing I needed was another savaging. The coast seemed to be clear, but there were so many hiding places on the site, he was probably watching me somewhere and sniggering. Unless, of course, it wasn't Louis I'd seen. Patting Rafferty on the head for reassurance, I took a deep breath and sneaked another peek. This time I saw Louis' face quite clearly. His right eye was bruised, he had a cut on his cheek, and he was staring forlornly into space, occasionally puffing on his cigarette. If he'd already seen me, he hadn't been bothered enough to move.

I ducked down again. 'He's hurt and he's sad,' I whispered to Rafferty, who was watching me expectantly with his china-blue eyes. 'I don't think Charlie is with him but, all the same, I think we should leave him alone.'

'First sign of madness, that is.'

I jumped to my feet, startled by Louis' sudden appearance. 'What is?'

'Talking to a dog.'

'I thought it was talking to yourself.'

'Same difference.'

'No, it isn't. Rafferty happens to be very understanding.' I smiled coyly. 'Are you okay, Louis? You look like you've been in a fight.'

He winced and turned away.

'Sorry. It's none of my business. I was worried, that's all. Anyway, I should go,' I added when he didn't reply. 'Mrs P will be wondering where I am. Come on then, Rafferty.' Tugging gently on his lead, I walked away, Rafferty trotting dutifully by my side.

'No, wait, Nat.' Louis ran after me. 'Don't go. Not yet.'

I stopped and shrugged. 'Okay!'

He flashed me the briefest of smiles, shifting his weight awkwardly from foot to foot. 'Want a smoke?'

'Sure, why not?' I said, trying cool for size.

He reached into his back pocket for the packet, prized out two cigarettes, popped them in his mouth, lit them both with a plastic lighter, and handed one to me. 'Here you go.'

'Where did you get them?'

'Vending machine at the station. Got a couple of cans of lager, too, if you fancy a drink. Borrowed *them* from my dad.' He grinned. 'Come on.'

I followed him inside the house, cigarette in one hand, Rafferty's lead and the rolled-up magazine in the other, and sat beside him. The cement floor felt chilly beneath the flimsy material of my school dress, I noticed, as Rafferty curled into a contented heap at my feet. I braced myself and took a drag. My head spun, and the smoke stung my eyes. I coughed uncontrollably.

'First time,' said Louis. 'Thought so.'

'That obvious?' I dropped the magazine and wiped my eyes with my sleeve.

'I was the same. You get used to it, though.' He ripped open the can and passed it over. 'I'm guessing it's probably your first lager, too, so take it steady.'

I blushed, wishing I wasn't such a goody two-shoes, and took a sip, as nonchalantly possible. The lager had a bitter, malty taste, but was easier going than the cigarette, and I managed to swallow without gagging. And just to prove I was up to the task, I had another swig and another puff. This time I didn't inhale.

'Any good?' he asked, motioning to the magazine.

Oh God, I thought, blushing again. 'Not really.'

'Why buy it then?'

'I suppose because Mum won't allow it in the house.' It

was true, she didn't, but even so it was a lame excuse and a lie. I loved *Jackie*. It was my guide to teenage life, a surrogate older sister who explained away the difficulties of adolescence. My bible. Without it I wouldn't have a clue about fashion, or boys, or periods, or makeup. And although I wasn't allowed my own copy, there was always someone at school who'd lend me theirs.

He picked it up and flicked through it. '*I'm really worried I'll never be able to kiss a boy. I'm fourteen and up till now, I've only ever had one boyfriend. What if Keith tries to kiss me? I don't know what to do. I'm so worried.*' Louis whistled. 'Wow! Heavy.'

I blushed and snatched the magazine back.

'How is your mum?' he asked.

I shrugged. 'Fine.' Last time I'd seen her she'd been decked out like Norma Desmond and having tea with Martha. Did that constitute fine? I doubted it. 'How's yours?'

'She isn't, though, is she?' pressed Louis. 'Mum says she had a breakdown, that she's on loads of drugs, and finds it difficult to get out of bed.'

It was like a punch to the belly. All the air went out of me, and my shoulders sagged. 'Dad told her then?' I mumbled. I didn't know why I was surprised. They were old friends. Why wouldn't he?

'I'm really sorry, Nat.'

My lower lip wobbled, and I dropped my gaze.

'Do you want to talk about it?'

I shook my head, left, right, left.

'It's okay, you don't have to if you don't want to.' He put his arm around me and squeezed. 'But talking about things sometimes helps. And just so you know, I'm a good listener.'

I nodded and sniffed away a tear.

'But not talking's fine, too.'

We sat in silence for a while, his arm around my waist. It was reassuring, having him hold me. I felt safe, a state of mind I hadn't experienced in far too long. 'If Ian had taken a right instead of a left …' My voice cracked.

'Ian?'

I squeezed my eyes shut. 'My brother.'

'Oh. Right.'

'It was over a year ago now. A hit-and-run. They never found the driver.' I spoke mechanically, without emotion. It was all I could manage. If I started crying again, I might never stop. 'He was only eleven. A child really.'

'Shit.'

'My mother broke down. We all did. He was such a good boy. Ian. Not a minute goes by when I don't miss him. We did everything together, you see. Dad and I … we try to get on with things. It's what Ian would want. But Mum said she couldn't, so she went to bed. She's been there ever since.' Until today, I thought. But how could I explain something I couldn't make sense of myself?

'How awful, Nat. If there is anything I can do to help you, ever, I will do it. You know that, don't you?'

Calm words, delivered with such force, I was in no doubt he meant what he said. It was like having a warm bath and slipping on a suit of armour both at the same time. I didn't reply. There was no need. It had all been said.

'What happened to your face?' I asked eventually.

Louis gave me a wry smile. 'Can't you guess?'

'Don't tell me. You walked into a wall.'

'Into Charlie's fist, more like.'

'Charlie hit you?' I inched around on my backside to get a better look. On closer inspection, it seemed Charlie might have broken Louis' nose as well. There was a nasty bump on the bridge, and it was slightly off-centre.

'You seem surprised?'

'But he's your brother. Your twin. You're so close. You do everything together.' I stopped, aware I was babbling. 'What were you fighting about?'

'You, amongst other things.'

'Me?' I did a double take. 'Why? What other things?'

'I like you, Nat. He hates that.'

'You do? He does?'

'I like you a lot.'

'Me? Why? But I'm so …' I'd been about to say ugly, flat-chested, dull, but the intensity of Louis' stare stopped me in my tracks.

'Beautiful?' He leant towards me. 'Are *you* scared to kiss *me*, Nat?' Without waiting for an answer, he pressed his lips on mine. They were soft and warm and slightly wet. I'd practiced kissing on the back of my hand, but this was entirely different. His tongue, inside my mouth, was teasing mine into a kind of dance, and every inch of my skin was tingling. It was the strangest sensation, like flying without wings.

All too soon he pulled away and smiled at me through heavy-lidded eyes. 'Now do you believe me?'

Before the kiss there'd been so many things I wanted to discuss with him: why Charlie hated me, what they'd been arguing about aside from me, whether Cee Cee or my father was the love of Martha's life? But they were unimportant now. All I cared about was Louis, his lips, his mouth, the strange fluttering sensation in my belly when he'd kissed me.

'I might,' I said, 'if you kiss me again.'

13

Bo Rivers wasn't wrong when he said Eel Pie Island would attract an enthusiastic crowd. The bar is a good draw, of course, especially since most venues don't serve alcohol. Martha glances at the two young men, propped against it, idly smoking and studying her intently over pints of beer. They were at The Marquee the other night and the Flamingo. Her third gig in a month and, already, she has a following of two. How cool is that? Must be doing something right. The brown-haired, better-looking one, winks at her and grins, while his smaller, auburn-haired friend presses his hand to his lips and blows her a kiss. She wonders if Cee Cee has noticed. Not that he'd mind. He's way too laid-back to care about some harmless flirting. Behind her, the band starts playing. She lowers her head, cups the microphone in both hands, and listens. Bo's solo sounds slick, despite his reservations. It was written for the trombone, but he'd cobbled something together because he felt the song was a perfect fit for her voice.

She peers at the dark-haired man beneath heavily mascaraed lashes. She counts in the bars, gyrating her hips as she waits for her cue. Drawing out the first word *I* for three counts, she tells him, and him alone, that she's 'Mad About the Boy'. The man, who must be in his early twenties, stares back wide-eyed, the cocky smile wiped clean off his face, the cigarette he'd been about to puff suspended in mid-air. His friend slaps him on the back, whoops, and falls silent. For the first time she's aware of the power of her voice; the emotions it provokes, the blind devotion. She is holding this man in the palm of her hand. He is hers, to do with as she wishes.

When she reaches the end, she fills her lungs, hanging on to the final note. Holding it. Holding it. And breaking off. Bam. The applause is deafening. She severs the connection with the young man and smiles at the audience, who are clapping and stamping their feet. She waits, soaking up the appreciation, savouring it, not wanting it to end. At the back of the room, Becky is jumping up and down and waving. It's a marked contrast to the broom handle she used to bang against the ceiling. Martha is delighted she's here and relieved they've made up.

The article had shocked Becky, but she'd been excited, too, and had immediately offered to do her makeup and help her out with her clothes. In her opinion, Martha needed a knockout look. Martha wasn't convinced. She wasn't some model to be primped and polished. She was a singer. She wanted to be taken seriously. But judging by the way the audience had ogled her at the Flamingo, she knew she needed to dress the part. Wasn't that why she'd headed over to Bazaar? Becky worked in the beauty and makeup department of the store and was always immaculately turned out. It had been one of the things which had so impressed Martha the first time they'd met. She'd do a good job.

Her reflection, when Becky handed her a mirror, had startled her. Creamy foundation and flesh-coloured powder covered her freckles and gave her skin a mask-like quality, with a swipe of blusher for a healthy glow. Her bushy eyebrows had been tamed, plucked to within an inch of their life and shaped into a tapering point, while the eyeliner on her upper lid flicked out and up at the end, like a cat.

'And last but not least, your lips,' Becky said, unscrewing a gold tube. 'Hot red for a luscious pout.'

Martha had hated it. She'd felt like an impostor. But Becky had insisted she was not only glamorous but the epitome of a very modern woman. A few hours later when, taking the steps to the underground, heads had turned her way, she'd felt like a freak. But Becky had laughed and said, *You're beautiful, Martha. That's all.*

The applause dies away. Her back to the audience, Martha glances at Cee Cee, beaming proudly. You gave me this, she thinks. You made it happen and you saved me. She smiles back, suddenly overcome with fondness for this kind, gentle man.

Last week he'd taken her to the cinema to see *Some Like it Hot*, followed by dinner at the Lyons corner house on Coventry Street where he told her about his childhood dreams of living in the Mother country, and the hostility he'd faced on arrival. Fortunately, he and Roly had bumped into Bo, who was also looking for work, at the Musicians Union on Archer Street. The three of them were hired for a gig, got on well, and on Bo's suggestion, formed a band. They put word out they needed a drummer and a bassist. Frankie and Mike showed up, and The Bo Rivers' Five was formed. Put like that, he made it sound easy, but she was under no illusions they'd worked hard to achieve their sound.

Later, he'd taken her to one of his friend's flats, a tall, wiry Jamaican called Alphonso, for a late-night, grass-fuelled jamming session, with half a dozen West Indian jazz musicians. It was the first time Martha had taken any sort of drug. She hadn't liked it one little bit, so probably also the last. But he hadn't kissed her again or even tried. Perhaps Bo had had a word with him about the 'band dynamic', too.

'You ready?' Cee Cee mouths.

She nods, and he gestures to Roly, poised at the piano. Martha closes her eyes and, determined to wring the soul out of each note, imagines herself in the heart of a woman being treated badly by the man she loves. Bo's trumpet gives way to Cee Cee's sax. She counts herself in: one, two, three, four.

'You're mean to me.' She opens her eyes and refocuses on her audience.

The song reaching its climax, Martha winks at the handsome man, adds a bit of scat singing, and repeats the last line a couple of times, like she's heard Ella do. Unfazed by this sudden departure, the band follows her lead to thunderous applause. Light-headed with relief, Martha inhales deeply then exhales the air and all the emotion with it.

'Ladies and gentlemen,' Bo says. 'Miss Martha Palmer will now take a short break. Her band, however, will endeavour to keep you entertained with an old favourite of mine, "Line for Lyons".'

My band? Goodness. Bo Rivers may be enigmatic and taciturn, but he sure as hell knows how to surprise her. She glances over at him, and he throws her a brief smile before turning back to the musicians to count them in. Making a show of clapping *her* band, she backs off the stage.

She's on her way to the ladies when the handsome young man intercepts her. 'Miss Palmer, you were … I mean, you are … magnificent. Please allow me the honour of buying you a drink.'

'I don't usually drink during a set.' The lie trips of her tongue. She doesn't usually drink, full stop. 'But for you I'll make an exception.'

'Gin and tonic?' his friend asks.

'Why not?' She spies Becky, weaving through the crowd towards them. 'Oh, and one for my friend, if you wouldn't mind.'

'It would be our pleasure,' the handsome one says. 'I'm Gordon by the way.' He reaches out and shakes her vigorously by the hand. 'And this is Rory.'

'And this is Becky.'

'Pleasure to meet you, boys!' Becky says.

Rory winks. 'Trust me, the pleasure's entirely mine.'

Becky cups a hand to Martha's ear. 'Where did you learn to sing like that?'

Martha laughs and shakes her head. She's asked herself the same question enough times.

'You'd better watch out or it won't be long before Dracula is sinking his teeth into your neck.'

Martha stares at Becky, nonplussed. 'Dracula?'

'Are you a singer, too?' Rory's eyes home in on the swell of Becky's breasts, set off by the low-cut crimson dress.

'No, I'm her manager.'

Rory raises an eyebrow 'Of course you are.'

'Here,' says Gordon, handing them the drinks. 'Your good health.'

They clink glasses. The song ends. The crowd claps, but not as loudly.

Emptying the condensation and saliva out of the spit valve, Bo introduces the band again by name as he always does, three or four times a set. 'And now one of my favourites. "Born to be Blue".'

'So, when can we buy your record?' Gordon asks.

'Sorry. What?' she asks, distracted by this late addition to the running order.

'Your album. Tell me it'll be in the shops soon.'

Martha screws up her nose. 'Well …'

'Next month,' says Becky.

Martha throws her a cautionary look.

'So, what do you boys get up to when you're not listening to the sensational Martha Palmer?' Becky asks.

Gordon shrugs. 'Nothing much. We're students.'

'Medical students,' says Rory, his gaze still fixed on Becky.

'Ooh! Life-savers!' says Becky.

Rory grins. 'But not a pool in sight.'

Martha laughs, covering her mouth with her hand. His head tilted, Gordon smiles goofily at her. They're overgrown schoolboys, and drunk, too, she thinks, as the sweet tones of a man's baritone fill the room. It's a flat sound, without vibrato, understated but beautiful. Nobody mentioned anything about another singer. She whirls around and is surprised to see Bo Rivers, eyes closed, lips pressed to the mic.

Becky's jaw drops. 'Goodness me. The Count can sing.'

'Perfect phrasing,' says Gordon, 'but not a patch on Martha.'

But Martha doesn't hear him. She only has ears, and eyes, for Bo.

14

August 1959

The Grind is packed again today, busier than ever, with people prepared to queue for tables out in the street in the blazing sunshine. It's been a sizzling summer, the hottest Martha can remember, with day after day of cloudless blue skies. Hovering out of sight in the kitchen, she is watching Giovanni who, having stopped short of rubbing his hands in glee, is lauding it behind the counter. A seasoned professional, he beams at his customers, praises them for their love of Italian coffee, and congratulates them on their choice of cake. No order is too small, and every wish is granted. Now and again, he checks his reflection in the mirror, runs a hand through his unruly hair, a finger over his moustache. He calls to mind a cockerel strutting through a courtyard in front of a brood of admiring hens.

And that's not all. Against this madness, Ella and Louis are belting out 'Isn't this a Lovely Day'. Since he found out about her *other talent* and, never one to miss a trick, Giovanni is now playing jazz records on the Dansette beneath the counter, non-stop. He's accumulated a stash of them, including some rare American imports he bought from Dobell's. He swears Miles Davis' new record, 'Kind of Blue', is his favourite. Martha doubts it. Whatever he might say, Jazz is not Giovanni's thing. Swing, maybe, but not this new craze. Modal jazz, the trumpeter is calling it, whatever *that* means. No, it's far more likely Giovanni, whose ear is fine-tuned to the latest fad, has latched on to the hype surrounding its release. It would be hard not to. Apart from all the teenagers sold on Adam Faith, the latest rock 'n' roll sensation, everyone else is listening to and talking about Miles Davis' record. Still, Martha isn't sure what to make of Giovanni's fervour. She loves the music – jazz, the blues, swing – it's her passion, but what was once an ordinary musicless coffee shop where she works, has become an entirely different environment altogether.

She's not a waitress anymore either. When Giovanni realised she didn't intend leaving, he announced she'd be working behind the counter with him. Luca hadn't wasted time in voicing his objection, rightly pointing out it was his job.

'Not anymore,' Giovanni said. 'But do not worry, Luca. I will not leave you to cope alone. I will advertise for another waitress.'

'You can't do this. Waiting tables is not in my job description.'

Giovanni thumped the counter with his fist. '*Basta*, Luca, *basta*! Do not spit in the plate you eat from. I can do what I bloody well like.'

'But it's not fair.'

'You are making an elephant out of a fly, Luca. Either eat this soup or jump out of the window.'

On the one hand, Martha is grateful to Giovanni. Since he found out about her budding career, he's supported her wholeheartedly. Back in February, when Bo announced the band would be touring for three months, she assumed Giovanni would blow a gasket and refuse to let her go. But he didn't. He made his irritation clear, then promised her job would be waiting for her on her return, if she still wanted it.

Bo, meanwhile, hadn't asked but simply assumed she wanted to tour with them. Never mind she had a job she didn't want to lose. But posing the question wasn't Bo's style. If he had an idea, he ran with it. Not that she cared. Only a fool would have turned him down. And when she thought about it, really it was the ultimate compliment. Bo considered her one of them. It was incredible. One minute she was waiting tables, the next she was travelling the country in a clapped-out VW camper van, with five fellas she barely knew. She should have been terrified, but whether out of respect for the 'band dynamic', or Cee Cee, or basic good manners, they not only treated her like a princess but also shielded her from the unwanted attention of several zealous male fans. They were quick to offer advice, too, if she asked for it, and geed her up on the days she was tired or down.

Crammed in with all the instruments, including Mike's drum kit and Frankie's double bass piled up on the bed at the back, it had been easy getting to know one another. Roly and Cee Cee regaled her with tales of their Jamaican childhood, smoking spliffs on the beaches of Ocho Rios, and digging the groove of the jazz club in town. Cee Cee honed his chops on a sax his uncle claimed had belonged to Bird, but which he'd probably chanced on in a junk shop in Kingston. Roly taught himself how to play on a discarded broken piano he found in the street and was soon comping with a jazz band in a run-down bar late at night.

Frankie's history couldn't have been more different. A classically trained musician, he swapped his violin for a double bass after graduating from the Royal College of Music and took up jazz, much to his parents' disappointment. Mean-while, ten-year-old Mike was driving his parents crazy, drum-ming on the furniture, the walls and the floor, with a pair of old drumsticks he dug out of a bin outside the Fullado Club. With money he saved from a paper round and shining shoes on the street, he bought a second-hand drum kit and, together with a couple of schoolmates, formed a skiffle band.

'And what about you, Martha?' Roly asked during a lull in the conversation. 'What's your story?'

'I ran away from home.'

'Why?' Roly asked.

'To seek my fortune as a singer.'

Everyone laughed.

Everyone except Bo, who fixed her with his searchlight stare. 'What happened to make you run?'

Martha's blush reached from the bottom of her neck to the tips of her ears 'Did I say run? I meant I left home. Dull really, by comparison to all of you.'

By the end of the tour, the five fellas, their habits – such as Roly's toenail picking and Frankie's incessant need to break wind – and the lingering odour of weed in the van's upholstery, were as familiar to Martha as the songs she sang.

They performed in dance halls, slept overnight in bedsits and AA hotels. The West End Café in Edinburgh booked them for a fortnight in February, the Corn Exchange in Berwick-upon-Tweed for a week, the Town Hall in Birming-ham, the Bodega in Manchester, the Essoldo in Newcastle, and the Gaiety Ballroom in Grimsby. And when Cee Cee's hero, Lester Young, died halfway through the tour, they drowned their collective sorrows in far too many bottles of Scotch.

With sell-out crowds at all the venues, the tour was a huge success. Martha was riding high on adrenaline, loving every second, her eyes well and truly opened. The only thing she found difficult to navigate was her daily proximity to Bo.

It started the night on Eel Pie Island when she heard him sing. His unique voice, the crystal-clear tenor tone, melancholic yet ultra-cool, sent shock waves through her body. His natural reserve only added to his aura. Unlike the others, who wore their hearts on their sleeves, he said little, seemingly content to listen. The nearer she was to him in the van, at dinner, or on stage, the greater the physical effect – butterflies, sweaty palms, racing pulse, and a strange tingling sensation creeping down her spine. Her budding romance with Cee Cee had fizzled out before it had a chance to get going. But, having lived on top of one another for months, she understands the importance of the band's dynamic now, which is why she hasn't breathed a word about her infatuation to a soul. Not even Becky. It wouldn't do to admit she's fallen for her boss, especially since Bo clearly doesn't feel the same way about her. All she can do is try and suppress the feelings and hope they go away. It's her shameful little secret, and she hides it as best she can.

Keeping busy helps and, in the four months she's been back, there's been no sign of a letdown. The band continues to be in demand. Giovanni has accommodated her new schedule, too – allowing her time off at weekends, working her shifts in and around her singing commitments – but she feels bad for Luca. He's right. It isn't fair he's given up his job for her. He's been doing it for years.

She'd had a private word with Giovanni and offered to

work in the kitchen instead, but he had waved his hand dismissively. 'Do not do the dead cat, Martha.'

She frowned. 'The what?'

'No, no, *tesoro*. Enough. It doesn't suit you. You are an intelligent *signorina*. Sofia is happy working in the kitchen. The Grind is your stage now. You are the leading lady, the main attraction. You know it. I know it. I am simply taking the ball on the bounce.'

And that's it in a nutshell. Giovanni is making the most of an opportunity which, quite unexpectedly, has come his way. Martha isn't a waitress anymore. She's an upcoming star; the coffee shop, her stage. These last twelve months, since she first performed with The Bo Rivers' Five, she's been gaining a reputation and, with the band's popularity growing daily following their sell-out tour, Bo has signed with manager, Leonard Sharp. A forward-thinking cockney with a pencil moustache and a penchant for trilbies, and something of an impresario, Len (as he prefers to be known), is convinced they have what it takes to go far in the business. Publicity, he maintains, is the means to achieving national fame. The band has already acquired a sizeable following, but according to Len, with the right exposure, it will become fanatical. This is due to their star quality, and Martha's, in particular.

'Your Hobson's one of the best in the business,' he explained, when he set out his plan. 'But you're also a tidy bird, Marfa. We need to get your beautiful boat in the linen. Course, once yer release a record, the stories will write 'emselves. You'll be an 'ousehold name and a lah-di-dah.'

This has been a lot easier than she imagined. Len seems to be best friends with almost all the journalists and photographers in town. Yesterday, to mark the launch of her first LP, her face stared out from the cover of the *New Musical Express*. It explains why crowds of people are now queuing outside the café, all of them armed with a camera, or an auto-graph book, or both. That Martha Palmer still works at the Italian coffee shop in Greek Street is common knowledge amongst their fans, but word must have got out to the public. She hates to think what it'll be like when the September edition of *Jazz Monthly* is published next week with her mug once again plastered on the front page.

In the café, someone calls out her name, and within a minute, everyone in the small room is chanting it. She is famous, just as Len predicted. Shame he didn't think to warn her about all this, though. It's utter madness. She rubs her clammy palms on her apron, takes a few deep breaths and, from the safety of the kitchen, dares to steal another peek.

The place is rammed to bursting. Several customers are brandishing her album sleeve, waving it above their heads. She catches sight of Dipper Da Costa, happily signing auto-graphs for anyone who asks. Milton Hyde, however, is cowering at a corner table, his face anxious and pale, an untouched slice of cake in front of him. Outside, the crowd is clogging up not only the pavements, but also the street. There must be at least eighty people out there, a hundred at a push. Giovanni is no longer smiling but windmilling his hands and issuing commands to the terrified waitresses he's recently employed. There's no way he can serve all these people. She only hopes he can control them.

The back door swings open with a whoosh, and a current of warm air eddies around her. She yelps and wheels around, fully expecting to see a fan. But it's only Luca arriving for his shift.

'Still skiving, I see.'

Ignoring the jibe, she slips past him and locks the door. When had it become unlocked? she wonders fretfully.

'What are you doing?' Luca asks, unhooking his apron

and tying it around his waist. 'And what the hell is that racket?'

Martha shrugs. 'World's gone mad.'

Luca cocks his head and listens. 'My God! It's you.' He stares at her open-mouthed, a preferable expression to the hangdog resentment he's been lugging around these past few weeks.

'I released a record. I didn't invent the wheel.'

He grins. 'Don't s'pose you've got a spare copy?'

Martha let's out a huge breath. She's hated being the cause of Luca's irritation. He's been a good friend to her since she started working here, supportive and loyal, funny, too.

'What was Giovanni thinking?' Luca continues. 'No. Don't answer that. It's obvious. Bloody parasite. One thing's for certain, you can't go out there. You'll be ripped to shreds.'

'I can't stay here, though. What if they come in?'

Luca shakes his head. 'Give me a minute. I'll think of something.'

Peggy, one of the new waitresses, rushes in, her face flushed. 'A young man asked me to give you this.' She hands Martha a piece of paper, wipes her forehead with her apron and, taking a deep breath, dashes back into the fray.

Martha opens the note, hastily scribbled on a leaf torn from a prescription pad. She reads it, and a slow smile creeps across her face

Don't panic, Martha, I have a plan. I'll be round the back in a jiffy.

Your affectionate Gordon.

PS congratulations on the record. Solid gold.

She hands Luca the note. 'Help is at hand.'

'Ah. Guess it's why he's training to be a doctor and I'm not.'

Right on cue, there's a knock on the back door. 'Martha? Are you in there? It's me. Gordon.'

Luca unlocks the door, grabs Gordon, who is clutching a plastic bag, by the arm, pulls him inside, and quickly locks it again.

'Bless you, Father,' Luca says, cocking an amused eyebrow as he takes in Gordon's dog collar. A well-thumbed copy of *On the Road* is sticking out of his pocket, which slightly detracts from the disguise, but otherwise it's pretty good.

'Best I could do on my budget.' Gordon turns to Martha, his face a picture of concern. 'You okay?'

She throws her arms around him. 'All the better for seeing you.'

'Aw! Shucks. You sure know how to make a man feel good about himself.'

Martha kisses him on the cheek and takes the bag. 'My disguise?' She pulls out the nun's habit and veil. 'Brilliant.'

'You'll attract some attention in that,' says Luca. 'Ever see a nun in Soho?'

Martha's heart sinks. 'You're right.'

'I'm kidding,' says Luca. 'It's perfect. No one will suspect it's you. Now hurry up and get changed.'

It's not until she's smuggled Gordon into her room and they're listening to Lady Day, something Martha's been doing a lot since the legendary singer's tragic death last month, and drinking the whisky from Gordon's hipflask which he poured into teacups, that Martha's tense shoulders relax and she can laugh about their mad escape. Fortunately, Mrs

Wilson, who believes Martha's recent three-month absence was because she'd been caring for an ill relative, is out, otherwise Gordon would never have made it up the stairs.

She and Becky have been spending a lot of time with the young medics in various bars and clubs around Soho. They're great company and enjoy shocking them with their gruesome med-school tales. Mainly they go out as a four, but once, when Rory was working a night shift, Gordon invited her to dine at Chez Auguste, alone.

'It's run by a likeable eccentric with a white goatee, and you can get a carafe of drinkable red for ten shillings, which is not to be sniffed at,' he explained in his straightforward, no-nonsense way.

Over dinner, they'd shared stories of their childhood dreams and ambitions, his of becoming a surgeon, hers of being a singer.

'You've pulled it off already,' he said. 'How does it feel?'

'Like I'm dreaming.'

'Trust me, you're not,' he said and pinched her on the arm.

She's never been gladder of his friendship. He knew her album had come out yesterday and that she had a shift at The Grind today. Typical of him to put two and two together. Always one step ahead, was Gordon. If only the same could be said of Giovanni.

'What a day,' Martha says. 'Can you believe it?'

'It could have been worse.'

'Impossible.'

'Delilah Moore could've shown up and thrown another punch. Imagine that?'

She smiles ruefully and shakes her head. For weeks Martha had feared she would but, since the afternoon in the café when the diminutive diva had turned the air blue, she hasn't clapped eyes on her. 'What's happened to her? She used to be everywhere, but now you never hear of her.'

'Rumour has it she's in rehab.'

'For what?'

'Her crushing drug addiction.'

Martha gasps. 'Flippin' 'eck. I'd no idea.'

'It's a well-kept secret. Let's hope she doesn't end up like poor old Billie. I read somewhere she had only seventy cents in her bank account, but hospital workers found seven hundred and fifty dollars taped to one of her legs.'

Martha slaps her hands to her cheeks. 'That's awful.'

'Yeah, it is. So, promise me you'll never do drugs.'

'No need. I tried grass once and hated it.'

'I mean it, Martha. When you're rich and famous and haven't the time for people like me, it'll be all too easy to go down that route.'

'What a low opinion you have of me.' She takes his hand and squeezes it and, leaning her head on his shoulder, hums along to 'Strange Fruit', the song about a lynching Billie made famous. Heartbreaking someone so talented died in such tragic circumstance. And Delilah Moore an addict, too. No matter how crazy things become, she will resist all temptations.

'Do you think it's going to be like this every day, Donny?'

He leans across and tucks a stray strand of hair behind her ear. 'Why do you call me that?'

'Dunno. Do you mind?'

'Not at all.' Gordon clears his throat and gives her leg a reassuring pat. 'But you can't work at the café anymore, Martha. I'm sure even Giovanni realises it's impossible now.'

'But … It's my job.'

'You really don't have a clue, do you.' He smiles again

and presses his forehead against hers. 'You're a singer, Martha. A star. You're going to be rich.'

She sighs and walks over to the box where she keeps her records and absently rifles through them. She doesn't feel the least bit like a star. Stars don't live in grotty fourth-floor flats or drink whisky out of chipped, china cups. She's plain old Martha Palmer, waitress and part-time singer. If anyone is a star it's Bo Rivers. It's his name they perform under, his band. All she does is turn up and sing. In between times she works in an Italian café. She doesn't need the extra money but she enjoys it … well, most of the time.

'It's going to be fine,' Gordon says. 'You'll see.'

'Easy for you to say.'

'It'll take some getting used to, but it's far more glamorous than working for a hyperactive Italian.'

She whirls around, frowning. 'Giovanni's not hyperactive. He's enthusiastic. I love working for him. I love the café. I love him. He's been so kind. Like a father, really. I wouldn't have survived a minute in London without his job. His help.' Her voice cracking, she turns back to the records.

'You can always visit. I'm sure he'd have no objections.'

She clenches her jaw. Stupid to think Donny would understand. Stuck in a hospital all day, surrounded by blood and gore, all he sees is the glamour and the fame. He has no idea about the business side of the music scene, the endless publicity rounds, the press intrusion, and the lack of anonymity. He saved her today, and for that she's grateful, but now she wishes he would go. She wants to be alone. Needs time to think. Wants to figure out if the good outweighs the bad, because if it doesn't, can she honestly say it's worth it?

'Right, well, time I went,' Gordon says, as if reading her mind. 'My shift starts in half an hour.'

She forces a smile and, muttering something about seeing

him out, follows him down the four flights of stairs. She opens the door and steps onto the pavement. The sky is a watery blue, the sun a faded yellow. In the ground-floor flat opposite, the landlady, Mrs Preston, is hard at work beating the dust out of her curtains.

Gordon pecks her on the cheek, and she manages a smile. 'Thanks again for saving me.'

He shrugs. 'It was nothing.'

Down the street, a man in a fedora hurrying towards them, catches her eye and waves.

Her stomach somersaults wildly. 'Bo!'

He breaks into a run, grinning from ear to ear, and opens his arms. Her heart flips. Oh my God. At last. The moment she's dreamt of. But just as quickly, they drop to his sides. Damn it, she thinks. Damn. Damn. Damn.

Gordon thrusts out his hand. 'I'm Gordon James. A huge fan of Martha … and … er … you.'

Bo shakes it, a blank look on his face. 'Pleased to meet you.'

Martha winces. She knows Gordon's only being his usual polite self, but for once she wishes he would forget his manners and go. His presence is awkward for everyone.

'Well, best be off. See you around then, gorgeous.' Gordon winks and marches away.

She cringes. Why? Why say that? And why wink?

'I heard what happened at the café,' Bo says distractedly, his focus fixed on the departing medic, whistling happily as he saunters down the street.

'Blimey, news travels fast.'

He faces her and smiles. 'Must've been a shock.'

'You could say that.'

'You seem irritated. Should I go?'

She grabs his arm. 'No, don't!' His eyes widen and,

blushing, she lets go. 'I … I'm sorry. It's just … well … you caught me off-guard.'

'Ah! I see.'

Martha frowns and throws up her hands. 'No, you don't. I just wasn't expecting you.'

'That guy …. Is he …? Are you …? Only, I seem to remember seeing him around you before.'

'God, no. Donny … I mean, Gordon is a friend.'

'Oh. Right. Good.'

She smiles coyly. 'Is it?'

Bo clears his throat. 'I have news.'

Her heart sinks. She'd thought she'd sensed a significant shift in their relationship, but it seems she was wrong. 'Oh.'

'Good news, Martha.' Bo tilts his head and regards her curiously. 'Is something up? By the look on your face anyone would think someone died.'

'No, nothing. Sorry.' She glances over his shoulder. Mrs Preston has finished her curtain beating, and the flat facing her lies in darkness.

'Great, because I've come to tell you "Fever" has sold more copies this week than any other record in the UK. Something to smile about, surely?'

She feels a flicker of something. Excitement? But it quickly subsides. I should be jumping up and down, she thinks. This is beyond my wildest dreams.

'You're shocked. Of course, you are. We need to celebrate. Muriel's bound to have a bottle of champagne on ice.'

She screws up her nose. 'Muriel?'

'A foul-mouthed lesbian I know. She runs The Colony Room. Trust me, no one will bother you there.'

'What about the band?'

His smile slips. 'I can call them if you want.'

A surge of happiness sweeps through her, and she beams. 'No. It's okay. I'll just get my bag.'

Thirty minutes later, they stride into Dean Street. The butter-flies have returned, dipping and diving with a vengeance. She wishes they would either fly away or settle down. Their constant flitting and flapping are unsettling. Why, after all the hours she's spent with this man, can't she control them? Her heart is racing, too, and her palms are sticky. What if he notices? Really, she should have told him she was busy. It was stupid to put herself in this position. Why does she never stop to think things through?

'Here we are.' He draws to a halt in front of a tattered front door flanked by a couple of overflowing dustbins. 'Now, up we go.'

She follows him, warily, up a dark staircase which reeks of body odour and urine. A man in a hurry rushes down from the floor above, and they press their backs against the grimy walls to let him pass. Rounding a bend, Bo leads her into a dark, dingy room with lurid green walls. In front of the bamboo bar, a woman with lank brown hair scraped off her pinched face is perched on a leopard-print stool. Drink in one hand, cigarette holder in the other, she appraises them for a moment, puffing on her cigarette.

'Hello, cunty,' she says, and without waiting for a reply continues her conversation with the man seated next to her.

Bo grins. 'See what I mean? Nobody cares who we are here.'

Martha takes in the plastic pot plants, the green banquettes, mottled mirrors, and the eye-catching art hanging from every wall. 'Is that why you chose to be a member?'

'You don't choose. Muriel allowed me to join because

I'm not considered boring. But I like it because there's no prejudice. Cee Cee and I can drink in peace.'

Martha flinches. She's witnessed the abuse hurled at Cee Cee plenty of times. On one occasion last September, shortly after the race riots, they were having a drink together, when the fella at the next table accused her of being a prostitute because, in his opinion, only a white whore would be seen with a black man. She can't imagine how he must feel, being an object of hatred simply because of the colour of his skin.

Bo leads her to a table in the corner, next to a couple of men chatting away in Polari, and orders some champagne. The barman delivers the bottle and two glasses, slides the cork out with his thumbs with a satisfying pop, and bubbly froth spills over the rim.

Bo pours and raises his glass. 'To you, Martha. Congratulations.'

Martha drinks. It's her first taste of champagne.

'Delicious, eh?' Bo is staring at her in his intense way, like he's not only reading her thoughts, but also analysing them.

One by one, the hairs on the back of her neck stand on end. Flustered, she takes another sip. The bubbles prickle her throat. She coughs and swallows far too quickly, and the liquid shoots out of her nose. Silently cursing herself, she gropes inside her bag for her handkerchief. She finds it, at last, and takes a minute to compose herself but, when she looks up, Bo is still watching her.

'Mm. Delicious,' she says.

Bo laughs and tops up her glass. 'Oh, I almost forgot. The BBC want to play "Fever" on *Juke Box Jury*, and the producer of *Tonight at The London Palladium* has been in touch with Len.'

Wait a minute, what? Television? Me? 'Flippin' 'eck.'

'So, you'll do it.'

'I guess so, if you will.'

He straightens up and smooths his tie. 'Ah. Well. They don't want me.'

'Why on earth not?'

'Because, Martha, you're the star.'

'Don't be daft.'

'I'm not. You're the one making records.'

She bites her lip. It's true, she has, but when she performs live it's always with the band. She thinks of herself as part of them. Is Bo really pleased for her? He gave her the break, after all. He might be annoyed. Or jealous. What if he doesn't want to work with her anymore? Oh, dear God, she couldn't bear it.

'Penny for them.'

She marshals her thoughts, for once carefully framing her answer. 'Do you mind?'

He laughs again, right from the belly. 'Mind? My dear, sweet girl, why would I mind? I'm delighted for you.'

A jolt runs through her. 'Am I?'

He peers at her, quizzically. 'Are you what?'

'Your dear, sweet girl.' Her mouth is dry, and her throat seems unnaturally thick.

'Look, Martha, I—'

'You know, if it wasn't for you, Bo, none of this would have happened. You gave me my break. My success is down to you. I owe you everything.'

He frowns. 'You owe me nothing. And anyway, it was Cee Cee who found you. Or have you forgotten?'

She fiddles with her sleeve. She should have kept her trap shut. He was in a good mood. They would have had a lovely evening. Now he'll probably suggest they both go home. Why did she always have to go and spoil things?

'Thing is,' he says, 'the second I heard your voice, I knew I was listening to something truly special.'

'Could've fooled me,' she says softly.

'I know and I'm sorry. But it wasn't only your voice. The second I set eyes on you … I … You … You are…' Wincing, he turns away.

She inches forward, aware the mood has changed. Her heart is pounding her ribs, and her cheeks are uncomfortably hot. 'What? I am what?'

His gaze settles on her again. 'You're beautiful, Martha, and I am head over heels in love you.'

15

In the days following Martha's visit, it quickly became clear the positive change we'd witnessed in my mother, and which had so excited my father, was not the start of the longed-for recovery we'd hoped for, but a passing interlude. The kaftan and turban had been the clues. Dressed up like some forgotten film star, she obviously wasn't in her right mind. I'd stop short of calling her out-and-out crazy, but she certainly wasn't herself. Sometimes, when I took her breakfast on a tray, she barely registered my presence. I found myself wondering whether her listlessness was a conscious choice, that by rendering herself mentally and physically numb, she was protecting herself from the pain, albeit to the total exclusion of pleasure. One thing was certain, she'd resolved to shirk a life that no longer held any joy because it was easier. Battling grief was tough. I knew only too well. I'd been trying to mend the fractured pieces of my heart long enough. But my mother's refusal to even try was infuriating. My father tried to reassure me. She was ill, he said, and her mind, like a broken arm, needed time to mend. But nothing he said made any difference. She'd given up and was taking the coward's way out.

I was furious with her, too, for neglecting her motherly duty to me, her only daughter. Clearly, she'd loved Ian more than she could ever love me. But Ian had been the epicentre of my world, too. I missed him. Grieved for him. Was angry he'd been taken so young. But, unlike her, I soldiered on. And just as well, because life had rewarded me with a get-out-of-jail-free card in human form. Louis Fairchild liked me and I liked him. I was happier than I'd been in far too long. Move over, Martha Palmer, I had a new object of my affection now.

Both of us were keen to keep our burgeoning romance private, particularly from Charlie. If he'd punched Louis in the face simply for liking me, who knew how he'd react if he heard we were going out. The hosepipe ban notwithstanding, the arrival of tenants at the Taylor's house meant their garden was out of bounds, but there was still the building site. We hatched a plan to meet there, every day after school at four-thirty, except on Wednesdays when I had my singing lesson. Rafferty and Mrs Pocock's injured hip were my cover. It was easier for Louis, who could do as he pleased, but he still had to work out how to give Charlie the slip. After much deliberation, he told his brother he was helping a sick neighbour, which wasn't a complete lie. And it worked a treat. As Louis had predicted, Charlie wasn't the altruistic type and never once asked to tag along.

Mrs P's hip was taking a long time to mend, and she couldn't thank me enough. 'How kind you are, and what a credit to your parents.' She pressed a bag of homemade butterscotch in my hand and whatever change she happened to have. 'Buy yourself a treat.'

That was when the guilt kicked in. I hated the idea I wasn't being entirely honest with her and tried to hand it back. 'It's a pleasure, Mrs P. I love walking Rafferty.'

But she wouldn't take no for an answer, and I left slightly richer than when I'd arrived. When I told Louis how I felt, he always took the same stance.

'You're not lying, Nat. Not really. You actually do love walking Rafferty.'

'Yes, but Mrs P doesn't know I'm meeting you.'

'I'm sure she wouldn't mind. You and Hayley used to walk Rafferty together.'

'It's not the same. What you and I are doing is du … duplicitous.'

'Duplicitous? Wow. Big word, Nat.'

I frowned, and Louis held my cheeks and kissed me. And as my knees weakened and every single one of my nerve endings tingled, Mrs P, my mother, and all the problems of the world simply melted away. Being with Louis was the only thing that mattered. I no longer questioned what he saw in me. There was nothing better than the two hours I spent with him every evening, eating Mrs P's butterscotch, talking, and kissing.

We carried on like this for a couple of weeks, until one day, when I was rolling on my favourite strawberry lip gloss, my father wandered into my room to ask me if I would drop by Greystones with a record Martha had asked to borrow. He'd promised to get it to her by four-thirty but had patients till seven. Would you mind? I sighed and made a show of studying my watch and explained that I was walking Rafferty at four-fifteen and was already late.

'And there I was thinking you were Martha Palmer's staunchest fan.'

'I am, but Mrs P is expecting me.'

'I'm sure Edie won't mind this once. Please, Natasha. It's important.'

'But Mrs P's relying on me.'

'And Martha is relying on me. I'll ring Edie right now and explain. You won't be late if you get a move on.'

I glanced at my watch again. It was ten past, which meant Louis would be waiting. He always arrived early because he didn't want me hanging around alone. It was typically thoughtful of him. But today I was stymied. If I continued to protest, my father would suspect I was up to something. The way I saw it I had two choices. Disobey my father, pick up Rafferty, meet Louis as planned, and give him the LP to give to Martha. Or deliver it, pick up Rafferty, and be late for Louis. The first option was fraught with difficulties. When I didn't show up, Martha would be worried and possibly cross. She might ring my father, who definitely would be. Chances are we'd be found out. And once my father knew about us there'd be no more sneaking to the building site after school. I simply couldn't let that happen. I had to deliver the record, pure and simple. Louis would understand.

Fifteen minutes later, and tapping my foot impatiently on the hall tiles while my father continued to chat away to Mrs P, I was still waiting for the LP. They'd discussed the change in arrangements in a matter of seconds, but five minutes had been taken up with Mrs P impressing upon my father how kind I'd been, and now the conversation had turned to the subject of her hip.

'Come *on*, Dad,' I muttered through gritted teeth.

'I'll drop by and see you next week, Edie.' Putting down

the phone at last, he caught sight of me and raised his eyebrows. 'Still here?'

I sighed. 'I'm waiting for the record.'

'Oh yes. The record. I'll go and dig it out.'

I folded my arms and bit my tongue as the first patient, Mrs Atkins from three doors down, arrived on crutches for her evening appointment. Mrs Bracken, with Barney in tow, followed closely on her heels. His face fell when he saw me. I knew better than to ask him what was wrong, so said *hi* and left it there.

'Found it!' My father rushed into the hall and handed it to me.

I glanced at the sleeve and did a double take. 'Martha Palmer Swings'. 'You've got to be kidding. Surely, she's got a copy?'

'She must have lost it or lent it to someone.'

'Brilliant. And now I'm really late.'

'For heaven's sake, Natasha. Calm down. Edie knows and—'

'For Martha,' I said quickly, in case he was catching on. 'You said she needed this by half past four, and it's almost a quarter to five.'

'Goodness. So, it is. Better get your skates on.'

I ran as fast as possible – the sooner I got there, the sooner I could leave – and consequently, by the time I arrived was out of breath. I was about to knock when voices floated towards me from the patio. I wandered around the back, past the rows of open French windows and the cream curtains rippling in the light breeze. Martha was there, lounging in a wicker chair and laughing hysterically. As I drew nearer, I saw she wasn't alone. The man in the pork pie hat sat facing her. He was smoking a long, thin cigar, and the blue-grey ribbons of pleasantly aromatic smoke which coiled around him afforded him a mystical air. Was it the saxophonist? I wasn't sure. I had no intention of intruding and had made up my mind to leave the LP by the front door, when Martha spied me.

'Tasha!' She rushed over and hugged me, her glossy hair shining in the evening sunshine. She smelt of lily of the valley, I noticed as she held me tight. 'Oh dear! You're out of breath. Did you run all the way?'

She released me, and I nodded and handed her the record.

'You're an angel, really you are.' She kissed me on the cheek.

Instantly, I forgot about Louis and being late and was simply glad I was here, with her.

'How's your dear mother? Is she well? Your father seemed to think she might be on the road to recovery.'

I screwed up my nose. 'Not really, no.'

Martha seemed neither surprised nor disappointed by this news, and I found myself liking her even more. 'How horrid for you all. It really is desperately unfair.' She picked up my hand and gave it a squeeze. 'But I'm here for you, if ever you need someone. You know that, don't you, Tasha?'

Unable to put my gratitude into words, I smiled and nodded again.

'Cee Cee, come and meet Tasha James,' Martha said, beckoning to the man. 'She's the pretty girl with the incredible voice I've been telling you about. Now, don't look at me like that, Tasha. It's true. Charlie can't take his eyes off you.'

My eyebrows shot up. 'Charlie?'

'You haven't noticed? How adorable. Oh dear, and now I've let the cat out of the bag. Still, I'm sure it's only a matter of time until he summons the courage to ask you out. And I shall be very pleased when he does.' She laced her fingers through mine and laughed her tinkly laugh. 'Won't it be fun, our two families entwined?'

My mouth opened and closed. Charlie hated me. Heat flared my cheeks, and yet I continued to stare at her exquisite face, the russet irises, the overlapping front teeth, her dark-brown hair. So like Louis.

'He's playing cricket,' she continued. 'More's the pity.'

'Stop, Marta. You're embarrassing her,' said Cee Cee.

It was true, she was, but I was far more terrified of betraying Louis. My mind was all over the place. What if she found out about me and Louis? Would she be just as pleased? Louis, who was waiting patiently for me at the building site. I winced, but fortunately Martha didn't notice, she was too busy introducing her guest.

'Tasha, this is the wonderful and legendary saxophonist, Mr Clive "Cee Cee" Campbell, the man who discovered me.'

'Not entirely true, but I'll take dat.' Cee Cee stubbed out his cigar, uncrossed his legs, and rose from the chair.

He doffed his hat, performed a semi-bow, offered me his hand, and smiled. His palm was pinkish brown, and his teeth were shiny and white. He had a small scar above his right eye and a fuzz of hair as short as Ian's Action Man. 'Pleased to meet you, little lady.'

I shifted my weight from foot to foot. I had no idea what to say to this man who seemed to be occupying more and more of Teddy's space. I wasn't sure how I felt about that either. Time was marching on. Louis was waiting. I had to get going. 'You, too, it really is, but I'm sorry. It's getting late. I have to go.'

'Oh no, you can't possibly leave us, can she, Cee Cee?

Not without your reward. And I do have a rather special one lined up. It'll only take a few minutes.'

'Reward? But I thought you needed the record urgently. I thought you had a deadline.'

She pulled a face. 'Oh dear, now I've made you cross.'

'No, you haven't. But I promised Mrs P … Mrs Pocock, I'd walk her dog. She's old and she's hurt her hip, you see, and Rafferty needs his walks. And … well … I'm a bit late and I really do have to go.'

'How sweet. Louis has been helping out a sick neighbour, too. Perhaps you should join forces.'

My heart flipped over. Sugar. I'd given it away.

'Thing is, Tasha,' Martha continued, tucking a stray hair behind her ear, 'we were hoping you'd sing for us. I've told Cee Cee all about your beautiful black voice, you see, and he's intrigued.'

I breathed a sigh of relief that she hadn't made the connection and glanced from one to the other, not understanding.

'She means you sound like a black sister.' Cee Cee grinned and slapped the back of his hand in the palm of his other. 'Like Miss Marta here. Black, breathy, and bright. Oh yes. All dem Bs.'

And Martha laughed her tinkly laugh.

Were they making fun of me? It certainly sounded like it. My cheeks burning, I pursed my lips.

'Hey, hey, hey,' said Cee Cee softly. 'We don't mean to upset you, little lady.'

'No, we most certainly do not.' Martha reached for my arm. 'Please say you'll stay five minutes and sing for us. It would mean so much to me if you did.'

I held her gaze and tried to think of a reason that would enable me to walk away. Louis was waiting, and I was desperate to see him. But at the same time, I was flattered. Martha Palmer wanted Cee Cee to hear me sing. She liked my voice. It would be mad to leave. I might never have another opportunity to sing to her again. Disrespectful, too. Louis would understand. 'Of course, I'll sing for you,' I murmured. 'And thank you.'

Martha clapped. 'So, what'll you sing?'

I didn't hesitate. '"Someone to Watch Over Me."'

Cee Cee raised his eyebrows, but Martha took no notice. 'It happens to be a favourite of mine.'

'I know,' I said, beaming. 'And I want to sing it at the school concert. If Miss Hendrik will let me, that is.'

Martha's hand flew to her chest. 'Why on earth wouldn't she?'

'It's not exactly school concert material.'

'Well then, we will have to do our best to convince Miss Hendrik. Go ahead, Tasha. The floor is yours.' Striding back to the wicker chair, Martha sat down and crossed her legs.

And so, on a warm evening in early June, nervously poised in front of my idol and the tall saxophonist in the pork pie hat, I sang the song I'd been practising like mad, about the man I longed to meet, who would love and take care of me. I'd only ever sung it in private – in the sitting room if my father was out, with the door closed so my mother wouldn't hear, or at the bottom of the garden when my father had his surgery – but I'd sung it so often it had become as natural to me as breathing. I closed my eyes and gave it my all.

After they'd applauded and congratulated me, Martha led me down a flight of steps to her 'precious haven', a large windowless basement. It had a wood floor, white walls, and was cluttered with instruments, including a piano, a saxophone resting on a stand, a guitar in a case, a set of drums, a microphone, and messy towers of sheet music; LPs stacked on shelves.

Martha sat at the piano and ran her fingers through a few arpeggios, finishing with a chord. 'Right, let's get down to work. You're good, Tasha, but in jazz, you need to be able to manipulate rhythm, interact creatively with improvising musicians, and transform the song into something distinctive and personal. If you're eager to learn, I'll teach you.'

The magnificent Martha Palmer, teach me? As if she had to ask. 'Yes, please.'

'Good girl. Now, first of all I want you to pay attention to the timbre of Cee Cee's sax. That's your voice.'

Martha played the opening bars, and Cee Cee began to blow. The sound was warm, smoky, and plaintive. Was it like my voice? I wasn't sure? After a while, Martha joined in. Rich and velvety, her voice lingered on the lyrics, at times hinting at despair, at others defiance and hope. It 'was powerful and affecting in a way mine hadn't been, as though she'd reached out and gripped my heart.

'Go back to the mic. Only, this time, imagine you're about to tell your own story,' she said. 'To move an audience, you must make them feel what you're feeling. They must believe you, too, as if you've lived what you're telling them. Be passionate, breathe life into the lyrics, take risks. And remember you don't have to sing loudly to have a strong emotional impact. Think you can do it?'

I rubbed my arms. It was a lot to take in, and I wasn't at all sure I was up to the task. 'I hope so.'

I sang the song over and over, Martha pulling me up on my phrasing or my rhythm, nodding or shaking her head, sometimes joining in. Time flew, but I was unaware of the passing hours. I'd forgotten all about Louis, Mrs P, and

Rafferty. There was only the music, Martha, Cee Cee, and me. It was all that mattered.

A knock at the door and the appearance of Mr Fairchild, dressed in a suit, brought me crashing back to earth. He appeared tired but greeted us all in his genial manner, shaking Cee Cee by the hand and offering us all drinks. Martha ran over and embraced him. He'd been away for three weeks on business, she explained, and she'd missed him. He didn't seem surprised to find Cee Cee in his house (or me, either, for that matter) and, although I looked, I couldn't sense any tension between them. Either they were very good actors or there wasn't any.

'Will you stay to supper, Tasha?' Martha asked. 'Charlie and Louis would love it if you did, wouldn't they, Teddy?'

Louis! The word was like a slap in the face. I'd been so excited by all the attention I'd forgotten about him.

'Yes, yes,' said Teddy, who clearly had no opinion on the matter. 'Now, please excuse me while I shower and change.'

'Thank you, but I really must go. Mrs P …' My voice trailed off. It was far too late to be calling on Mrs P, and Louis was bound to have given up and left. He might even be here already.

'Come back and practice,' Martha said. 'You're welcome anytime.'

I thanked her and hurried upstairs, along the corridor past the kitchen towards the hall. Half of me hoped I'd find Louis in the sitting room so I could explain. Half of me hoped I wouldn't. Charlie might be around, which would make talking awkward. But there was no sign of either of them, so I headed down the drive, vowing to myself I'd make it up to Louis tomorrow.

If he turns up, my conscience nagged.

I'll ring him and explain.

Charlie might answer the phone.

Then I'll ask for Martha?

So, Louis will be none the wiser.

I'll write a note then.

And what if Charlie sees you deliver it?

Head down and lost in this argument with myself, I didn't see Louis approaching. He grabbed hold of my arm so suddenly I jumped. 'Nat!'

'Oh my gosh. Louis!'

'What are you doing here? I've been waiting for you for hours.'

'I'm so sorry. Dad sent me here on an errand. I tried but I couldn't get out of it and when I got here, Martha … your mum insisted I sang for Mr Campbell.'

He flinched. 'I see.'

'Don't be like that.' I reached for his hand, but he tucked it behind his back.

'I was worried, Nat. Really worried.'

His face crumpled and, for a second, I thought he was going to cry. I hadn't meant to hurt him. I hadn't meant to stay. If only he understood. I considered telling him I loved him. But something held me back, and I bit my lip instead.

'Will I see you tomorrow, Louis? At the building site?'

He shrugged. 'If you like?'

'Oh, Louis. I do. I like a lot. It's my favourite part of every day. But I had to go along with your mother today. Don't you see? Otherwise, our secret would have got out.' It was mostly true. No point in telling him I'd enjoyed myself so much I'd forgotten all about him.

At last he smiled.

I leant in and kissed him. 'See you tomorrow?'

'Course.'

Determined not to be late the following day, I picked up Rafferty ten minutes earlier than usual. Mrs P batted away my apologies and pressed a bag of butterscotch and three ten pence pieces in my hand.

'Truth be told, I wasn't expecting you yesterday anyway,' she said. 'Dr James told me you might be delayed.'

It was a sultry evening, and the heavy air teemed with flying ants which settled on my face and in my hair. One even tried to climb into my ear. I flicked it away and batted at the others while Rafferty, excited at the prospect of an unexpected snack, snapped at them greedily. I perched on the doorstep of the half-built house for an hour until I decided Louis wasn't coming. The onslaught of insects hadn't let up, and I'd grown increasingly irritable with them and their bites, and more and more upset with Louis. Why had he retaliated like this? Tit for tat, like a child.

It was still light by the time I returned home, hot, sweaty, and itchy, but I was in no mood for anything except a bath and bed. Even with all the windows open it was stiflingly hot and, try as I might, I couldn't sleep. My thoughts were in disarray, and my heart ached with a different kind of pain than I was used to. The idea of splitting up with Louis was unbearable. If only I hadn't been so selfish and sung for Martha, none of this would have happened.

But then again, was it really all my fault? Dad had sent me on the errand. And Martha had insisted I sing for her. What was I supposed to do? Besides, Louis knew singing was my passion. We'd talked about it often enough. I'd have been an idiot to pass up the chance. Martha Palmer was a legend. It was a golden opportunity. No wonder I'd lost track of time. Surely, he'd forgive me this once?

I slid out of bed and dug out Ian's old teddy bear, hidden beneath my jumpers in my bottom drawer. He'd called it Joe because one of its eyes had been replaced with a button. He'd never gone to bed without it. Consequently, it still smelled of him. I crept back under the sheet, pressed the soft fur against my cheek, and breathed in the familiar scent of my brother.

'I'm so lonely without you,' I whispered. 'But I met this boy, and he was kind, and I really, really liked him, and things got better. Only now he's gone and left me, too. And I don't know what to do.'

Of course, I knew full well Ian would have no idea what to do either. He'd died too young to have had a crush on any girl, let alone understand what it felt like. But he would have listened to me and would have said something funny, and we would have giggled, and some of the pain would have gone away.

'If only you were here,' I whispered. 'If only you hadn't gone and left me all alone.'

The next few days were a struggle. I lost my appetite, couldn't be bothered to practise my singing, and snapped at my father whenever he asked me what was wrong. I continued walking Rafferty, though, and not just to help dear old Mrs P. It was good to be alone with him because unlike almost everyone else in my life, he didn't ask irritating questions. He loved me unconditionally, too, and it lifted my flagging spirits to see his tail wag when he saw me. He also gave me a reason to return to the building site every day. I went in case Louis was there and hung around for an hour or so, throwing a tennis ball for Rafferty to keep him amused, sucking a piece of Mrs P's butterscotch. Occasionally, some other kids turned up to play, but not Louis. He never showed up.

On Tuesday of the following week, five days since we'd last met, the truth finally dawned. Whatever it was we'd had was now well and truly over. I sank to the floor and blubbed like a baby. Rafferty dropped the ball I'd thrown for him at my feet and nudged at my hands with his cold, damp nose. When I didn't stop, the poor dog circled me and whined. But the tears continued to fall.

'What's up, Nat? Want a hug?'

I recognised his voice immediately. My tears turned to laughter. I leapt up to throw my arms around Louis but froze.

'Judging by your expression, I'm guessing you weren't expecting me.' Charlie smiled sheepishly.

'No. I …' The words dried up. What other explanation could I possibly give? Pleased I was back on my feet, Rafferty barked and bounced around between us.

'Well, I'm sorry anyway.'

I wiped my cheeks with the heels of my hands. 'For what?'

He shrugged. 'For not being Louis.'

'Why would you want to be Louis?' I snapped.

'Because you'd have hugged me.'

Really? Did Charlie really expect me to believe him? He couldn't stand me, showed me up at every available opportunity. And now he had the nerve to stand there and lie to my face. It was the last straw. I squashed my lips together and glowered.

'Don't look at me like that, Nat.'

'Like what?'

'Like you hate me. You don't hate me, do you?'

'I don't hate anyone,' I whispered. If I didn't hate him, what I felt was pretty close.

'But you don't like me.' Charlie's mouth turned down at the corners. He seemed genuinely upset, and yet I didn't quite believe it.

'Well, it's only because you're always so mean to me.'

He tilted his head. 'I'm only mean because I like you.'

I rolled my eyes. This really was too much. How on earth did he expect me to believe him? What was he playing at? I was about to tell him to shut up and go away, when I remembered what Martha had said. What if she hadn't got it wrong? What if Charlie had confided in her? My cheeks burned. Out of irritation, or because I was flattered, I wasn't sure.

'How about that hug?' he said eventually and, without waiting for an answer, flung his arms around me.

'Charlie, no,' I said, but I wasn't sure I meant it. After the pain of the last few days, it felt comforting to be held. He smelled good, too, of vanilla and pine. I rested my head against his chest, closed my eyes, and listened to the gentle beating of his heart. I knew it was wrong, that I was leading him on, that it was Louis I cared about. But Louis wasn't here. Louis had dumped me. It didn't matter what I did.

Charlie's heart was beating faster now, in time to mine. He let go of me, cupped my cheeks, and pressed his soft, warm lips on mine. Just like Louis, I thought, as he eased away and stared at me intensely. My head spun; my body tingled. I honestly thought my legs might give way.

'I love you, Nat. Have done since the second I first saw you.'

I wanted to tell him he was being daft. He couldn't possibly be in love with me. He didn't know me. And I didn't know him. Love at first sight was the stuff of fairy tales and romantic films. He'd been nothing but horrid to me. But I was lost for words.

'Do you mind?'

It was such a funny question, and the situation was so strange, I wanted to laugh. Instead, I smiled and shook my head. His handsome face, taut with tension, relaxed. And I thought again how ethereal his beauty was, the blond hair, pale-blue irises, and golden skin.

'You taste of butterscotch,' he whispered and kissed me again.

16

Martha is thinking about her father for the first time in ages. She is wondering whether he'd like the record she and Becky are listening to. She thinks he probably would but, because she's not sure, she's hit by a pang of homesickness. She squeezes her eyes shut and concentrates on the music, 'Mingus Ah Um', a gift from bass player, Frankie. Charles Mingus, the angry man of jazz, is Frankie's hero, and he's determined everyone understands why. Bo's been won over. He loves Mingus' emotional range – the swing, bebop, the shades of gospel, and twelve-bar blues – Cee Cee, too, and so does she. She's been playing it on a loop, much to Frankie's delight, but this is the first time Becky has heard it.

'So, what do you think?' Martha asks.

'It's fun. Energetic and upbeat but intimate, too. I much prefer it to "Kind of Blue". Now hold still. It's time for your eyelashes.'

Martha tilts her head and opens her eyes wide. The tube of cream mascara with the spiral-tip wand is the latest addition to Becky's makeup bag and is much easier to apply than the cake. She is doing her 'homework', practicing on Martha for her new job as a fashion makeup artist. This change in her career is due, in part, to Rory. Becky has been seeing him a lot these past few weeks, having finally caved in to his constant badgering to go on a date. He'd taken her to dinner at Quo Vadis where, to her astonishment, she'd fallen in love with him. Martha has seen plenty of besotted men throw themselves at Becky's feet, but Rory has succeeded where all else have failed. According to Becky, unlike his predecessors, he'd been genuinely interested in what made her tick. And when he'd suggested she expand her line of work, Becky, normally so stubborn, had handed in her notice at the department store and had been hired, immediately, by *Vogue* on a freelance basis. Next week is her first fashion show. Understandably nervous, Becky is using Martha's face as a blank canvas upon which to experiment. Martha is pleased to help. Any excuse to spend time with Becky. It's a rare treat these days and, with their lives diverging, is set to become even rarer.

Things are happening so fast. Her life has changed beyond recognition. Martha has Bo, her newfound fame, and a bank account with more money in it than she'd ever have imagined, and Becky has Rory and a new job. Martha is happy, but at times she feels she's struggling to adapt, unlike Becky who has. Gone are the endless streams of boys and wild nights partying in Soho, the reckless decision-making and spontaneity. Martha realises this is a good thing, but she still finds herself reflecting on the past. Life seemed less complicated before. More innocent. Still, at least Becky has finally stopped pushing Martha into dating Donny. For some reason she'd got it into her head that he was madly in love with her. To shut Becky up and to stop herself going mad, she'd finally come clean about Bo. She hadn't wanted to, not because she wanted to keep it a secret – she didn't; she wanted to shout about it from the rooftops – but because she was worried Becky, who referred to Bo as the Count, might disapprove.

But instead of reeling in horror, Becky had clapped and hugged her and said, 'No wonder you're so radiant.'

The cat well and truly out of the bag, it seems the whole world knows about Martha and Bo. The press has labelled them the hottest couple in town. And thanks to Len, it's rumoured that, at their upcoming performance at the Royal Festival Hall, they'll sing together for the first time. She's excited, can think of nothing better, but it's weird being discussed by people who don't know her. Worse still is reading about the life the journalists have invented for them. It's like she isn't a real person anymore, but a character in a novel. Bo advised her to stop looking at the articles, which she has, but Becky insists on reading them to her anyway.

'I can't help thinking what if I'd taken the job at the Raymond Revuebar,' Becky says, reaching for the hot-red lipstick she insists suits Martha so well, 'I'd have strutted about wearing next to nothing, serving drinks, and being ogled at by all and sundry.'

Martha winces. She still hasn't told Becky about posing for Stan. Or anyone else for that matter. 'You were only going to do it for the money. It's not as if you were thinking of it as a career.'

'I know, but it's so demeaning.'

'Says the girl with the well-paid new job. Some girls have no choice.'

'You really believe that?'

'Yeah, I do. And if it is their choice, then they're the ones holding the power.'

'Utter tosh. Men hold all the power. Keep still,' Becky says, leaning in. 'They always have and they always will.

Vogue would never have employed me if I had a seedy history. Here.' She hands Martha a tissue, screws the lipstick back into its gold case, and snaps on the lid.

'You wouldn't have told them.'

'Ah, but what if they found out? I'd be sacked on the spot.'

Martha blots her lips, balls up the tissue, and tosses it in the bin. 'Well, you didn't take it. So, there's an end to it.'

'One of my better decisions,' says Becky wistfully. 'For which I'll be eternally grateful.' She passes Martha a mirror. 'There you are. Beautiful. Giovanni will be bowled over.'

'It's not a date. It's a family dinner with his wife and children.'

'Trust me, he'll be lost for words.'

Luca is shutting up shop when Martha arrives at The Grind. His face lights up, and he drops the cloth he's holding, rushes over, and kisses her on both cheeks, once, twice, three times, as is his way.

'You look like a film star. Giovanni won't know what's hit him.'

'Don't you start. Becky's been practicing again. Think it's too much?'

He stands back and admires her. '*Bellissimo*. It's perfect. You're perfect.'

'I can assure you I'm not. Becky's talented, that's all.' She glances around, taking in the familiar gingham tablecloths, the Gaggia machine, the plastic orange bobbing about in the tank on the Formica counter. 'How's it going? Business still good?'

'Business is great, but Giovanni's moodier than ever since you left. Please come back. I miss you.'

'You won't believe it, but I miss you all, too.' It's true, she does. She felt safe here, cocooned. 'Is Giovanni still playing records? I can't see the jukebox he said he'd ordered.'

'There was never going to be a jukebox. But yes, he's still playing records. Mainly yours, of course. Since you scored a hit on *Juke Box Jury*, he hasn't shut up about it.'

'Thank the Lord. Imagine if they'd hated it.'

'As if! It was number one in the charts. By the way, I thought you were amazing at the Palladium. Was it terrifying being on the telly?'

She casts her mind back. Backstage, before the performance, she'd felt sick and edgy and had contemplated leaving by the back door. Becky, Rory, and Donny were in the audience, but even that hadn't helped. Bo had clasped her sweaty hands and encouraged her to take long, deep breaths. Her pulse had slowed, she'd stopped perspiring, and her churning stomach had calmed. Thank God Len had persuaded the producers to allow The Bo Rivers' Five to back her. If Bo hadn't been there, she might have lost her nerve and left, and her career would have been over before it had really got going. Crazy in hindsight, because once she'd walked on stage to the audience's applause, her nerves had evaporated.

'It felt like any other performance. And with all the lights, I hardly noticed the cameras.'

Luca tilts his head. 'I was scared fame would alter you, but you're just the same.'

'Becky has a habit of keeping my feet on the ground.'

'And Bo, I should think. How is the gorgeous man?'

'He's fine.' She gives him a playful thwack. 'Are you invited tonight?'

'Nah. I'm merely a waiter. You've always been the

special one. Or haven't you noticed?' He prods her playfully in the ribs and grins.

'Ha ha, very funny.'

'Oh, I almost forgot. A woman was asking after you.'

'Please God, not Delilah Moore.'

'Nope. She was blond and older, but a real looker, I'll give her that. What was her name? Loretta, I think.'

Martha tenses.

'Yes, that's it, Loretta.'

It's a warm night, but an icy shiver runs down her spine. 'Did she say what she wanted?'

'Nah. She was friendly, though, and from her description of you, seemed to know you, although she called you Martha Parker. I explained you didn't work here any longer. She insisted on giving me her number.' He reaches over to a jam jar stuffed with receipts and crumpled-up slips of paper and roots around for it. 'Here it is. Do you want it?'

She shakes her head as nonchalantly as possible. Without further questioning, Luca scrunches it up and flicks it in the bin.

Footsteps thudding down the stairs signal the arrival of Giovanni. He rushes into the café, throws his hands in the air, and chatters loudly in Italian. Grasping Martha tightly on the arms, he covers her cheeks in kisses. 'Ah, an old man in love is a madman who is done for,' he says, the hint of a tear in the corner of one eye.

Martha's mouth falls open.

Luca grins. 'Don't panic. What he actually means is there's no fool like an old fool.'

Giovanni throws him a pained look. 'That is what I said.'

Martha giggles. 'Oh, Giovanni, it's good to see you.'

. . .

Sofia is putting Matteo, Pietro, and Luigi to bed when Martha and Giovanni head up the stairs to the flat. The three Fiori boys, aged from five to ten, sleep in what used to be the servants' quarters on the fourth floor of the old building. Sofia and Giovanni sleep in the larger of the two bedrooms on the third, which also boasts a sizeable bathroom. If either of them mind living above the shop, they never let on. It's not unusual. In Soho most people do, although often it's not their own.

'To every bird his nest is beautiful,' Giovanni says, leading her into the living room, which is directly above the café at the front of the house.

'It's very kind of you to invite me.'

'Ah, I think not. You see, Martha, it is very kind of you to come. I am sure you have far better things to do now than be entertained by a couple of middle-aged Italians. Here, sit down. I will kick-start your digestion with a Negroni. You drinking now? Eh? Now you are leading the life of old Mick.'

She laughs. 'Occasionally.'

'*Bueno*. Because the Negroni, it is the best.'

Giovanni pours red vermouth, Campari, and gin, over some ice and a slice of orange peel and stirs it. He presses his fingers to his lips and blows a kiss. '*Et voila!*'

'Thank you.' She takes a sip. It's strong, far stronger than anything she's used to, and bittersweet.

'You like? It is delicious? No?'

'Mmm. Delicious.'

Giovanni mixes another for himself and flops in a chair beside her. 'Sofia will be down in a minute. She has not told the boys you are here. They would never go to bed if they knew.'

She is reminded of how excited she and her brothers used to get on the rare occasion friends of her parents dropped by in the evening. Confined to their room, nevertheless they crawled across the small landing and peeked through the banisters. Sometimes they dared one another to creep downstairs to steal some nuts or an after-dinner mint. There'd be hell to pay if they were caught. She wonders how they are, what they are doing. Peter would be thirteen by now, Thomas ten, and Mark almost eight. She hasn't seen them for nearly three years. Would she even recognise them? A lump lodges in her throat. It's the second time today she's thought about home. Why, when she's the happiest she's ever been? Her career is going well, and she's in love. She takes another sip of Negroni and tells herself not to be so stupid.

'I am proud of you,' Giovanni says. 'You have achieved so much in your young life. You are like a daughter to me, Martha. The daughter I never have. I cannot imagine how your true parents must feel.'

She's surprised by this declaration and slightly irritated. Apart from the fact her parents are poor and live in Yorkshire, Giovanni knows nothing about them. So why mention them? For all she knows they might be dead. She frowns and stares at her hands.

'What is wrong? Did they not come and see you at the Palladium?'

Martha shakes her head.

'*Mamma mia*! You still have not spoken to them?'

She blushes. 'Not for three years.'

He sighs. 'Far from the eyes, far from the heart. But there has been much written about you in the papers. I expect they know.'

Still frowning, she bites her lip. The thought has occurred to her, but unless she gets in touch, there's no way of knowing. And anyway, too much time has passed for her to try. 'It's complicated.'

Giovanni nods. 'Of course. Of course. I apologise. Water that has passed no longer grinds. But why not send them tickets for your next performance. There's an ocean between saying and doing.'

Martha mulls it over. It's not a bad idea. At the very least it would break the ice.

Mistaking her expression for disapproval, Giovanni holds up his hands. 'I must learn to keep my big mouth shut. It is a bad habit. But I think I do not need to tell you that.'

Sofia wanders into the room. She greets Martha with a flourish of kisses, rattles off a succession of compliments, and announces supper is ready. Pasta with a *sugo finto* sauce, is followed by a robust fish stew called *cacciucco*, accompanied by homemade, wood-fired bread, with *tiramisu* to finish, all washed down with a couple of bottles of Chianti. Each course tastes exquisite. Sofia explains it's the type of food they used to eat in the Tuscan village where they lived before moving to London. Generous and jovial, Giovanni and Sofia are the perfect hosts. Martha has never eaten so much in her life. She feels completely at home.

Once they've cleared the dishes, they move back into the living room. Giovanni pours them all a large brandy, digs out some cards, and teaches Martha how to play the Italian game, Briscola.

All too soon, it's time to leave.

'If I don't go now, Mrs Wilson will lock me out.'

Giovanni starts to protest, but Sofia throws him a look. 'Giovanni will walk you home,' she says.

'Really, there's no need. It's not late.'

She raises her palms. 'I insist.'

The Soho streets are heady with the aroma of foods from a dozen different countries, and flush with theatre-goers on their way home: Indian, Chinese, and Turkish waiters; Black

GIs, pimps; and a couple of heavily made-up transvestites. A trio of Maltese gangsters in dark suits lean against the wall of a club, smoking cigars and scrutinising the passersby and, floating up from the basements, the blue notes of jazz and the backbeat of rock 'n' roll reverberate in the cool, late September air.

'I love this place, this little patch of brilliance,' Martha says. 'I never want to leave.'

'Ha. There will come a time when you cannot wait to see the back of it.'

'Never.'

'Ah, the ignorance of youth. Trust me. It will happen sooner than you think.'

'You're wrong, Giovanni. I intend to live within this square mile forever.'

'And what about the young man you are seeing, eh? This Bo Rivers. Does he have a say?'

'None whatsoever.'

'But you like him? You have a glow about you like a woman in love.'

'Yes, I like him. I like him a lot. He makes me very happy.'

Giovanni stops suddenly and grasps her arms. 'You are young, *tesoro*. When I took you on as a waitress in my café you were not much more than a child. I sensed something bad had happened for you to leave your family behind, and I promised myself I would watch over you. I would not let any harm come to you. I would be a father to you.'

'I know, Giovanni, and you have.'

'No, listen to me. I am serious now. I am no longer in the position where I can take care of you, although you know you can call on me any time of the day or night, if ever you might need me. You are standing at a crossroads in your life. You must choose which road to take even though you do not know where it is going. It is long with many twists and turns on the way. It is exciting but it is also frightening. You are blessed with a beautiful face and a beautiful voice. A great many people will want a piece of you. They will ask you to do things you do not want to do. Sometimes you will make the wrong decisions. You must be careful, *tesoro*. Make sure you have the right people around you. I do not want to see you get hurt. Bo Rivers is older than you. You are a girl. He is a man.'

She pulls a face. 'He's twenty-seven. Not that old.'

'But does he have your best interests at heart? Will he do what is right for Martha Palmer? Or will he do what is right for him?'

'For me, of course. He loves me. We're happy. Life is good.'

'And do you also know you do not have to sleep with him if you do not want to?'

'Yes, I know. And I won't.' Martha wriggles free from Giovanni's grasp and sets off again, this time at a brisk pace, the door to her lodgings in sight. This is not the sort of conversation she wants to have with her old boss. Why did he have to go and ruin a perfectly lovely evening? What she does or doesn't do in her spare time is no business of his. Why can't he keep his nose out of things?

She reaches for her key and is about to put it in the lock when it swings open and Becky strides out.

She sees Martha and claps excitedly. 'Perfect timing. Come on.'

'Why? Where are we going?'

'A quick drink in the Queen's Head followed by an all-nighter at Cy Laurie's.'

'I don't know. I'm pretty tired.'

'Oh, go on. It's only a quarter to eleven. Rory and Gordon are going to be there. We'll have a great time.'

Becky's mood is infectious. Her anger dissipating, Martha smiles and turns to Giovanni. 'Fancy joining us, Giovanni?'

Giovanni holds up his hands. 'No, I do not. *Ciao, tesoro.* You take care of each other now.'

The club is heaving with arty bohemian types, dancing as if their lives depend on it. In amongst them a smattering of cats, all in black, sway to the rhythm. Almost everyone is puffing on a cigarette, the cloying air fuggy with smoke. It's hot, too, and damp with sweat. So hot, the trumpeter has ripped off his shirt and is playing bare-chested. Perched on a dustbin close to the stage, a man, stripped to his underpants, nods in time to the rhythm. Becky nudges Martha and points to Gordon and Rory holding fort with a bevy of girls a few feet away. They inch their way through the revellers, and a man flogging purple hearts. Catching sight of them, the medics cheer and offer them whisky from a flask they're handing round. Martha has already consumed more than usual at Giovanni's, followed by a gin and tonic at the pub on the way here, but she takes a sip anyway. Laughing, she flings her arms around Gordon and attempts to kiss him on the cheek but misses and ends up kissing him on the ear.

'Steady,' he says, holding her.

She throws back her head and laughs. How lucky she is to be here in this room with these lovely people, dancing to the best music in all the world. 'Dance with me, Donny.'

'Are you sure you're up to it?'

'Couldn't be surer.'

They whirl round the dance floor for ages until, exhausted and overheated, Martha suggests they take a breather. 'I love this place,' she says. 'Nobody cares who you are, whether you're rich or poor, if you're black or white, if you're into boys, or into girls, or both.'

Gordon grins. 'Famous or not, beneath the street where the jazz is hot, we meet as equals.'

'Well said, Donny.'

A woman with dark hair rushes over and pokes Gordon in the ribs.

'Oh, hello,' he says.

The woman smiles and nudges him, with her elbow this time. 'Well? Are you going to introduce us?'

'Oh yes. Rightio. Martha, this is Elizabeth. Elizabeth, Martha.'

The woman smiles and links her arm through Donny's. 'Hello, Martha. I'm so excited to finally meet you.'

Martha hiccups, tilts her head, and squints at them, but her vision is off-kilter. 'Oh 'eck. I'm sorry. Need the little girl's room. Back in a bit.'

But when she comes back, Donny and his friend have gone. She doesn't mind. Life is good, and the evening is for dancing.

Martha and Becky emerge from the basement, a pair of moles blinking in the early morning light. The dawn is breaking, and the milk floats are out on their rounds, the drunks staggering home from the clubs. At a quarter past six, when they're sure Mrs Wilson has left with Elsie, they sneak into their rooms. Still smiling, Martha flings herself on her bed. She's seeing Bo for a drink at The French later, followed by dinner at his flat. She can't wait.

But then Giovanni's voice rings in her ears.

Frowning, she rolls onto her side. How many actual

fathers discussed sex with their daughters? Surely Giovanni was taking the whole surrogate dad thing a step too far. How could he begin to know what's right for her anyway? He doesn't know the first thing about Bo. And he can't possibly have guessed she's been wondering what it would be like to sleep with him. Bo's mentioned it a few times, but she's not sure if she's ready. He keeps saying she's not under any pressure but each time he brings it up is pressure enough. Should she want to talk about it, though, she has Becky. Instead of wasting time deliberating the whys and wherefores, Becky had jumped into bed with Rory on their first date.

'Does it hurt?' Martha had asked.

'A teeny-weeny bit the first time, but after that it's magical. You should try it. It's what we were designed for, after all.'

'What if something goes wrong?'

'Nothing will go wrong unless Bo's a masochist, which I doubt. But I'd strongly advise against lying back and thinking of England. It's a real turnoff. Ew! Like screwing a corpse. You need to move to the rhythm, so to speak. Perform. Should be easy for you.'

But Martha isn't sure. What if she doesn't enjoy it? What if she does it all wrong? What if she can't *perform*? It might destroy the relationship. Why not carry on as they are, kissing and cuddling?

Perhaps Giovanni's right, she thinks, as she drifts off to sleep. Perhaps it would be best to wait. We're happy enough as we are.

17

I spent the night following Charlie's declaration of love wrestling with my thoughts. Why had I returned his kiss? Had a supernatural force possessed me temporarily? It made no sense. I was torn up about Louis. Distraught. I didn't even like Charlie. How could I, when all he ever did was bully me? He might be good-looking, but he was mean. At least he had been, before Jack-the-lad had morphed into Little Prince. Then he'd been sympathetic and kind. He'd told me he loved me. Had I been shocked into submission? Was I so weak, all it took to turn my head were three small words?

But was it true? Or was it yet another one of his nasty jokes I'd fallen for hook, line, and sinker? And if it was, what did he hope to gain?

I peered at the Davids, five of them now, including Starsky. According to the scribes at *Jackie*, they'd been around the block a few times. If only they could speak, they'd help me make sense of it all. Had I missed something? Think, Nat, think.

I racked my brains. Charlie had appeared out of nowhere. Had he been following me? Or had he stumbled upon me by chance? What was the probability? I was no mathematician, but the building site covered a vast area. It would be an astounding coincidence if he happened to be exploring the same house as me, at the same time. He didn't seem as surprised to see me as I was to see him either. Almost as if he'd known I'd be there. What if Louis, now he wasn't bothered about me, had let slip our meeting place? Charlie might have dropped by on a whim, just in case. Martha was convinced he was keen on me. He was her son, so she probably knew him better than anyone. Better than Louis. Perhaps better than Charlie knew himself. What if it wasn't some skewed joke? What if Charlie really was in love with me?

The flaxen light of dawn filtered through the crack in the curtains. I rolled onto my back and groaned. Determined to figure out the cause of my irrational behaviour, I tried another angle. Assuming Charlie was in love with me, did I want to go out with him? Could I switch my emotions from one twin to another, just like that? Was I that fickle? Or was it simply the case that I'd been hurting and Charlie had been there?

Oh God, had I made a massive mistake?

I must have drifted off to sleep because I was awoken by the alarm. There were tell-tale dark patches beneath my eyes, I noticed, as I stared at my reflection in the bathroom mirror and, as I wandered down to breakfast, the beginning of a headache was gnawing at my temple. To make matters worse, my father bounded into the room with a broad smile on his face.

'Good morning, Natasha. How are you this fine, sunny day?'

'Tired.'

'Well, maybe this will wake you up.' He whisked his hand out from behind his back and handed me an envelope.

I stared at it in a daze. The only people who wrote to me

were my grandmother or Hayley. But this handwriting was unfamiliar. Frowning, I turned the envelope over a couple of times and placed it on the table.

'Aren't you going to open it?'

I shook my head, picked a piece of toast from the rack, scraped some butter over it, and took a bite.

'Ah, it's like that, is it?'

'Like what?' I asked, my mouth full.

'You have a secret admirer and you want to read it in private.'

'I do not!' I said, spitting crumbs. I slid down in my chair and peered at the letter again. It couldn't be from Charlie. He'd have missed the last post. Unless … unless he'd written it before he'd kissed me. But that would mean he'd planned the encounter.

I shuddered and glanced at my watch. If I got a move on, I'd have enough time to read it in private before I left for school. I bolted the toast and a glass of orange juice, snatched the letter, ran to my room, and tore open the envelope.

But it wasn't from Charlie. It was from Louis.

With trembling hands, I began to read.

Dear Nat,

Don't worry, I'm fine. I got back today and the first thing I did was phone you. Your father said you were out walking Rafferty. I'm really pleased you're still doing that. I don't think he guessed anything, by the way. Your dad, I mean, not Rafferty.

Anyway, I was desperate to tell you I miss you like crazy. All I could think about in hospital was you.

All my love and everything,

Louis xxx

Hospital?

I dropped the letter and doubled over, head in hands. The room was spinning. My stomach churned. Louis hadn't dumped me. He'd been in hospital. But why? What had happened? And why had no one told me? Or had Martha told my dad, and he hadn't passed it on? He'd forgotten to tell me Louis had rung, so it was entirely possible. Wait a minute. What about Charlie? Did he know? Stupid question. Of course he did. But why keep it from me? Did he think I already knew? Or was it because I was crying and he thought it would upset me more?

Or was it all part of his plan?

Oh God. What had I done? I'd never have kissed Charlie if I'd known. I should have rung Louis to ask why he hadn't shown up. It would have been the sensible thing to do. And if it meant people finding out, so what? Instead, I'd let him down big time. Everybody seemed to know about Louis but me. Why had nobody told me? Why?

'Get a wriggle on, Natasha. We're going to be late,' my father called.

My mouth was dry, my heart thumping, my palms sweating. And it was in this state of general panic I tucked the letter into the pocket of my skirt and ran downstairs.

'Oh, I almost forgot,' my father said, flicking through his pile of post. 'Louis Fairchild phoned yesterday evening. Probably wanted to tell you all the gory details about his accident.'

I stopped dead in my tracks and clenched my teeth to stop myself screaming. 'What accident?'

'A game of dare that went wrong. Martha was terribly worried.' Flick. Flick. Flick. 'Sounds like it was quite a fall. He lost consciousness.' Flick. Flick. 'The doctors at the hospital were worried about his neck, so they kept him in.'

Flick. 'Seems he only broke his nose. Silly idiot. But there we are. Boys will be boys.' Flick. Flick. 'I promised Martha I'd pop round tonight to see how he's getting on.' Flick. 'You could come, too.'

'Why didn't you tell me?' I spoke as calmly as possible, a struggle, under the circumstances.

'Must have slipped my mind.' He threw the letters on the hall table where they spread out like a fan. 'Still, now I have. Anyway, he's back home and fine. Come on. We really must get going.'

To say I was in two minds about accompanying my father to Greystones that evening would have been an understatement. The visit was fraught with such dizzying potential for disaster I spent the entire day trying to figure out a way to avoid going. On the one hand, I was desperate to see Louis. I wanted to explain why I hadn't been in touch, that I'd had no idea he'd been in an accident, that I'd missed him dreadfully. And, in the likely scenario we weren't alone, my contingency plan was to slip him a note. Easy.

On the other hand, there was Charlie to consider. Clearly, he knew about Louis and me. My father was Louis' doctor, so Charlie must have assumed I knew about the accident – not everyone knew about the Hippocratic Oath. If he really did love me, he wouldn't want to hurt me. At least, not until he found out I didn't want to break up with Louis. But what if he tried to kiss me again? The awful truth I was a two-timing cow would be out in the open. Louis would hate me, and most probably Martha, too. Was it likely, though? Would Charlie be brave enough to kiss me in front of his parents? My father? It seemed implausible even for him. In fact, the more I thought about it, the more I saw my father as the perfect foil.

The third scenario was equally alarming. What if Charlie had already bragged about our kiss to Louis? I'd be the last person Louis would want to see. With a bit of luck, Charlie was as secretive as his brother. Although, thinking about it, keeping our relationship a secret had been my idea. The twins were close. Until I'd come along, they'd done everything together. What if I'd driven them apart?

Crikey, what if they wanted to share me?

I shook my head and groaned. Whichever way I looked at it, I saw only trouble. Perhaps it would be better for everyone if I stayed at home.

By the time I got back from my singing lesson – in which I forgot to ask Miss Hendrik if she'd let me sing 'Someone to Watch Over Me' at the summer concert – I was nursing a full-blown headache. I plonked myself at the kitchen table, where my father was enjoying a cup of tea, and told him I was unwell and therefore wouldn't be able to accompany him tonight.

My father, being the stoic, stiff-upper-lip type of doctor – apart from when he was dealing with my mother – wasn't having any of it. 'Nonsense. A bit of fresh air and a change of scene will do you the world of good.'

'But—'

'No buts. Martha is expecting you. She has news she wants to share. Sounds exciting, doesn't it?'

My stomach churned. 'What news?'

'I've no idea, but your face,' he said, chuckling, 'is a picture.'

Charlie's told her, I thought miserably. And Martha wants to celebrate.

· · ·

The walk to Greystones seemed to take forever, and my legs seemed to grow heavier with each step. I dreaded reaching my destination, but at the same time wished the ordeal over with. When my father suggested we call in on Mrs Pocock, my agony was prolonged still further.

Mrs P looked thinner but was, as usual, pleased to see me. 'Why don't you play in the garden with Rafferty while I'm being checked over.' And Rafferty, at the mention of his name, wagged his tail enthusiastically.

I found an old grey tennis ball in one of the flowerbeds and threw it across the lawn. Rafferty tore after it, leapt into the air to catch it in his mouth, then galloped back and dropped the ball at my feet, dribbling saliva. I scratched him behind the ears. 'You're a clever boy, aren't you, Rafferty? Not an idiot like me.'

Minutes later, my father called. We were off. I said bye-bye to Rafferty, gave Mrs P a hug and told her I'd see her tomorrow at the usual time, and continued to Greystones, weighed down by an increasing sense of doom.

Teddy greeted us at the door. 'Ah, the good doctor and his able assistant. Come in. Come in. It's kind of you to call, Gordon. Much appreciated, although the patient seems to be back to his usual self. Still, you can't be too careful with head injuries. Dangerous things. Yes, Martha. Gordon's here. Splendid. Splendid.'

Martha breezed into the hallway in a sleeveless denim sundress, barefoot as usual. My chest tightened. It was the first time I'd seen her since I'd sung for her and, terrified I was about to disappoint her, considered hotfooting it home. If I hadn't already, now I appreciated the influence she held over me. I was in her thrall and would do anything to please her. To fail her would be cataclysmic. I couldn't. I mustn't.

'How wonderful to see you both.' Martha kissed us and led us down to the sitting room.

'What'll you have to drink?' Teddy asked.

'Champagne, I think,' Martha interjected. 'As we're celebrating.'

Teddy touched his nose. 'Oh yes, of course. Right you are, darling.'

A violent shock wave ran through me. Oh God. Charlie's told her, I thought, and clenched every muscle in my body to stop myself falling over.

Outside on the patio, Louis and Charlie were bouncing towards one another on space hoppers, jousting with broom handles. My heart sank. This was it. The moment I'd been dreading all day had finally arrived. I was going to have to face the two of them together. May my death be quick and painless, I thought, as my father, who was also looking in their direction, arched an eyebrow.

Teddy rushed through the open French windows. 'Oh, for heaven's sake. Will you stop it. Mindless clots, the pair of you.'

Out of the corner of my eye, I noticed Martha scoot after my father and whisper something in his ear, and he smiled. But I was too caught up in my personal crisis to pay them much attention. I dug my hand in the pocket of my shorts and clutched the note hidden there. Somehow, I had to get it to Louis, without anyone seeing and before the awful truth came out.

'Hurry up with the champagne, won't you, Teddy,' Martha said.

'Just having a word with the boys, darling.'

'Don't worry. Donny's more than capable.'

I loitered by the sofa and watched my father peer at

Louis' pupils with a small torch. He had a nasty cut near his temple, but no other injuries I could see.

'Any pain? Visual disturbances?'

Louis shook his head. 'Nothing.'

'Good.' My father patted him on the back and pocketed the torch. 'He's fine, but I'd strongly advise against further jousting. Any fighting of any kind, in fact. And no alcohol, of course.'

'Of course,' said Martha. 'Now where *is* the champagne? Teddy!'

'Coming, dearest.' Teddy rolled his eyes, hurried into the house, and had to swerve to avoid colliding into me. 'Oh, hello, Natasha. Aren't you going to join them?'

I held my breath, lowered my gaze, and walked outside.

'Hi, Nat,' they chorused.

Cautiously, I lifted my head. Louis had moved towards me and was smiling broadly. Charlie, a foot behind, was eyeing me intently, arms folded. I willed myself not to blush, but by the heat in my cheeks, I knew I already had. 'Hi, Louis. How's your head?'

Louis took a step closer, and for an awful minute I thought he was going to kiss me. Here, in front of everybody.

'Give me a hand, won't you, Charlie?' Teddy yelled from the kitchen.

I shot a sideways look at Charlie, but he brushed past me without a second glance. Was it a good thing? I thought, perhaps, it was. Quick as a flash, I pulled out the folded-up paper and pressed it into Louis' hand.

'I've missed you, Nat,' he whispered, his mouth millimetres from my ear, as he closed his fingers around the note.

I leaned back. But he took hold of my hand and drew me to him.

'It's okay. Charlie knows.'

I stifled a gasp. 'He does?'

'I wrote you a letter at the hospital and told him to wait for you at the building site. I figured he owed me. But you weren't there.'

'You did?' My heartbeat thundering in my ears, I tried to make sense of it all. A note? So, Charlie had known I'd be there? But why hadn't he given me Louis' letter? Oh God. This was too awful for words.

Martha touched my arm, and I jumped. 'Well, aren't you the dark horse.'

Dizzy now, I crossed my arms tightly over my chest. Did she know about Charlie?

'Our secret's out.' Louis eyes were sparkling.

My stomach lurched.

'Secret?' said Teddy, who'd reappeared with a tray of champagne flutes, followed by Charlie with the bottle. 'How intriguing.'

'Louis has got himself a girlfriend.' Charlie was grinning. He seemed happy, but his eyes, fixed on mine, bored into me.

Mortified, I unfolded my arms and stared at my shoes.

'Poor girl doesn't look all that happy,' said Teddy jovially.

Louis reached for my hand again and held it tightly. I tried to smile, but my lips wavered at the edges.

'Are you happy, Nat?' Charlie asked.

I froze. Was this the moment he was going to come clean? Here, now, in front of everyone? He'd lied to Louis about seeing me, so I wouldn't put it past him.

Martha gave him a playful shove. 'Stop with your teasing.'

'Sorry, Nat,' Charlie said.

Louis gave my hand a reassuring squeeze. I lifted my head and prayed my cheeks weren't as red as they felt and caught the eye of Charlie, who winked at me and walked away.

'You've embarrassed the poor girl,' Martha said. 'Of course she's happy, and so am I. It's wonderful news, isn't it, Donny?'

I'd been so preoccupied with Charlie's machinations and motives, I hadn't given a thought to how my father might react.

His expression was stony. 'Well. Natasha is very young.'

Martha linked her arm in his. 'Oh, Donny. Don't be so old-fashioned. She's fourteen, for heaven's sake. A child no longer. Hurry up with the champagne, Teddy.'

Louis chuckled, and I finally managed a smile. My ordeal seemed to be over. I could breathe again. Emboldened, I snuck a peek at my father, but despite Martha's reassurances, his lips were pursed and he was frowning. For once, Martha's influence had failed. It didn't bode well.

The glasses filled, Teddy handed them round to everyone bar Louis. I clutched mine as if my life depended on it.

'And now for my announcement,' Martha said. 'Darling Teddy is throwing me a party and—'

The twins sighed. 'Another one.'

'Yes, another one,' said Teddy. 'Only this one is special because it's to celebrate your mother's fortieth.'

Martha raised her eyebrows. 'Darling, it's awfully rude to refer to a woman's age.'

'There's no shame in turning forty. Hard to believe, I know. My beautiful wife doesn't look a day over thirty.'

Charlie groaned.

Martha waved her hand dismissively. 'Don't let's talk about age. It's depressing.'

'Congratulations, Martha. You really don't look it.' My

father, who was still smarting but trying to hide it, raised his glass.

'If I could get a word in,' Martha said. 'We're not celebrating because of my advancing age. We're here because of Tasha.'

I rubbed frantically at my forehead. What now? Really, I couldn't handle anything more.

Teddy laughed. 'You haven't asked her the question yet.'

'I know, now will everyone please shush.' Smiling, Martha turned to me. 'You will sing at my party, won't you, Tasha?'

18

The heavy drapes are drawn, and the dark room is lit by candles. There are at least twenty of them, scattered around the place in jam jars and glasses, a couple of bowls. A fire burns in the grate, and a Chet Baker record is playing on the turntable beside a tall, slim vase bearing a single red rose. Martha's attention, though, is drawn to the bed. She can't take her eyes off it. It's huge. Wide and long and higher than her waist with a dark mahogany headboard and a plump, paisley eiderdown. Its size seems to mirror the significance of the moment, like a headline written in bold and underlined. **The First Time**. It's not an ambush, though. They've talked about it a lot of late. Only she wishes he hadn't gone to so much trouble. She understands why he has. He wants to make it special. Memorable. But isn't it always? The First Time. How easier it would be to stumble home drunk and accidentally fall into bed. Not that anyone could fall into this one. They'd have to climb. And that would involve a conscious act.

Bo's hand is on the small of her back. To comfort, or cajole her?

'Are you sure you want to do this?'

No, I'm not. I'm not sure at all. But she smiles at him and says, 'Of course.'

'There's no pressure.' He leans over and kisses her neck.

His lips are soft and warm, but all the same she shivers. Like hell there isn't.

'Don't be scared,' he says.

She's aware of his laser-like eyes on her back, his searchlight stare. What will they make of her naked body, her flaws; the mole on her stomach to the right of her belly button, her dimpled bottom, and her mismatched breasts? Her gaze strays to the ashtray on the bedside table, a packet of Craven A and a much-thumbed copy of Jack Kerouac's *On the Road*. Wasn't Donny reading it, too?

Oh God, why am I thinking about Donny at a time like this?

She refocuses her mind on the present: Bo, the candlelit room, the giant bed. She knows exactly why she's here. It's because she loves this man. She's besotted with him. Cannot bear to be apart from him, not even for a minute. And if this is what love involves, naked sex on a colossal bed in a too-hot room, this is something she must do. There's a chance she might even enjoy it. Best to be honest, though.

'I'm not.' She turns to face him and smiles coyly. 'Not *really*.'

'It's okay.' Slowly, silently, he gently cups her face in his hands.

His breath is warm and sweet. She tilts her head and parts her lips, but still he hangs back. His translucent eyes fixed on hers are heavy-lidded now. Is it desire she sees there, or lust? She feels a fluttering below her ribcage, a swirling emptiness. He hasn't laid a finger on her, and yet it's as if she's flying. Her body aches. It's hungry for him, ravenous. She wants him to reach out and touch her. But still he waits. She can't bear it. Her breathing deepens. She thinks if he doesn't touch her soon she will burst. She longs to feel him, skin on skin. She will beg him if she has to.

'Please,' she whispers.

And now, at last, he kisses her.

The candles which haven't burnt out flicker in the jam jars. Martha lies on her side, facing Bo, who is looking at her as if she's the only thing in the world worth seeing. She doesn't mind. Not anymore. It pleases her to be the sole object of his attention. Makes her feel valuable, treasured. They are nose close. She breathes in his citrus smell. Beneath the paisley eiderdown, their hands and feet are touching, their fingers and toes intertwined like links in a chain. She wonders what it was she'd been frightened of. Making love to Bo had been the most natural thing in the world. Beautiful, too, and special. So very special. There'd been pain, of course, when he'd slid inside her. A sharp pain which had taken her breath away but had lasted barely a heartbeat. Overwhelmed by a weightless desire, she'd given herself over to him. She'd felt at peace but at the same time more alive than ever before.

Bo lets go of one of her hands and strokes her cheek. 'I've never seen anyone as beautiful. I love you, Martha Palmer.'

She smiles. And in her smile are all the words she cannot find but longs to say. They are part of one another now. Complete. She will never love anybody as much as she loves this man. Never. She has given him her body but right now she would happily offer him her soul. She wants to freeze time, to stay in this room with the too-large bed for all eternity.

Bo leans in and brushes her lips with his. 'Now, what say we try that again?'

Martha is perched on one of the threadbare sofas in Mac's rehearsal room, another sweaty basement that reeks of stale sweat and nicotine, and which morphs into Cy Laurie's Club at night. A mug of coffee in hand, she studies the grey liquid suspiciously. The building's water is off, so she'd popped into The Harmony, a greasy spoon on Archer street, with her own mugs. The proprietor had been more than happy to fill them.

'It'll save me 'aving to wash 'em up, luv,' he said, wiping his nose on his sleeve.

It's lukewarm and odourless and barely recognisable as coffee. Giovanni would be appalled, but she has a raging thirst, so it'll have to do. In for a penny, she thinks as she takes a sip. Ew! It tastes as bad as it looks. Still, if her singing is to be any good tomorrow, she needs to keep her vocal cords lubricated. She takes a deep breath and, holding her nose, gulps it down.

The thud of leather on skin, as a couple of burly men beat seven bells out of each other, filters through from the gym on the floor above. Her boys are hard at it, too, their coffee untouched. The room is only booked for another hour, and they still haven't got to grips with 'La Vie en Rose' – a song Edith Piaf wrote in a Paris pavement café shortly after the Second World War. A romantic vision of love seen through rose-tinted spectacles, it's the latest addition to their repertoire. They'll be performing the Louis Armstrong version on Saturday at the Royal Festival Hall. It's important they get it right. A few glissandos from Roly, a sleepy solo from Bo, her vocals, and a trumpet finale to finish which ends on an almost unreachable high D. This is Bo's sixth attempt, and he's only hit it once. He doesn't seem particularly concerned, though.

And if he isn't, she thinks, I'm not either.

There's a physicality to Bo's playing, his upper body working to produce his sound. He goes for the note, and she holds her breath. Almost there. This time he makes it. She blows him a kiss and claps. Cee Cee slaps him on the back, and Roly, Mike, and Frankie whoop with delight.

Bo grins. 'One more time from the top.'

And off they go again. Martha taps her foot on the wooden floorboards, occasionally murmuring the lyrics. As with most of the other songs on their playlist, 'La Vie en Rose' is Len's idea. It's a good choice. She likes it. The trouble is, every song he's chosen is about love. She thinks the evening is in danger of becoming saccharine, but Len disagrees.

'Ain't nuffink new, duck, apart from "La Vie". It's the meanin' behind them dickies what's changed.' Which was her point exactly, only put a different way. 'You and Bo, togever, is roman'ic. The punters wan' a butcher's.'

It's odd that Bo, who's always maintained a desire to keep his private life out of the spotlight, has agreed to go along with it.

'It's just a few songs,' he said when she questioned him. 'It's not real.'

But it is real, she thinks, as she runs over the words in her head. Every word.

She glances at her watch. Not long until she and Bo pick up their passports. They're off to France at the end of November on a three-date mini tour, playing at Le Caveau de la Huchette, Chez Inez, and La Rose Rouge. It's her the French public are clamouring to see, but as was the case when she performed at the Palladium, she's insisted The Bo Rivers' Five accompany her. Nothing more was said until Len called her into his office the following day and suggested she persuade Bo to change the name to The Martha Palmer Band.

'Why on earth would I? Bo's the bandleader, for heaven's sake,' she snapped. 'He's a brilliant trumpet player and singer and deserves equal billing.'

And Len had left it at that.

Martha has all but moved in with Bo since she first slept with him, three weeks ago. To explain her prolonged absences, she has come clean with Mrs Wilson. Unable to keep up the pretence she's working as a waitress, she's told her landlady she's been away on tour. Mrs Wilson had been surprised but not the least bit curious as to how or why this had come to pass.

'You've certainly got a decent pair of lungs on you, Martha Palmer,' she said, arching an eyebrow. 'I can vouch for that.'

'You don't mind?'

'Mind? Why would I mind? As long as you pay the rent and abide my rules, I couldn't care less what you do.'

In the New Year, Bo wants to take her to the jazz clubs on 52nd Street. It's been a lifelong dream of his to visit the New York basements and see his heroes perform. Before the band's success, he'd planned to take a job on a cruise ship from Southampton to pay his way over. Now, he can easily afford his fare and wants her to go with him. All they need is a visa. They've booked interviews at the US Embassy next week. So, it's busy, busy, busy as usual. If she wasn't riding high on adrenaline, she'd be exhausted. They've been working non-stop for eighteen months. Somehow, Bo's managed to convince Len they need to take a break. Martha is excited. She's hoping for the chance to see Carmen McRae, Sarah Vaughan, or any one of her idols. To watch them perform live would be a dream come true.

The session over, the band pack up their instruments,

apart from Cee Cee who sidles over. 'How goes it, little lady? Mi old bredrin taking care of you?'

She blushes. It's no secret they're a couple, but she and Cee Cee had been close. They'd been on a date, and he'd kissed her a couple of times. Sure, he'd never pushed for anything more serious but, all the same, he had feelings. What must he think of her?

'Yes, he is, Cee Cee,' she says quietly. 'Thank you.'

'You excited about Saturday? And di next few months? It's gonna be a busy time.'

'Yes, I am, and yes, it is.'

'Sure you got di stamina? What wid your extra-curricular activities.' Cee slaps one hand in the back of the other and howls with laughter.

Out of the corner of her eye, she sees Bo nodding at Roly on the other side of the room. But despite the racket Cee Cee's making, he doesn't look over. She's relieved he hasn't heard their conversation. If she could go any redder, she would. Angry now, she moves away.

'Hey, little lady. I'm kidding.' Cee Cee touches her arm. 'You and Bo go together kinda perfect. Like salt fish and ackee.'

The tension broken, she smiles. 'What the 'eck is that?'

'Breakfast, Jamaican-style. You'll have to try it sometime.'

'It's a deal.' She reaches for her bag, hooks it over her shoulder, and makes to leave.

'Marta, wait.'

Startled he's called her by name, she turns. He has taken off his shades and is looking at her with his deep-brown eyes and no hint of a smile.

'I wanted to say dat we, di band and me, dat is, appreciate

everyting you've done for us. You've changed our lives.' Without waiting for a reply, he replaces his sunglasses and heads over to the chair where he's left his saxophone, hat, and coat.

Kind of him. But did I do it for them? she wonders as she follows Bo out the door. Or for me?

The fire is lit, and the small living area is cosy and warm. Sitting at the square table, Martha is attempting to write her diary, something she's wanted to do since moving to London. She's stopped and started so many times, the sporadic entries lack any form of continuity. Her attention strays to the flames licking at the fireplace bricks. In the tiny white-tiled kitchenette, Bo, a keen and capable cook, is baking bread and waffling on about the art of 'swing'. Her mind wandering, she's barely heard a word until now.

'You're rhythmically sophisticated, Martha.'

She pulls a face. 'Am I?'

'It's the way you attack the notes surrounding the beat, falling behind, sometimes getting ahead of it, implying rather than expressing it. You beguile your audiences. You're clever. It's why you're so irresistible.'

'You do that, too.'

'Darling, I'm not in your league.'

She hates it when he talks like this, building her up while putting himself down. It's simply not true. He's far superior a musician to her. For a start, he blows as well as sings. He's a skilled bandleader, too, with the speed and agility to take the head one minute and improvise the next. She wishes he'd stop with the flattery. It's as annoying as the knickers she found under his bed this morning. And it's the discovery of these knickers, now stuffed in a bag in the bottom of his wardrobe, which is the cause of her distraction.

She wasn't snooping, far from it. She was trying to find the sheet music for 'It's Always You.' Bo wants to perform it as a duet tomorrow. Trying to remember where she'd seen it involved turning out every drawer and cupboard, peering behind every cushion. The vast bed was the last place she'd searched. And there it was, underneath, next to the knickers. She'd reeled backwards, bumping her head on the bedsprings. Black lace. Sexy. Nothing like the white silk pairs she wears.

Whose are they? she wonders, still staring at the fire. A past lover? They spend all day together, so Bo can't possibly be two-timing her. And if that's the case, which she's sure it is, why is she so upset? She can't be jealous. Whoever they belong to is long gone. He's with her now. He loves her. Doesn't he?

Yes, he does, she reasons, and I love him.

But it's not enough. Their existence is proof she's not the first woman Bo has made love to. Before her there was someone else. Someone he cared enough about to sleep with. No doubt about it. No woman would remove her underwear if she weren't about to have sex. Unless she was a friend staying over, and Bo was sleeping on the couch in the other room. But really, what was the likelihood of that?

'Penny for them?'

She looks up, startled. 'You can't ask that. I'm writing my diary.'

'You've been staring at that page for a good ten minutes without writing a word. What's wrong?'

Tell him, she thinks. He'll explain he's had other lovers, but so what? It'll be nothing, and I can forget all about it.

But what if it isn't? You're performing together tomorrow in the biggest concert of your life, singing a whole heap of love songs. What if you don't like what he has to say? her conscience nags.

Her smile falters. She shrugs. 'Nothing. Nerves, I suppose.'

He eyes her doubtfully. 'And you're sure that's all?'

'Isn't that enough?' she snaps.

'Right! I think it's about time I distracted you, don't you?' He reaches out his hand and, without uttering another word, she lets him lead her to the bedroom.

Martha is pacing the dressing room in her floor-length, bottle-green gown. It's been specially commissioned for the occasion at vast expense, and there's no denying it's a thing of beauty. The velvet bodice fits her like a glove, but the fishtail skirt makes moving difficult. Like a mermaid trying to walk on dry land, she's practising, shortening her stride to tiny geisha-like steps.

Got it, she thinks, glancing at the clock on the wall. Forty minutes to go. Now all she needs is her makeup. Where was Becky? She should be here by now. What if she doesn't show up? If her nails weren't already varnished, she'd be biting them.

She sighs and fans herself with her hands. It's hot in the small room and heady with the scent of flowers. Everyone she knows, it seems, has sent her a floral gift, plus plenty of people she's never met. There's an enormous bunch of red roses from Bo, a pretty posy from Donny, bouquets from Becky and Rory, Giovanni, and Sofia, and an exotic, tropical plant from Cee Cee, Mike, Roly, and Frankie. Even Mrs Wilson has sent her a dainty magenta cyclamen. But by far the most unexpected, it fair took her breath away, is the spray of pink and white carnations from her parents. A gift loaded with inference, she stares at it, trying to make sense of its sudden appearance in her life. Her parents have received the tickets she sent them, which means they know about her new life, where she is and what she's doing. But what they feel about it, or about her, she has no way of telling. The brief note attached, *Best of luck, from Pa and Ma,* gives nothing away. She glances at it again, and her insides quiver. Are they here?

A brief knock on the door, and Becky breezes in with her makeup case in one hand, a spiky green cactus in the other. 'Goodness. It's like a jungle in here. I've never seen so many flowers.'

Martha draws her into a hug. 'Yours, though, are special. Thank you.'

'Ooh, careful, or you'll get pricked.' Giggling, she strides over to the roses, reads the card, and whistles. 'How romantic. Ooh, and rather a special one from Gordon, too. Poor bugger's still in love with you then.'

Martha rolls her eyes. 'How many times do I have to tell you, we're just friends.'

'Sure, *you* are, but *he's* in love with you.'

'Rumour has it, he's bringing a date.'

'Oh, you mean Elizabeth. They've been dating a while, so at least he's pretending to try to get over you. You must have met her.'

She shakes her head. 'Don't think so.'

'You'll love her. She's the life and soul. Clever, too.' Becky takes a step back. 'My, what a fabulous dress. You look stunning, Martha. Give us a twirl.'

'I'll try. But it won't be easy.' Standing on tiptoes, arms out to the sides, she spins around.

'Heavenly.' Beaming, Becky hands Martha the cactus.

'The man on the door asked me to give you this. Bit weird, but there's no accounting for taste. Who's it from?'

Martha places it next to Mrs Wilson's cyclamen, opens the little white envelope, and pulls out the note.

Break a leg,
L x

'Charming!'

'It's theatre speak for good luck.'

'I'll take your word for it.' Plonking her bag on the floor, Becky switches on the mirror lights. 'So, who is L?' she asks as she picks out palettes of foundation, eye shadow, tubes of lipstick, and mascara from her bag.

Squinting in the sudden glare from the naked bulbs, Martha settles on the stool, reaches for a hairband, and scrapes her shoulder-length hair off her face. 'Luca. Must be. It's his sort of humour.'

Becky picks up a brush and sets to work on Martha's face, covering the dark patches under her eyes with the concealer and applying the foundation. 'I'm going to use liquid eyeliner. It's best for the cat flick. And I thought brown eye shadow, for a smoky effect.'

'Okay.'

'How are you feeling? Still nervous?'

'I am now. Thanks a lot.' Since Becky's arrival, Martha had forgotten all about her nerves. She feels them suddenly in the pit of her stomach, a horrible lunging sensation as if she's falling from a great height.

'Well, don't be.'

'Easy for you to say. This place is huge.'

'Bo will be behind you. Close your eyes.' Becky reaches for a cotton bud and lays it diagonally, at the corner of her eye, to create a perfectly straight line. 'Now the lips, and we're done. What do you think? Hot red again?'

'What else?'

Becky leans across, runs the lipstick over Martha's lips, and stands back to admire her work. 'Beautiful as ever.'

Martha stares at her reflection. The stage version of herself she's grown used to. 'Thanks, Bex.'

There's another knock on the door, and a man calls out, 'Five minutes, Miss Palmer.'

'Shit.'

'Deep breaths,' Becky says, rubbing her back. 'That's right. In through the nose and out through the mouth.'

They're waiting in the wings. Bo and Cee Cee, heads together, are talking through the set. Martha is relieved they haven't included her in the conversation. Her legs are shaking, and her heart is thudding against her ribs. She only hopes the microphone won't pick it up.

The stage is immense. Far bigger than the Palladium or any of the others she's performed on. The biggest stage she has ever seen, in fact, as is the auditorium which Len claims seats three thousand. To stop them rattling around and to help with the acoustics, the orchestra, which accompanied the last act, is going to remain on stage. The conductor glances towards them and nods. He picks up his baton, and the orchestra ready themselves to play them in.

'Good luck, everyone. And don't forget to enjoy yourselves,' Bo says. 'Two, three, four, and we're off.'

She takes a deep breath, stretches her lips into a smile, and steps onto the stage to the first few bars of 'Sing, Sing, Sing'. It seems to take an age, her usually brisk gait hampered by the length and cut of her dress. Please God, do not trip, she thinks as she shuffles forwards to polite applause. She reaches the microphone in the centre and clutches it for support. The lights are down, but the people in the first three or four rows, and the boxes nearest the stage are visible. She catches sight of Giovanni, Sofia, Luca, and Milton Hyde but avoids their gaze and focuses on a point in the middle distance instead. After what seems an eternity the band strikes up the intro to 'Mad About the Boy'. Her nerves settling, she raises her head and starts to sing.

The stage vibrates with the thunderous ovation, and a shiver runs down her spine. Is it really for me? Sofia is smiling, and Giovanni is giving her a discreet thumbs-up. Beside him, Milton Hyde, head on one side, a dreamy faraway look on his face, clasps his hands to his heart. Luca catches her eye and winks. In the box nearest the stage on the right, Becky, Rory, and Donny are on their feet, clapping enthusiastically, as is the striking, dark-haired girl with them. Hovering at the back of the same box, distinctive in his trilby, Len, too, is nodding his approval.

The noise dies down. Martha thanks the audience and step backs to stand alongside Bo. Behind them, Roly's fingers glide over the keys for the opening bars of 'It's Always You'. He reaches Bo's cue, and Mike and Frankie, on drums and bass, join in. Normally, she loves this song. It's romantic and poignant; particularly the cool, unaffected way Bo delivers the lyrics. But today there's an awkwardness to it, as if the vast audience is eavesdropping on a private conver-sation. She takes over the second verse, juts out her chin and, inwardly cursing Len, reminds herself it's a performance. It's not real. But she can't shake the feeling she's revealing too much of herself and is relieved when she completes the song without a glitch. She turns to Bo, who tips back his head and blows.

They've been on stage an hour and forty minutes and are nearing the end of 'All of Me', an energetic arrangement broken up by another solo from Bo, followed by one from Cee Cee on tenor sax. Her worries about the playlist have proved unfounded. The audience have lapped up every song. Somehow, they've captivated the imaginations of almost three thousand people. They are officially a success.

She turns to applaud Bo as she backs offstage. He's performing 'I Fall in Love Too Easily' as a solo. At sixteen bars it's too short for her to do anything other than wait in the wings until she takes to the stage for the final number. It's her favourite number because it reminds her of how easily Bo fell in love with her. The first time he saw her, he said. Is that even possible? Can you fall in love with someone you don't know?

He's singing the fourth line about his love not lasting, when the image of the black lacy knickers pops into her mind. She screws up her eyes, but the lingerie loiters. Had Bo been in love with their owner, too? Had he fallen out of love with her and immediately fallen in love again? And if he had, who's to say he wouldn't do it again?

Why now? she wonders miserably. Why here? If only she hadn't found the wretched things.

Someone whispers congratulations in her ear. Startled, she topples back and steps on their toes.

'Ouch!'

'Sorry. I'm sorry.'

'You're back on in sixty seconds,' the stage manager says, righting her.

Damn those knickers. And damn the owner, she thinks as, jaw clenched, she shuffles back on stage.

Bo hits the last note of 'La Vie En Rose', and a glissando-like thrill runs through her. The climactic end isn't lost on the audience. Springing to their feet as one, they roar their approval, clapping their hands in a deafening wall of sound. She hardly dares breathe. It's absurd, the stuff of fairy tales. No longer Martha Palmer, the miner's daughter from Barnsley, she's feted. Adored. Life doesn't get any better than this. She glances at Bo beside her. His trumpet dangling by his side, he is lapping up the hysteria like a newly crowned king. None of this would be happening if it wasn't for him. She reaches for his hand, and they bow, one, twice, three times. They part and gesture to the band who move between them and, all together, they bow again. A second time, a third and fourth.

The applause continues. This is it, she thinks. This is what I was born to do.

Bo guides her off the stage and leads her towards the green room. The stage crew pat them on the back. They walk in, and there's a loud pop. Len holds up the bottle, champagne foam spilling over the rim. Everyone cheers. Len hands her a flute and toasts her. The guests raise their glasses. Some of them clap. In a dreamlike state she takes a sip. Smiling, she glances around at the familiar faces. There is Giovanni, arms open wide. He embraces her, as does Sofia. Luca is there, kissing her on both cheeks. Milton Hyde is weeping openly. The other girls from the boarding house – Jenny, Maud, Stephanie, Janice – congratulate her. Rory shakes her hand. Donny beams. And now Becky has hold of her and is spinning her around and around.

'My dress,' she says. 'Be careful of my dress.'

She is laughing. Becky is laughing. Someone hands her another glass of champagne. It's Cee Cee, and he's kissing her on the lips. Rory follows suit, and Mike. She doesn't mind. They're her brothers now. Frankie grins at her and refills her glass.

Len sidles over and pinches her cheek. 'You beauty.'

His eyes are glistening. Are they pound signs she sees in his irises? She giggles as he tops her up. Bo whispers something in her ear, words only she can hear. Private words. She smiles and reaches up and kisses him. Becky drags her away. There's someone she wants her to meet.

'Elizabeth Dawson,' Becky says, grinning. 'Gordon's date.'

Elizabeth Dawson is tall, slim, and dark-haired. 'We've met,' she says as she shakes Martha's hand.

'Have we?' Martha screws up her nose. 'I'm terribly bad with names.'

'And faces,' mutters Becky.

'Can I bother you for an autograph?' Elizabeth asks. 'I'm a huge admirer of yours.'

Martha smiles and signs Elizabeth's programme. A friend of Mike's asks her for her phone number. She doesn't have a phone, so he writes his on a cigarette packet and hands it to her. A photographer from *The Times* takes her picture. The flash blinds her. When she opens her eyes, he asks if she would mind if he takes another. This time she is ready. Len appears and steers him away. Someone taps her on the arm. It's Donny. He gives her a hug and kisses her on both cheeks.

'Martha Palmer, you are magnificent,' he says and pours her another drink.

She giggles and pecks him on the lips, spilling champagne.

'I love your laugh,' he says. 'It makes me think of sleigh bells.'

The room spins. Faces have become a little blurred. She giggles and hiccups. I'm drunk, she thinks.

'Steady there, superstar.' Luca hands her a sandwich. 'Eat before you fall over.'

Somebody has put one of her records on the turntable. Giovanni is telling her it's her battle horse. She has no idea what he means, but it's funny, and she laughs and tells him she loves him.

'Wine in, truth out,' he says.

She is drinking another glass of champagne and eating another sandwich.

Everyone is happy.

They're all dancing to Cliff Richard's 'Living Doll'.

Everyone is celebrating.

Out of the corner of her eye, she sees a commotion in the corner of the room. A familiar-looking woman, her face contorted with anger, is prodding Bo in the chest. Or is it two women? She can't be sure. A pair of Cees Cees appear by her side.

'Let's dance,' they say as they grab her hands and spin her round.

Martha giggles.

What a party. What a night.

It's late Sunday morning, and Martha is in bed. In the kitchenette, Bo is singing quietly and beating eggs in time to the rhythm. The mouth-watering smell of bacon, sizzling in a pan on the gas ring, drifts under the door towards her. Taste buds primed, her tummy rumbles. She's hungry. And not only for breakfast but for him. They've made love twice already. But today she can't seem to get enough of him. She's in love, and so is he. They are fit, healthy and happy and, since their performance at the Royal Festival Hall a fortnight ago, critically acclaimed also. Adjusting to this level of fame has been a struggle. She can't go anywhere without someone approaching her for an autograph. Still, in a little over a week, they fly to France. Although she's enjoying her success, she's looking forward to walking anonymously through the streets of Paris. But she's nervous, too.

Her mind drifts back to the concert. Not for the first time she wonders if her parents were there. They haven't been in touch, but how could they when they don't know her address? The flowers and the note hinted at their pride. Perhaps she should pay them a visit. She loves them, but shame is holding her back; the fact she left without a word, the reasons why.

Bo shoves open the door and saunters in with a tray of food and a single red rose in a vase. 'Hungry?'

She smiles and thinks she must be luckiest woman alive. 'Mm. Starving.'

'Sit up then. Not even a superstar can eat lying on her back.'

Martha sticks out her tongue.

'Here you go.' He places the tray gently on her lap, props her up with pillows, and stares at her in his intense way.

'What?'

'Just admiring your unmatchable beauty.'

She kicks out at him, laughing. 'Oh, do shut up.'

He grins and dodges out of the way. 'Eat up or it'll get cold.'

She forks up some egg and pops it into her mouth. 'Mm. As delicious as it looks.'

'How do you fancy playing the new club in Gerrard Street on Wednesday?'

'Ronnie's place?'

'Yeah. He approached Len yesterday. We could use it as a rehearsal for Paris.'

'Sure, why not.'

'Excited about next week?' He sits beside her and pats her leg.

She nods half-heartedly, her mouth full of crispy bacon melting on her tongue.

'Really? That excited.'

'I'd rather stay right here with you.'

He grins. 'You'd get bored soon enough.'

'Never.'

'They have beds in Paris, too, you know.' He leans across and reaches for the shiny new passports on the bedside table. He flicks one open. 'Hmm. What a beautiful photo. Oh … Oh shit!' He grimaces and stares at her, as if she's a stranger. 'Shit.'

She drops the fork as if he's punched her. It lands with a clatter on the plate.

'God, Martha. Why didn't you tell me?' All colour has drained from his face. 'Fuck's sake,' he shouts. 'You're just a child.'

19

Instead of goading us at every opportunity as I'd feared, Charlie left us alone. He didn't tease or mock me when our paths crossed but smiled and asked me how I was. He didn't refer to 'the kiss', or his wild declaration of love, or why he hadn't delivered Louis' letter either. Not that I asked. Some things were best left well alone. And as the weeks wore on, I started to think I'd imagined the evening on the building site when I'd tumbled into his arms. My relief was boundless. Louis and I could see each other without fear of being ambushed. And I could practice my singing with Martha without fear of being ridiculed. It was an idyllic time, happy and carefree. The sun shone without fail, and not even my father's stern disapproval, or my mother's depression, could cast a shadow.

The days being long and warm, Louis and I spent all our time outside, away from the grownups' prying eyes. Not that we considered Martha a threat. She seemed to enjoy our budding relationship as much as we did. In her opinion we were young adults whom she trusted enough to leave alone. We were neither too young nor too naïve to have fallen in love. Because we *were* in love, of this I'm sure, tender teenage love, passionate and true.

But I had other things to be grateful for. Martha noticed I was growing out of my clothes and took me on a shopping spree. She bought me trendy flares, a crop top, platform shoes, my first bra with lilac flowers embroidered on the white lace, and a pink gingham bikini. For the first time since Ian died, I was at peace with the world.

My father, on the other hand, was not so sanguine. As far as he was concerned, it was impossible his fourteen-year-old daughter had fallen in love. Criticism came in the form of thinly veiled advice. *You're too young*, his favourite refrain. *I started seeing girls when I was a lot older. You'll regret it later. Your schoolwork will suffer. You should be out with your girlfriends. If you don't you won't have any left.* But his 'advice' fell on deaf ears. The more he complained, the more I avoided him and the deeper in love I fell. We'd always been close, but now we were drifting apart. Consequently, when school sent me home with a letter about the summer concert, I threw it in the bin. It didn't matter. Miss Hendrik had vetoed 'Someone to Watch Over Me' and replaced it with 'Somewhere Over the Rainbow'. I was unenthusiastic and unwilling to learn the lyrics, so Miss Hendrik had no alternative than to drop me from the event. I couldn't have cared less. Why would I when Martha had asked me to sing at her birthday party? School singing lessons were a drag. Miss Hendrik wasn't a patch on Martha Palmer. The school concert seemed infinitesimally childish by comparison.

Time became a precious commodity, every second to be used wisely. Every day after school, I'd meet Louis outside Mrs Pocock's house. We'd take Rafferty for his walk and head to Greystones, sometimes with Rafferty in tow. On those days we'd laze on a rug in the orchard, chatting and listening to Louis's LPs – Fleetwood Mac, ELO, Queen, and The Rolling Stones – which he'd taped on his brand-new cassette player. On the days without Rafferty, we'd swim in the pool and climb into the treehouse. It was too hot for clothes, so we'd lie on one of the bunks in our swimming costumes and kiss until our lips were sore and our jaws ached. Nobody ever disturbed us there. And as the days passed and we grew more confident in each other's company, we'd slip our hands, tentatively, beneath each other's swimsuits. My body tingled under Louis' touch in ways I'd never experienced. We were never naked, though, and despite the arrival in the treehouse of a poster of a girl in a tennis dress scratching her naked bum, Louis put no pressure on me to go further. I was grateful. All I knew about sex were the snippets Hayley had revealed on the top deck of the bus home from school. It sounded terrifying. I was too young, too innocent, too scared.

There was the party to think about, too, and my performance. I had no idea why Martha wanted me to sing and seriously doubted I was up to it. But the more I practiced with her the better I became and the bolder I felt, until I reached the point when I could honestly say I was looking forward to it. It made it easier knowing Martha had sought my father's approval. I wasn't surprised he'd agreed. He'd always encouraged me to sing and enthused about my talent, but I was relieved when, during one of the rare evenings we spent together, he let slip he was proud that Martha held me in high regard. Coming from my father, this was praise indeed.

But this was where his enthusiasm for my interests began and ended. A man unafraid to offer his opinion, he said it like he saw it, whether it proved popular or not. His outlook on life and his style of parenting contrasted so completely with Martha's I wondered how two such different beings had ever been friends. And as the weeks flew by and I grew closer to Louis, I couldn't help but notice the shine had worn off their relationship. The idea I'd entertained that my father had once been the love of Martha's life seemed ludicrous now. I desperately wanted to ask her if they'd been more than friends, there were opportunities enough when we were on our own but, although I adored her and was growing increasingly confident in her company, I lacked the precocity to broach such an intimate subject.

By now, the summer holidays were upon us. It was swelteringly hot, the mercury hitting ninety day after day. Lawns cracked, tarmac melted on the roads, plants withered in the parched fields and flowerbeds and, with fewer aphids to feed on, there was a plague of ladybirds, who took to feasting on human sweat to stay alive. The country was running out of water. The government's advice was to bathe with a friend, put a brick in the cistern, let wilting flowers die, and cars go dirty. People queued at standpipes. With his elderly patients struggling in the oppressive heat, my father was busier than ever and, with my mother still in bed, had hired a secretary to help with the paperwork. His waiting room was, most probably, a hive of idle gossip but, as I was never at home, I wasn't privy to it.

The Fairchilds, meanwhile, had removed to the beach. Quite unintentionally, I'd initiated this change in their routine when, during one of my rare conversations about Ian, I'd mentioned how much I missed the seaside now he was gone. We'd spent our summers there, digging convoluted waterways and giant pools protected from the incoming tide by sandy walls reinforced with huge pebbles we'd heaved across the shingle. When the tide was high, we'd bob about in the foaming surf in our rubber inner tubes, riding waves that dumped us onto the rolling hissing pebbles while my mother, blind to our antics in her Jackie O sunglasses, lay on a lounger and gorged on the latest Harold Robbins.

'How about we go today?' Martha suggested. 'It sounds enormous fun, and I bet it's cooler on the coast.'

I'd loved it with Ian, but it was even better with Louis, Martha, and Charlie, whom I now considered a friend. We piled into Martha's white open-top sports car, equipped with anything we could possibly need: bats, balls, inflatables, and shrimping nets. We played beach cricket and volleyball and had a picnic on the rocky reef when the tide was out. At high tide, we dived off breakwaters into the surf and floated around on lilos. Some days, we walked to the pier to play on the slot machines, hook ducks on long sticks, and eat pink fluffy candyfloss which melted on my tongue. Best of all, though, were the evenings we spent on a remote beach, accessible only by a steep, narrow cliff path. Transporting all the food and paraphernalia we needed was backbreaking, despite Teddy doing the lion's share of the work. But it was worth it. A cooling dip in the sea was followed by a mad dash to collect as much driftwood as possible for the campfire. The sausages and burgers Teddy cooked in the flames were the best I'd ever eaten. We slid them inside Martha's spongy, homemade buns, with mustard and ketchup, and ate coleslaw and salad on the side. We played rounders on the sand, and when it was dark, we'd go swimming. Later, by the light of the campfire, cuddling up to Louis, my hair tangled into knots by the saltwater and sea breeze, we'd listen to Martha sing until it was time to pack up and go home. I was in heaven.

'Are you excited about performing at her birthday?' Teddy asked me one night. He'd opened a second bottle of red wine and was, by his own admission, feeling more relaxed than he had in weeks, the big contract he'd been working on successfully signed and sealed.

'Oh yes. It's a huge honour.'

'She's one of the true greats, you know. Incomparable, in my opinion.'

'Oh. Teddy. You do exaggerate,' Martha said, but she was smiling.

'Went to all of her concerts, back in nineteen-sixty. I was her biggest fan.'

'Is that how you met?' I asked.

'Not exactly,' said Teddy.

'I needed a solicitor. My manager introduced us. Teddy hadn't a clue who I was, let alone heard me sing. He'd been living and working in Singapore for years.'

He pulled a face. 'You make it sound so unromantic.'

'Oh, darling, I'm sorry. I should have mentioned the flowers. A whole barrowful from Covent Garden. Can you believe it?'

I shook my head and grinned.

'You're nuts, Dad,' Charlie said.

'Bonkers,' agreed Louis, and put his arm around me.

'Ha. The vendor thought I was joking, but he couldn't disguise his glee when I handed him the cash.'

Martha laughed her tinkly laugh. 'My house smelled like a florist for days.'

'Three months later we were engaged.'

'Fast mover, Dad,' said Louis.

'Or desperate,' added Charlie.

'Martha had a band,' Teddy continued, ignoring his sons. 'Very good, they were, too. Cee Cee was in it, of course. They never played on her records, though. Why was that, darling? Can you remember?'

Martha glanced out to sea. 'Oh, I don't know. Something to do with the record label, I think.'

'The Bo Rivers' Five, they were called. Bo Rivers discovered Martha, you see, gave her her first break. Never met him, though. Never heard him play either. He'd left the band by the time I came on the scene. But I gather he was a gifted trumpet player.'

'Where is he now?' I asked.

Teddy shrugged and turned to Martha who was still staring at the horizon. 'Any ideas, darling?'

'None,' said Martha briskly. 'Now what say we roast some marshmallows.'

20

B o thrusts the passport at her. 'Look, it's here in black and white.' He points to her date of birth. 19th August 1942.

She stares at him blankly. She doesn't understand why he's shouting at her.

'You didn't think to tell me. Why, Martha? Why?'

'I'm seventeen. I'm not a child.'

'But you were fifteen when you first sang with us.' His face contorts, and he wrings his hands. 'And ... Jesus Christ ... sixteen when I first slept with you.'

He looks at her with such distaste, Martha quakes. She slips out of bed but realises she is naked and reaches for the first item of clothing she sees. His shirt. She puts it on, fumbling with the buttons. 'Please. Don't be like this.'

Bo turns his back on her but doesn't reply. She wraps her arms around him from behind, but he shrugs her off. 'I don't understand why you're so upset.' Her voice is little more than a whisper. 'You haven't broken any laws.'

'By some miracle.' He whips around, his expression

pained. 'I wanted you the moment I set eyes on you, or have you forgotten?'

'Yes, but you didn't … we didn't—'

'How could you be so deceitful?'

Martha recoils, the barb like a slap to the face. She wishes she could understand why he's so angry. 'I wasn't. I haven't—'

'I trusted you, Martha.'

She stares at him helplessly.

'You don't have a clue, do you?'

Her lower lip trembles as she shakes her head.

'No, of course you don't. Why would you? You're a child.'

'I'm sorry,' she whispers. Is that what he wants her to say?

Eyes bulging, he scratches his jaw. 'You're sorry! Jesus! I'm ten years older than you, Martha. Have you any idea how it makes me feel?' Throwing up his hands, he steps back several paces. 'You should have told me. You should have told … wait a minute.' He strides over and clasps her arms. 'Have you told anyone?'

She shakes her head. 'No one.' Except Becky, she thinks. 'No one asked.'

'Are you quite sure? Not even Len? No journalists? All those interviews you've done. Someone must have asked, surely.'

She'd thought so, too, had dreaded it in fact. It was odd, though, no matter who she spoke to, no one ever did. Not even her friends. 'Nobody.'

'Okay. Good. You'll have to lie. Yes, that's what we'll do. We'll pretend you're … what … twenty-two, twenty-three? Twenty-three. You'll remember, won't you? You'll remember to tell anyone who asks that you're twenty-three.'

'If it's what you want.' She'd agree to anything right now if he'd stop shouting.

'It is, Martha. It absolutely is.' He stops pacing and rests his hands on her shoulders, calmer now, the anger ebbing away almost as quickly as it had erupted.

She wants to ask him if he still loves her but she dares not. 'Okay,' she whispers. 'I will.'

'Promise me.'

'I promise.'

'You do understand?' he asks, cupping her face in his hands.

She nods. Another lie. She doesn't. Not one little bit. She just wants him to kiss her and for this terrible misunderstanding to be over.

Martha jumps at a sudden loud knocking. Bo yelps and covers his face with his hands, as if it's the police come to arrest him.

'You in there, Bo?'

Martha presses a hand to her heart. It's Keith, the trainee surveyor who rents the flat next door.

Bo exhales long and loud, rushes into the sitting room, and opens the door. 'Yeah, I'm here.' His tone is forced-casual, his fists, clenched. 'What's up?'

'Your crazy ex-girlfriend's downstairs throwing one hell of a tantrum.'

'Fuck. This is all I need.'

'Want me to get rid of her?'

He frowns and runs his hand through his hair. 'I do, Keith. Please. And tell her not to come around here anymore while you're at it. God sakes, when is she going to get the message?'

'Right you are, Bo.'

Groaning, Bo shuts the door and circles the room, once

twice, three times. 'I thought I'd made myself clear,' he says, more to himself than to Martha, who's watching him, bewildered. 'I've told her often enough. She's completely and utterly deranged.'

A question is on the tip of her tongue, but she swallows it. She may be young but even she can see now is not the time to ask if the crazy girlfriend has lost a pair of knickers.

He smiles at her, but it's awkward and strained. 'I need some air to clear my head.' He strides over and kisses her on the mouth. A passionless kiss.

'I'll come with you.'

'No,' he says, grabbing his coat. 'I want to be alone.'

She bites her lip. 'But—'

'You can wait here, if you like. I won't be long.' And without a second glance, he marches out of the room, closing the door behind him.

Martha didn't hang around. She couldn't bear the thought of just sitting there, twiddling her thumbs. What if he didn't come back? So, she wrote him a note, dashed outside, and set off walking, but almost immediately a stranger recognised her. His triumphant whoops attracted the attention of several other passersby eager to engage her in amicable conversation and, within seconds, she was surrounded. Normally, she wouldn't have minded. Her fans were curious but always gracious, never rude. But, right now, she wasn't in the mood. Apologising profusely, she'd flagged down a cab. Back at her lodgings, she'd flung her coat on her bed and locked herself in the lavatory on the top floor.

She slumps on the toilet, head in hands, mind swimming. Bo's absurd behaviour makes no sense. Her fame, a leaden weight, bears down on her. Who am I? she wonders, staring blindly at the chipped white tiles. Martha Palmer the miner's daughter from Barnsley? Martha Palmer the famous singer? Or Bo Rivers' girlfriend, the man I work with and whose bed I happen to share? What if he doesn't need me anymore? Could I exist without him?

She's angry, too. Angry with herself for not telling Bo her age. Angry with Bo for reacting the way he did. Angry his ex-girlfriend appeared out of the blue. Angry that, having lost his temper with her, he wanted to be alone. She's never seen this side of him before. Perhaps he has other sides she doesn't know about, too.

If he'd asked me my age, I'd have told him. It's not a secret. Just something I choose not to mention.

It had evolved naturally after she'd arrived in London and was looking for work. The way potential employers had spoken to her, it was obvious they'd assumed she was older. Even Becky had (although, later, Martha had told her the truth). How else could she have got a job? Some lodgings? If Mrs Wilson had found out, she wouldn't have thought twice about throwing her out. Rules were rules. And then the interviews had started. She'd lost sleep, worrying about the repercussions if her true age got out. For peace of mind, she'd resolved, if the question came up, to simply add three years. With her parents out of the picture, no one would be any the wiser. But not a single journalist had asked.

And now she's seventeen. An adult. A star. Her age of no consequence.

Unlike Bo's ex-girlfriend showing up. Atrocious timing, but why had she come? What did she want? When had they split up? Can't have been all that long ago if she was still trying to win him back. If that's what she'd been doing. Bo hadn't mentioned any past girlfriends. At twenty-seven, he must have had a fair few. Was it unusual for a man not to mention his past lovers? She didn't know. This subject, like so many others, had never arisen. Apart from his love of jazz, the trumpet his uncle had given him, his chance meeting with Delilah Moore, and the strange quirk he has of holding an unlit cigarette because he gave up smoking two years ago, Bo has told her nothing about his past. She hasn't a clue where he's from, what his parents do, where he went to school, the company he keeps. All she knows is what they have together.

I've been too afraid to ask, she thinks. How sad does that make me?

The sound of footsteps on the landing has Martha holding her breath. Someone tries the door handle. She thinks if she stays quiet they'll give up and go away. She waits. A minute passes. And then the banging starts.

'What on earth's the matter with you?' Becky says. 'What are you doing, hiding away in there?'

Her mouth clamped shut, Martha crosses her fingers and hopes Becky will get bored and leave. It's not as if she knows it's her. It could be Maud, or Jenny. Or any one of the other girls

'What's wrong, Martha? Are you ill?'

She clenches her teeth and glares at the ceiling. 'Go away, will you. I'm fine.'

'No, you're not. Come on, open the door. Talk to me. I might be able to help.'

'Leave me alone.'

'MARTHA! OPEN THE DOOR.'

Slowly, Martha slides open the bolt. Arms hanging uselessly, she props herself against the wall and stares glumly at her shoes.

'What's happened? Come on, you can tell me.'

Martha sighs but doesn't look up. 'I found a pair of

knickers under his bed,' she says in a small, flat voice. 'Sexy knickers.'

'Okay. He's had sex before. So what? It's nineteen fifty-nine, for heaven's sake.'

Martha cringes. It's true but it's not what she wants to hear. She raises her head. 'Do you think he was in love with her?'

Becky smiles and puts her arm around Martha. 'Maybe. Maybe not. What does it matter?'

'I don't know. But … I don't think I can bear it.' Martha tilts her head until it's resting on Becky's shoulder. 'What if he still loves her?'

'Oh, Martha,' Becky says, stroking her hair. 'First love can be bewildering, but it's also rather wonderful. Has it not occurred to you this other relationship ended because he fell in love with you?'

Martha looks up in surprise. 'You think?'

'The man is gaga about you. Totally and utterly besotted.'

Martha takes a deep breath. 'There's more,' she says. 'Much more.'

Martha lies on the bed in her room. Beside her, fingers steepled, Becky shifts back and forth in the rocking chair Martha bought last week. Most of the flowers have long since died, but Bo's long-stemmed roses remain, the faded leaves curled and brittle, the petals darkened to a deep blood red. An omen, perhaps? She'd intended to keep them forever; a romantic memento. Now, she's not so sure. How could she have been this naïve? This stupid?

On her dressing table, Mrs Wilson's magenta cyclamen is still going strong, and the cactus – which turns out wasn't an ironic gift from Luca – shows no signs of dying either.

'You should have told him your age,' Becky says eventually. 'I know I didn't show it, but I was gobsmacked when you told me you were fourteen. I kept quiet because I could see you had enough on your plate, what with running away and being homeless. My point is, you're still very young.'

Martha heaves herself up on her elbow. 'Seventeen isn't young. Girls are married with babies at seventeen, become prostitutes.'

'They do, but if Bo had slept with you when you were fifteen, it would've been illegal.'

'But he didn't. That's the bit I don't understand. He hasn't broken any laws.'

Becky stops rocking and raises her finger. 'Ah! But he thought about it, didn't he? You look older. You look …'

'Twenty-three?'

'Exactly!'

Martha groans. 'I think he's going to split up with me.'

'Don't be ridiculous. He adores you. And right now, he's probably terribly worried. Pull yourself together, go back and tell him you love him.'

'He was moody as hell. I was scared.'

Becky frowns. 'Bit of an overreaction, if you ask me. But that's men for you.'

'But what if he ends it? We're off to France next week. What'll happen to the band?'

'That's it in a nutshell, Martha. Never mix business and pleasure.'

'You're not helping.'

'So, what was she like?' Becky asks. 'Pig ugly or drop-dead gorgeous?'

'I didn't see her. She was downstairs.'

'What, you didn't peek out of the window? Blimey. I would've.'

'It didn't occur to me,' says Martha, scrubbing her face with her hand. Where is he now? she wonders, miserably. With her?

There's a rap on the door.

'Lover boy's downstairs waiting for you,' Jenny shouts from behind it. 'He wants to take you to dinner. It's important, apparently. Martha? You hearing me?'

Martha stares at Becky, wide-eyed. Her heart is going like the clappers. Is this it? Has he come here to finish with her?

'Yes, she's hearing you,' Becky yells. 'Ta for this, Jen. She'll be down in a minute.'

Martha screws up her nose. 'What do you think he wants?'

'To apologise for behaving like a twat.'

'D'you think?'

'Or he wants to bite your neck and drink your blood.'

Martha picks up her pillow and hurls it at Becky.

Becky laughs and throws it back. 'Only one way to find out. Get your arse downstairs and listen to what he has to say.'

A scattering of dried leaves, caught up in a flurry of wind, swirl around her legs as she steps outside Mrs Wilson's boarding house. Wrapped up in an overcoat, Bo stands on the pavement, swinging his arms and stamping his feet. His face lights up on sight of her.

'I thought you weren't coming,' he says.

'I had to change. Do my makeup. That sort of stuff.'

He smiles sheepishly. 'You don't need makeup.'

She rolls her eyes and slips her hands in the pockets of her coat.

'I'm sorry,' Bo says. 'I shouldn't have lost my temper. It was unfair of me.'

Martha screws up her nose and squints at him. She'd hoped he'd apologise but she hadn't expected it to tumble out of him this quickly.

'I think you kept it from me because it has something to do with why you left home. If you wanted to, we could talk about it over dinner.'

She clenches her jaw. A discussion about why she left home is not top of her list of priorities. But she doesn't want another fight either.

'Come to dinner,' he persists. 'Please. I have a surprise for you.'

She stares at the ground and prods at a leaf with her toe. She doesn't think she can take any more surprises. She's had a bellyful today.

Bo reaches for her arm, but she moves out of the way. She looks up. He's eyeing her forensically, scouring her face for clues. She holds his pale gaze and tries to read his mind. But of course, she can't. His expression, as usual, is impenetrable.

'Could we at least eat? I've booked a table. It'd be a shame to waste it.'

She lets out another, longer sigh. 'Okay.'

Martha glances at the gilded mirrors, the sparkling chandeliers, and the marble columns. The Ritz Restaurant is the last place she expected Bo to take her. He didn't seem the ostentatious dining type. If she needed any more proof she knows nothing at all about her lover, this is it. Still, no one will bother her here. At least a dozen fans must have stopped them on the way, asking for an autograph. To be fair, Bo had suggested they come by cab, but she'd insisted they walk.

Not because she wanted to but out of sheer bloody-mindedness. Today she'd make up her own mind, thank you very much.

One of the many waiters attending them removes the silver cloche covering her Steak Diane with a triumphant flourish. The sommelier follows, filling up her cut-glass flute even though she's only had a sip. Champagne. The Ritz. As apologies go, it's completely over the top. What little conversation they've had has been strained. Hardly surprising. With all these waiters buzzing around them, it's not the place for a heart-to-heart. None of them appear to have recognised her, but even so she can't understand why, if he wanted to talk, Bo has brought her here. They've engaged in idle chitchat – the concert at the Festival Hall, Ornette Coleman's revolutionary new record, 'The Shape of Jazz to Come', and the article in *Jazz Journal* about how influential a year nineteen fifty-nine has been – everything except themselves. All the same, scratching around like a hen knowing the fox might strike but hoping it won't, Martha is on tenterhooks.

When coffee and petit fours arrive, and the subject still hasn't been broached, it occurs to Martha tonight is all about grand gestures. A fancy dinner at the Ritz is Bo's way of saying sorry. Pleased to have escaped unscathed, she breathes a silent sigh of relief.

'Why did you leave home?' Bo asks gently.

Martha starts. Having expected a question like this the entire evening, she is, nevertheless, caught unawares.

'Did something happen? Is that why you ran away? You did run away, didn't you?'

She rolls her lip between her teeth and scrutinises the napkin on her lap. White and starched, not a single crease.

He reaches across the table and touches her arm, lightly. 'I only ask because I care. I want to know everything about you. I love you, Martha, with all my heart. You know that, don't you?'

She wonders later if those were the magic words, the proof she needed that what they had transcended all obstacles. He wasn't worried about her age. There was no one else, and it was Martha the person he loved, not Martha Palmer the singer. At that precise moment, however, she is beset with doubts.

'You were so young when I met you. You mentioned something about running away when we were touring. I'm guessing something bad happened to you.'

His tenderness touches her deeply, but still she dithers.

'I promise I won't judge.'

'I found some underwear,' she says evenly. 'Black lace.'

'Oh! Great. I—'

'Under your bed.' She pauses, watching for a reaction, but his baffled expression doesn't change. 'Are they hers? Your girlfriend's? The one who came to your flat?'

He retracts his hand. 'You're my girlfriend, Martha.'

'Did you love her?'

He sighs. 'God, no. It was a fling. Nothing more than sex, really.'

She flinches. He's twenty-seven, she reminds herself. What did you expect?

'Is this what's been bothering you?'

Is it? she wonders.

'Don't you trust me?'

His expression is pained. What point is she trying to make, exactly? Whatever it is she's going about this all wrong. She loves him. She trusts him. He's never given her any reason not to. But … 'You were so angry about my age. And I didn't know where you went. I suppose I was scared you were going to leave me. For her.'

'I'm sorry, I needed some space, that's all. I was shocked but I overreacted, and it was stupid of me. You really don't look seventeen, but I can't stop loving you just because you're ten years younger than me. It's not a switch I can turn off.'

'You mean it?'

'Cross my heart and hope to die.' He makes the gesture, and she smiles. 'Tell me what happened to make you leave home, Martha. Please.'

She winces. More than anything she wants to believe him, but she's not sure she can. *I must, though*, she thinks, miserably. *If I don't, he'll never trust me again.* She glances around, but none of the waiters are anywhere near. She takes a deep breath and stares him directly in the eye. 'I was fourteen. A schoolgirl who loved to sing. My father was a fan of Sarah Vaughan, you see, Ella Fitzgerald, and Billie Holiday. All the greats. We used to listen to their records together on Sundays. I guess his enthusiasm rubbed off on me. Whatever the reason, I tried to imitate them. My father heard me one day. He couldn't believe his ears. *You'll be a somebody*, he said. Anyway, one evening on my way home from school, I saw a sandwich board outside the local pub advertising for a singer. I could do that, I thought. Trouble was, I was wearing my uniform, and there wasn't time for me to change and come back without making my mother suspicious. That night as I lay in bed, I kicked myself, furious for not even trying to think of an excuse. But, lo and behold, the following evening the board was still there. This time I didn't think twice. I dashed home and put on a frock. *Where do you think you're going dressed like that?* Mum asked. *Meeting a friend*, I said. *Oh no you're not, young lady. You've chores to do.* But I yelled at her that she was always trying to ruin my life and ran out of the house before she could stop me.

'I had second thoughts when I reached the pub and almost didn't go in. But the barmaid saw me and asked me if I'd come to audition. I must seem like a singer, I reasoned, and followed her inside. The landlord didn't ask my age, just told me to sing. I remember him smiling. He said I had a beautiful voice and the position was mine. Could I start on Friday? Well, of course, I said yes.

'My folks grounded me for being rude and disobedient, but I didn't care. I was so excited and couldn't wait for Friday. I was going to sing no matter what. I took my frock to school and hung around at a friend's until eight. I was incredibly nervous, but the landlord was pleased to see me, which put me at ease. I told him I needed to freshen up, and he showed me to the ladies ...' Her voice cracks. She can remember it as if it were yesterday, the leer on the landlord's face, his chipped yellow teeth and foul breath.

'I'd no idea of his intentions until he'd pinned me against the wall. *You're a pretty little lass*, he said as he grabbed my breast with one hand and pulled down my knickers with his other. I tried to wriggle free but I was wedged between his body and the wall. He tried to kiss me. But I wasn't having it and kneed him in the groin. He doubled over, and I shot out of the ladies, out of the pub, and didn't stop running until there was a mile's distance between us. I felt dirty and ashamed. I'd lied to my parents, for what? So some dirty old man could get his filthy hands on me? I packed my bags and left before the sun was up and caught the first train to London.' Martha pauses, the pain still raw three years on, the humiliation still strong. She'd cried her heart out for hours, an endless stream of tears until, exhausted by the effort, she'd drifted off to sleep, waking, an hour later with a salty crust on her cheeks.

'It was stupid of me. That's why I don't talk about it. I'm ashamed. I let my family down.'

A lone tear trickles down Bo's cheek. It clings to his chin for a moment, elongating before it drops onto the tablecloth and disappears, and all that remains is a small damp circle. She holds herself upright and waits for him to speak. He seems upset, but perhaps he's disappointed, too. She wants to know but doesn't want to ask. She's too scared of what he might say.

His hand reaches inside his pocket, but instead of the handkerchief she's expecting, he pulls out a small box. He opens it, places it on the table, and pushes it towards her. A diamond, sparkling in the light.

'Martha Palmer, will you marry me?'

'Oh.' She clasps her hands to her chest. 'Yes, Bo Rivers. Yes, I will.'

It's a bitter Monday evening in December. Martha and Len are waiting on the King's Road, outside the Chelsea Palace, for the car Granada Television has hired to take her home. It was due five minutes ago and, although she is wrapped in a thick wool coat with a fur collar, her stockinged feet are numb.

We should have waited inside, she thinks, clapping her hands in a futile attempt to stave off the cold. She scans the area for fans. She'd been expecting a crowd, but the road is deserted. Perhaps they stayed home to watch her on television instead. She's tired, too, having spent all day in a studio in Tin Pan Alley recording her third album; not the ideal preparation for a live television performance. And she's without the band. Despite their recent successes in London and Paris,

The Bo Rivers' Five are honouring a year-old booking in a Surrey pub. Bo hadn't wanted to, but Len had insisted.

'Don't go getting a reputation for being a trilby. Never mind it ain't your boat they wanna butcher's at.'

Always nervous about performing without them, she realised turning down a slot on *Chelsea at Nine* would have been mad. Billie Holiday, may she rest in peace, had appeared on the show last February, so getting the call had been a big deal. Thankfully, the moment she took to the stage the adrenaline had kicked in, and she'd produced an above average performance. She checks her watch. Eleven-fifteen and still no sign of the cab. Coming off stage tonight, the letdown had been huge, her tiredness now bordering on exhaustion. She needs to slow down. She can't go on like this.

Since the concert at the Royal Festival Hall, Martha has been in constant demand. There are not enough hours in the day for her to fulfil every request put Len's way. A canny operator and the master of strategic planning, he somehow manages to tweak her schedule so she can undertake the majority. When she suggested she was running the risk of overexposure, Len was quick to reassure her. It was, he said, in her best interests to strike while the iron is hot.

'Your fans 'ave short memories. We've gotta graft to keep your boat in their loafs.'

She understands but sometimes she wishes the world would stop spinning so she could step off and catch her breath. Still, it's not long until she and Bo leave for America. She can't wait to have him all to herself. Since he proposed to her, they've hardly spent any time alone. Bo says things will change when they get back. They're going to buy a flat in Chelsea, or a terraced house like the one they viewed last week, and get married in the spring. Becky will be her bridesmaid and Cee Cee his best man. It's happening so fast she can barely keep up. She glances at the solitaire diamond ring on her fourth finger. It isn't a dream. She really is engaged.

Len notices and raises an eyebrow. 'I thought you was keepin' schtum.'

'Don't you miss anything?' she asks irritably. She'd meant to take it off before the performance, but it had skipped her mind in the rush.

'Nope!'

'Well, you needn't worry. Nobody noticed.'

'Don't you Adam and Eve it. Millions of viewers 'ave just 'ad a butcher's.'

She stares at him for a moment, computing what he's said. Damn it, she thinks, her heart sinking. He's right.

'What's with the mardy boat?' Len asks, straightening his garish tie as the door to the theatre swings open behind them. 'It's good news. Sales'll go through the bleedin' roof.'

'And that's all you care about, isn't it?'

But Len isn't listening. His attention has been grabbed by the diminutive and instantly recognisable figure of Delilah Moore. Eyes glinting, she glares at Martha with intense loathing. Grateful for Len's presence for the first time this evening, Martha looks to him for reassurance. But Len, frozen to the spot, stands there, opening and closing his mouth. Her insides turn to water. Knees trembling, she steps back and covers her face. She hasn't forgotten what happened the last time they met.

'You stupid little bitch,' Delilah hisses. 'Can't you see he's using you?'

Taken aback, Martha lowers her hands and glances at her manager. Did Delilah know Len? Had they worked together, too?

'Do us all a favour and go 'ome, luv,' Len says.

'Can't bear to hear the truth. Is that it? Well, tough, because I'm—'

A car screeches to a halt beside them, bringing Delilah's rant to a halt. The driver winds down his window. 'Martha Palmer? Sorry I'm late.'

Quick as a flash, Len opens the rear door and, before Martha has a chance to reply, bundles her inside. 'Lock it,' he says as he slams it shut.

Martha does as she's told and is glad she has because Delilah bolts forward and grabs the handle. Finding it locked, she raps her knuckles on the window. 'IT'S WHAT HE DOES.' Delilah's hands are flat against the glass. She is nose close. Martha can see every spidery vein in the whites of her bulging eyes, the tops of each molar in her mouth. 'ONCE HE'S GOT WHAT HE WANTS HE'LL GET RID OF YOU. BY FORCE IF HE HAS TO. BUT DON'T TAKE MY WORD FOR IT. ASK HIM YOURSELF.'

'Isn't that Delilah Moore?' the driver says. 'Well, I never. What a night.'

Len opens the passenger door and jumps inside. 'Step on it,' he says, slapping the dashboard.

The driver throws him a questioning look, but Len stares, steadfastly, ahead. Without uttering another word, the driver stamps on the accelerator. Craning her neck, Martha turns to peer out the rear window. Arms folded, Delilah Moore stands motionless, glaring at the car as it speeds away.

21

M y father and I had taken to eating supper in silence.
It wasn't a conscious decision, rather that neither of
us had anything to say to one another anymore. To make
matters worse, I'd started avoiding eye contact as well. Dad's
disappointment in me was all too plain. I didn't need to be
constantly reminded by his narrowed eyes and furrowed
brow. I was surprised, therefore, when he put down his knife
and fork one night and told me he'd invited Martha and the
twins to tea.

'Why?' It had come completely out of the blue. There had
to be some ulterior motive.

'You've been spending an embarrassing amount of time
with the Fairchilds. I thought it high time I reciprocated.'

'Martha doesn't mind,' I snapped. 'She enjoys having
another girl about the place.' It was true. She told me often
enough. She made me welcome, as well, and included me in
every aspect of Fairchild family life. I liked it better at Greystones. It was more fun than home. There were trips to the
beach, there were parties, there was music and laughter.
Musicians from London, exciting sophisticated people,

dropped by on a whim. Home was dull by comparison. With my mother in bed and my father wedded to his work, nothing ever happened here. Consequently, I never saw the point in inviting Louis over. A boring old tea party in our back garden, in the stifling heat, sounded horrendous. 'And anyway, I'm not sure she's interested in drinking tea. She's not that sort of person. She likes Pimm's.'

My father's expression darkened. 'I never thought I'd say this about you, Natasha, but you're selfish. What about your mother? When did you last think of her?'

'That's just stupid,' I retorted, stung by the jibe. 'When did she last think about me?'

'She is ill, and you are not.' He rose from the table, stormed into his consulting room, and closed the door.

I clenched my fists and stamped my feet. 'I hate you,' I yelled. 'I hate you both.'

The day of the tea party seemed hotter and more airless than any day of the summer so far. My father's only afternoon off, he wasn't going to be deterred by the weather. I came home from school to find plates of finger sandwiches – cucumber, and egg and cress – fondant fancies, chocolate éclairs, Viennese whirls, and a homemade three-layered Black Forest gateau, oozing cream. It was quite some spread. And although I was still harbouring a massive grudge, I couldn't help but be impressed. Maybe the afternoon wouldn't be so bad after all.

'That looks good,' I said. 'I didn't know you baked.'

He winked. 'Neither did I.'

'Martha …' I was about to say she baked her own bread but stopped myself. 'Martha will love it.'

His face lit up. 'Do you think so?'

'Yes, Daddy, I do.' Overcome with a sudden burst of affection, I rushed across the room and gave him a hug.

Once I'd changed out of my uniform into my new clothes, I went outside to help. The old table tennis table, and the Swingball my parents had given Ian on his eleventh birthday, were set up on the sun-scorched lawn. Ian's face had lit up when he'd opened the box. He'd loved any game involving balls – table tennis, football, cricket, rugby, and latterly tennis. Trouble was Dad, the only other member of the family who played, was often too busy to take him to the park. The beauty of Swingball meant Ian could play it on his own. In any event, he'd hardly used it because a month after his eleventh birthday he was dead.

'No swimming pool,' my father said, misreading my expression. 'But it might be fun to run around a bit when it cools down.'

I swallowed the lump in my throat. 'You kept it.'

'We kept everything. Your mother couldn't bear to be parted with a single thing. I understood. It's not natural for a mother to bury their child.'

It was the first time he'd articulated the physical suffering he and my mother had endured. Too young to know how to reply, I stared at my brand-new platforms and willed the moment to pass.

As luck would have it, the doorbell rang. I dashed towards the house. 'I'll get it.'

'Careful in those, or you'll break your ankle.'

Martha's glossy hair cascaded down her back in waves. She was dressed in another white flowing creation and had donned a pair of silvery sandals for the occasion. She kissed me on both cheeks and wafted into the garden, leaving a trail of lily of the valley in her wake. In a house suffocated by grief, she was a breath of fresh air. And as they had so often in the past, my father's eyes brightened at the sight of her.

'Darling Donny, how heavenly,' she said, taking in the scene.

Louis and Charlie stuck their fingers in their mouths and pretended to vomit, and I giggled, happy they were all here.

'Is it just us?' Martha asked as she ducked under the parasol and took her place at the garden table.

My father nodded. 'For the moment.'

Louis threw me a sympathetic look, but nothing more was said on the subject.

Sitting in the shade, we drank tea from my mother's pretty china cups and stuffed our faces with food. When the heat waned, Martha challenged my father to a game of table tennis.

'Okay, but you won't stand a chance.'

I watched them for a bit while the twins messed around with the Swingball. They were totally mismatched, but I noticed that my father, a talented player, took care to let Martha win a few points. When they'd finished we all joined in a game of Around the World. It was chaotic but fun and had us all sweating and gasping for breath by the end. Later, Martha and my father went inside to do the washing up. Left to our own devices, Louis suggested we play a game of hide and seek.

'Inside or out?' Charlie asked.

'Both. If it's all right with Nat.'

'Fine by me.'

'Cool,' said Louis. 'Now close your eyes, Nat, and get counting. Sixty should be long enough.'

I started in the garden, peering into the dark, cobwebbed

corners of the shed and the small orchard at the bottom of the lawn. If past form was anything to go by, they'd be hiding up a tree. I looked but I couldn't see them, so I headed inside. With four storeys I had my work cut out but at least I knew where the best hiding places were. I was deciding whether to search the attic, the large spare room cupboard on the second floor, or behind the suitcases in the box room on the third, when I overheard my father arguing with Martha in the kitchen. I no longer thought they'd been past lovers, but their relationship still intrigued me. I crept towards the half-open door and listened.

'… told her I don't approve,' my father said.

'And yet you invite us for tea.'

'It's like you're punishing me.'

'I'm not punishing you. I care about her. She needs a mother.'

I flinched. They were talking about me.

'Do you think I don't know that?'

'Of course not.'

'She's only fourteen. Louis is a full year older. Why must you encourage them? You know what boys are like at that age.'

'Louis is different. He's kind and sensitive. And anyway, they spend most of their time with Charlie.'

'Kind doesn't come into it. Fifteen-year-old boys are one-track minded. I should know. I was one once. She could get pregnant.'

I gasped and quickly covered my mouth with my hand. How dare he talk about me like this?

'If you're worried, which clearly you are, you should discuss it with her.'

'It's not that simple.'

'For heaven's sake, you're a doctor. You must have those sorts of conversations all the time.'

'This is different, as well you know. The sensible thing to do would be to forbid her from seeing him.'

I clenched my fists. *You can't do that. And if you do, I'll run away.*

'If you rush in there all heavy-handed it will only lead to trouble. If you're that worried, why not put her on the pill?'

I winced. This was unbearable. How could they possibly know what was best for me? And yet … Martha's defence of me was positive. Wasn't it?

'She's far too young. Don't you go putting any more ideas into her head. I've cast a blind eye to the clothes, the singing lessons, but I honestly don't know what to make of it. Are you being kind, or are you trying to mould her?'

'I'm going to ignore the last remark. Your daughter is growing up without a mother. All I did was help. Amongst other things, the poor girl was in desperate need of a bra.'

My father let out a long, anguished sigh. 'Yes, I know. I was wondering what to do about it.'

'And now you don't have to.'

There was a brief pause, during which I imagined my father staring blindly ahead and Martha taking his hand and giving it a squeeze.

He sighed. 'I'm sorry. That was unfair. It's not easy bringing up a teenage girl alone. And I worry. I try not to but I can't help myself. What if something happened to her, too?'

The conversation had already provoked a raft of emotions – anger, bewilderment, irritation, gratitude – but now I experienced something altogether different, guilt perhaps, or pity. It had never entered my head that my father's overprotection stemmed from fear. That he was terrified he might lose me as well.

'No need to explain. I understand. Really, I do. My world revolves around my boys. I love them just as much as you love Tasha.'

'Oh, Martha, I may be cranky and old-fashioned but, believe me, it's good to have you back in my life.'

'Thank goodness for that. I was beginning to wonder.' Martha's familiar tinkly laugh rang out. They were friends again.

Would my life be easier now? I wasn't sure.

'No, I mean it. I thought I'd never see you again. And when Rory eventually told me what happened after I left, I was devastated.'

My ears pricked up. Something had happened between Martha and my father. I leaned in closer and held my breath, certain I was about to find out.

'It was kind of you to write,' Martha said.

'I wish I'd done more. But by the time I heard, I was married and living down here. And, well …'

'Did you ever …?'

'No, Martha, I didn't. I'm a man of my word.'

'I know, and thank you."

I exhaled quietly. Something had happened between them, but what exactly?

'How are things?'

My father sighed. 'Her depression is getting worse. I'm not sure how much longer I can manage on my own. She needs specialised help.'

Mum? I gasped. Was he saying she should be in hospital?

'I'm so terribly sorry, Donny. It must be awful. If there's anything I can do.'

'It's Natasha I feel sorry for. As you so rightly pointed out, she needs a mother.' My father cleared his throat. 'This is the point when I apologise for my earlier outburst and thank you for filling the void.'

'Shush. There's no need.'

'It's uncanny, but Teddy looks a lot like him, you know,' my father continued. 'I thought it was him when I first met him. Is that why you—'

But my father never completed the sentence because my mother, dressed in the same kaftan she'd worn when Martha last visited, but mercifully minus the turban, decided to make an appearance. Wandering down the stairs, she was waving her arms wildly and remonstrating loudly to my father.

'Gordon! Gordon! Oh, dear Lord. Where are you, Gordon? Why didn't you tell me he was coming?'

Instead of rushing to my mother's aid, I slunk into the dining room, horrified by her crazed appearance and her manic mutterings. Fortunate, because my father, who darted out of the kitchen at the sound of his distressed wife, didn't see me and therefore couldn't have known I'd been eaves-dropping. He didn't notice Charlie, either, who was peering through the third-floor banisters at my mother, as if she was an escapee from a lunatic asylum. It was bad enough having a mother who hid herself away in her room, but making a spec-tacle of herself like this, in front of my friends, was the stuff of nightmares. I shivered and prayed Louis wasn't watching, too.

'I was always such a big fan. You remember, Gordon?' She tugged my father's sleeve. 'It gave me such a shock seeing him standing there at the end of my bed.'

'At the end of your bed?' echoed my father.

'I thought I'd seen a ghost. But he said hello, so I knew he was real.'

'Who? Who did you see at the end of your bed?' He was trying hard to remain calm, but I knew he was rattled. He glanced around for Martha, probably out of some vain hope the sight of her might bring my mother back to her senses but, wisely, she'd chosen to remain in the kitchen.

'You know perfectly well who,' my mother snapped. 'You've just had tea with him. He told me so himself. I asked him for an autograph, but he ran away. Now where on earth has he gone?' Her eyes flitted about, searching for the ghost she'd thought she'd seen.

'Look! There he is.' She smiled, triumphantly, and pointed to Charlie, staring through the banisters at her with a combination of terror and disbelief. 'There's Bo Rivers.'

22

It's another freezing morning, and the sun has yet to rise. Her teeth chattering, Martha switches on the lamp and gets out of bed. Her breath is visible in clouds, and a thin film of ice covers the inside of the attic window. She blows on her hands, marches over to the four-bar electric heater, turns it on and, shivering, cosies up to it. I should move out, she thinks. We should buy a place of our own. It's not as if we can't afford to.

When some semblance of feeling has returned to her limbs, she sprints across the room and ignites the Ascot. She's barely slept a wink, but the chilly air has driven away the fatigue. All night she's tried to make sense of Delilah Moore's sudden reappearance and the accusations she'd hurled at Len. Clearly, she still hasn't forgiven her. But why this concern about Len? She assumes Delilah means he's using her for financial gain. She's lost track of quite how much money she's earning because Len oversees her finances. Sure, he's a bit of a spiv but, like Bo, she thought he had her best interests at heart. Is he creaming off more than he should? *Ignore every last goblet of cherry what comes out of that brandy's north and bleedin' south*, he'd said in the taxi. Was that because he was guilty? It seemed unlikely.

She fills the basin and thrusts her face into the lukewarm water, rubbing her cheeks with her hands. If only she could talk it through with someone. But Becky is at Rory's, and there really isn't anyone else in Mrs Wilson's boarding house she can confide in. If only she'd stayed at Bo's last night. He'd have got back late, but at least she'd have been able to talk it over with him. She might even have slept.

I'll head over there now, she thinks, dabbing her face with a towel.

It's a couple of minutes past eight when she rings the bell of Bo's flat, and a weak sun is rising in a dove-grey sky. She paces the pavement until the door opens. But it's Keith who opens it, not Bo.

'Oh! Hello,' he says.

She takes in his pyjamas and dishevelled hair. 'I'm sorry, I woke you.'

He yawns. ''Bout time I was up. Be late for work if I don't get a move on.'

'Can I come up? I'm sure Bo won't mind if I wake him.'

'No, he wouldn't, if he was here.'

'He's not back?'

'Not yet.'

'Oh!'

'Wanna wait for him?'

'Er …' Martha racks her brains. She thought he'd said he'd go home after the gig. He had, hadn't he? Her life was incredibly hectic. Maybe she hadn't heard him properly. 'No. It's okay. I'll drop by later.'

'Great show by the way.'

'What?'

'Last night. On the box. Blew me away actually.'

She shifts awkwardly. 'Oh! Right. Thank you, Keith.'

'See you later then.' Smiling, he closes the door.

Martha wanders along the street with no clear idea of where she's going. Her first appointment, over at the recording studio in Tin Pan Alley, is not until ten-thirty. At least she thinks it is. Perhaps she should check with Len, in case she's got that wrong, as well. Len would know Bo's plans. He knows everything. For a moment she thinks about dropping by his office. But, with last night's shenanigans still fresh in her mind, he's the last person she wants to see right now.

She traipses through Soho Square in a daze, down Greek Street, past the Gay Hussar, the Pillars of Hercules, and L'Escargot, drawing to a halt outside The Grind. The sign reads CLOSED, but the lights are on. She raps on the door and, pressing her face to the window, peers inside expecting to see Luca setting up for the day. But it's Giovanni's head which pops up from beneath the bar. Seeing her outside, he hurries over and unlocks the door.

'*Ciao, tesoro.*' He hugs her, kisses her on both cheeks, and studies her probingly. 'It is good to see you, but something is wrong.'

She smiles sheepishly. 'Who said anything's wrong?'

'It is twenty past eight. Last night you were on television and, if I remember correctly, recording all day. You must be exhausted and yet here you are. Young, and yet so famous. I fear it is neither easy, nor wise. Come inside, and I will make you the perfect cappuccino.' He leads her through the café to the kitchen where a dark-haired youth of about nineteen is buttering bread. On sight of Martha, his jaw drops and the knife clatters to the floor.

'Ignore Stefano. He is like a mouse in a bell tower.' Giovanni cuffs the youth lightly on the head and mutters something in Italian.

'*Scuse*,' Stefano says and, blushing like a teenage girl, dashes into the shop.

Giovanni shakes his head. 'He is not a bad boy, but one must eat what the convent provides.'

'Has Luca left?'

'*Santo cielo*! No! IIe has an appointmcnt with thc dcntist, but the young girl, Peggy, has gone. Ah, but it is good to see you, *tesoro*. Sofia and I watch you on the television last night, and we cannot believe it is our little Martha. You sing like an Italian, so loud, so strong. We are like the proud parents.'

For the first time today, Martha smiles. The familiar sound of the Gaggia machine springing into life reassures her still further. She is glad she came.

'Now, tell old Giovanni what is wrong. Is the engagement off?'

'The engagement?'

'Last night you were wearing the ring. This morning you are not.'

Martha sighs. She's not sure why she's surprised. With eyes all over his head, Giovanni never misses a thing. The bell above the door signals the first customer of the day. Milton Hyde, perhaps, or one of the other regulars.

'No, it's not off. It's supposed to be a secret.'

'Ah, I see. Mr Bo Rivers wants a full casket and a drunken wife.'

'Flipping 'eck, I hope not.'

Giovanni waves his hand. 'It is an old Italian saying which means … the best of both worlds. In other words, he wants you but he does not want the world to know it.'

She sighs and shakes her head. 'We just want some privacy.'

'So, he has nothing to hide?'

'No, of course not. Why would you say such a thing?'

'Because it is twenty-seven minutes past eight in the morning and you are here.'

Stefano reappears with two cappuccinos. He places the cups on the table and steps back as if afraid to get too close.

Giovanni scrutinises them, his surprise evident. '*Bellissimo*!' he exclaims, and Stefano beams.

'Perhaps I am wrong about him,' Giovanni mutters as the boy leaves the room once again.

'Perhaps he has a good teacher.' Martha takes a sip of coffee.

'How is it, eh?'

'Delicious.'

Giovanni puts his fingers to his lips and blows a kiss.

Smiling, Martha puts down the cup and rests on her arms on the table. 'Something odd happened last night.'

It doesn't take long to tell Giovanni, who listens without interrupting. He leans on his elbows and, nodding to himself, steeples his fingers. 'It is the behaviour of someone who is jealous.'

'She can't still be angry about the night at the Flamingo. It was ages ago. And why she's worried about Len is beyond me. Len thinks she's mad but—'

'Have you ever considered Delilah Moore might be jealous about your relationship with Mister Bo?'

'What do you mean?'

Giovanni shrugs. 'You know.'

'You think they were together? No, he would have said?'

'Would he? You are sure about that?'

'One hundred per cent,' she says crossly.

'Well, maybe it is true. Perhaps Delilah Moore really is mad. It is not so crazy. I have seen her in action. You are drowning in a glass of water. But I would suggest if you are suspicious, you ask Mister Bo. While the dog scratches itself, the hare escapes.'

'You might be right.'

'*Caro bambino*, have you ever known Giovanni to be wrong? Oh, I almost forget. I have something for you.' He walks to the sideboard and picks up a buff Manila envelope, her name written across the front in large capitals. 'This was delivered early this morning. A coincidence, no?' Giovanni drops it onto the table in front of her. 'Well, are you going to open it?'

'Signor Fiori,' Stefano calls from the shop. 'Signor Fiori. A mister De Marco to see you.'

'*Uffa*!' exclaims Giovanni.

Martha winces. She recognises the Maltese name all too well. 'Trouble?'

'I expect he is here to remind me who is the boss,' he says and, grumbling, stomps out of the room.

Martha stares at the envelope and sighs. She receives a lot of correspondence like this, letters and photos from besotted fans, most of which are sent to her via Len's office. Weird, though, this one was hand-delivered here. It's common knowledge she stopped working at The Grind a while back. She tears open the envelope, reaches inside, and pulls out a small slip of paper and a single page from a magazine. She looks at the picture and gasps.

It can't be.

No.

No. This isn't happening.

The room falls away. She thinks she might faint. She

takes a few deep breaths, her heart banging against her ribs, and reads the brief note.

> *I thought you might be interested to see this.*
>   *Pretty good, don't you think?*
>   *L*

She stuffs the picture into the envelope and screws up the paper, just as Giovanni plods back into the room.

He throws up his hands. '*Mamma mia*! Sometimes I do not know which dead saint to pray to. Eh? You okay, *tesoro*? You look like you have just seen one.'

'I have to go, Giovanni.' She springs to her feet and sweeps past him into the shop. From his table in the corner, Milton Hyde glances up from his newspaper and smiles. But she forges ahead without acknowledging him.

Giovanni follows. 'Go where?'

'An appointment.' And without a backward glance, she rushes into the street.

23

Martha sits on a frosty park bench in the winter sun, clutching the envelope and staring blindly at the bronze mermaids curled around the feet of a sea god blowing into a conch shell. She has no idea where she is or how she got here. She should be heading to Tin Pan Alley Studios for the recording session, but she can't seem to summon the enthusiasm. If only Becky was around to give her some advice. She'd be shocked, of course, because she hadn't known. She'd be annoyed, too, hurt Martha had kept it from her. *No more secrets*, she'd said. But she'd understand. She always did. More importantly, she'd know what to do. But Becky is at work, and the only other person she can conceivably talk to is Bo. The thought of admitting she'd posed naked at the age of fifteen makes her shiver. He'd be appalled, might even hate her for it. Not that she conceivably can, because she hasn't a clue where he is.

Why did I do it? she wonders, burying her head in her hands. How could I be so stupid? I've ruined everything.

She starts at a tap on her arm.

'You all right, dearie?'

She flinches, and her head droops lower. The last thing she needs right now is a chat with a fan.

'Sorry, luv. Didn't mean to startle you. I wanted to check you're okay. It's awfully cold to be sitting out here, no matter how pretty the view. Are you all right?'

'Yes, thank you,' Martha mumbles into her hands. She thinks if she remains hidden, the woman will go away.

'Thing is, you don't look too good. How about I take you for a cup of tea. Warm you up if nothing else.'

Her breath hitches. Wiping her tears, she raises her head. The woman's face is lined, her hair grey, her blue irises paled with age. 'No, but thank you.'

'Bad news, eh?' She nods at the envelope and hovers, waiting for a reply. 'How about that tea? I don't like to leave you like this. It's really no trouble.'

Martha tries to force her lips into a smile – the woman has been nothing but kind – but all she can manage is something akin to a grimace. 'I'm fine. Please, don't worry. I'm due somewhere, in fact.' She makes a show of checking her watch and prises herself to her feet. 'I really must get going.'

'All right, but you take care now, dearie.'

'Yes, thank you. I will,' she mutters. 'Goodbye.' Waving stiffly, she hurries down the path out of the park, regaining her bearings as she walks through Chester Gate. She can't talk to Bo or Becky but she needs to talk to someone. She takes a right turn to the Marylebone Road, crosses it, and heads into Fitzrovia, stopping only when the red baroque building of University College Hospital looms into view.

A nurse on her way into work brushes past.

'Excuse me,' Martha says. 'I wonder if you could help?'

The nurse swings around, and her hands fly to her cheeks. 'Oh, my goodness, Martha Palmer. Well, I never.' She inches closer. 'It is you, isn't it?'

Martha's stomach clenches. If only she'd thought to bring her sunglasses. A scarf. 'I'm looking for Don … er, Gordon James. Do you know him?'

The nurse beams. 'Yes, of course. He's been working the night shift, but I'm sure he won't mind if you wake him. I mean, who would? You're Martha Palmer after all.' She screws up her nose. 'I don't suppose I could bother you for your autograph? It would mean the world to me.'

Bracing herself, Martha signs the book the nurse produces from her handbag.

'Ooh. Thank you. My friends will be unbelievably jealous.'

'Gordon's lodgings?' Martha asks. 'Which way?'

'Down there, second door on the right.' The nurse points towards another, smaller building.

Martha glances at her watch. Damn. It's past eleven. She shouldn't be here. She should be in Denmark Street by now. She peers around and spies a telephone box further up the road. She rushes to it and dials Len's office. His secretary, Nora, answers, and Martha explains, in a faltering voice, that she has a headache and won't make it to the recording studio until late this afternoon.

'I told him you were overdoing it,' Nora says. 'Take the day off, duck.'

Martha sits in an armchair, gripping the buff Manila envelope while Gordon, bleary-eyed with sleep, hands her a cup of tea.

He pulls a face. ''Fraid the milk's a bit off.'

She rests the envelope in her lap. White globules are floating on the top, she notices, but she takes a sip anyway. It's warm, and for that she is grateful.

Gordon watches her curiously, head on one side. 'Elizabeth sends her love.'

She frowns. 'Who?'

'My girlfriend. Dark hair. Pretty. Likes jazz. Loves you.'

'Oh! Right.'

'She's fine, Martha. Thanks for asking.'

He's angry with me, she thinks, her teeth chattering.

'You're freezing.' Without waiting for a reply, he lifts the tartan rug off his bed and drapes it around her. 'Better?'

Is it? she wonders.

'So, are you going to tell me what's wrong?'

I shouldn't have come here, she thinks. I should go. But instead of getting up, she draws the rug tight around her shoulders, sinks further into her chair, and closes her eyes.

Gordon crouches beside her and pats her leg. 'What's wrong, Martha? What's happened?'

His voice is gentler now. She can hear the worry in it. 'I…' She shakes her head.

'What's in the envelope?'

'I shouldn't have done it.' Her voice is hoarse, her throat tight. 'Cee Cee told me not to. I promised I wouldn't …'

'Are you in trouble?'

'I needed money. I didn't think … I …'

Gordon leans over and lifts the envelope out of her lap. She doesn't attempt to stop him but watches, wide-eyed, as he slides the contents out.

His eyebrows shoot up, and he whistles. 'Bloody hell. I wasn't expecting that. Is it you?' He glances from her to the photo. 'Wow! Different hair, but yes, most definitely, you. Blimey, I'd never have guessed.'

She jolts. 'You've seen it before?'

'Bound to. Plenty of these floating around med school. Jesus Christ, Martha. It's fairly explicit. Cleverly positioned vase, though. Otherwise … Well!' He whistles again and shakes his head. 'I'm guessing you posed for this. That it was consensual.'

She nods and sinks a little lower. This must be how it feels to drown in shame.

Gordon frowns. 'Right.'

Martha squirms and focuses on the crumpled dressing gown, lying on the floor beside a copy of *Punch* perched on top of a pile of magazines.

'Judging by your reaction, this is the first time you've seen it?'

She nods again.

He flicks back to the cover. 'May 1958. Nineteen months ago. A one-off?'

Her hands fly to her face. 'Jesus. Yes. What do you take me for?'

'Okay, okay. Just trying to get a handle on it. I'd no idea you'd been a pornographic model.'

Martha's skin crawls. Put like that, it sounds so seedy. 'I was behind with the rent. I needed a haircut and an outfit. I wanted to get noticed. As a singer not a … Don't you see? It funded me and now it's going to ruin me.'

'It's not going to ruin you, Martha. Nobody is going to remember a nineteen-month-old photo if they didn't put two and two together at the time. And even if they do, how will they know it's you? Your name isn't credited.'

'Well, somebody has. Why else would they have delivered it to The Grind?'

Gordon strokes his chin. 'Ah, I see.'

'What? What do you see?'

'You're being blackmailed.'

Her heart is thrashing about. She thinks it might pop out of her chest. 'What makes you say that?'

'No note. Anonymous sender. Classic.'

'Actually, there was a note.'

He peers inside the envelope. 'Where?'

She rubs her clammy hands together. 'I threw it away.'

He pulls a face. 'Right.'

'But I remember it said they thought it might interest me and that it was very good. Something along those lines. And it was signed *L*. I wondered if it was Bo's ex-girlfriend. She turned up at his place recently. Maybe she knows about us. I wore my engagement ring on television last night. She might have seen.'

'What's her name?'

'Don't know. Didn't ask.' She bites her lip and stares at her fingernails, resisting the urge to bite them. 'Giovanni thinks he dated Delilah Moore.'

'Her name begins with D.'

'Yeah, I know, but at the Flamingo, Bo referred to her as Lila. She ambushed me again last night outside the theatre. She was crazy mad. Said Len was using me and would get rid of me when he'd got what he wanted. Giovanni is convinced she was referring to Bo. Oh God, I'm so confused.'

'Bo's asked you to marry him. Pyscho Moore probably found out. Clearly, she's insanely jealous of you.'

'Insane enough to send me an out-of-date picture? I hadn't even met Bo when it was taken. And, anyway, where would she have found it? I doubt she reads men's magazines.'

'Hmm. It does seem unlikely. What about the photographer?'

'His name was Stan. Stan Waterfield.' She closes her eyes again and sighs.

'Did you recognise the handwriting?'

Has she seen it before? *Think, Martha. Think.* A memory stirs. She opens her eyes. 'Someone sent a plant when I performed at the Festival Hall. A cactus. The note said *Break a Leg*. It was signed *L*. I thought it might have been from Luca. A joke to put me at my ease. He knew how nervous I was. It wasn't his writing, but sometimes the florist writes the message on the card, don't they? But, it wasn't from him, and I'm pretty sure the handwriting was the same. Whoever wrote it knows who I am.'

Gordon screws up his nose. 'Odd choice of plant. Prickly and unattractive. Exotic, though. An ironic gift, perhaps, like the saying.'

But Martha isn't listening. At the mention of the word exotic, something clicked. 'Loretta.'

'Loretta?'

'Stan's assistant. Luca mentioned she'd dropped by. Perhaps she wanted to give it to me in person but gave up because I was never there.'

'That's it. Bet she thought you'd like a copy. It is pretty good. I imagine Loretta is rather proud of Stan.'

Cheeks blazing, Martha sinks even lower and glowers at her hands.

'Sorry,' Gordon says and quickly slips it back into the envelope. 'Here. Burn it before anyone else sees it.'

A thought enters her mind, invidious and unbidden. 'But what about the other copies?'

'Ah! Collectors' items. Bound to be.'

The bald statement is like a punch to the gut. Martha thinks she might be sick.

'But your name isn't credited, and with a bit of luck, Stan and Loretta have never heard of Martha Palmer the jazz singer.'

'I told them I was Martha Parker, but Loretta knows I worked at The Grind. That's where we met. What if Luca gave her my real name?' Martha cradles her head and moans.

A victim of blackmail, and all because of one stupid mistake. Bo will break off their engagement now, for sure. She can't bear it. She can't. 'Oh God! What if she sends it to the newspapers?'

'The press can't print it. Not without some serious doctoring.'

'It would still be obvious what I'd done.'

'Okay. Okay.' Gordon clicks his fingers. 'Here's what we'll do. We'll talk to Len. Assuming it's not from him.'

Martha jerks upright and opens her mouth, but no sound comes out.

'Sorry. Bad joke. It's not from Len. He wouldn't shoot himself in the foot.'

'You think?' she asks, Delilah's threat reverberating in her ears.

'Definitely. More importantly, he'll have dealt with hundreds of similar scenarios. Damage limitation is part of his job. He'll know what to do.'

Yes. Yes. Of course. Len will sort it out. *Dear Lord, but he'll see me naked.* She grimaces. 'I don't know if I can bear it.'

'It'll be awkward, but not half as embarrassing as being splashed all over the newspapers.'

She covers her mouth with her hand. Put like that, what choice did she have? Bo was always saying Len was the best in the business. Now she was about to find out. Thank God she'd had the foresight to come here. Thank God for Donny. For the first time since she'd received the picture, Martha feels able to breathe.

'Look lively,' he says. 'We'll head over there now.'

She stands and flings her arms around him, burying her face in his chest.

He kisses the top of her head. 'Not so bad in the end, eh?'

'Thank you. I'm sorry for waking you and for involving you in this horrible, sleazy nightmare.'

'Don't be. You know I'd do anything for you.'

She raises her face and kisses him briefly on the lips. Gordon wraps his arms around her and squeezes her tight. His heartbeat seems unnaturally fast. She's wondering if he's really as confident as he's making out when someone knocks on the door.

'I'm sorry, Martha. I'm on call.' Gently, he peels her off him and, smiling reassuringly, opens it. 'Elizabeth. What a lovely surprise.'

'Well?' Elizabeth says. 'Are you going to invite me in?'

'Of course, of course,' Gordon says, hurriedly stepping aside. 'You'll never guess who's dropped by.'

Elizabeth's jaw drops on sight of her. 'Martha Palmer. Good heavens. What on earth are you doing here?'

Martha blushes and shifts from foot to foot. She thinks this is Donny's girlfriend, although she's not entirely sure. 'I … er … I—'

'She's unwell and wanted some advice,' Gordon says and pecks Elizabeth on the cheek.

'Oh, I see,' Elizabeth says, but it's quite clear from her tone she doesn't. Her attention drifts to the envelope, and she frowns.

Martha bites her lip.

'X-rays,' Gordon says.

'Oh dear. Well, I'd better leave you to it.'

'Actually, we were both on our way out. Martha has an appointment, and I'm due back at the hospital, but I'll walk you to the road. Let me grab my coat.' He half closes the door and whispers to Martha as he ushers her out of the room. 'I'll meet you outside Len's office in half an hour.'

Martha mouths her thanks, astonished how easily the lie

slips off his tongue. 'Goodbye, Elizabeth. Lovely to meet you,' she says, and strides down the corridor as confidently as her shaky legs will allow.

Apart from posing for the picture in the first place, watching her manager stare at her naked form is the toughest thing Martha's ever endured. Her toes curling, she grits her teeth and prays for the ordeal to be over. To his credit, Len doesn't bat an eyelid. He doesn't comment either, or ask why she did it, but makes it clear he understands why she doesn't want it getting out. She's astonished when he tells her not to worry, that he'll get hold of the negative and retrieve as many back copies as he can. The plus side, he points out, is that it's uncredited, and as she used an alias, it would take a Martha Palmer aficionado to figure out it was her.

'Oh, and Nora finks you should 'ave tomorrow off as well. Finks I've been workin' you too 'ard. I've cleared it wiv the studio.'

By the time Martha and Gordon leave Len's office, it's dark. Too tired to talk, they walk through the unusually deserted Soho streets in silence. Clustered around the brazier belonging to a man selling roasted chestnuts, a group of people warm their hands. Workers wrapped in thick wool coats, hats, and scarves pass by, too intent on getting home to give them the time of day. Martha barely heeds them. Cee Cee made her promise not to go back to Stan's studio, but she'd gone against her word and done it anyway. And now her past has not only caught up with her, it has tripped her up and slapped her hard across the cheek. Her mother would say she'd brought the whole sorry mess upon herself, and she'd be right. She had. There was no shying away from it. She was the loser here, no one else. She'd been stupid enough to do it.

She'd regret it for the rest of her life, but she had to learn to live with the consequences.

'It'll be all right,' Gordon says as they reach her door.

'And if it gets out?'

'People have short memories. But Len's your man. He'll sort it out.'

'Right.' She wishes she believed him, but if the last twelve hours have taught her anything, it's to expect the unexpected. 'And you won't tell … er …'

'Elizabeth? I promise.'

'Yes, Elizabeth. I'm sorry you had to lie to her, by the way.'

'I know you are. I don't think you should be on your own, though. Do you want me to stay over? Elizabeth won't mind.'

Martha is unconvinced, but she smiles and shakes her head. 'Becky'll be here, and Bo will probably come over.' She winces. She'd forgotten about him.

'You'll tell him, won't you?'

'I don't know.'

'You shouldn't keep secrets from him. You're going to marry the guy.'

'You're going to be keeping a secret from Elizabeth.'

'That's different. It's your secret not mine.'

'Hmm.'

'He loves you, so he'll understand.'

'Ah, but will he forgive me?'

'There's nothing to forgive. You were young. You were poor. You made a mistake. You're sorry.'

She pulls a face. Donny has no idea quite how young she was. Not so Bo. He won't forgive her a second time.

'See you soon.' He bends down and kisses her on the cheek.

'I couldn't have got through this without you. You're a brick, Donny.'

He grins. 'A brick. Wow!'

'Sorry, a life-saver then.'

'Hmm, I seem to remember hearing that before. Might have it engraved on my headstone.' He winks and, blowing her a kiss, sets off down the road. 'Take care, and try not to worry.'

She thrusts the key in the lock, frowning. Donny's right about one thing. Len will sort it out. But he's wrong about Bo. There's no way she can tell him. She closes the door and drags her weary body up the stairs. She's reached the second floor when Becky's stricken face appears over the banister of the floor above.

'Thank God, you're back. Bo came around when you were out. He was in a foul mood.'

'What? Why?' But Becky has disappeared.

He knows, she thinks. No, he can't. It's impossible. What then? Her pulse racing, she hurries up the stairs and runs through the events of last night, racking her brains for something that might have upset him. The only thing that comes to mind is that she'd worn her engagement ring on television. Surely, he'd understand it had slipped her mind. Oh, and Delilah's outburst. But that was hardly her fault. Perhaps something else had happened. Dear Lord, please not. She hasn't the energy for any more drama.

Becky is waiting on the fourth floor. Her cheeks are pale, Martha notices as she catches her breath, and she's holding something.

'I explained you were out, but he dashed upstairs,' Becky says. 'Seconds later, he rushed back down and left without so much as a how's your father. I thought it was odd so I went upstairs and found this pinned on your door. I took it down immediately. Nobody saw it but me. Here.'

Martha can hardly breathe. She takes the all-too-familiar photograph, torn from another magazine, and reads the hastily scribbled note pinned to the corner.

My God, Martha.
  How could you? You were 15!
  I can't trust you anymore. Gone to New York.
  Don't wait for me.
  Bo

24

Tensions at Greystones were on the rise. Not, I hasten to add, because of my mother's extraordinary outburst but because the date of Martha's party was drawing near. The sun continued to shine. The land was parched and, with the rivers and reservoirs drying up, water had become a precious commodity, more valuable than gold. The plants were suffering, the lawn was bald, cracked, and dusty, and the trees were already dropping their leaves. And to Teddy's dismay, the Fairchild's brand-new swimming pool was evaporating to such an extent if he didn't do something and quick, the sides would cave in.

'From now on I want you to scoop out your bath water and transfer it to the pool,' Teddy told the twins.

Charlie pulled a face. 'Ew. Disgusting.'

'We only have two inches,' added Louis. 'It'll be dirty.'

'Not once I've treated it. Here. Two buckets.'

'Must we?' moaned Charlie.

'You want to carry on swimming, don't you?'

No one mentioned my mother's crazed behaviour. Odd, because it had caused much consternation at the time, most notably for Martha who, while my father dealt with my mother, had dragged Charlie into the kitchen, where I'd retreated, and had given him a stern dressing-down.

'What on earth were you playing at?' she'd yelled. 'Why were you in her room?'

'Nat was taking such a long time to find us, I thought I'd pop in and say hello.'

'What an incredibly stupid thing to do. Honestly, Charlie, I despair of you, I really do.'

I was shocked. It was the first time I'd seen Martha lose her temper. I couldn't understand why she cared two hoots about my mother's opinion. Unless she was worried Charlie's behaviour might reflect badly on her.

Charlie jutted out his lower lip. 'I was being polite.'

I was pleased when my father returned and had the good grace to explain away her ramblings as the confused mind of a woman on strong medication, and in the throes of a mental breakdown. This seemed to appease Charlie, Martha, and Louis, who'd popped out of his hiding place in the spare room cupboard to see what all the fuss was about. The crisis over and equanimity restored – although some way off the good mood of earlier – the Fairchilds had bidden us farewell.

Pleased though I was with my father's account, I wasn't sure it was entirely true. I'd overheard too many conversations between him and Martha to dismiss my mother's words as nonsense. She'd been convinced Bo Rivers was standing at the end of her bed. Bo Rivers, the trumpeter who'd discovered Martha Palmer and whose name I'd committed to memory the evening on the beach when Teddy had mentioned him. My mother didn't know Charlie, had never met him, but, clearly, she knew Bo Rivers. There were elements of his father about Charlie – blue eyes, blond hair – and so, putting two and two together as I tossed and turned in bed, I concluded Teddy must look a bit like Bo Rivers, too. My mother may have lost her hold on reality, but there was nothing wrong with her eyesight. She'd been in no doubt whom she'd seen. According to Teddy, Bo Rivers had disappeared before he'd met Martha, and yet, although she'd performed with his band, Martha had no idea where he'd gone. On reflection, considering the influence he'd had on her career, it seemed odd, as did her apparent lack of interest when Teddy had brought him up. Or had it been a ruse, a way of avoiding the subject because she knew exactly where Bo Rivers was and why he'd gone. Which led me back to the all-important question. Was Bo Rivers the missing link in the mystery of Martha's past? Was he the love of her life?

Did she love him still?

This last question I dismissed as impossible. If she was still in love with him, she wouldn't have married Teddy.

So far so logical. But it didn't explain Martha's sudden loss of temper. She was the master of cool, calm collectedness, so it seemed astonishing something as trivial as a case of mistaken identity had caused her to fly off the handle. Unless she'd been concerned about the backlash, the effect the sudden appearance of a stranger in my mother's bedroom would have on her, not to mention the repercussions for my father, and for me.

Of course, it was entirely possible the reason for Martha's outburst was more prosaic. Charlie knew my mother was ill but had gone into her bedroom anyway. Had he intended to alarm her, just for a laugh? It was the kind of prank 'old' Charlie would've pulled but, judging by his obvious remorse, I was inclined to think he was telling the truth and it was idle curiosity which had drawn him there.

And if that wasn't enough food for thought, there was the conversation I'd overheard between Martha and my father to consider, too. He'd been sorry about whatever had happened after he'd left that famous night. Had promised Martha he'd keep it a secret. Was it because he'd been involved? Did it have something to do with the woman I'd overheard them talking about in the treehouse? What was her name? It was on the tip of my tongue. Deborah, Deirdre. I clicked my fingers. Delilah. But who was she? And where did she fit in?

Round and round I went. The more I mulled it over, the more tangled my thoughts became. I longed to broach the subject with my father, but when he wasn't working he was holed up with my mother, only leaving her room to turn out my light. I was old enough not to initiate a conversation at bedtime. He must be worried, not to mention tired, and my questions would only make him cross. Better to wait for a more suitable moment.

A couple of days later, having overslept, I strolled into the kitchen and was surprised to find my father still at the break-fast table. He was reading the newspaper, his face a study in concentration. I sensed an opportunity. But I didn't want to arouse suspicion, so I poured myself some orange juice, buttered a slice of toast, and sat down.

'How is Mum this morning?'

'Fine.'

'No ill effects?'

He pulled the newspaper tight with a snap. 'None.'

'Oh good, because I was worried.'

He eyed me warily over the top of the paper. 'I'm sure you were.'

'Is she getting better?'

'She's not quite there yet. No.' He spoke in the tone he used when a subject was off limits.

Talk about stating the bleeding obvious, I thought, as I glared at the paper barrier he'd erected between us. What about the specialised help he'd told Martha my mother needed? When was he going to tell me about that? These were subjects for another time, however. Adopting an innocent expression, I said, 'Does Charlie look like Bo Rivers?'

My father lowered the newspaper and scrutinised me suspiciously. 'Actually, yes, he does.'

I whistled. 'What are the chances?'

He shrugged and disappeared again.

Somehow, not being able to see his eyes emboldened me. 'Was Martha in love with him?'

'Enough, Natasha.'

'Before she married Teddy, I mean?'

'Wherever it is you think you're going with this, stop now. Bo Rivers disappeared almost seventeen years ago, at least six months before Teddy and Martha got married.' He folded the paper, slapped it on the table, and marched out of the room.

I stared at his departing back, mystified as to what he thought I'd been about to say.

When I went around to Greystones later, I was surprised to hear Martha was in bed.

'One of her heads,' Louis explained.

'Has more than one, does she?' I joked, to disguise my disappointment.

'Ha ha. Very funny,' he said and tickled me until, with tears streaming down my face, I begged him to stop.

Charlie was nowhere to be seen either. Part of me was

relieved. Being mistaken for someone else by a madwoman, and being publicly reprimanded by his mother, must have been humiliating. He might be upset and angry, might take it out on me, if he hadn't already on Louis. I was curious to know how Louis felt about it all but thought better of asking. We talked endlessly about almost anything, but the nitty-gritty stuff – my mum, his mother's past – we steered well clear of. If one of us brought up either subject, the other batted it away. Which explains why, when he asked how my mum was, I simply replied, *same as always*. I didn't bother asking after Charlie, deciding to leave well alone.

Bored of hanging around the house, Louis and I decided to drop in on Mrs Pocock to see if she needed any groceries. It was a while since we had because it was too hot to walk Rafferty, and with his thick coat, we'd all agreed he was probably better off lounging in the shade.

We rang the bell, but when she didn't answer I was worried and said as much.

'She's probably gone out,' Louis said.

'Her hip,' I reminded him.

'Maybe it's better.'

While we were deliberating, Mrs Bracken arrived. She had on a headscarf and was carrying a caddy full of polishes, bleach, and surface cleaners. 'Hello, Natasha dear. How are you? And how's your poor mother? Any improvement?'

The villagers always referred to Mum as my poor mother. I should've got used to it by now, but I hated it. It made her seem more pathetic than she was.

I screwed up my nose. 'Not really, no.'

'Oh dear. How's your father bearing up?'

'Oh, he's fine. You know Dad.' Although I doubted she did. She was his patient, so I suspected most of their conversations revolved around her.

'If you're looking for Edie, I'm afraid I've bad news. She took a turn for the worse and was admitted to hospital.'

A sudden coldness struck my core. 'Oh no. Will she be all right?'

'Let's hope so, eh?' Mrs Bracken patted me on the back. 'I've come to keep an eye on the place while she's there. Do a bit of cleaning, that sort of thing.'

'Where's Rafferty?' I asked.

'He's gone to stay with her niece.' She slotted the key into the lock. 'Having a wonderful time by all accounts.'

I flinched. Why hadn't they thought to ask me? But the answer was obvious. My mother, of course. Everything began and ended with her.

'Barney's at home at a loose end if you want company. Might do you good to have a bit of fun with an *old* friend.' And without acknowledging or uttering a single word to Louis, she strolled inside.

Mouth open, I stared at her departing back.

'Do you want to go and see him, Nat?' Louis asked.

'No, I do not.'

'Barney's all right. It might be fun.'

'She only suggested it because she doesn't want me hanging around with you.'

'You think?'

'I don't think, I—'

Louis was grinning.

I biffed him playfully in the belly. 'I don't know how you can be so calm.'

'Getting angry won't help. And anyway, why would I care what the stupid old bat thinks? Come on, let's take a trip to the building site.'

But the half-built houses were stuffy, the exposed

concrete floors burning hot, so we headed back to Greystones for a swim.

We messed around in the hall-full pool for ages, flopping on and off the slippery lilos like seals, until we grew bored. Martha still hadn't appeared, and with nothing better to do, Louis took a couple of beers from the fridge, some cheese and half a loaf of bread, and suggested we head over to the treehouse. It was hot in there as well. Too hot for rolling around on the bunk. Too hot for kissing. Too hot to eat. So, we opened the beers, put on some music, and talked instead.

'Are you looking forward to the party?' There were only three days to go, and although I was excited, I was nervous, too.

'Are you? You're the one singing.'

'Yes and no.'

'Funny. But I think I know what you mean.'

'Have you and Charlie never sung?' I knew they didn't now, but I found it hard to believe they never had.

'Nope.'

'So, you take after your dad.'

'Crikey, no. Dad's not musical in any way whatsoever. It's more a case of we can't be bothered. Charlie plays the drums, I'm okay on the piano, and we can both play the trumpet.'

'Really? You never said. Wasn't Bo Rivers a trumpet player, too?'

Louis shrugged.

'You must want to know all about him, though, seeing how he discovered your mum. I wonder why he left? Where he went? Weird Charlie looks like him, don't you think?'

Lying on his back, hands behind his head, Louis closed his eyes but said nothing.

'Aren't you a tiny bit curious where he went?' Now I'd

broached the subject, I was determined to find out what Louis thought. 'I mean, he played a big part in Martha's life. And Mum clearly knew him. Why else would she have confused Charlie with him? Come on, Louis. Say something. You must have an opinion.' I prodded him with my foot. 'I've never seen Martha angry. Why was she, Louis? What do you think? Speak to me, Louis? Louis!'

I was kneeling over him now, on the point of shaking an answer out of him.

Louis opened his eyes. 'Charlie's really upset about it.'

I sat back on my heels. 'I bet he is. Mum can be very unsettling. But why do you think Martha reacted like that?'

'You know why. He shouldn't have gone in there.'

'I think there's something else. Something she's not telling us.'

Louis sat up and clasped my arms. 'Shut up, Nat.'

'Don't you—'

But Louis silenced me with a kiss.

I'd agreed a deal with my father at the beginning of the holidays that, if I went out for the day, I'd always be home for the evening meal at eight. If the Fairchilds invited me for supper, I was to let him know by lunchtime. The river of casseroles, lasagnes, and pies the villagers had delivered to our house following Ian's death had long since dried up, and my father had assumed the role of cook. He said he enjoyed it, and I didn't doubt him. Years before Ian died, he'd proved himself a dab hand in the kitchen, whipping up such wonders as chicken Kiev, beef curry, and spaghetti Bolognese. In the past I'd nagged him to allow me to have a go but, this summer, with my days taken up with Louis, I was happy to let him get on with it. The novelty must have worn off, but he continued to take his role seriously, assiduously planning and shopping for each meal. This ate more time out of his already busy schedule, so it was only fair I let him know my plans.

With the balmy weather showing no signs of breaking, he was barbecuing most nights. Greeted by the familiar, smoky aroma of chargrilled chicken as I walked up the drive, the prospect of Dad's tender, succulent kebabs and hickory sauce had me salivating in anticipation. I rushed through to the garden and was surprised to find my mother seated at the table, sipping Pimm's from a tumbler laden with fruit and mint. She had on the pretty black-and-white pinstriped sundress which suited her so well. Her dark hair, now flecked with grey and longer, having not been cut or styled since Ian's death, was washed and pinned neatly back. Even more astonishing was the smile on her pale face. She seemed as near to her old self as I could remember. I glanced at my father. His expression flickered. Was he uneasy?

But he winked at me and said, 'Well, isn't this lovely?'

Was it? I wasn't sure. I tried to assess the dramatic change in her demeanour. If I hadn't been a witness to her depression, the darkened bedroom, and her endless absence, I would never have guessed there'd been anything wrong.

'Have you had a good day, darling?' she asked.

'Yes. Thank you.' I looked to my father again who nodded reassuringly. It was my cue. I was to behave as if nothing out of the ordinary was happening. 'And you?'

'Wonderful.' She picked up the jug of Pimm's and poured another glass.

I smiled, uneasily, as if witness to a miracle I couldn't quite believe. I should have been happy, but there was something disconcerting about her transformation. Was it possible for a person to recover this rapidly from a breakdown? Was it normal? Should she be drinking?

'Here you are.' She handed me a glass.

I hesitated. I wasn't usually offered alcohol at home.

'Go ahead,' Dad said and winked again.

My mother laughed. 'I'm sure she drinks plenty of Pimm's round at Martha's place. Do you, darling? Or does she prefer champagne?'

At the mention of Martha's name, I flinched.

My mother noticed. 'Guilty as charged.'

This isn't happening, I thought. This can't be real.

My father placed a reassuring hand on my shoulder. 'We've been talking about Martha. Your mother knew her, too, you see.'

'Oh!' Although I'd suspected as much, this was news to me.

'She was engaged to be married back then,' my mother continued, breathily. 'December nineteen fifty-nine, wasn't it, darling? Her fiancé was a trumpet player. He had the most startling eyes I'd ever seen, and the blondest hair. A very striking man.'

'Bo Rivers,' I said, intrigued by this latest development.

Her eyes widened. 'Goodness. How on earth did you know?'

I was on the verge of reminding her that she thought she'd seen him yesterday but thought better of it.

She turned to my father. 'Funny they never married. They were so devoted, weren't they? Performing together, living together—'

'You knew Bo Rivers, too?' I couldn't help myself. Finally, I'd found someone who was prepared to talk about him.

'Well, not exactly. I was a fan, had been long before Martha Palmer came on the scene. Before I met your father, in fact.'

My father frowned. 'Darling, I'm sure Natasha isn't the least bit interested.'

It was a warning shot intended for me, but I wasn't going to pass up the opportunity. With a bit of careful questioning, I might even crack the mystery. 'Oh, but I am.' I set my glass on the table and slipped into the chair next to her. 'I'm terribly interested. Why did they split up?'

'No one knew. It happened suddenly. Overnight, it seemed at the time. Rumour had it she'd been seeing someone else and he found out.'

'You don't know that,' my father said. 'It was idle conjecture put around by the tabloids.'

My mother sniffed. 'Yes, well, the upshot was Bo Rivers fled to New York. No, don't look at me like that, Gordon. It's true. He did flee. Such a shame. He became quite successful over there, I gather, which is something, I suppose. Martha Palmer carried on without him, though. The critics always maintained she was the real star so it didn't hurt her career. The Beatles did that, and the Rolling Stones, of course. We saw her perform in the West End in the early sixties but we didn't see her again. At least not until we moved down here.'

'Does Bo Rivers still live in New York?'

My father's eyes bored into me. 'Natasha. Don't worry your mother.'

'Oh, I doubt it.'

I was on the edge of my seat. 'What makes you say that?'

Father cleared his throat. 'Natasha, can you help me with the plates.'

'The boy I saw yesterday.'

'Charlie.'

'Yes, Charlie,' she said. 'He's the spit of his dad. Bo would hardly stay in New York—'

'Darling, I really think you—'

'Well, he wouldn't, Gordon. He'd want to see his son.'

My hand flew to my mouth. It was one thing imagining Martha had a past and secret love, but this was something else. This changed everything. 'No, Mum, you're wrong.' I stood so quickly the chair toppled over.

My mother's right eye flickered. 'Am I? But I distinctly remember you telling me the same thing moments ago.'

I stamped my foot in frustration. 'No, I didn't.' My father reached for my arm, but I dodged out the way. I was angry. I had a point to make. 'Teddy Fairchild is the twins' father.'

'Natasha, please,' he said. 'This isn't helping.'

'Twins?' Mother glanced from me to Dad and back again, her eye twitching rapidly. 'Teddy who?'

'Martha would never have cheated on Bo, or Teddy or anyone,' I continued. 'She's not like that.' She wasn't. The light shone out of Martha Palmer. She was beyond reproach. She was perfect.

At least she had been.

'It's okay, Natasha. Your mother's confused. Teddy bears an uncanny resemblance to Bo Rivers, that's all. Teddy is the boys' father.'

25

I've always wondered whether things would have turned out differently if I'd heeded my father's warnings that evening. There was no doubt I'd provoked my mother into revealing all she knew about Bo Rivers, and that she was innocent in so far as she hadn't intended any harm. How could she when she'd removed herself from reality for so long? She'd never been to Greystones, had never met Teddy Fairchild. In her disturbed mind, Martha Palmer was a figure from her past, a sepia-tinged and carefree time forever lodged in her memory. In those days she was not the mother of a dead child but an eager young woman looking forward to a rose-tinted future with the man she loved and who loved her back. She was to be the wife of a GP. She would live in a large house, in a pretty village. She would start a family. Her life was an unchartered map of infinite possibility.

My father's words and common sense, however, struck a chord. Of course Teddy was the boy's father. Martha married him and not Bo Rivers, who'd gone to America never to return. Instead of storming off, as I'd intended, I sat down again, albeit somewhat subdued. No further mention was made of Martha Palmer and the Fairchilds and, although, clearly agitated by my outburst, not only did my mother's eye relax but she also recovered some, if not all, of her newfound composure, and the remains of our little family enjoyed our first supper together in far too long.

I came down to breakfast with an added spring in my step only to discover my mother remained in bed. My disappointment was crushing. She'd been exhausted by the efforts of last night, my father gently assured me. It was normal, but over the next few weeks he was confident she'd gradually return to her old self. When I arrived home that evening and saw her outside sipping Pimm's, a pattern which was to continue for the next few days, my relief was boundless. She was always pleased to see me and didn't seem in the least bit bothered that my every waking moment was spent with the Fairchilds. Perhaps she didn't know. And if my father hadn't told her, I certainly wasn't going to. Martha had been an incredible substitute, but having my actual mother back in my life, even if she wasn't quite as I remembered her, was the best thing to have happened all summer. The last thing I wanted was to upset the status quo.

The villagers quickly caught wind of my mother's recovery. Although she wasn't up to entertaining her old friends, she'd pop into the waiting room to say hello. Her improved health and the upcoming party at Greystones, to which the entire village had been invited, were the main topics of conversation amongst my father's patients. I'd catch the occasional snippet as I rushed past the waiting room on my way out of the house every morning,

'It's good to see her back on her feet,' said Mrs Jenkins, the pub landlady on a rare visit to the doctor.

'Will she go to the party?' asked Mrs Jones.

'I don't think she'll be up to it,' declared Mrs Fitzwilliam. 'She's awfully frail.'

'Might do her the world of good,' countered Mrs Jenkins.

'I gather Martha Palmer is going to perform,' said Mrs Jones. 'Who'd have thought we'd have a bona fide star living in the village.'

There was no mention of marijuana, no talk of nude swimming or lewd behaviour. Thanks to her all-inclusive invitation, Martha's stock had risen dramatically.

My home life wasn't the only thing to have altered. The atmosphere at Greystones had changed noticeably, too. Martha was increasingly busy with the party – making endless lists, chatting on the phone to the caterers and the flower-arrangers, gardening, and practising her singing – and didn't have much time for me anymore. Charlie, too, seemed different. I wondered whether he was struggling to come to terms with the bizarre case of mistaken identity he'd unwittingly provoked. Or if he'd simply grown tired of playing gooseberry to Louis and me. He didn't say anything, at least not to me, but I saw the effect of whatever was troubling him in his behaviour. He spent long periods of time shut up in his room, was reluctant to join us when we went swimming, and no longer joined in the games we tried, in Martha's absence, to organise. Even Louis was subdued, but I sensed this had a lot to do with Charlie's mood. Didn't twins feel each other's pain? I was pleased, therefore, when, one morning a few days before the party, I arrived at Greystones to find Martha in high spirits, baking bread in the kitchen. The back door was open, and the room glowed with golden-yellow sunlight.

She saw me and smiled. 'You look especially pretty today, Tasha.'

I blushed. 'You always look pretty.'

She laughed her tinkly laugh. 'You should see me first

thing in the morning. Trust me, I'd scare the living daylights out of you.'

I was trying to imagine Martha appearing anything less than perfect, when a shot rang out in the garden, closely followed by a scream. A tight, high-pitched scream. The kind that stops your heart and sets your teeth on edge. The bag of flour Martha was holding slipped from her fingers, and a white cloud billowed around her.

'Oh my God, the twins.' She bolted outside and rushed over to Louis, who was lying prostrate on the ground, clutching his head.

I followed hard on her heels but pulled up sharp and screamed. Bright-red blood seeped through his fingers onto the dried grass. Motionless beside him, his face deathly white, stood Charlie, a smoking pistol in his hand.

26

Martha, who was visibly trembling, knelt beside her bleeding son. Specks of light flashed in front of my eyes. I was going to faint. It was important I didn't. It would only add to the chaos. So, I stabbed my fingernails into my palms and lowered my gaze.

When I looked up, Martha had peeled Louis' hands away and was muttering gentle words of encouragement. Was he breathing? I couldn't see his face. All I could see was blood. So much blood. Bile rose in my throat. I swallowed it down and gulped up air.

'He shouldn't have moved,' Charlie said, his voice cracking. 'The bottle fell off his head, and I shot him instead.'

Bottle? Head? My breath coming in short bursts, I scanned the area. Sure enough, a few feet away, the lopsided neck of a milk bottle sat in a nest of shattered glass.

Martha, who'd showed no signs of having heard Charlie, had switched her attention to me. 'Tasha. Call Donny.'

I stared at her blankly.

'Quick. Call your father.'

I couldn't move. My legs had been rendered useless.

'Charlie! Take Tasha inside. She needs to telephone Doctor James.'

Oh yes, I thought, nodding. He can help. I swept my hand across my forehead and glanced at Charlie, who was walking towards me, gun in hand. I yelped and backed away. I wasn't going anywhere with him. He'd just shot his brother. Chances were he'd shoot me. If only I'd told Martha about the gun in the first place, this wouldn't be happening. Louis was going to die. Me, too, more than likely. Stupid. Stupid. Stupid.

'Give me the gun, Charlie,' Martha said.

I held my breath, but he handed it to her without a word.

'Do as I say, Natasha, please. NOW.'

I trudged after Charlie, trying to control my breathing and my thoughts. Once Dad got here, everything would be okay. All I had to do was phone him. Charlie wasn't going to do anything. He'd caused enough trouble already.

We'd barely stepped a foot inside when Charlie spun around. His cheeks were flushed, his eyes sparkling. 'I'm still in love you with you, Nat. You know that, don't you?'

I reeled backwards and collided with the doorframe, hurting my arm. Charlie took a step closer. I balled my hands into fists and raised them in front of my face. 'Get away from me.'

'I mean it, Nat.' He reached out to touch my cheek, but I dodged out of his reach. 'And I'll wait for you. For however long it takes.'

My scalp prickled, and my teeth were chattering. Why was he telling me this now? He'd just fired a gun at his brother. Did he honestly think I'd fall for his lies again? I didn't trust him. Unless … My breath hitched. 'Is … that why you … shot Louis?'

'What? No, of course not. I wouldn't hurt Louis.'

'Liar!'

'It was an accident.'

'I … I should call the police.'

A shadow passed across his face. 'You should call your dad. I wasn't trying to kill him, Nat. We were playing a game. A stupid game, which went wrong.'

I rubbed absently at my arms. 'A game?'

'Yes, I know. I'm an idiot. But whatever you think of me, please call your father. Please, Nat. Louis needs a doctor.' There were tears in his eyes. He wiped them away, walked over to where the phone hung on the wall, and lifted the receiver. 'Tell me your number, and I'll dial it myself.'

My father, crouched over Louis, was speaking to Martha in a gentle but matter-of-fact manner. 'The bullet missed his head and nicked the fleshy part of his ear, which is why there's so much blood. He'll need stitches but, otherwise, he'll be fine.' He delved into his bag, pulled out a roll of bandage, and smiled encouragingly. 'Natasha, fetch me a glass of water, please.'

I frowned. I couldn't go back inside. Charlie was there, and I wanted to stay a million miles away from him.

'Chop-chop.'

He can't hurt me, I told myself as I rushed into the kitchen. Not with my dad outside. I checked the room, but there was no sign of him. With a bit of luck, he was doing the sensible thing and keeping out of everyone's way. I let out a huge sigh, grabbed a glass from the draining board, and filled it up. By the time I reappeared, Louis was sitting up. His face was pale grey, but he had a clean white bandage wrapped around his head. I handed him the water, and he grinned.

'Natasha was with me the whole time. She was never in any danger,' Martha said.

My father rose to his feet. 'I'm pleased to hear it.' He winked at me, drew me towards him, and kissed the top of my head.

I hugged him back and breathed in his familiar smell.

'What must you think of us, Donny?'

'I'm a doctor. It's not my job to judge.' He let go of me, picked up the gun, and turned it over in his hands. 'Enfield revolver. Standard army issue.'

'It's Teddy's,' Martha said, although he hadn't asked. 'It belonged to his father. He fought in the war.'

I couldn't believe my ears. She'd known about the gun all along.

'I thought he'd locked it away.' She sighed and shook her head.

My father raised his eyebrows.

'It was an accident,' Louis said, struggling to his feet.

I rushed to his aid, linking my arm through his to heave him upright. 'He could've killed you.'

'But he didn't.' My father's voice was firm but kind. 'No harm done. Let's be grateful for that.'

As he handed Martha the gun, I wondered whether he meant it, or if he'd said it for her benefit. After all, this was the second time he'd attended to Louis after an 'accident'. Her face was sheet-white, her hands trembling. Clearly, she'd been as scared as me.

My father wiped a smudge of flour off her cheek and stroked her back five, maybe six times. 'I'll drive you to the hospital. Louis is still bleeding. Best we hurry and get him stitched.'

The following evening we were sitting down to supper, when Teddy Fairchild showed up unannounced with a brown paper parcel. The unexpected sight of Louis' father prompted an unwelcome mental rerun of the terrifying events of yesterday – Louis lying on the grass, a crimson halo circling his head. I lowered my gaze, but one glance at the lamb chops on my plate oozing blood had me quickly looking up again.

'I'm terribly sorry to disturb you,' Teddy said. 'But I felt compelled to come.'

My mother, unused to strangers, glanced nervously at Dad who smiled reassuringly. 'Darling, this is Teddy Fairchild, Martha's husband.'

She eyed him curiously. 'Oh! I see.'

I wondered if what she saw was an uncanny likeness to Bo Rivers, or whether she realised that this man was, indeed, the twins' father.

'My wife, Lizzie.'

'Super,' Teddy said. 'Delighted to meet you, Lizzie. I do so hope we'll be seeing you on Saturday.'

My mother's right eye twitched. 'Saturday?'

Dad hasn't told her, I thought, rubbing my hands down my shorts.

Teddy shifted awkwardly. 'Oh … er … We're having a little do for Martha's fortieth. We'd be delighted if you came.'

My mother's face relaxed into a broad smile. 'Oh, we'd love to, wouldn't we, Gordon?'

I stared at her in amazement. She hadn't been out of the house for so long I'd given up hoping she ever would.

'Splendid. Martha will be thrilled. She was terribly worried about the goings-on the other day. Thought you might never speak to us again.'

I held my breath. My mother didn't know about *that* either.

'Don't be silly,' Mother said. 'The poor boy didn't mean any harm.'

My eyes almost popped out of my head. Dad must have told her. But why was she so composed? I glanced questioningly at Dad who shook his head. My mother didn't know. And then it clicked. She thought Teddy was talking about Charlie's bedside visit.

'No, he didn't,' Teddy said. 'He was playing silly buggers, as usual. It was Louis' idea, apparently. Doesn't surprise me. They will egg each other on. They've been getting into scrapes since they were toddlers.'

And I thought, maybe he's right. Perhaps I'm being unfair on Charlie. With his declaration of love ringing in my ears it had seemed too much of a coincidence. But maybe it was an accident. Martha certainly thought so. And Louis, who'd since tried to convince me that 'shooting the bottle off the head' was a game they often played. My father, too. The twins were pranksters. Hadn't they proved it often enough? Perhaps Charlie wasn't a potential killer. Perhaps my guilt had clouded the issue. I'd cheated on Louis. And willingly. Charlie hadn't made me. Sure, he hadn't given me Louis' letter. He'd just told me he loved me, and I had dived right in.

My mother batted the air with her hand. 'Consider it forgotten.'

Teddy beamed, his bonhomie restored. 'You're very kind, dear lady. Really. Incredibly understanding. Thank you.'

'Boys will be boys.' Taking Teddy by the arm, my father steered him towards the house.

'I've brought the damn thing with me,' Teddy said as they walked away. 'Thought it best if you kept it safe. Out of sight, out of mind, if you catch my drift. And the ... you know ... ammo. What do you say?'

'Wouldn't it be better to get rid of it?'

'Well, it's a family heirloom so…'

My father sighed. 'Okay, I'll do it. For the time being, anyway.'

I glanced nervously at my mother, but she'd showed no signs of having heard. Or if she had she couldn't have realised what the *damn thing* was, or the ammo. All hell would break loose if she knew we were taking possession of a gun.

Instead, she picked up her knife and fork and said, 'What a lovely man. A party. How exciting. I shall look forward to it.'

And I breathed a silent sigh of relief.

The following morning, I accompanied my father to Greystones on the start of his rounds. While he was checking Louis over, Charlie sought me out.

'I was out of order the other day,' he said. 'And I'm sorry.'

'You scared me.'

'I know.'

I bit my lip. 'I'm sorry too. I shouldn't have kissed you.'

Charlie shrugged. 'It's cool. You love Louis. I understand.'

I blushed, embarrassed by his candour and my lingering guilt.

'Don't worry,' he added. 'I won't tell him. I love him, too, remember.'

My conscience at least partially clear, and the twins' accident consigned to memory, I began to look forward to the party in earnest. Greystones was a hive of activity. The continued lack of water had left the lawn dusty and brown, and the withered shrubs and flowers had deprived the garden of colour. Never one to admit defeat, Martha taught us how to make roses, hydrangeas, peonies, and sunflowers out of tissue paper and floral wire. We scattered them among the dying plants and brought the bed to life. The lanterns and fairy lights, which she dug out of the loft, we strung across the patio and in the trees, while Louis and Charlie hammered the flaming torches into the hard ground. When I wasn't busy helping with the decorations, I'd find a quiet spot to rehearse. I'd sung 'Someone to Watch Over Me' so often I was growing bored of it. The lyrics, too, had lost their poignancy. I didn't need to find someone anymore because I had Louis.

On the day of the party, I woke early with a rolling feeling in my stomach. My big day had arrived. Tonight, I was going to perform on the same stage as Martha Palmer in front of a hundred guests. There'd be musicians, singers, and actors. Who knows what opportunities might arise if I impressed. A glamorous life as a singer, perhaps, with my own band.

During one of our practice sessions, Martha had let slip she'd appeared on television several times. She'd been offered a part in a film, too, but had turned it down because she'd been pregnant with the twins. 'I ballooned to the size of a house,' she said. 'So, it was a wise decision.'

'But why did you stop?' It was the question I'd been longing to ask but hadn't dared voice.

'The industry changed, and my kind of music went out of

favour. I didn't want to schlep around the clubs, so I retired. Best decision I ever made. Oh dear. You're disappointed?'

I was. It seemed odd for someone at the height of their fame to simply walk away.

'But I'm making a record with Cee Cee and his Crusaders. A comeback, I hope. So, not quite game over. Ah, a smile. That's better.'

I kicked off the sheet and leapt out of bed. I couldn't wait to get over to Greystones. The party was starting at two in the afternoon and, according to Louis, was bound to go on until the early hours. They usually did, and this one was special.

By the time I arrived at noon, the band were warming up on the small covered stage and Martha and Teddy were rushing around with brooms and buckets, sweeping up leaves and dead insects.

'She looks very young for forty,' I remarked to Louis as Martha breezed past in tight white shorts and a bikini top.

'What does forty look like then?'

I thought of my own mother who, like my father, wouldn't reach that milestone for another two years. Martha's forehead was smooth, but Mum's was lined. There were grey flecks in her hair, and crows' feet crisscrossed the corner of her eyes. I screwed up my nose. 'Old.'

Louis chuckled. 'Good point, Nat. Spot on.'

Cee Cee arrived a few minutes later in an uncharacteristically morose mood. A beaming Teddy intercepted him and whispered something in his ear. Cee Cee nodded, but instead of smiling, as his host continued to do, his expression darkened.

'What's up with Cee Cee?' I asked.

'No idea. Nerves, I guess.'

Charlie sidled over and said hello. He kicked at a loose stone and frowned. Seemed he had a lot on his mind, too. The reason soon became clear. 'Dad tells me your mum is coming.'

'Yes. She is.'

He hesitated. 'How is she?'

'She's much better. No more crazy talk.'

Charlie's face relaxed. 'Oh good. I mean, I'm glad.'

'Yeah. Me, too.'

The kick off fast approaching, my nerves were getting the better of me, which was why, when the doorbell rang and the first guests arrived, I was in the cloakroom by the front door.

Martha screamed with delight. 'Oh, my goodness. Becky. Rory. What a wonderful surprise. It's been how long?'

'Sixteen years, four months, three weeks, and two days,' the woman, Becky, said. 'But who's counting?'

Martha laughed her tinkly laugh. 'I'm so pleased you're here. Dear Teddy. How clever of him. But it's such a long way to come. You must be exhausted.'

'Wouldn't have missed it for the world.'

'And our families are extremely grateful,' added Rory. 'They've been begging us to visit for years.'

'I've a surprise for you, too. Donny's here.'

'Donny? Oh – Oh!! Gordon James!' Rory's voice rose, excitedly. 'How on earth did you manage to track him down?'

'I didn't. He's a neighbour and my doctor.'

Becky snapped her fingers. 'I thought the village sounded familiar.'

'Goodness, how clever of you,' said Martha. 'I'm hopeless with names.'

Rory whistled. 'Haven't seen the old chap for years. Quite made my day, that has.'

'Hello, hello.' Teddy's voice came booming down the

hall. 'Ah ha. Becky and Rory. Splendid, splendid. Good journey? Not too tired? Excellent. Now let me take your bags and I'll show you to your room.'

Teddy's voice growing faint, I was about to unlock the door when the woman, Becky, spoke.

'Congratulations on your fortieth by the way. Funny, I had it down as your thirty-fourth.'

Martha giggled. 'Shush. Teddy might hear.'

'But surely you've told him … No? But he must have seen it on the marriage certificate.'

'Ah! Well.' There was a pause. 'We're not actually married.'

I stuck my fist in my mouth to stop myself crying out. Not married?

'But you told me the date? I sent flowers. What on earth happened?'

'I was late. Missed our slot at the registry office.'

'Late? Why? What were you doing?'

'I lost track of time.'

'On your wedding day? Honestly, Martha, do you have any idea how ludicrous that sounds? Poor Teddy. He must have been distraught.'

I imagined Teddy pacing the pavement outside the Town Hall as he waited for his beautiful bride, wondering whether she'd turn up.

'Actually, he was remarkably calm. The wonderful thing about Teddy is he takes everything in his stride.'

'Sounds like a saint. But, Martha, why were you late? What is it you're not telling me?'

Another pause.

'Did you ever intend marrying him?' Becky asked.

'Yes. No. I don't know.'

I clasped my cheeks in my hands. This was news indeed.

'And what about the twins, Teddy's parents, do they know?'

'Nope. Nobody does, apart from you. Oh, and Teddy of course.'

'And your age? Why continue the charade?'

'We'll talk about it later but, for now, come on in and have some champagne.'

It struck me, as I wandered into the garden to find Louis, that Martha Palmer was the keeper of a great many secrets. First, there was the mystery surrounding her fiancé's disappearance, Bo Rivers, who might also be the love of her life and who may or may not live in New York. Her true age, six years younger than she claimed. Her pretence at marriage. Why had she missed her own wedding? Why not marry Teddy at a later date? It was mind-boggling. None of it made any sense.

I flopped onto the bank beyond the patio. Almost immediately the band struck up the opening bars of 'Goodbye Pork Pie Hat'. The party had begun. It wasn't long now until I'd take to the stage and sing. But instead of excitement, or nerves, I had the unshakeable sense that something was off. I couldn't put my finger on it, only that the day wasn't panning out quite as I'd hoped. Had the conversation I'd overheard stripped the gloss off? Perhaps I'd feel better if I spoke to Louis about it. Trouble was, Martha was one of our off-limits subjects. And anyway, now wasn't the time to go telling tales. He was bound to be shocked. I'd talk it through with my father later. Since my mother's recovery, he was far more approachable. Chances were there was a simple explanation.

'There you are,' said Louis, running over. 'I've been

looking for you everywhere. Oh, Nat, what have you done to your arm?'

I'd forgotten all about the big black bruise, a lingering reminder of my confrontation with Charlie. I bit my lip and covered it with my hand. 'Walked into a door.'

'Bit careless, but that's nerves, I s'pose. Thought you were having second thoughts. You're not, are you?'

I smiled sheepishly. 'Of course not.'

'Fab,' he said and hugged me. 'Have you told your mum yet?'

'No, I want to surprise her. Is she here?' I glanced about and saw her, standing alone on the periphery. She had on a pretty shade of lipstick and a stylish floral dress, but was shifting her weight from foot to foot as if she didn't know what to do with herself. Even from this distance I could see her right eye was twitching. It didn't bode well. I scanned the guests for Dad, but I couldn't see him anywhere.

'Don't you think you should?'

I frowned. 'She's not mad.'

'I know.' He laced his fingers in mine. 'Come on. Let's go and say hello.'

I shook my head. 'Think I'll wait until after I've sung.'

I peered at Mum again. Still hovering on the fringes, she was staring ahead as if in a trance. I followed the line of her unfaltering gaze to my father, chatting animatedly to Martha and a man and woman I didn't recognise. Becky and Rory perhaps? Dad had his hand on the small of Martha's back and was laughing right from the belly. He was happy and relaxed, as he always was when he was with her, and all of a sudden it occurred to me that, even though *he* wasn't the love of Martha's life, *she* might well be the love of his.

The band stopped playing. Teddy picked up the mic. 'Cee

Cee Campbell and his Crusaders, ladies and gentlemen.' The guests cheered and clapped, but Teddy held up his hand and called for hush. 'It's wonderful so many of you have joined us here today to celebrate my beautiful wife's fortieth birthday.'

I counted the lies. One. Two.

'Darling, you don't look a day over thirty.'

There was a general murmur of agreement, and somebody wolf-whistled.

'You have brought me such joy and happiness over the years. Truly, I am the luckiest man alive.'

As the guests barracked and applauded, it occurred to me this magnificent woman, who attracted so much admiration and attention, and who'd given him this wonderful life, was enough for Teddy. Nothing else mattered to him, not her past, her age, or the lack of some silly piece of paper, because she was his and his alone.

'So, without further ado, ladies and gentlemen, I give you Miss Martha Palmer.'

Cee Cee Campbell's Crusaders struck up the opening bars of 'That Ole Devil Called Love'. Teddy beamed and passed the mic to Martha who kissed him on the cheek. It was plain for all to see that he adored her. Mulling things over in the weeks that followed, I thought it was because he did, and because he treated her like a goddess, that Martha, in her own way, adored him, too. I turned to Louis, curious to see what he made of it all, but he rolled his eyes as if to say he'd seen it all a thousand times.

The song nearing its end, my nerves kicked in. Only one more until my big moment. But wait, Teddy was back on the stage and holding the mic again.

'Now, darling, I know you're supposed to sing 'Mad About the Boy'. A favourite of mine, I hasten to add.' More laughter, more cheers. 'But I've organised a little surprise.' He turned to Cee Cee. 'Everything ready?'

Cee Cee nodded. He was frowning, his shoulders stooped. Was he unwell?

'Martha, it's been almost seventeen years since you last performed together, but to celebrate your fortieth birthday in style, a very special person has flown all the way from New York to be with you here, today. I give you MISTER BO RIVERS.' Elongating the last three words, Teddy stepped back, applauding triumphantly.

Louis and I, and several other guests, gasped, others cheered, while those who had no knowledge of Martha's history exchanged bemused looks. Sensing something was horribly wrong, I glanced at Martha. Her hand was over her mouth. Her cheeks drained of colour. A reaction totally at odds with her husband, who was preening and smiling as if he'd won the pools.

But when a tall, handsome man in his mid-to-late forties (it was hard to tell), walked onto the stage, trumpet in hand, Teddy's mouth dropped open, and he shuddered, a visible tremor coursing through his body. There was a collective intake of breath. Someone screamed, short and sharp, and the guests fell silent. Louis let go of my hand and started clawing at his cheeks. Blinking rapidly, I scanned the crowd for my parents. I couldn't see Dad, but my mother, still standing alone, was nodding emphatically, a knowing smile on her parted lips.

27

June 1960

Martha is in bed listening to Dave Brubeck's 'Time Out'. It's her favourite record from last year. She loves the extra little beat added to the normal 4/4 time. It's a brilliant piece of innovation. She's hoping it'll calm her. She's restless, unable to sleep. Tomorrow she is marrying Teddy Fairchild, a man she met three months ago and who bears an uncanny resemblance to the man she loves. But unlike Bo Rivers, who is noble and principled, Teddy, much like his name, is a lovable, big-hearted bear of a man. She's in no doubt he loves her. She can see it in his eyes, the way he looks at her as if she's the loveliest, most precious thing he has ever seen. He has placed her firmly at the centre of his world, would do anything for her. Her life with him will be without drama. He is as honest as the day is long. He will keep her safe. He will keep her secure. Tomorrow, when they sign the register, he will find out she is not, as she has told him, twenty-three, but only seventeen. He will ask her why she lied to him about her age and she will explain she had to for professional reasons. She will not tell him about the photograph. There is no need. Nothing more has come of it, and isn't likely to. True to his word, Len extracted the negatives from Stan – she has no idea how, she'd been too afraid to ask – and gave them to her. She'd burned the celluloid strips over a candle in her room, the perforated plastic curling at the edges as it melted in the flames. Heaven forbid another copy comes to light. If it does, she is certain Teddy will understand. He will forgive her anything. She hasn't told Teddy she was once engaged to Bo Rivers. They have not met, nor are they likely to. Bo Rivers left six months ago and, with each passing day, all hope he'll return. She has licked her wounds and is getting on with her life. She thinks she will be happy with Teddy. She is marrying him because she loves him. She's not *in* love with him. Not yet anyway. But she's sure she will be before too long.

She glances at the clock on the bedside table. A quarter past eleven. Becky advised an early night – she'd done the same before she married Rory apparently. Beauty sleep, she called it. She wishes Becky was here to be her bridesmaid as she had been for her. But Becky and Rory are living in Australia now, and it's too far for them to come.

Without her best friend by her side, she'd decided against a church wedding. Hadn't wanted much of a celebration at all. If Teddy was disappointed, he hadn't shown it. The registry office was his suggestion. His only stipulation concerned her dress. It didn't have to be long or particularly bridal. Simply white. According to Teddy, she looks particularly gorgeous in white. She wonders whether he thinks she is a virgin. They haven't slept together yet. Tomorrow will be the first time. She shivers. What if the sex isn't as good as it was with Bo?

I'll make tea, she thinks. That'll calm me.

She leaps out of bed and heads downstairs to the kitchen. She turns on the light, picks up the kettle, fills it with water, and places it on the stove. 'My stove,' she says, striking a match. 'My kitchen, my house.' She says this most days because she still can't believe the small terraced house is hers. She and Bo had thought about buying it and, after he'd left and with Giovanni's help, she'd gone ahead and bought it anyway.

'You have enough money. Why not?' he said. 'You would have to have crickets in the head to go on living in Mrs Wilson's lodgings.'

I should have invited Giovanni, she thinks, as she takes the milk from the fridge. He'd have given me away.

Giovanni, Cee Cee, Becky, and Rory are the only people who know she's getting married. She hasn't told her parents or her brothers. She'd have told Luca, but he's in Italy visiting family. She'd have told Donny, too, but since the incident with the photograph, he'd written to tell her he couldn't see her anymore. His girlfriend – what's-her-name – had been upset finding them together. He'd gone on to say he'd miss her terribly and wished her well in her marriage to Bo. He would know what had happened now. The whole world knew. It had been in the papers, quite the scandal, according to the *Mail* who claimed she'd left Bo for another man. Pure fiction, but at least the truth behind the breakup hasn't come to light. In her last letter, Becky mentioned Donny was married and had moved south, somewhere near the coast, to start up a GP practice. He was doing well.

The whistling kettle rouses her from her thoughts. She picks it up, but a loud knock on the front door startles her, and she almost drops it. The thumping continues, emphatic, urgent. She wonders if it's Teddy having second thoughts. Or perhaps he's been in an accident. She rushes into the hall, her pulse racing.

'Who is it?'

'Me.'

She reels backwards as if electrocuted. 'Bo?'

'Yes. Me. Bo. Are you going to let me in?'

She opens the door, not daring to believe it. But there he is, the man of so many of her dreams. Her knees go weak. With shock or desire? She isn't sure.

'Sorry! I know it's late but I had to come.'

Three months too late, she thinks, frowning. Impeccable timing as ever.

He fumbles in his jacket pockets. 'You're getting married today. Cee Cee told me.'

'I am?' She glances at the thin gold watch on her wrist, a gift from Teddy. It's five past midnight. 'I am.'

He winces. 'Can I come in?'

She leans on the console table to steady herself as, without waiting for an answer, he enters the house and closes the door.

'Please don't,' he says.

She frowns. She knows what's coming. She can feel it, a growing tension in the air around her.

'I love you, Martha.'

He moves closer, but she folds her arms, as if to protect herself. 'You left without giving me the chance to explain.'

Bo flinches. 'I was hurt. Shocked. But I've thought about it, and I was wrong not to trust you. You were young. You didn't know what you were doing.'

'Yes, I was, and yes, you were. I didn't lie to you. I just didn't tell you. There's a difference. I feared losing you but I wanted to protect you. I knew the pictures would upset you. They upset me. Not a day passes when I don't regret posing naked for sleazy Stan Waterfield. But I needed the money. And if you think that's dishonest, what about you? You kept something from me, too. Who was she?'

Bo raises his chin from his chest and cocks his head. 'She?'

'Your lover. The one before me.'

He shrugs. 'Lila. Lila Moore.'

Martha gasps and raises her hands to her cheeks.

'Jesus, Martha, I thought you knew. I thought everyone did. It wasn't a secret. She was nuts. A lunatic. An addict. Thought because she looked a bit like Billie Holiday she had to act like her or something. She used to fall over and bruise herself but couldn't remember and would accuse me of hitting her. She was high on something the night she was supposed to perform at the Flamingo. It was the last straw. I couldn't deal with it, so I called off the relationship. She took it very badly, which is why she refused to show up.'

Suddenly it all makes sense. Somebody had been with him the evening she'd called him from the phone box all those months ago. Delilah. It's why he'd rung off so abruptly. He hadn't wanted Delilah to hear. And the knickers. Delilah's. No wonder she was pissed off with Martha. She hadn't just stood in for her on stage. She'd snagged her boyfriend, too. A succession of images flash in front of Martha's eyes: Delilah Moore calling her a bitch and hitting her in The Grind; a woman laying into him after the gig at the Festival Hall; Bo's ex-girlfriend turning up at the flat and upsetting him; the evening outside the television studio when Delilah Moore had ranted incoherently. *He's using you*, she'd said. *Once he's got what he wants he'll get rid of you. By force if he has to. It's what he does.* She'd been talking about Bo not Len. Well, she'd been right about that. Bo had left.

'She was angry you stepped in for her at the Flamingo, but when she found out I was seeing you she hounded me. Kept telling me I'd made a mistake. Called you a whore. Crazy stuff.'

The penny drops with a loud clang. *It was Delilah who blackmailed me.* 'She sent you the photo, didn't she?'

'I'm sure she did.'

'Didn't you recognise the handwriting?'

'Handwriting?'

'On the note.'

'There wasn't one. Just a blank envelope.'

She tilts her head. 'How can you be sure it was her?'

'It's the type of mean, spiteful thing she'd do.'

'And yet you fell for it, hook, line, and sinker.'

'Yeah.'

She screws up her nose. 'But how did she find it? And how did she work out it was me? It doesn't make sense.'

'I've no idea but, Martha, do we have to talk about her? I'm here because I love you. Only, you're about to marry another man. I've been an idiot. Please forgive me. I beg you. There's no one else. There never will be. I love you and only you.'

These last few months, as she struggled to recover from the shock of Bo's harsh words and his abrupt departure, Martha has lain in bed, night after lonely night, dreaming of their time together, wishing she hadn't made such a mess of things, hating herself that she had, praying for the chance to share her life with him as she'd always hoped she would. Theirs had been an abbreviated affair. Her love cut short. She wanted more. Now here he is, the man of her dreams.

The love of her life.

'You broke my heart.'

'Can I at least try and mend it?' A tear rolls down his face.

Her breath catches. She reaches out and wipes it away. He clasps her wrist, draws her close, and kisses her. She gasps and kisses him back. Her body floods with heat as he steers her across the hallway and pins her against the wall. She feels the plaster, cool on her back as he unbuttons his jeans. She knows she should tell him to stop but she can't. All the breath is gone from her lungs. And as he lifts her, she wraps her legs around his waist. His warmth inside her, she moans and closes her eyes.

Martha wakes at twelve, her head on Bo's chest. For a split second she is disoriented. But then it hits her. She should be at the registry office saying her vows. She glances at Bo, deep in sleep. He's flown all the way from America to stop her from marrying Teddy. He wants her to marry him instead. He loves her. She loves him.

Life, though, is rarely that simple. Bo sets the bar so high, what if she can't live up to his expectations? What if they fight? She couldn't bear it if he walked out on her a second time, a third.

They'd made love all night. In between times, she'd bombarded him with questions, and he'd answered every single one. His mother was Swedish, his father Scottish. They'd divorced when he was ten. His mother had gone back to Malmö, and his father had brought him and his elder brother up alone. They'd lived in Surrey. His father died of lung cancer six years ago. His brother lived in California. He'd had three girlfriends before her.

'Did you fall in love with them?' she'd asked.

'The only person I've ever fallen in love with is you. I loved you the moment I set eyes on you. I will always love you.'

She flicks away the tear trickling down her cheek. She wants to believe him, she really does. But she doubts he loves her as much as Teddy does. Could anyone love her as much? She'll be safe with Teddy. She can be herself. No more Delilah to worry about. No more heartache, no more confusion.

She slides out of bed and takes the dress, hanging on the door, into the bathroom. She slips it on and peers at herself in the mirror. Teddy's right, white does suit her. She wipes her eyes, puts on her makeup, and brushes her hair. That will do, she whispers to her reflection.

Quietly, so as not to wake Bo, she tiptoes out of the bathroom and down the stairs. At the door, she glances at her wristwatch. By the time she reaches the Town Hall she'll be well over an hour late, but Teddy will be waiting. Of this she is certain. She closes the door with a sigh and, head held high, walks away from her turbulent past towards a peaceful future.

Later, once she and Teddy have agreed there's no real need to get married, they make love for the first time, but without the passion she shared with Bo. She's not surprised. She expected it somehow. What does it matter anyway? There is no room in her life for regret. The past is her secret. She has made her choice. She will live her life to the best of her ability. She will be happy.

28

An eerie hush descended, so quiet I was sure everyone could hear my heart thudding against my ribs. The guests, including Bo Rivers, were staring at Martha, who'd frozen rigid.

'Was it something I said?' Bo was smiling, which was odd, under the circumstances.

Martha didn't move, not even a flicker.

His smile wavering, Bo tore his eyes from Martha and threw a questioning look at Cee Cee. But the saxophonist shook his head and stared glumly at his shoes. It seemed to me he'd anticipated this scenario, so why on earth hadn't he tried to prevent it?

'Shit!' said Louis, recovering his senses. 'I need to find Charlie.'

'I'll come with you.'

'No, Nat. Don't.' And with that, he sprinted off towards the house.

The guests muttered and gathered up their things, the chatter increasing in volume the more of them realised the party was over. I glanced around, fretfully. This wasn't meant to happen. They mustn't leave. To go now was akin to betrayal. I wanted to scream at them to stay. Didn't they know? This was to be my big moment. I was going to sing. I opened my mouth, but the only thing to come out was a whimper.

'I am afraid this last drop has caused the vase to over-flow,' said the man standing next to me. He had a genial face and a bushy moustache and was shaking his head.

I clutched his arm. 'Please don't go.'

'*Signorina*, the party *è finite*. We must all go home.'

'But I was going to sing.'

He smiled indulgently. 'Ah! Martha's *piccolo prodigio. Mio caro*, from the hand to the mouth the soup is often lost. Another time, I think.'

I had no idea what he was talking about. Tears of frustration welling in my eyes, I clenched my fists. 'But I've been—'

He put a finger to his lips and shook his head.

I spun back to the stage. Bo Rivers was deep in conversation with my father, but there was no sign of Martha and Teddy, or Cee Cee and his band. Around me the guests were trooping towards their cars. All except my mother who, like a boulder standing firm against the current, stood spellbound, her attention zoomed in on Teddy, who was talking to his boys on the far side of the pool. Were they his boys? I wasn't sure anymore.

I curled my arms over my head and groaned. I was drowning in questions. It dawned on me then, that the person with all the answers was Martha. I dashed across the patio, through the French windows, but pulled up sharp. Martha and Cee Cee were sitting on a sofa, talking. I ducked behind an armchair, close enough when I peered around it, to see Cee Cee's initials embroidered on the corner of the white handkerchief he handed her.

'He came back, den,' Cee Cee said.

I held my breath.

Martha sighed. 'The night before my wedding. He begged me not to go through with it.'

'Is dat why you were late for di ceremony? Sweet Jesus. And Teddy didn't suspect a ting?'

'Nothing. But he wouldn't, would he? He's not the suspicious type.'

'Mi bredrin worshipped you. Why Teddy, though? He's a good guy, but ...'

'I thought I'd be happier with him.'

'And are you?'

'He loves me warts and all, and yes, I have ... I mean I *had* ... a good life.'

Cee Cee sucked his teeth. 'I would never have agreed to it if I'd known Teddy hadn't even seen a photo. Or if I'd known he'd come back to see you. We must have had a hundred conversations over the years, but he never once mentioned it. Neither did you.'

'Bo keeps things close to his chest, and Teddy lives in the present. And as for me, I only wish I had.'

'Yeah, mon. Me, too. Would have saved you a whole lotta trouble.'

At last, I had the definitive answer to the question that had bugged me all summer. Bo Rivers was the mystery man. The love of Martha's life. The twins' father, too. Was she still in love with him? Had she been all this time? My chest tightening, I sat back on my heels and wrapped my arms around myself.

'When did you first realise Bo was—?'

'Natasha!' My father's shout, which had me jumping out of my skin, brought an abrupt end to Cee Cee's question. 'What the hell are you doing?'

Cheeks aflame, I crept out of my hiding place. Martha's glare burning a hole in my back, I focused on my father. 'Nothing.'

'Come on. It's time we left.'

There was no way out of it. So, off I traipsed, my tail between my legs and my song unsung.

The next few days I was the loneliest I'd been since Ian died. I didn't hear a word from Martha. Why would I? She had far bigger problems of her own. My father was, once again, preoccupied with his patients, and my mother was back in her room. Lights off, curtains drawn, she hid herself away like a deserter fleeing a war.

The following night, desperate for information, I parked myself on the bottom stair, opposite my father's study, and waited, determined not to budge until I'd spoken to him. It wasn't until midnight that he finally emerged. He jumped when he saw me and placed his hand to his heart.

'Good grief, Natasha. Why aren't you in bed?'

I frowned. Wasn't it obvious? 'I want to talk to you about Martha.'

He sighed. 'It's late, Natasha, and I'm tired.'

Oh no. He wasn't going to fob me off. Not this time. I sprang up and stamped my foot. 'I don't care. I'm not moving until you've told me what's going on. Please, Dad. I'm worried.'

He released a drawn-out sigh. 'It's complicated.'

'I know, but please try because, in case you've forgotten, Louis is my boyfriend.' Even as I said it I realised how pathetic I sounded. So, I was surprised when my father put a protective arm around me and eased me back onto the stair.

'I know,' he said.

I listened, enthralled, as he revealed snippets about his younger days. How he'd met Martha after one of her early concerts, while he was at med school. How he'd had a ring-side seat to her career, watching her bloom into a successful singer. How beautiful she was. How magnificent. Her engagement to Bo Rivers which they'd tried to keep private. But something had happened to make Bo break it off. Here, my father stalled.

'What?' I prompted.

He took a deep breath. 'An unpleasant photograph came to light.'

It was the first I'd heard about a photograph. I opened my mouth to speak, but my father beat me to it.

'That's all you need to know.'

'Did it ruin her?'

'No. Thankfully, the newspapers didn't get hold of it. But Bo was sufficiently upset to move to New York. His leaving was tough on Martha. She was dealing with a broken heart, and with Bo no longer on the scene, it didn't take long for the journalists to find out they'd been engaged, and Bo had called it off. One newspaper insinuated Martha had been unfaithful, but no name ever came to light. I don't know how, but she soldiered on.'

It struck me then, that although there was plenty I didn't know about Martha, there were details I knew which my father didn't.

'She saw Bo Rivers the night before her wedding,' I said.

His mouth fell open. 'How on earth do you know that?'

He'd caught me spying, but I didn't want to admit to eavesdropping so I shrugged. 'He's the twins' father. Not Teddy.'

He sighed with relief, perhaps because, on top of everything, he wasn't going to have to explain the process of reproduction. 'It looks that way but, Natasha, we have no proof, so I don't want you to go chatting about this with anyone. Do you understand?'

Even as he uttered the words, the irony wasn't lost on me. His patients, the source of so much gossip over the years, were bound to.

Eager to hear what they had to say, I hung around outside the waiting room the following morning. Judging by the fragments of conversation I caught, it was a subject they clearly relished discussing.

'It's slutty behaviour like this that gives musicians a bad name,' said Mrs Fitzwilliam whom, it transpired, was a budding pianist.

'It's not exclusive to musicians,' said Sarah Salt, the primary school teacher. 'Politicians are equally depraved.'

'And vicars,' Mrs Anderson, the postmistress, added.

'Vicars? Don't be daft,' retorted Mrs Fitzwilliam. 'God wouldn't allow it.'

Sarah Salt sniggered. 'That's rather a naïve view.'

'Oh dear,' said Mrs Fitzwilliam. 'I don't think Reverend Josephs would be best pleased to hear it.'

'Reverend Josephs isn't here, Marjorie,' muttered Mrs Anderson.

'I heard they put the house on the market,' said Mrs

Fitzwilliam.

Mrs Anderson sniffed. 'Just as well, if you ask me. Poor man probably can't wait to get away.'

'He'll leave her,' declared Mrs Fitzwilliam.

'I'd have thought so.'

Sarah Salt sighed. 'It's the children I feel sorry for.'

There was a general cooing of agreement.

'Is *he* still around, Marjorie?' asked Mrs Anderson.

'No idea.'

'I heard he hotfooted it to London with the coloured gentleman,' said Mrs Fitzwilliam.

'Good riddance to the pair of them, I say.'

'Hear, hear.'

'The cheek of the man, turning up out of the blue like that,' blurted Mrs Anderson. 'Talk about making an entrance. Hello, you don't know me, but I'm your father.'

'Actually, I don't think he knew either,' said Sarah Salt.

'Good heavens. Really?'

'That's what I heard.'

When I wasn't hanging around the house, waiting for the phone to ring or the post to arrive, I sat on the swing my father had built for me when I was five. It was cooler beneath the branches of the gnarled apple tree, and peaceful. I spent hours there, thinking about Martha. The woman I thought I knew and the woman she'd turned out to be. The sheen of perfection surrounding her had dulled. Considering what she'd had to conceal, it must have taken a great deal of effort to maintain the shine. In her attempt to be all things to all people, she'd become the keeper of a great many secrets. I couldn't bring myself to call her a liar. The word had too many derogatory connotations. She was too kind, too generous with her time and talent, to be labelled selfish or a fraud. But she wasn't honest either. She'd dodged the truth; had allowed people, myself included, to believe what they liked about her. Time and time again she'd seen how happy this made us, how preferable our imagined perception of her was to the truth. She had tried to do the impossible. She had tried to live up to every single one of our expectations. For a while, she'd succeeded. But, in the end, she had failed spectacularly. Had I been older and wiser, as I am now, I would have told her that just as there will always be people who love, respect, and admire you, there will also be plenty of people who don't. Some will be jealous, others will disapprove, or feel threatened, because, no matter how hard you try, you can't please everyone. No one is beyond reproach. That's the reality of being human.

Over the next few days, as the weather turned humid and sleeping became increasingly difficult, I spent the nights trawling my secret copies of *Jackie* for advice about what to do when your boyfriend discovers his father isn't who he thought it was. But of course, there wasn't any. The subject was too niche. Exhausted by my efforts, I turned to the five Davids. What dark truths lay hidden behind their obliging smiles? Were their reputations as shiny and bright as their pearly-white teeth? Was I being foolish to invest so much faith in them?

By the time the early morning light streamed through the windows, I was even more fractious and upset. Hanging around was getting me nowhere. I had to do something. But the only scheme I came up with was to sit on the wall and wait.

It took me an age to find my flip-flops, which I eventually remembered I'd left on the doormat. An envelope was lying next to them. A prescription request from one of the neighbours most likely. I picked it up and was about to toss it on the hall table when I noticed it was addressed to me. What's more, I recognised Louis' handwriting. I tore it open, squealing.

Dear Nat,

I miss you like mad. It's awful at home. Everyone is sad and angry all the time. Please meet me at the treehouse this evening at 7. Come the back route, via The Laurels. But don't get caught. The new tenants are really mean.

I love you.

Louis xxx

'I love you, too,' I whispered and kissed the letter, once, twice, three times. Pressing it to my heart, I smiled for the first time in ages and tried to imagine what idiotic thing he and Charlie had done to upset their new neighbours. Not that I cared. Louis loved me, that's all that mattered. And I was going to see him. Today. Now all I had to do was devise a plan to reach the treehouse without being spotted by the tenants or arousing my father's suspicions. Still, I had all day to think of one and, actually, it was really rather thrilling.

I was still on the swing at six-thirty, trying to work out how to give my father the slip, when he rushed outside.

'I'm sorry, Natasha, but I've been called out. I've taken your mother up her tray, so help yourself to supper when you're hungry.'

It wasn't unusual. My father was often called out to his

patients, but up until then I couldn't remember ever having been this pleased about it.

'Okay, Dad,' I said, trying to keep the excitement out of my voice.

I waited until the car engine fired and rushed inside in time to see him pulling out of the drive. I hung on for five more minutes, in case he'd forgotten something, and quietly, so as not to alert my mother, crept out of the house. The hole in the hedge had almost, but not quite, grown over. I peered at the Taylor's house. Not a single light was on. The tenants were out for the evening. I clapped my hands and, looking heavenwards, thanked God.

It was uncomfortably hot in the treehouse, but we flung our arms around each other and toppled onto the bunk. Knotted together, we rolled around, tugging at each other's clothes while our tongues collided in a desperate dance. His skin was slippery with sweat, and his hands were everywhere, my breasts, my neck, my belly. My body ached with a ferocious hunger, as if I wanted more of Louis than he could possibly give. One of his knees prised my legs apart. I moaned. This was it. This was what I wanted. I loved Louis. After this there could be no going back.

Reality hit. I gasped and pushed against him. 'No, Louis. Stop.'

'It's okay. I've got protection. Give me a second.' He slid off me, reached for his shorts, and fumbled inside a pocket.

Had he planned this? Was this why he'd asked me over? 'No,' I said. 'I don't want to.' I snatched my knickers and T-shirt and, turning my back to him, put them on. My cheeks were burning. I felt stupid and ashamed but, more than that, I was worried I'd annoyed him. He touched my arm, and I flinched.

'It's okay, Nat,' he said gently. 'I don't mind.'

'Really?'

'Course not, stupid. I thought you wanted to.'

'One day,' I said, meaning it. 'But not yet.'

He drew me to him and hugged me. 'Don't worry. I don't love you any less,' he whispered.

We held hands and drank the beers he'd brought while, unprompted and in a small voice I barely recognised, Louis told me how, after the guests had left, his parents had argued all night, but by the morning, Martha had gone.

'Where did she go?'

'I don't know. But she came back the next day with your dad and left again.'

My jaw dropped. 'With Dad? Why?'

He frowned and looked away, biting his lip as he relived the memory. After what seemed an age, he turned back. 'I don't want to talk about it anymore. I can't.'

'It's okay. I understand,' I said, although I didn't. Not one bit. The events of the last few days had strayed far outside the realms of my understanding. Had my father thrown his hat into the ring and professed his love for Martha, too? It didn't seem likely. Dramatic flourishes weren't his style.

'Where is she now?' I asked.

'No idea. Dad's beside himself with worry.'

'Do you think she's with *him*?'

He shrugged and flicked away the tear that had spilled onto his cheek. 'I just hope she'll come back.'

I slipped my hand in his and gave it a squeeze. 'Of course she will.' I was confident no mother would choose to leave her children behind. Mine had come close, mentally if not physically, but I was pretty sure that was different. And, anyway, I'd witnessed, first-hand, Martha's devotion to her boys. 'I've never known a mother love her children as much. You and Charlie are her world.'

'You really think so, Nat?'

I didn't know what else to say so I kissed him instead.

Eventually, I broke away. 'I have to go.' It was dark and getting late. I'd have some explaining to do if my father had come home. 'But I'll come back tomorrow.'

I arrived home, hot and sweaty, but luckily there was no sign of my father's car. I unlocked the door. Immediately, the crunch of gravel signalled his return. I dashed inside, darted into the sitting room, switched on the television, and threw myself on the sofa. When the set eventually flickered into life, as luck would have it, *Starsky and Hutch* was still on. I leant back against the cushions, crossed my legs, and glued my eyes to the screen. My father wouldn't suspect a thing.

'Hello, Nat,' he said, popping his head around the door. 'Everything okay?'

'Fine. How's the patient?'

'All good. Have you eaten?'

'I wasn't hungry.'

'Nat, you must eat. I'll check on Mum then I'll make us both a sandwich.'

I flopped back, thanked God, and settled down to watch the episode, my heart bursting with love for Louis, his scent lingering on my skin.

A minute later, maybe less, my father's footsteps thundered down the stairs, and he rushed into his study, cursing. Cupboard doors slammed. Drawers banged. And then the sitting room door flew open.

'Your mother's gone.' He was breathless and pale, his panic evident.

I stiffened. 'She can't have.'

'For God's sake, Nat, you must have heard her leave? What were you doing?'

He hated liars, but I couldn't tell him the truth. Not when he was like this. 'Watching television.'

'I'm going to try and find her. Stay here! Do not leave the house! Do you understand?'

'Yes, but shouldn't we call the police? She could be anywhere.'

'Not yet,' he said, hurrying out of the room.

I stared at the screen for a few moments. Starsky said something to Hutch that made him laugh, but my fractious mind had rendered me deaf to reality. Was my father worried she'd gone to the cliffs? Since the party, I'd been so preoccupied with thoughts of Louis and Martha I'd all but ignored the dip in my own mother's health. She ate little, hardly spoke, unless to answer yes or no. A wave of nausea ran through me. I'd lost Ian. What if I lost her, too? She might be a paler imitation of her former self, an almost-stranger, but she was still my mum.

During that agonisingly slow half hour, my father didn't return. He didn't telephone either, which he would have done if he had news. At a loss to know what to do with myself, I went into his study. At first glance, the room looked the same as always – neat piles of paper either side of his blotter, pencils lined in a row – but rounding the desk I noticed the locked middle drawer had been forced open. Was this the cause of his anger? And if so, why? What did he keep in there? Who had forced it open? Had an intruder come in when I was out and stolen something? Had he kidnapped Mum? Would he come back for me?

My mind unravelling, I ran frantically around the house. The back door was unlocked. I turned the key, but my hands were shaking so violently, I couldn't get a grip. Tears streamed down my face. I tried again. And again. At last, it was done. Failing a madman with an axe, I was safe. Time had slowed down to such an extent, I couldn't sit still. With nothing to do but wait, I went up to my bedroom, sat on the sill, and peered out the open window. Storm clouds were gathering in the heavy humid air. It was unnaturally dark, and I couldn't even see the lawn. Thunder rumbled in the distance. I held out my hand, and a fat drop of rain burst on my palm. After forty-five days, the drought had broken.

'Nat! Nat!'

'Louis!' I strained my eyes, but I couldn't see him in the pitch-black.

'Nat, quick. Come down, there's been an accident. We need your father.'

Every single hair on the back of my neck standing on end, I ran downstairs and opened the front door. The rain was falling hesitantly, the engorged drops exploding as they collided with the earth. I peered into the gloom. 'Louis? Where are you?'

'Nat!' He grabbed my wrist, drew me to him, and enveloped me in his arms. 'Oh my God, Nat.' And suddenly he was kissing me as if it was the last time he ever would.

I pushed him away. 'What are you doing?'

'I'm sorry I—'

'My father's not here.'

A flash of lightning seared the night sky. In the bright light, I caught a glimpse of white-blond hair. 'Charlie!'

Blood was smeared across his shirt. And his hand was covered in it, too.

'What have you done?' I staggered backwards, the answer all too clear.

The broken drawer.

The gun.

Charlie's killed someone.

He's killed his father. He's killed Bo Rivers.

I opened my mouth and screamed.

29

The moment Martha returns from Cee Cee's place in London, where she'd stayed while she sorted things through with Bo, she telephones Gordon. He's the most sensible person she knows and, right now, she needs his counsel. He'd helped her before, a long time ago. She's extremely relieved he's prepared to help her again.

They have met on the seafront and are sitting on a bench, staring out over a placid sea. She is wearing sunglasses and a scarf, to be on the safe side, and has told him everything. Typically, he's listened without batting an eyelid.

'Goodness, that's extremely rare,' he says.

'So, I gather.'

'And Bo knows?'

'Yes, he does?'

'How did he take it?'

'Actually, he was very understanding. Once he'd got over the shock. He wants to meet them, of course.' She sighs. It's only fair, but she has no idea how she'll make it happen. Her life is in tatters. Her future uncertain.

'And you're sure it's Teddy you want to be with?'

Martha closes her eyes. It had been tough seeing Bo again after all these years. She'd almost fainted with fright when, like a ghost, he'd appeared out of thin air. He'd been the last person she'd been expecting to see at her party. Apart from a few crows' feet and some fine lines either side of his mouth, he was no different to the last time she'd seen him. Same blond hair, same piercing eyes. Later, in London, he'd taken her to dinner. She'd experienced the familiar frisson of excitement, the butterflies and racing heart she'd always felt when she was close to him. But she'd been surprised when he'd clasped her hands and told her that he loved her, that he always had, and that it wasn't too late to change her mind. She'd wanted to tell him she loved him, too. It was true, she did. She would always love Bo Rivers. He was the man she loved above all others. But what good would come of it? It was far too late for them now. Too many people stood to get hurt – Teddy, the twins whom she loves above all else. But they would always have the memories. Romantic and gilded with nostalgia, they were the stuff of fairy tales. They could never be real. Not now.

'In another life, perhaps,' she said.

He recoiled, as if she'd slapped him. 'I never married, you know. I couldn't.'

She sighed, sad to be the cause of his pain. 'Then you must promise me you will. I won't be happy until you do.'

Martha winces and shakes her head. It won't do any good to dwell on it. Not when there is so much at stake. The past is the past and must remain there. The future is all that matters.

She opens her eyes and turns to Gordon. 'I'm certain I want to stay with Teddy. If he'll have me, that is.'

'He loves you. Anyone can see that. You'll talk to him? Tell him everything?'

'Uh-huh.' She rolls her bottom lip over in her teeth and

glances at her hands. Knowing she must has caused her sleeplessness nights, robbed her of her appetite. 'Do you think he'll find it in his heart to forgive me?'

'That, my dear, is the six-million-dollar question. But, Martha, I'm curious …'

She raises her head. 'Go on.'

'… did you marry Teddy because he looked like Bo?'

She wonders if now's the time to admit to Donny she and Teddy never married. No, she thinks. Things are complicated enough already. 'Perhaps. But I knew he'd be kind and care for me, no matter what. Until now, that is.'

'Steady Teddy. Yes, I see. You wanted stability. You followed your head and not your heart.

'And look where it's got me?'

'Don't be too hard on yourself, Martha. You never meant to hurt anyone.'

She loops her arm in his and rests her head on his shoulder. 'Ah, Donny. Not everyone is as understanding as you.'

Gordon chuckles. 'Don't I know it. So, you'll tell him everything?'

'Everything.'

At the far end of Potter's Lane, Martha grips the steering wheel of her white sports car and stares blindly into the black night. She is gearing up to talk to Teddy. Intermittent raindrops splatter the dusty windscreen, trickling down the glass in dirty streaks. Looks like the drought is over, she thinks, turning the key in the ignition. That's good.

She runs over the conversation she's about to have one last time. It's important she's word-perfect. I am, she thinks. She takes a deep breath, presses the accelerator, turns into her driveway, steers the car into the garage, and slips in through the back door. The lights are on, but the house is deathly quiet. Too scared to call out, she wanders into the sitting room. The French windows open, she heads out onto the patio and immediately sees Teddy. He has his back to her and is staring at the inky starless sky, a glass of red wine in his hand.

'Hello, Teddy,' she says quietly, so as not to startle him. 'I'm home.'

Teddy spins around. 'Martha.'

Without his familiar smile he looks like a little boy lost. Is he pleased to see her? She can't tell. He hesitates. An awkward silence hangs between them. Eyes narrowed, head cocked to one side, he seems to be willing her to speak.

Because speak she must.

She rubs the back of her neck and clears her throat. 'A sperm can survive for up to five days. Did you know that? I didn't.' It is not the speech she's practiced. But there it is.

Teddy puts down the glass and, fumbling with his clothing, peers at the flowerbeds as if the answer is hidden somewhere amongst the withered shrubs.

'It's got a name,' she says. 'Heteropaternal superfecundation. It can happen if the woman ovulates twice. I didn't know that either.'

Teddy throws up his hands. 'What are you talking about?'

Martha braces herself. 'Louis is your child, but Charlie ... Bo Rivers is Charlie's father.'

He squishes his eyebrows together and clasps his head. 'What? I ... I don't understand.'

'I slept with Bo the night before we were supposed to get married. We were engaged, you see, before I met you, but he broke it off and went to New York. When he heard I was getting married, he came back. I should have told you.' Her chin quivers. There. She's said it. There can be no turning back.

'Yes, you should.' His voice is quiet, barely audible.

The pause that follows seems to last forever. Martha waits, scared to speak in case she wounds him some more. Thunder booms overhead. She glances up at the billowing black clouds. The storm is gathering momentum. Soon there'll be lightning. She wills it to come. More than anything she wants to bring an end to the conversation. The humid air is suffocating, as if the night, too, is full of malice.

'Did he ask you to marry him?' Teddy asks eventually.

'Yes, he did. But I wanted you. I still do, if you'll have me.'

But Teddy is snapping his fingers. 'Charlie is his son, you say? And you know this because?'

Her chest tightens. 'I first suspected it when the twins were four. Charlie, although he resembled you, had more and more of Bo about him. But I thought, so what? You loved them as much as I did. You were bringing them up. You were their father. But when Bo turned up out of the blue, looking so much like Charlie, I had to find out, for the twins' sake.

'Donny took blood from both twins and told me to take the phials, together with samples from Bo and I, to a clinic where they'd run a paternity test. Bo's and Charlie's blood had identical isozymes. Louis' didn't. Bo is Charlie's father. You can do the same test if you want proof, but Louis is your son.'

'I … I thought it would be … the most wonderful surprise,' Teddy says, wringing his hands. 'Cee Cee wasn't keen. He didn't think you'd want to see him. But I wouldn't listen. And now your secret is out and our marriage … well, we aren't married, are we?' His eyes bore into her as if he's seeing her for the first time. 'How convenient.'

'We may as well be. I could have married him but I chose you. It was you I wanted.'

Teddy's face crumbles. 'Wanted but didn't love.'

Martha steps closer and reaches for his hands. 'I love you very much, Teddy. I should have told you I'd been engaged before. But I was so young—'

'Young! For heaven's sake, you were twenty-three,' Teddy says, yanking free from her grasp.

She sighs. 'I was seventeen.'

''Fraid you've got the maths wrong, love. It was your fortieth birth—'

'I was born in nineteen forty-two,' Martha continues in a small voice. 'I'm thirty-four years old. I was seventeen when you asked me to marry you.'

'You lied to me? Why would you do that? Tell me, Martha. I don't understand.'

Martha takes a deep breath. 'I was fifteen when I met Bo, sixteen when we started dating. He found out and was horrified.'

'What do you mean he found out? Did you lie to him, too?'

Martha winces. 'My age never came up until we planned to go to America. He saw my passport.'

A knowing smile settles on his lips. 'He didn't trust you then?'

Martha squirms. It's the truth. Bo said as much in his note. There can be no denying it. 'It wasn't like that. We were … well, famous. We were in the news. Bo was worried about the age gap. He thought it reflected badly on him. It was crazy really, but he did. He suggested I add on a few years and made me promise to keep up the pretence. I couldn't see the harm.'

Teddy folds his arms. 'Tell me, Martha. Why did Bo Rivers break off the engagement?'

Martha frowns and rolls her lip between her teeth. She's promised herself she'll tell Teddy everything, but she's not sure she's ready to talk about the photograph. Not tonight. Not while he's like this.

'Must have been something pretty bad if he left the country.'

She lowers her gaze. 'I don't know.'

Teddy throws up his hands. 'You don't know? Christ, you must take me for an idiot. Do you still love Bo Rivers? Tell me?'

A twig snaps in the bushes. Martha flinches. 'Where are the twins?' She casts around frantically, scanning the area. It was one thing to be the object of Teddy's loathing, quite another to be despised by her own children.

'In the treehouse, I expect. But you're right to be worried because they will find out. You realise that, don't you? You can't keep it from them. They have a right to know.'

'I must go to them.'

Teddy grabs her wrist. 'Does he want to see Charlie? Does he want to be a father?'

'Please, let me go. They'll want to see me. They must be upset. I've never been away from them this long.'

'Oh no you don't. Not until you tell me the truth. And I mean all of it.' Martha tries to wriggle free, but Teddy's grip is too strong. 'You're keeping something from me, Martha. What is it?'

Drops of warm rain bounce on the paving stones around her. One lands on her cheek, uncomfortably close to her eye. She flicks it away with her free hand. If only the downpour would begin.

'Tell him, Martha.'

Martha starts at the woman's sharp, shrill voice.

Teddy lets go of her and peers into darkness. 'Who's there?'

'Go on, Martha,' the woman continues. 'Tell him about the photograph.'

Teddy's head snaps back and forth. 'Who is it? Who's there? Show yourself.'

'The pornographic photograph.'

Martha gasps and clasps her hands to her chest. 'Delilah?' No, she thinks. It can't be. Delilah died of a drug overdose some years ago. Didn't she?

The woman barks a hollow laugh. 'You posed naked for Stan Waterfield in his grubby little studio, and Bo found out. That's why he left you. Go on, Martha. Tell Teddy the truth. He's a good man. He deserves to know.'

Her heart skips a beat. Loretta? A jagged flash of silver clefts the darkness. In that split second, Martha sees her. Sees the gun. She recognises both. Donny's wife. Teddy's gun. 'You!'

Donny's wife draws back her lips. 'You never could remember my name.'

'Lizzie,' Teddy says. 'Dear lady. Put the gun down.'

'Lizzie,' mutters Martha, her mind spinning. Short for Elizabeth. She remembers it now.

Teddy walks slowly towards her and holds out his hand. 'Hand me the gun. You're scaring my wife.'

Lizzie snorts. 'Why on earth are you protecting her?'

'Where did you get it?' Martha asks. 'The magazine? Who showed you the picture?'

'Really, Martha? All those times you visited, you never noticed them on Gordon's floor.'

Martha clutches her cheeks. 'Donny didn't give it to you. He didn't know.'

'Donny! Honestly! His name is Gordon, and no, of course he didn't. I was looking for something to read to pass the time. I spent hours waiting for Gordon that summer. He always claimed he was at the hospital, but I knew he was out gallivanting with you. He was always going on about you, always playing your records, going to your concerts. I found it under a pile of clothes. An old edition, dog-eared and torn. I'd never seen a dirty magazine before. The picture of you stood out. I didn't realise it was you at first. But something clicked. Your mouth, I think, the top lip thinner than the lower.'

Martha is trembling violently. A crazed woman is pointing a gun at her, but she needs to make sense of it all. 'But you had more than one copy.'

'For heaven's sake, Martha. The medics passed them around. It was easy to find another one.'

'But why did you do it? I don't understand?'

'I'd always been a massive fan of yours. But the photograph. What kind of girl would strip naked for all the world to see? The sort who wouldn't think twice about stealing another girl's man. You see, Teddy, Martha is a liar and a cheat. She's been cheating on you with my husband all summer, exactly as she did seventeen years ago. Only, this time, I've been too sick and you've been working too hard to notice.'

Martha legs are shaking, her knees weak. She wishes she could sit down. 'That's not true. Donny and I are just friends.'

'Donny and I are just friends,' the woman mimics.

'Dear lady, you're confused—'

'I confronted Gordon that night, told him I'd spoken to Rory and knew he wasn't at the hospital. He came clean, said he was with you, but it was a private matter, and he'd been sworn to secrecy. Ironic, really, because I knew perfectly well what was in that envelope. And then he told me he loved me and asked me to marry him. He wouldn't see you anymore. His proposal took me completely by surprise, but joy was tinged with guilt. I'd pinned the photo to your door as a warning to stay away. I never meant any harm. I was furious when you showed up again. But then you turned up for tea with Bo's son. No harm done, I thought. But at your party I saw you and Gordon together. He was touching you, and you were whispering to one another, like you used to. I knew exactly what you'd been up to. I'd been right all along.'

Another streak of lightning rents the sky. Her teeth bared, Lizzie cocks the trigger, raises the revolver, and aims at Martha.

She's going to kill me. Martha's palms are sweating. Her heart is pounding.

'Lizzie,' says Teddy, walking towards her. 'Dear lady. Please, hand me the gun. This is not what you want. Think of Tasha.'

'Her name is *Na*tasha. And she's precisely who I'm thinking of. Your bitch of a wife stole her from me, too. I have nothing left. NOTHING.'

'You're unwell, Elizabeth,' Martha says gently. 'You need help.'

There's a crack as the bullet leaves the gun. Her abdomen stings with a burning pain. She lets out a sharp cry and, touching the hot, wet wound, falls to the ground.

She hears voices. Distant voices, detached from reality. She is discombobulated, as though she's been drugged.

Screams echo around her.

'Mum! Mum! Is she dead, Dad? Has she killed her?'

'Boys, stay away. It's not safe.'

The children. Oh my God, my boys.

A woman shrieks, shrill and loud.

'Drop the gun, Lizzie.'

A man's voice. Donny?

'Well done. Now sit down. Good. Louis, call an ambulance.'

Somebody is telling her not to leave. As she drifts away, she wonders where they think she's going.

And now she is a child again, running barefoot in the field behind their home. Her mother is calling her, telling her it's time for tea.

Her mouth is dry. She is terribly, terribly cold.

She opens her eyes and blinks.

'She's back,' Teddy says.

She wants to tell him she never left, would never leave him. Not ever. But she can't. She's too tired.

Her mother is calling her. Or is it her father? *Martha, Martha,* he says. *Come back home, will you. There's a good lass.*

'It's okay, Martha. Hang on in there,' Donny says.

Is it okay? She wants to ask him but she can't seem to move her mouth. She tries again, but no words come out.

Somebody is gripping her hand. 'Don't leave me, Martha. Please don't leave me. I love you. With all my heart I love you. And it'll be okay. You'll see. We'll work it out.'

That's good, Teddy, she thinks as she closes her eyes, because I love you, too.

EPILOGUE

M any months later, my father filled in the gaps, most notably Martha's regretful decision at the age of fifteen to pose naked. I knew then, for certain, that all of Martha's lies had been told in good faith. She had meant to protect the people around her, not hurt them. And yet hurt she had, and the list was long: the two boys she loved; her husband, Teddy; her lover, Bo Rivers; my father, her friend; and me. But there was one other on the list who was, perhaps, the most cruelly affected of us all. My mother. Racked with grief over the untimely death of her son, Lizzie James was insanely jealous of the magnificent Martha Palmer. Blind to Martha's goodness, she saw only the bad. She'd convinced herself her husband was in love with her. And, because she'd lost her mind, she'd shot her.

But worse was still to come.

After my mother went missing, my father, putting two and two together, dashed over to Greystones. The shot had already been fired, a lightning strike had cut off the power, and Charlie had been dispatched to find him. When she saw her husband, my mother dropped the gun and screamed hysterically, tearing at her face. My father tried his best to console her. But with Martha dying and Teddy begging him to save his wife, he had his work cut out. Later, he told me he was determined not to fail. It was vital Martha lived, for my mother's sake – who'd go to prison if she died – as much as Martha's. With Charlie gone, it was left to Louis to try to calm her. But Louis was far too worried about his mother to waste his energy on the crazy lady who'd shot her. And she was left to her own devices.

By the time we arrived at Greystones – once Charlie had convinced me my mother had taken the gun and it was Martha who'd been shot and, with the power down at Greystones, we had to call an ambulance – my father was working hard on Martha to stem the flow of blood. My mother, however, was nowhere to be seen. And as the storm clouds burst and the rain cascaded down and soaked us to our bones, Louis and Teddy held Martha's hands and begged her to stay alive.

We didn't know that, while we waited for the ambulance, my mother had picked up the gun, walked to the end of Potter's Lane, and blown her brains out.

My mother's funeral was a quiet affair, but that was to be expected. Most people did the decent thing and stayed away, but a few stalwarts braved the service. I have no idea who, because my eyes were trained on my shoes for the full half hour it took to cremate her. In the same way as I'd struggled to understand her illness, I couldn't make sense of her death. It was inconceivable my mother had had such a major part to play in Martha's story. Although, I shouldn't really have been surprised, when all things in those days seemed to start and end with her. If I'd known how the narrative would play out, I'd have done my utmost to keep them apart. Ignorant of the power of love, I had no idea of the destruction it could bring.

Guilt gnawed at my conscience. I wondered whether, in the moments before she'd squeezed the trigger, she'd given me a second thought, and if she had, was it to blame me? Was it down to me that she'd shot Martha? Had I driven her to suicide? My father tried to convince me it was no one's fault. She was ill. Her mind was damaged. She had reimagined the past. A past in which Martha was the villain and she the victim. Had skewed the unalterable to see things that were not there.

I wanted to believe him, but I had my doubts. It seemed to me that he'd been in love with Martha all along. And, when he told me Mum was reunited with her darling son and at peace, I struggled to believe that, too.

The second funeral was a far more ordinary affair. Although with only my mother's and brother's to compare it to, I could hardly judge. But Mrs P's felt different. For a start, almost all the villagers were there. Plenty of other people I'd never met had come to pay their respects and to celebrate a long and happy life lived to the full. I tried to join in, but I couldn't. My young life, already fractured and torn, had been ripped apart some more. Tears streamed down my cheeks, but I made no attempt to stop them. Edie Pocock had been a constant, steadying presence for as long as I could remember. I missed her terribly, and I missed Rafferty, too.

I took comfort in the fact Martha survived. Had she not, my mother would forever be remembered as a murderer. Perhaps, in the end, what drove her to kill herself, was the awful realisation she was so damaged by grief, she'd spiralled out of control.

Our lives had changed dramatically, blown apart as if by a

bomb. And even though life marched relentlessly on, there was no way any of us could simply pick up where we had left off. The day after she was discharged from hospital, Martha, Teddy, and the twins moved to France, departing our lives as abruptly as they'd arrived. Left to salvage what we could from the wreckage, my father and I endeavoured to forge a future for ourselves. Unlike the Fairchilds, we couldn't up sticks and leave. My father's business had taken years to build, and although, once again the villagers offered us their unconditional support, daily I faced cruel reminders of all I'd lost. Only the weather was different, and as my resilient and, at times, super-human father guided me through the long and lonely days that followed, I was grateful for the rain. It helped not to be reminded of the eternal sunshine of those unforget-table days when, intoxicated by the magical new world I'd discovered and blinded by first love, I had constructed a fantasy around a beautiful woman with a mysterious past.

I never set eyes on Martha Palmer again, although I never tried to find her. Perhaps because I hoped she'd seek me out herself one day. In truth, I still believe she might. And so, despite the tragedy and heartache my dangerous obsession had unwittingly unleashed upon my family, I find myself scouring the audiences at my concerts, hoping for a glimpse.

Perhaps, still craving her approval, even after all these years.

A Song Unsung Soundtrack - Spotify

A Kiss to Build a Dream On – Louis Armstrong
Mean to Me – Billie Holiday
April in Paris – Sarah Vaughan
Tenderly – Sarah Vaughan
Round Midnight – Thelonious Monk
Salt Peanuts – Dizzy Gillespie
A Night in Tunisia – Miles Davis and Charlie Parker
At Last – Etta James
Mad About the Boy – Dinah Washington
Someone to Watch Over Me – Ella Fitzgerald
West End Blues – Louis Armstrong
The Man I Love – Peggy Lee
Line for Lyons – Gerry Mulligan and Chet Baker
Born to Be Blue – Chet Baker
Isn't This a Lovely Day – Ella and Louis
Strange Fruit – Billie Holiday
Fever – Peggy Lee
La Vie en Rose – Louis Armstrong
Sing, Sing, Sing – Benny Goodman
It's Always You – Chet Baker
All of Me – Dinah Washington
I Fall in Love Too Easily – Chet Baker
Goodbye Pork Pie Hat – Charles Mingus
That Ole Devil Called Love – Billie Holiday
Take Five – The Dave Brubeck Quartet

Miles Davis: Kind of Blue
Ornette Coleman: The Shape of Jazz to Come
Charles Mingus: Mingus Ah Hum
The Dave Brubeck: Quartet *Time Out*

AUTHOR'S NOTE

To describe the Soho of the late fifties, and to gain a rudimentary understanding of jazz, as well as the singers and musicians of that era, the following books were the most useful: *A New History of Jazz* by Alyn Shipton; *Let's Join Hands and Contact the Living: Ronnie Scott and His Club* by John Fordham; *Louis Armstrong: An Extravagant Life* by Laurence Bergreen; *Owning Up* by George Melly; *An Unholy Row: Jazz in Britain and its Audience, 1945-1960* by Dave Gelly; *Mama Said There'd Be Days Like This: My Life In The Jazz World* by Val Wilmer; *Up West: Voices from the Streets of Post-War London* by Pip Granger; *Never Had It So Good: A History of Britain from Suez To The Beatles* by Dominic Sandbrook; *The Story of Soho: The Windmill Years, 1932-1964* by Mike Hutton; *London Calling: A Countercultural History of London since 1945* by Barry Miles.

And for Giovanni's Italian proverbs, *You Can't Get Blood Out of a Turnip: Non si può cavar sangue da una rapa and other Italian proverbs with English equivalents* compiled by Ilia Terzulli Warner and Christopher Arnander with illustrations by Kathryn Lamb, proved invaluable.

ACKNOWLEDGMENTS

*A Song Uns*ung was inspired by my father who was such a huge support to me, not only in life, but also in my career as a writer. The first person to read my manuscripts, he never shied away from telling me exactly what he thought of them. When I told him the subject for my fifth novel was partly centred around a jazz singer in the late fifties, he was thrilled. A gifted pianist, he enjoyed all types of music, including jazz, so much so that, after he retired, he took up the trombone with, I might add, varying degrees of success. In the last few weeks of his life, when we had no idea quite how ill he was, he kept asking me if I'd finished the novel. It broke my heart that he died before I had. And while I'm pleased to have made the decision to publish, three years after the book's completion, it is, nevertheless, tinged with sadness that my dear father never had the chance to read it. Thank you, Dad, for always being there for me. I miss you terribly.

A massive thank you to my friend and fellow author, Dreda Say Mitchell. Without her endless support, patience and encouragement, *A Song Unsung* would never have seen the light of day. Thank you Dreda for believing in me, for guiding me, and for holding my hand through the long and complicated publishing process.

Andy Davies, award-winning trumpeter and leader of Ronnie Scott's house band, was the inspiration behind Bo Rivers. He was kind enough to invite me to Wednesday's Late Night Jamming Sessions to watch him perform on several occasions. A consummate showman, with a pork pie hat and penchant for waistcoats, it was a huge privilege and enormous fun to have a ring-side view of his scintillating talent. On hand to answer my many questions, he taught me all I know about playing the trumpet. Thank you, Andy, for everything you did to bring the jazz, in this novel, to life.

A huge thank you to the wonderful Fran Kazamia. She has taken over my father's role of first reader, and I don't know what I'd do without her input, insight and wise counsel.

My other fabulous beta readers, Lesley Frame, Sarah Page and Roh Visick, I hope you know how much I value your feedback and the precious time you devote to my work. Thank you.

Thank you to the phenomenal Adrian Newton for designing the outstanding cover. You are one in a million, Ade. Thanks for putting up with my unusual thought processes, and for being a true friend to me all these years.

Emmy Ellis my editor, for your forensic eye and attention to detail, I applaud and thank you. You truly are an inspiration.

Hugs to Sam and Holly for listening to my bleatings, and for helping me out with all things technical and arty.

And finally, a special thank you to my husband, Simon, for his continued loyalty and unstinting support. I couldn't have done any of this without you.

ABOUT THE AUTHOR

Born and educated in Sussex, Fiona graduated from Exeter University with a degree in Philosophy. She worked in London in film and entertainment PR, before moving back to Sussex where she divided her time between coaching tennis and writing books. To date, she has published two mysteries – *Killing Fame*, and *The Gate* – the psychological thriller – *When the Dove Cried* – and the critically acclaimed literary thriller, *The Other Side of the Mountain*.

Thank you for reading *A Song Unsung*. If you enjoyed it, please post a review and help other readers discover the story.

Fiona Cane at Amazon

Printed in Great Britain
by Amazon